SHANGHAI FLAME

Alex Cloud knows he's being followed. He only has a short period of time to find Flame and bring her back to the ship in order to leave Shanghai alive. China has turned Red, and an American newspaperman's life has turned worthless. Dodging from one risky situation to the next, Cloud runs into Haigmann, a canny middle-man who seems to think Cloud has something of value. Eventually Cloud finds Flame, but she wants nothing to do with him. Undaunted, he's sworn to get her out of Shanghai, but now finds himself carrying a lethal pack of cards with a microfilm of names glued into them. Now they're both on the run, trying to stay one step ahead of the spies and thieves who want that film—ready and willing to kill anyone to get it.

COUNTERSPY EXPRESS

"Don't get ... mixed up with a woman. My mistake..." The dying words of Jim Cabot's European contact ring in his ears as finds himself being trailed by one woman and tempted by another. His mission is to locate Borsilov, a defected Russian scientist. His predecessor, Max Becker, died trying. And already Cabot has been knocked senseless and his life threatened by two gunmen as he tries to track down the missing scientist. Behind the threats is an Italian Red named Major Racasoli. Pitted against them all is an English opportunist, Sydney Jardine, who wants to sell Borsilov to the highest bidder. But those dying words of warning mean nothing to Cabot now, because he has met Pia-- and all bets are off.

SHANGHAI FLAME

— · · — · · —

COUNTERSPY EXPRESS

A. S. FLEISCHMAN

INTRODUCTION BY GEORGE KELLEY

Stark House Press • Eureka California

SHANGHAI FLAME / COUNTERSPY EXPRESS

Published by Stark House Press
1315 H Street
Eureka, CA 95501
griffinskye3@sbcglobal.net
www.starkhousepress.com

ISBN-13: 978-1-944520-14-4

Book design by Mark Shepard, SHEPGRAPHICS.COM

First Stark House Press Edition: December 2016

FIRST EDITION

"The Magic of A. S. Fleischman"
By George Kelley

When a kid has his first book published when he's just 19-years-old you know he's going to turn into something special.

Albert Sydney "Sid" Fleischman was in fifth grade when he first saw a magician. "He flipped the deck into falling waterfalls of cards, spun them into fans, and trust a sword through a shower of cards to impale the seven of diamonds—selected a moment before. I was dazzled…I knew what I wanted to be. Someone else could be president of the United States. I wanted to be a magician."

Sid Fleischman pursued his love of magic by inventing magic tricks and, as a teenager, joined the San Diego Magicians Club. Fleischman wrote up the mechanics of his sleight-of-hand magic tricks and sent the manuscript called *Between Cocktails* to Abbott's Magic Company, a publisher of books for professional magicians. "When the book landed on my doorstep, with my name on the cover, it impressed the hell out of me. The thought of becoming a writer had never crossed my mind. But my aspirations took a shift." *Between Cocktails: With a Packet of Matches* (1939) has been in print for over seventy years.

After graduating from high school, Sid Fleischman toured as a professional magician in vaudeville shows. Fleischman also performed in nightclubs and became a member of the touring Mr. Arthur Bull's Francisco Spook Show. He then decided to go back to school and enrolled at San Diego State College where he met Betty Taylor. They fell in love. When Sid Fleischman's Naval Reserve unit was activated after the attack on Pearl Harbor, Sid Fleischman and Betty Taylor disappeared from college and reappeared in Yuma, Arizona where they secretly got married on January 25, 1942. She was 20 and he was 21. Their parents were initially not happy with this turn of events. But this action set the pattern for Sid Fleischman doing the unexpected.

Sid Fleischman reported to the *Albert T. Harris*, DE 447, a destroyer escort. He served as a yeoman during his tour of the Far East where he visited Shanghai which became the setting of his first Gold Medal novel, *Shanghai Flame* (1951).

After World War II, Fleischman graduated from college with a degree in English and worked as a reporter at the *San Diego Daily Journal* until the newspaper went out of business in 1950. With Betty's encouragement, Sid Fleischman turned to writing. Using Betty's red Royal portable typewriter, Fleischman wrote a detective novel called *The Straw Donkey Case* (1948). It was followed by a sequel, *Murder's No Accident* (1949). Both books were published by tiny Phoenix Press. Fleischman was paid $150 per book. When Phoenix Press went bankrupt, Sid Fleischman turned to the growing paperback market. He decided to write a mystery novel for Gold Medal which was breaking new ground in publishing by soliciting original manuscripts instead of merely reprinting hardcover books as inexpensive paperbacks.

"I tried writing Henry James sentences, but it was too much like pulling taffy, and I settled on the quicker pulse of Hemingway prose, trim and unpretentious." Sid Fleischman's approach to writing a novel was also unique. He didn't use an outline. He just made it up as he went along. But Fleischman worked on each page until he thought he had it right before he would write the next page. Using this method, he rarely had to revise his work when he was finished.

Fleischman decided on writing a suspense story about an American newspaperman in Shanghai. After three months of work, Fleischman mailed *The Man Who Died Laughing* to Gold Medal. Dick Carrol, bought the novel but changed the title to *Shanghai Flame*. "When my first copies arrived they blazed forth with a baffling new title, *Shanghai Flame*. Shanghai I could comprehend, but *Flame*? There were no fires in the yarn. Upon examining the text I discovered that to support his newsstand title, Dick had an underling go through the manuscript and change the name of my red-headed heroine…to Flame. Gold Medal was no place for those who regarded their prose as chiseled in anything but quicksand."

Fleischman knew his knowledge of the Far East gave him an advantage over the other Gold Medal writers and based several of his paperback novels in the Orient. "I laid out a claim. The [Asian] background seemed made for intrigue and mystery and suspense, the shadowy stuff that, as a magician, I found seductive."

Shanghai Flame features an American journalist named Alex Cloud who searches for the woman who dumped him, Paula "Flame" Forrest. Flame, also a journalist, got involved with political groups in Shanghai and is now hunted by the Communist Reds. Sid Fleischman introduces a MacGuffin, a pack of playing cards holding dangerous secrets, and the plot takes off. Cloud and Flame have to escape from Shanghai, avoid assassins, and discover the secrets of the playing cards. It all makes for fun reading.

The original striking cover artwork of *Shanghai Flame* by Barye Phillips shows a couple from an overhead vantage point. Fleischman received a cent-and-a-half per copy on a first print order of 200,000 copies. That's about $3,000. Big difference from the $150 per book from Phoenix Press!

"With reprint following reprint, and check after check, I felt rich enough to pack up my young family and take off for Europe in the early 50s." The European trip provided the basis for *Counterspy Express*. Where Fleischman's *Look Behind You, Lady* (1952) is set in Macao, *Danger in Paradise* (1953) is set in Indonesia, and *Malay Woman* (1954) set on a rubber plantation in Malaysia, *Counterspy Express* (1954) reflects Fleischman's experiences in Europe instead of the Far East.

Perhaps the change in setting was the reason Gold Medal rejected *Counterspy Express*. *Counterspy Express* was published by ACE Books in 1954. ACE published a series of paperbacks in a unique format called *tete-beche* (from the French meaning "back-to-back") where two books are bound together, each with a separate reversed cover.

ACE Double D-57 has *Counterspy Express* by A. S. Fleischman on one side and *Treachery In Trieste* by Charles L. Leonard (a pseudonym of M. V. Heberden) on the other side. Both covers show a beautiful woman in a threatening situation defended by an armed man.

Top of Form
Bottom of Form
Victor Welles is given the mission of finding the bolt hole of a runaway Soviet atomic-scientist. Then, after he locates the hidden scientist, Welles needs to navigate the risky escape route despite the Soviet agents hunting for their missing scientist and deliver him and the super secrets he carries to American authorities. *Counterspy Express* turns into a murderous race across Europe. From the alleys of Genoa, the casinos of San Remo and Monte Carlo, the dangerous roads to Occupied Austria, and spy haunts of sinister Switzerland, Fleischman writes a high-octane thrill-ride full of action and romance.

On July 20, 1958, the movie based on *Counterspy Express* showed up in American theaters under the title *Spy in the Sky!* The film was directed by W. Lee Wilder with a script by Myles Wilder. Steve Brodie, Sandra Francis, and Andrea Domburg star in this adaptation. The "atomic" secrets of *Counterspy Express* are transformed, because of Sputnik, into "satellite" secrets. A captive German scientist, working on the classified Russian satellite program, escapes to "The Free World" where he finds himself kidnapped by agents who plan to sell him and his knowledge of satellite technology to the highest bidder.

After reading *Shanghai Flame* and *Counterspy Express* it's obvious that Sid Fleischman plotted these novels with a magician's perspective. His characters encounter surprises, unexpected events, and illusions in each chapter. Fleischman also ends each chapter with a cliffhanger so readers will want to read on to find out what happens next.

The best way to learn about Sid Fleischman's writing method is to listen to the twelve short (about two minutes each) video interviews available at www.scholastic.com/teachers/contributor/sid-fleischman where Fleischman shares details about his writing methods, where his ideas came from, and insights about writing books for five decades.

Sid Fleischman's children—Paul, Jane, and Anne—wondered what their father did for a living. The fathers of their friends went off to work while their father stayed home all day and played with a typewriter. Fleischman decided to show his children what he did so he wrote a children's book where Paul, Jane, and Anne appeared as characters. In typical Fleischman fashion, he read each finished chapter out loud to his children and used their suggestions to improve the book. Sid Fleischman said of the experience, "As a father I wanted to hear the kids laugh, and I began reaching out for funny scenes and comic villains and dialogue with flashes of humor. This novel changed me forever. It was the first sustained comic writing I had done; it fixed my style and gave me a literary voice of my own."

Fleischman sent *Mr. Mysterious & Company* to his agent and the book was published in 1962. The success of his first children's book led Sid Fleischman into a new career as an author of books for children and young adults. In 1975, *Mr. Mysterious's Secrets of Magic* appeared, a book of magic tricks for children.

In 1987, Sid Fleischman received the Newbery Medal for *The Whipping Boy*. The Newbery Medal is awarded to the author of the best book for children in that year. Two years later, Fleischman's son Paul won the Newbery Medal for his book, *Joyful Noise*. Sid Fleischman and his son are the only father-son winners of the Newbery Medal.

Over his long writing career, Sid Fleishman's production was impressive: 8 books of magic, 10 novels of mystery and suspense for adults, 45 books for children and young adults, 6 screenplays, one play, 3 biographies, and one amusing autobiography.

Sid Fleischman died on March 17, 2010, a day after his 90th Birthday.

August 2016,
North Tonawanda, NY

REFERENCES

Fleischman, Sid. *The Abracadabra Kid: A Writer's Life.* Greenwillow Books, 1996.

Fleischman, Sid and Gary Lovisi. "An Interview with A. S. "Sid" Fleischman." *Paperback Parade*, January 2001.

Shanghai Flame

By A. S. Fleischman

Chapter One

I waited.

Outside, the black rickshas and pedicabs streamed by in an endless, jingling herd. This was Shanghai, Red Shanghai, and no place for an American newspaperman without a gun in his pocket.

I waited. I had been waiting two days at a glass-topped table in a small bar on Avenue Joffre, in the former French Concession. It was September and the air was hot and moist like New York in the summer.

She might walk in any minute, any hour, any day. Sooner or later she'd walk in and I'd be here.

"You want to rent that table by the month, m'sieu?" Georges, the mountainous bartender-owner, picked up the empty beer bottle and scowled professionally at the game of solitaire laid out in front of me.

"You can do me a favor," I said. "Get lost."

A patina of sweat gave Georges's face an extravagant look of cunning like a wrestler's. His head was large and round, burnished by the Shanghai sun, with hair clipped within an inch of his scalp. I counted five assorted rings spangling his fingers.

"Go home," he said. "Georges is tired of looking at you. You don't talk, you don't smile, you just sit there with the cards. You got trouble on your mind, m'sieu. Georges don't want trouble here. Go home."

"You won't have any trouble if you bring me another bottle."

He stared at me for a moment with contempt in his glistening blue eyes and walked away. His flat feet had him shifting his bulk awkwardly from the shoulders with every tired step.

I scooped up the cards and began to shuffle them. The cards were thick, a European make, and felt clumsy in my hands. The backs were a dark blue with a Maltese Cross tangled in a filigree of wiry lines. I started another game.

Georges came back with the beer and I let it sit. I felt reasonably safe and inconspicuous at Georges's. It was a small place, with a one-man bar and tables against the mirrored wall. There was a cage full of canaries in the corner behind me and every so often Georges would go over and comfort them in French. His customers were largely Frenchmen and Czechs and Swiss who somehow managed to get along with the Reds, with an occasional swaggering Russian and once in a while an intrepid British businessman who had stayed on for his intrepid British firm.

I abandoned the game after a few more minutes. I was bored with waiting and the chatter of the birds behind me was getting on my nerves.

I took a puppet French newspaper out of my coat pocket and reread the classified ad I had placed on Monday, the day before yesterday.

"Flame," I translated. "I'm alive and waiting for you at Georges's Bar. Cottardo."

Cottardo. The name would scare hell out of her. Cottardo was dead and she knew it. But I knew she would come running after him, dead or alive.

It was a cheap trick, but it would bring Flame to me. I wasn't in love with the idea of walking the streets of Shanghai without identification papers on me, looking for her. I had left Hong Kong too impulsively to get forged papers; all I had with me was a roll of *jen min piao*, inflated Red Chinese bank notes. This was one city in which I had to stay out of trouble, and looking back upon the last couple of haywire years I knew I had developed a talent for doing just the opposite. For once I was trying to play it smart. For once I gave a damn about myself.

In about an hour it began to rain the way it does in Shanghai this time of year. The sudden downpour washed too many Shanghailanders into Georges's and the place began to jam up. And then the little guy in the dirty linen suit came in.

He had a boyish face with glasses in polished steel rims; his skin was coarse and he moved with a mincing step. He came in with a sketch pad under his arm. He laid it on a corner of the bar while he removed his glasses and dried them with a wrinkled white handkerchief. Then he began pestering the customers to let him sketch them. And finally he got to me.

He spoke German first, but I shook my head and he switched to English. I gave him a cold blank stare, but I don't think I fooled him. He tried French, and I told myself to get rid of this character fast. He looked Russian to me—maybe one of the white Russians who had happily turned Red when Chairman Mao came to town.

"Don't bother me," I said in French.

He stood there smiling at me through those thick lenses. "You have a strange face," he said. "That is my business, m'sieu, faces. And my pleasure. No charge for the m'sieu with the strange face." He sat down, flipped the cover off the pad, and immediately set to sketching.

I started to get out of my chair, but held back. I was on good behavior. No trouble wanted. I settled back with annoyance and lit a cigarette. He kept a set smile as his pencil darted over the paper in a blocking-in movement. What the hell, I tried to tell myself, it would pass the time.

After a while he held out his pencil and moved his thumb along it to measure my nose. I saw that the pencil had a hard lead, but it didn't mean anything to me then.

"A bit of Greek in your nose, *mon ami*." He smiled. His teeth kept appearing between nervous lips, short and dull white, like bad Japanese pearls.

He had a fast hand and I puffed irritably at the cigarette. I was an idiot to be here, to give a damn whether Flame turned up or not. We had broken up in Rome two years ago, and it was meant to be for keeps. After that I began coming apart at the seams. Unless I pulled myself together I knew I'd soon be right back where I started—at some rewrite desk in the States, turning out obits and weather reports. When Flame left me I stopped living. I had been dead for two years and the funny part was that I knew it. Funny as hell.

The little guy kept flashing his eyes at me and moving his pencil. I thought back to that poker game at the press club in Hong Kong two weeks ago. Someone said, "What in hell ever became of Flame Forrest?" and Guy Adams piped up, "Hell, she turned Commie. Stayed on in Shanghai after the Reds came. Still there, as far as I know. Serves her right. Probably couldn't get out now if she wanted to." He chuckled and turned to me. "Flame. That nickname you gave her matches her politics now, as well as her hair and her temper. What the hell's her real name, Alex? I've forgotten. And didn't you used to bed down with her in Rome?"

"Her name is Paula," I said, "and I never heard of her."

I left the game early, ignored a couple of cables on my desk from New York, and uncorked a four-day sabbatical. When I came out from under the hangover there was a cable from the World News Syndicate putting me on a month's probation. The chief advised me my heart didn't seem to be in my work. I tore the damned cable up and found myself a British freighter running the Nationalist blockade up the coast to Shanghai.

The artist ripped off the sheet, grinned solicitously, and laid his work before me.

I looked at the drawing and grimaced. It wasn't a handsome face. The jaw was all right, maybe a little too angular, but all right. It was the eyes that did it. I saw for the first time how hard and cynical and tired they were; I remembered now a copy boy who described them recently as limpid pools of whisky. The dark hair looked in need of a trim. It wasn't a handsome face, but it was me. Alexander Cloud.

When I looked up, little Picasso was already picking his way out of the bar and into the downpour.

I looked again at the picture and sensed something was wrong. It took me a long time to see it. When the idea connected, I saw that the sketch cut deeply into the paper. He had pressed hard—hard enough to make an impression beneath. The bastard had made a carbon copy of my face!

I picked up my trench coat and got out of there.

I stopped for a second under Georges's dripping striped awning. There was already an inch of water flooding the street, and it was going to get deeper. The street lights penetrated about as far as you could spit, and I couldn't pick him out at first. Then I saw him hurry past the yellow window of a café across the street. My first thought was to get over there and drown the jerk in the gutter. I saw him look around once, but he didn't recognize me.

I buckled my trench coat and threw the collar up around my neck. Then I started down my side of the street, keeping an eye on him.

I figured he'd take me straight to Flame or to the Reds, and maybe that was one and the same. I didn't want to believe it; if it were true that she had gone over to them, I'd break her neck before they chained me to a rewrite desk.

The ricksha traffic had thinned, but a few struggled against the downpour. My lead kept to Avenue Joffre, and I became dimly conscious of persons huddled in wet doorways and under awnings. It gave me that chill feeling you get in an unfriendly city.

He couldn't be leading me far, I figured, or he'd have signaled for a ride. I decided to cut across the street to bring up the distance between us. A form loomed up and its bicycle bell broke the air. I jumped aside to let the pedicab go by. When I got to the sidewalk the little guy was crossing the streets at the end of the block.

I had already learned that the Reds had set up operations in the French quarter in the old jai-alai building on Avenue Du Roi. I decided I'd jump him if he got within a block of the place.

But he turned left on Route Père Robert and hastened his step the two short blocks to the Rue Corneille, and I saw we were coming to the end of the line. He crossed the street and I fell into the doorway of a darkened bakery to watch.

He stopped and looked around, the sketchbook clamped under his coat in an effort to keep it dry. He must have been satisfied that the coast was clear. The street appeared deserted. Then he walked toward the unlit entrance of a small, glazed-brick building with a candy shop and tobacco store set in its narrow ground floor.

It happened before he got to the entrance. They were waiting for him under the tiled archway that joined the next building. One light-footed man in a raincoat snapped a short length of wire around the artist's neck and twisted. I think I heard a short, tortured gasp for air. The other man dug the sketchbook from inside the coat, and then they tossed him face down in the shallow waters of the street.

Chapter Two

I had never felt like a coward before. I stood there and did nothing while they killed the little guy, and let myself feel like a coward. My heart pounded as I watched and held back, but I knew it would be madness to interfere.

When they were gone I realized I could never safely go back to Georges's. My name was in no one's little black book, but my picture soon would be.

I stood there until the insistent ringing in my ears died away, feeling the sting of warm rain on my face and telling myself I was a fool to bother about Flame. Even if I found her I knew what she would say to me: "The door is over there, darling."

I remained in the shadow a long time, knowing every second I lost compounded the danger of my being there at all. I finally crossed over to him and dragged the limp body into a narrow lane under the tiled arch. The blood was still flowing where the garrote had opened his neck.

His steel-rimmed glasses had been knocked off. I went back to the curb and fished around in the water until my fingers found them. Then I put them on him and walked away.

I stood for a moment at the entrance to the building the artist had seemed headed for. Apartments stood above the ground-floor shops and I fished out a match to read the names beside the buzzers. They were French and Russian names and none of them was Paula Forrest.

I dropped the match when the door opened. A short Oriental, fixing his military rain cape, came through. He gave a start when he saw me. Then he touched his red-starred cap and moved off. The door closed gently.

I heard a girl laugh distantly above. I tried the door, and it was unlocked. I walked in.

The stairway was unlit, but I saw light above along a traverse hall. I squeezed the loose water out of my hair and turned down the collar of my raincoat.

When I reached the top landing the hall was deserted. But only for a moment. A tall woman with long earrings and ridiculous black bangs stepped out of a lounge and into the hall. I surprised her.

"*Bon soir*," she said, and then snapped her fingers sharply. "Leta, Leta!"

Leta appeared, a Chinese girl of perhaps fourteen in the blue cotton gown of the amah. She tried to help me off with my trench coat, but I refused. The tall woman invited me into the lounge. It was lighted only by a hurricane lamp against the drawn curtains on the street side. As I came in a chunky little man looked up from a newspaper, examined me casually, and then got up and left.

The tall woman smiled professionally. "You would like to see some girls?"

I looked around and realized I was in a small flesh shop of perhaps four or five rooms.

"Just one will do."

"You are new to Marie's," she said, eyeing me carefully. It was clear she wasn't too pleased with what she saw.

"Yes, I'm new to Marie's," I said.

The room was warm, and my wet shoes felt like boots. I lit a cigarette slowly, trading cautious looks with her. Unnaturally tall, she betrayed a sensitive contempt in her eyes, as though her destiny was to run a house but never to perform in one.

"I hear you've got an American girl here," I said. "I'd like to see her."

She eyed me tartly, and I think I was relieved for a moment when she shook her head. "No, no Americans. There are few left in Shanghai."

But I didn't believe her. "The one I'm looking for is here," I said.

The woman turned and snapped her fingers. "Leta!"

"Shut up," I whispered, catching her bony wrist in my hand. "This business was outlawed by the Reds. I'll have you raided in an hour."

She looked at me hatefully. "Who are you?"

I let go of her wrist. "Never mind that. Let me see her."

She turned without a word and I followed her along the hall. She stopped at a door on the street side and knocked softly. There was no answer. She turned the knob and we walked in.

A girl lay alone face down on the Grand Rapids bed. She wore a loose pink kimono and her head was buried in the pillow. The tall woman walked to the bed and pulled her over.

"Drunk," she said. "This one always gets drunk when it rains."

"Leave me alone," the girl mumbled.

The voice was from Texas. It wasn't Flame.

"She'll do," I said to the woman. "Get out."

"You pay first."

"I'll send you a check."

The woman picked a red shoe off the dressing table and threw it at me. Then she spat and slammed the door. I walked over and turned the key.

The girl had long brown hair, pale skin, and long, well-cared-for hands. She was trying to catch me in focus. "What you doing here?" she muttered. "I've retired from business for the night, mister. Go 'way."

"I only want to talk to you," I said. "Nothing professional."

"Drop dead."

"What's your name?"

She got up on an elbow. "Why you botherin' me, mister?"

"I'm a guy in trouble," I said. "Want to help me, baby?"

"Not especially." She paused, looking at me a long time. "You an American?"

"Is that a crime?"

"It is around here."

"Where you from?" I asked.

She lay back and pulled my hand to her lips. She took a deep drag on my cigarette. "The gutter, U.S.A. That answer your question?"

I walked over to the window and looked down at the street below. The rain was passing and a coolie was pulling a ricksha through the water. Then I saw that someone had taken up my old stand in the doorway of the bakery across the street.

"I'm looking for a girl," I said, turning. "I thought you might be the one. I think now maybe you can give me a line on her."

She turned over on her stomach with the long, full lines of her back toward me. "I don't know nothing about anybody, mister."

"Her name's Paula Forrest. Does that mean anything to you?"

Her hand crawled along the edge of the bed to an empty bottle on the floor. "Ain't this a hell of a time to be out of a drink, mister, when it's raining?"

"It's not raining any more. Snap out of it, baby. Paula Forrest. Think about that name for a minute. Or maybe you know her as Flame Forrest. It's a nickname she uses."

She looked at me with sudden resentment. "Why don't you get out of here? I don't know you. Maybe you're a phony. Maybe you could get me in trouble. Only Marie knows I'm an American. My papers say I'm Russian."

"Look, baby, I'm in too much of a hurry to get you in trouble. If I don't get out of here quick be in plenty of trouble myself. Flame Forrest. What does the name mean to you?"

"Not a thing."

I took her shoulders in my hands and brought her to a sitting position. My fingers dug in. "You're lying."

She twisted away and got off the bed. "Christ, there are five million people left in Shanghai—count 'em, five million. Am I supposed to know 'em all?"

"She was a newspaperwoman. Red hair. Maybe she used a different name. You'd remember an American newspaperwoman, wouldn't you?"

She hung there a moment. That lit something in her mind. She went to a drawer in the dressing table and pulled out a scrapbook.

"Yeah. There was a girl told me she wrote for newspapers, and she had red hair. I was a taxi dancer at a joint in Hongkew. She only worked there a little while and then the Reds closed us down. Maybe I got a picture."

She sat on the edge of the bed with the book and turned the pages of clippings and pictures in alcoholic slow motion. She kept stretching her eyes to keep them open. I sat beside her and read date lines from all over Asia and the Middle East. She had been a cabaret dancer.

She stopped at an eight by ten group picture of about two dozen hostesses in evening gowns.

"That's me here." Then her finger began tracing other faces with set smiles and then went over them again. "No. She's not here. I guess she came to work later."

I took the album out of her hands and examined the faces myself. Flame wasn't there. I flipped through the rest of the book slowly. I stopped at a blown-up candid shot of the girl from Texas doing a strip under a spotlight. You could see café patrons in the shadows around the edge of the dance floor. Two guys caught my eye because the photographer had caught them in an unusual pose. They weren't watching the stripper, and she was already down to three lotus buds. I held the picture closer and my heart began picking up extra beats. One of the men was gesturing excitedly with his hands, a thin, brown-faced man in a Panama hat. The other was staring daggers through a casual smile. For a moment I thought I must be crazy. My pulse shifted into high gear. There was no mistake about the second man, the slick hair, the sharp, handsome nose, the long-lashed eyes.

It was Cottardo.

I ripped the picture out of the book. "Where was this taken?"

"What the hell do you think you're doing, mister? That's my picture."

I grabbed her wrist. "Hurry up."

Hostility flared in her eyes for a moment, and then it passed. "I told you. In Hongkew."

"Where in Hongkew?"

"The Viennese Club. The Reds closed the place down, like they did everything else where people could have fun. All they want to do is re-educate everybody."

"When was it taken?"

"About nine months ago. Just before I came here to work."

I folded the picture and put it in the pocket of my coat. "Who owned the place?"

She grimaced. "A stinking Austrian named Haigmann. We found out later he had peepholes cut in our dressing rooms and used to bring military brass to watch us."

Haigmann. The name meant things to me. He was a guy with a gold thumb. When I reopened the Shanghai bureau in 1946 you couldn't dig up a story of graft or get-rich-quick schemes without finding his thumb print.

When I looked at the girl again she was sobbing softly.

"You suppose someday I can go back?" she said. "I'd like to see it rain in Dallas again. I murdered a guy."

"My guess is he deserved it."

"Thanks, mister." She straightened up suddenly and walked uncertainly to the dressing table. She began brushing her hair. "Can I bum another cigarette?"

I threw her the pack and walked to the window again. The guy was still standing there in the doorway. I moved across the room and kissed her on the shoulder. "Thanks for everything, baby." She watched in the mirror.

"Any time," she said. "Any time at all, mister. Come back and see me any time."

"Don't wait up," I said. I unlocked the door and found the hall deserted. I buckled my raincoat on the way down the stairs. It had started to rain again.

I walked across the street and stopped before the man in the doorway. He was a short guy with a broad, pasty face, and my directness startled him. I jabbed him hard in the stomach and a cigarette catapulted out of his mouth. As he hunched with the blow, I clipped him on the back of the neck with the edge of my palm. I hit hard and he fell hard. He was out.

I patted over his pockets until I found the gun he hadn't had time to reach. It was a Mauser that looked as old as World War I. I slipped it into my raincoat pocket and walked to Avenue Joffre. I picked up a ricksha and told the boy to take me to Hongkew.

Chapter Three

Rain, dripping inside, struck the black hood of the ricksha like an incessant drumming of fingertips. The cotton seat was soaked and puddles soon collected along the creases of my coat. The ricksha coolie had attached brown oilcloth across the face of the cab, enclosing me in a dark, private world of my own. I lit a match and peered at my watch. It was almost midnight.

Two years ago Cottardo had been shot to death in Greece after skipping out of Italy. My story had sent him running; but that news obit was in error. Cottardo had been caught nine months ago in Shanghai by a night-club photographer. He looked very much alive in the picture, Cottardo and Flame in Shanghai. Find Cottardo. Find Flame.

Cottardo's type, I was thinking, never dies of anything but old age. When I knew him in Rome he was a young purchasing agent with aristocratic manners and too much money in his pocket for a young purchasing agent. When Flame and I split up, my fault as usual, he sold her a bill of romantic goods, nonsense as usual, but she went for it. I poked my Greek nose into his Italian affairs and came up with a bribery scandal, but he was tipped and was across the Adriatic and flying south two hours before my story broke. When the news cropped up two days later that he was dead, we speculated that someone had wanted him shut up for good. A few weeks later Flame suddenly quit her job and left town and I lost track of her—until two weeks ago.

The carriage began to slow and I pulled up one corner of the flapping shield to look out. We were beginning the rise over Garden Bridge. I could hear the coolie's breath bark with the pull, and I felt like a perfect bastard just sitting there letting him lug me. Then we were across the crest and starting down. I looked below to Soochow Creek, where sampans were nestled for the night, lifeless as a log jam.

The coolie followed Broadway East, past silent go-downs and the endless procession of luggage shops that lead to Hongkew, Shanghai's Little Tokyo. I sat back, remembering 1937, the first time I saw the streets of Hongkew. Seven weeks earlier the Japs had burst from their quarter in the struggle for all Shanghai: I was a raw kid with no paper behind me; I had worked my way across with the bright idea of free-lancing the war. I made out. After the last war I came back and found that during the Japanese occupation the little men had turned Hongkew into a ghetto for European Jews who had flocked to China to escape Hitler's ghettos.

Originally, Hongkew had been laid out as the American settlement more than a century ago.

We had been in Hongkew about ten minutes when the ricksha stopped at a corner and let me off near the river. I paid the coolie and waited until he pulled out of sight. Then I crossed the street and walked one block north. I knew my way.

It was a plaster, two-story building the color of mud and as old as Hongkew itself. There was no sign of life about. A wooden sign over the lower windows told me Haigmann was still keeping up pretenses. It said: "Haigmann Margarine Mfg. Co.," with translations in Chinese and Japanese along the sides. I found the passageway that led around back, passed under an arch dripping with bougainvillea, and started up the outside stairway to the second-floor quarters. August Haigmann lived there.

A dog inside the apartment began to growl before I reached the landing. I rapped on the door and waited.

There was a shuffling inside, and pretty soon Haigmann called through the door, "Who is it?"

"An old friend," I said.

"Who?"

"Let me in. I want to talk to you."

There was a long pause and finally the door opened the short length of the safety chain. The police dog nosed out defiantly. "*Sha*," Haigmann commanded, gripping its leather collar. He looked out, but couldn't see me clearly in the darkness of the landing.

I lit a match. Haigmann examined me in the brief glow. "Ah, the fool American journalist."

Fool is right, I said to myself. "Let me in."

He unhooked the chain and held back the dog as I walked in. The room, brightly lighted, smelled faintly of vegetable oils from the small manufacturing plant below. A woman stood apprehensively in the center of the room, her eyes fixed on me. They were Oriental eyes, large and shy, but her skin was smooth and white and she was taller than the race from which she had partly sprung. She was strangely beautiful, as Eurasian women are apt to be.

"Sit down." Haigmann smiled, and then gave a command in German to the dog. The tawny animal growled briefly and leaped onto the bed in one corner of the room. Haigmann chose to live modestly.

"So you come back to Shanghai." Haigmann grinned, sitting down heavily in a leather chair and selecting a pipe from a rack beside him. "As you see, much has changed. My European wife is dead. The woman who looks at you so curiously is now my wife, Herr Journalist. A beauty, eh?"

I nodded self-consciously. I had known Haigmann's European wife, a Jewess named Stella. He had been a colonel in the Austrian army and was faced with the choice of divorcing her because of her blood or fleeing to China with her. He chose the latter; he hadn't been a rogue all his life. China changed him.

Almost at once I sensed I had come at a bad time. I saw Haigmann's young wife hastily gather three cups of coffee off an oak table and take them into the pantry. Haigmann saw it too, but laughed comfortably.

"That one, she is beautiful but lazy. Those cups have been here since tiffin." Then he called to her with superficial kindness, "Ariadne, some coffee now, eh?"

Haigmann drew flame into the bowl of his pipe. The feeling crept over me that we were not alone, that I was intruding, that another person was still in the apartment. But where? There was only the large studio room, the pantry, the bathroom.

"Why do you look about so?" Haigmann smiled. "There is no one here but us."

"What about the pantry?"

"You come with suspicions on your mind, eh? Please look, my friend, and the bathroom too. I do not lie to you."

I got up and looked. I felt foolish, but settled back in the chair feeling better for having taken the precaution. "Sorry," I said.

"Not at all, Herr Cloud. In these times, it is best not to trust anyone. Why, I do not trust even my beautiful Ariadne. As you see, she is young enough to be my daughter, but old enough to make a cuckold of me. I must watch her, eh?"

His laughter soared as Ariadne eyed him coolly. I eyed him too, a towering figure, large-boned and crudely masculine. His thick calves were cased in polished leggings; a broad belt held up an old pair of faded riding trousers. An acre of hairy chest was bared by the open neck of his shirt. Haigmann was a man in his fifties. He moved with the spirit of a man twenty years younger.

Ariadne brought an aluminum pot of coffee and set delicate Spode cups before us. They had been Stella's cups, vestiges of a former life.

"Now then," Haigmann said, his eyes searching me with good humor, "you come at this late hour for a proper purpose. A story, perhaps? I have no stories. Influence? I have no influence. Just to talk? Yes, we can talk."

I sipped the hot coffee and glanced at Ariadne, who had taken a chair at her sewing machine and begun work on a silk garment. There was dignity in the way she sat, the way she held her head. A button had come undone along the back of her dress and white skin flashed with every stretch of her arms.

"I'm not in Shanghai on a story," I explained. Haigmann offered me a cigarette from an opened pack on his tobacco stand. He lit it for me. "I'm looking for someone."

"A woman?"

I nodded.

"Always a woman, eh?" He sucked at the pipe, his blue-gray eyes shining with amusement. "If you come for advice, I give it to you. Go back before you find her. No woman is worth risking your neck for, Herr Journalist."

"I never take good advice," I said.

"Of course," he said, tamping the hot coals in his pipe with an index finger. "And once you find her, do you think you can get out of Shanghai—alive?"

"I found my way in. We'll find our way out." I smiled to myself. The Sassoon, under a brown-bearded old China hand named O'Rafferty, was at the moment tied up to a dock on the Pootung side of the Whangpoo River. The Sassoon had brought me to Shanghai, together with a cargo of Malayan rubber, and was due to leave Friday on the return trip to Hong Kong. The day after tomorrow.

"You make it sound so simple, Herr Cloud. Do you suppose I would remain in this hole of a place if I knew how to get out?"

"I don't think you want to leave."

"Ah, you are right, I do not."

I traded smiles with him. "I remember that you got along well enough with the Japs, and my guess is you have made friends with the Reds. If I knew August Haigmann, he is in the middle—scraping gold off both sides of the political fence."

"You flatter me, my journalistic friend. I am a small businessman. I leave politics alone. But the Reds, they are country bumpkins. They are more frightened of Shanghai than we Shanghailanders are of them. The big city bewilders them. Still, they police it well."

"I understand they closed your cabaret. What was it? The Viennese Club?"

He took the pipe out of his mouth and peered at me with some surprise in his eyes. "You keep well informed, Herr Cloud. Yes, they closed me up three weeks ago, but what matter? One must change with the times, eh?"

Three weeks ago. I had assumed from what the Texas girl told me it had been nine months ago.

"It is the second time they closed me up," Haigmann went on. "But this time it is for good, I am afraid."

I took the photograph out of my pocket and unfolded it. I held my fingertip to Cottardo's throat. "Recognize this guy?"

He took the picture out of my hands and examined the faces for a long time, sucking at the pipe. "Where did you get this?"

"Never mind that. It was taken in your place just before they closed you up the first time. Where can I find this guy?"

He broke into an innocent laugh and handed the picture back to me. "Herr Cloud, I cannot be expected to know everyone who came into the Viennese Club."

"I think you know this character. He's just your type."

"You talk like a fool." He got up. "Sorry, Herr Journalist. You have come to the wrong man. I cannot help you."

"August Haigmann is never the wrong man," I grinned, "if there is a loose buck to be made." I pulled out a wad of *jen min piao*.

"You overestimate me. Put the money away. It's dangerous that you are even in my house."

"For you or for me?"

"For both of us."

The sewing machine purred against our conversation. It was almost as though Ariadne didn't understand the language we spoke. Every time the back of her dress popped open my eyes were drawn to that teasing bit of flesh.

Haigmann watched me closely. When he understood my glances he laughed lecherously. "A bit of woman's skin, it charms you, eh, American?"

"I was just thinking," I said, "how desperately she must want to escape you."

"Of course. In the East a wife is a slave. This one had a French father and she thinks she should be treated like a European."

"I should treat her like a princess."

"You are a fool."

"I know."

Haigmann knocked the ashes thoughtfully from his pipe and replaced it in the rack. The low ceiling made him seem a giant. The leggings creaked as he paced slowly, the trousers flared and bagging, the hair on his arms bleached almost invisible by the sun. He stopped across the room from me. "You say you can get out of Shanghai at will, eh?"

"I didn't say that."

"But you have a way out—a matter of being at a certain place at a certain time, perhaps."

"Something like that."

"How long have you been in Shanghai?"

"What difference does it make?"

"How long?"

"Since Monday."

His eyes began to narrow, as though a sudden plan were developing in his mind. I began to sour on the idea of getting his help. In another moment his face cracked in a cheerful smile.

"Herr Cloud, I think we can do business together."

The statement sent an unexpected chill along my spine. "Forget it," I said, pushing my coffee cup aside and getting up. "The guy in the picture means something to you, doesn't he? Look, I don't give a damn about him except that he can lead me to someone I do care about. I didn't smuggle myself into this Red squirrel cage to do business with you. I want to find that guy, Cottardo. Don't get any elaborate ideas. That's all I want—Cottardo."

"Sit down, Herr Cloud. You are too tense. We must be friends if we are to do business together."

"I remember the sort of business you do."

Haigmann's eyes held a sagging grin that seemed a warning. I had seen that grin the first time shortly after the war, when he appeared suddenly in my office. During those days Shanghai was tremendously DDT-conscious, and several outfits were flooding the shops with beer bottles of kerosene labeled DDT. Haigmann wanted to trade me facts for immunity; I traded. He was safely back in margarine when my story broke and the arrests were made. A year later, when speculation in rice was fattening a few and starving the coolies, he appeared again in my office to trade. He had a faculty for seeing the handwriting on the wall first and always withdrew, covering up his tracks, before the ax fell. He became a valuable news source; I cultivated him.

I walked to the window and turned, facing his laugh.

"You are a devious person, Herr Cloud," he said. "You look for a woman and ask me about a man. Does that make sense?"

"In this case it does."

"And the woman's name?"

"Let's leave her out of it." I knew Haigmann too well to trust him with that. He had the sort of honed mind that found ways of putting stray information to work for him, and I didn't want that mind working on Flame. "You wouldn't know her. Out of your class."

"I have angered you, and now you say childish things." Haigmann paced thoughtfully before the shallow entry hall, as though to tell me that I couldn't leave if I wanted to. The leggings creaked softly, leather against leather, and it seemed to me now an ominous sound. "Perhaps I know this woman after all."

"You're free to guess."

"I don't have to guess, Herr Journalist. The woman you hunt is dead."

I moved impulsively. I strode across the room and grabbed the front of his shirt in my hands. "I'll kill you," I whispered in his face. "I'll kill you if you're faking."

"Flame Forrest has been liquidated." He smiled evenly. "Now take your hands off me. I shouldn't want the dog to tear you to bits."

"I don't believe you," I said.

He peeled my hands off him and grinned. "You do have spirit, eh? That is an excellent virtue, Herr Cloud. We will make use of your spirit."

I turned away angrily. "Forget it. I'm not interested in being useful to you."

He laughed outrageously, standing feet apart before the entry. "But, of course, you will be. And to yourself as well, for we will make money together."

I picked up my trench coat from the back of the chair and started toward him. His words stopped me short.

"It is too late for you to turn back, Herr Cloud. Do you know you are wanted for murder? Only Haigmann can get you out of Shanghai alive."

The sewing machine stopped and Ariadne's eyes, soft and frightened, watched me.

"What do you mean?"

"The Polish artist."

"I didn't kill him."

"What does it matter?" He chuckled and moved forward in the room. A sinking feeling came over me. If the Shanghai police were looking for me, they had a sketch to go by. And it looked a hell of a lot like me. If they wanted me, it wouldn't be on a phony murder charge. In the syllogism of their thinking, Americans are spies, I am an American, therefore I am a spy. Haigmann was right. What did it matter that they chose to start with murder?

He stopped at the tobacco stand and picked up a pipe from the forest of stems in the rack. "Ariadne will fix more coffee and we will see what can be done about you."

"Never mind the coffee. What's your current racket?"

"I have no racket, Herr Journalist. Merely a problem in transportation. Come, I show you."

He got a flashlight and I followed him to the entry hall, I saw a second door at right angles to the one I had entered by. He opened it, flicked on the light switch, and started down an inside stairway to the plant below.

A draft swept up the stairway and brought with it the fresh, salty fumes of the factory. When we got to the bottom, he used the flashlight instead of lighting the place up. I followed him through hogsheads of lard and oleo oil, and then to the back of the room, where two giant metal churners were silent for the night. Nearby stood a cutting machine that led onto a narrow, waist-high platform, where Chinese hands would do the packaging.

"In here," Haigmann said shortly. He fumbled through his keys and held the light on a door lock. When he got it open we entered a narrow, refrigerated storeroom stacked to the burlap ceiling with pound cartons of margarine. He turned on a dim light, dangling from a long cord, and locked the door after me.

"I trust no one," he said, as though the gesture needed explanation. "But tonight I am going to trust you because you must trust me, eh? I tell you everything, like before. Everything."

My skin perspired despite the chill air.

He began unstacking a vertical row of margarine and let the cartons pile about his feet like discarded bricks. Soon he reached his arm through the opening and brought out a package like the others, but I knew it would not be so innocent.

He opened the flap and slowly emptied four yellow cubes in paper jackets onto his massive palm. He discarded three. The remaining unit looked indistinguishable from the others.

He began unpeeling the jacket. I saw at once he held a molded lump of gold.

His laugh was little more than a chuckle. "I suspect you want to return to Hong Kong," he said. "This will return with you."

"You've got it all figured out, haven't you?"

"Gold on the Hong Kong black market is fifty-six dollars an ounce—so this lump almost doubles in value. A proper business. One of transportation."

I felt the weight of the Mauser in my pocket, and it felt good. When I brought it into the open, he gave it only a passing glance.

"You have a gun," he said. "That is good. You may need it."

"Unlock the door."

"Your temper is amusing. American righteousness, eh? You are a child, Herr Cloud. Perhaps that is why I trust you. My problem, as I said, is simply one of transportation. That is a proper business, you must agree. Yours, at the moment, is one of murder. Would you kill me rather than engage in proper business? I think not. But hold the gun, if it gives you comfort."

His playful manner in the face of the gun was maddening. He had lived on wits so long he was ready to match them against bullets. I could almost admire him for it. He ignored the gun completely now.

"I do not have to tell you that the Reds dislike gold to disappear from China. They give the death penalty to the foolish ones. We will not be among the foolish. I have friends. We will see to it you arrive in Hong Kong safely. You wonder, perhaps, why I wish to involve you when I already have established channels, eh? For six months I have dispatched gold out of Shanghai. But it must pass through so many hands that when my small cargoes reach Hong Kong the scales tell the story. A friend takes a scrape here, another friend a scrape there—my gold loses weight in passage. One must be an opportunist, Herr Journalist. You are an opportunity. This gold will not scrape off in your righteous hands."

"And if I turn you in—a foreigner smuggling gold out of China?"

"That would be a mistake." He smiled broadly, and I saw his trump card coming. "My friends who will protect you—they are the Reds. Officials who trust me to see this gold converted to accounts in Hong Kong banks against a rainy day. I am but a middleman. I do not think they would like you to interfere, eh?"

Chapter Four

I shot out the light globe and pitched the storeroom into blackness. Haigmann was a sitting duck in a narrow aisle. "Stand where you are," I said. "I can't miss if I want to hit you." Then I backed to the door and found the lock with my fingers. I put the tip of the gun against it and fired.

I anticipated some show from Haigmann. But all he did was laugh. I pushed the door open into darkness as blinding as before. "Good luck, Herr journalist," Haigmann said. I closed the door after me, and then it came. The rustle. The flash through my mind that there *had* been another person about. The thick grunt and the slice through the air. Lights came on, but they were in my head. They died quickly, even as I began to fold....

I awoke face down on the floor of the apartment upstairs. I felt as though I had been out for hours. Nevertheless, Ariadne was still working at the sewing machine; I could hear its uneven whine. I opened my eyes and a deep ache hammered inside my head when I began to move. I saw Haigmann in a flickering double image and I blinked my eyes and pretty soon the two Haigmanns fused. He was seated at the table, drinking coffee, his back to me. I rose to my elbows and saw someone else.

I think I saw the flash of rings on his fingers first. I looked beyond them to the massive hand, the cropped hair, and the small, glistening eyes banked by flesh. His lips sucked noisily at a cup of coffee. I closed my eyes, but my mind wasn't playing tricks because he was still there when I looked again.

It was Georges. Occupation: bartender.

Haigmann turned. "You are rested, eh?"

I got to my feet and felt the back of my head. It felt like hell. Ariadne stopped to look at me. She was no longer working on the silk. She was sewing at the shoulders of my raincoat.

Georges tells me you've met before," Haigmann said. "That spares the introductions, eh?"

"Next time we meet," I said, "I'll remember to duck."

Haigmann laughed in good humor. Georges's unsmiling eyes avoided me as he drank his coffee.

I looked at the table. Piled near the center were the Mauser, my wallet emptied, the money, comb, deck of cards—everything.

Haigmann poked through my things and withdrew the cards. He slipped them out of the case and shuffled them aimlessly.

"Do you understand about human patterns, Herr Cloud?" He grinned. "Everyone has a pattern, even my young half-caste wife, who sits so rebelliously at her work. When something doesn't fit into a man's pattern, it leaves room for suspicion, eh? Like a pack of cards in your raincoat pocket. I cannot fit into your pattern. It is the last thing I might expect to find in your pocket. Now, what shall I make of it?"

I steadied myself with a hand against the sideboard. "What are you getting at?" I exercised my neck and closed my eyes with pain.

"Perhaps you are bored easily, eh? And so the cards."

"You can let it go at that." I moved to the table and poured some coffee. I looked at my gun. Had he unloaded it?

He cased the deck and pawed through my other things. "You have no identification with you," he commented, "That fits the pattern. You are a hopeless amateur. Another man would carry forged papers. Forged papers are better than none. Since you have none, we must keep you out of sight, eh? For your own safety."

"Your concern for me is touching." The coffee felt good going down, and I began to pull myself together.

He lit his pipe through a smile. "A chance argument with a coolie over a ricksha fare, the police ask for your papers, and you cannot produce anything but a pack of cards." He touched the gun to illustrate the next step. "They have your picture—that was extremely foolish of you. Dead, you would be of no use to me."

The information at his fingertips angered me. It was uncanny. He knew about the dead artist only a couple of hours after it happened. He knew about the picture. He knew I was looking for Flame. The only blank was Cottardo, and I suspected he knew plenty that he wasn't sharing.

He got up and gestured toward my things on the table. "Put this stuff back in your pockets. Be careful of the gun. It is still loaded."

His self-confidence was megalomania. But Georges was more cautious. He laid his fat hand on the Mauser and snapped it up. It went out of sight in a pocket of his wrinkled tropical coat. Haigmann laughed.

"While you slept we have been busy," Haigmann went on. "Everything is arranged. A friend will keep you out of sight in a sampan on the Pootung side. The police will not find you." He walked to Ariadne, who was still working on my raincoat. "You would appear ridiculous carrying a lump of margarine, eh? We have a better plan. I have melted down the gold into flats, which Ariadne sews into the shoulders of your coat. The weight will not hinder you there."

I started putting my stuff back in my pockets; it was all there—but the picture.

I started to say something, but held back. If he had thought to keep the picture, it told me what I had only suspected: He knew Cottardo.

Georges sat back in the chair, balancing it on its creaking hind legs and skillfully rolled a cigarette. For a man of his bulk it struck me as remarkable that you could so easily forget he was in the room. He never seemed to be listening. He said nothing. His mind seemed detached from his surroundings.

I lit one of Haigmann's cigarettes and moved to the window. The rain pelted against it in sudden gusts of wind that died and returned. Haigmann was kidding himself; I wasn't going to leave Shanghai until I found what I came for. Flame.

I said, "You're damned certain I'll deliver the gold when I get to Hong Kong, aren't you?"

Haigmann turned an eager face on me. "But of course. You will have no alternative. You will not have to deliver it. The gold will be picked up from you."

"I see."

Haigmann knocked the ashes from his pipe. "Now, we must know when your transportation takes you out of Shanghai."

"You seem to know everything about me. I'm surprised you don't know that."

"I shall find out if you prefer not to tell me."

I didn't doubt that he could. "Early next week," I lied.

He pulled at his nose thoughtfully. "That is a long time to keep you hidden." He looked at the clock. "Ha, it is already Thursday morning."

"That's your problem," I said.

He smiled confidently. "So it is. But I am used to solving problems, eh?" Then the humor went out of his eyes. "The rest is simple. When you reach Hong Kong, go to the Imperial Hotel. A room will be reserved for you. An agent will contact you, and your job will be finished."

He told me that the gold being sewn in my coat weighed sixty ounces. I could fill in for myself where it had come from: the teeth of the dead, the rings on their fingers, the heirlooms in their homes. Melted down, the impurities and alloys rendered.

Then Haigmann added in a tone of friendly warning, "You would be very foolish to tell anyone en route of your private cargo. Life is cheap here. Gold is dear. Men have been murdered for a handful of coppers."

"I'll try to stay alive," I said. It struck me then that there was more than gold involved. At $56 an ounce, I would be transporting metal valued at $3,360. That was too trifling a sum for Haigmann to take any risks for. I had missed something.

The raincoat was finished and Haigmann helped me slip it on with elaborate courtesy. The added weight at my shoulders was comfortably distributed. Even then, Ariadne had sewn cotton padding under the bars of gold to prevent chafing. I thanked her with a glance.

"You have no identification," Haigmann said. "The pack of cards will be your identification. Keep them with you. Georges will accompany you to Pootung."

Georges put on his raincoat and then took the gun out of his pocket, checked it, and put it back. I smiled halfheartedly and we left.

Georges walked slightly behind me down the stairs and into the fresh, wet wind. His face, a heavy, stupid face, was a deceit. His alert eyes gave him away, brown, venal eyes. They had obviously watched out for him, whatever the political winds that blew him to Asia.

He kept that half step behind until we got to the street and found a pedicab. As I was getting in his arm held me back and his eyes gave me a long silent warning.

I got into the cab and he maneuvered his wide hips and heavy shanks beside me. It was a tight fit, as his body relaxed it pressed against me. The rain was becoming a steady drizzle and the coolie fixed a shield across us. Georges told him to take us to the China Lumber Company wharf.

Haigmann had given me a pack of cigarettes and I began hunting for it. The pack was in my trench-coat pocket. As my fingers closed around it I was pricked by a pin Ariadne had apparently left behind. It was stuck in a small loose piece of silk cloth. I drew it out with the cigarettes with passing curiosity. The pin was obviously there to call my attention to it.

"Cigarette?" I asked.

Georges grunted a refusal. He wasn't happy with this little chore Haigmann had sent him on. Neither was I.

I spread the swatch of cloth in my right palm, concealing it from Georges. I lit the cigarette casually.

In the flickering light of the match I saw that Ariadne had stitched two words for me to read. They were clumsily done on the machine.

FLAME CATHAY H

I put it away with the matches. The pedicab turned right at the corner and Georges lurched against me even as his feet and thighs tensed to ballast the turn.

We rode in silence and I smoked thoughtfully. Then the opportunity came: We turned left. I threw my weight against Georges and felt the pedicab rise suddenly to a teeter on its left tire. Georges tried to grab me. The carriage crashed on its side to the street and I heard the coolie yell. I ripped the shield away, kicked myself loose, and ran.

The streets were dark and wet and quiet. I sprinted around the corner and after a couple of dozen steps slipped into a residential lane stacked with plaster apartments. I worked my way to the next street, across, and into another lane. Within a couple of minutes I paused at Wayside Road and saw a few lights. I ducked into a doorway to catch my breath. Across the street and half a block down I spotted the wet haze of a green neon sign.

"Cathay H" meant Cathay Hotel, I reasoned. Flame was at the Cathay Hotel. I waited for about five minutes. Georges had lost me. I crossed the street. The place was a small Italian café, almost empty, but open even in these dark hours of the early morning. I strode through the door and found the phone against the back wall. I looked through the book for the number of the Cathay Hotel.

From where I stood I could see the street and be seen. But that didn't seem to matter now. I called the number.

The hotel operator must have been asleep. I hung on and lit a cigarette. Then a man's voice came through.

"Cathay."

"Paula Forrest."

"One moment."

It wasn't a moment. It seemed an hour before his voice came back. "She's not registered here," the man said.

I tossed the cigarette away. "Maybe she's registered as Flame Forrest. Look again."

He looked again. Finally, "She *was* registered, but Miss Forrest has checked out."

"When?"

"Early this afternoon."

"Did she leave a forwarding—" My eyes were on the street, and Georges passed, trotting heavily. He stopped. "Did she leave a forwarding address?"

"No."

Georges stood at the door. He started across the wooden floor, throwing those shoulders of his from his flat feet. One hand was dug in the pocket of his dripping raincoat. I hung up.

"You're a hard guy to lose," I said.

He stopped in front of me. His free hand whipped out and caught me across the cheek. I took it. He had brought the coat pocket upright and I think he was mad enough to shoot. The startled Italian behind the counter watched us as we walked out together.

It wasn't far to the China Lumber wharf, and we went by foot. Georges wanted it that way, despite the discomfort of walking for him. He didn't want to take another chance in a pedicab or ricksha. It made him vulnerable, boxed him in, and he obviously was the type who never makes the same mistake twice.

The long dock was almost bare. The Whangpoo, rising to flood tide, raced by in a chocolate torrent. I could see the bleak decks of lighters tied up, and small junks and sampans hovering in their protection from the swift current. The drizzle fell silently against the creaking wooden dock as we walked toward the flickering lights of the Ming Wha Sugar Factory in the distance.

"*Nous y voici*," Georges muttered. We stopped beside an ancient Gantry crane, its long metal arm poised in the night sky.

Georges brought the Mauser out of his pocket. I looked at it and laughed. "Put it away," I said, slipping off the coat. "The gold's all yours, with my compliments. If there's going to be a double cross, it couldn't happen to a nicer bastard than August Haigmann."

"Fool," he mumbled between thick, trembling lips. "The gold is a trifle. The cards. *Donnez-moi les cartes!*"

The words stunned me. "Give me the cards!" Haigmann had been strangely solicitous about the deck. It was to be my identification, he said. The images of the last few hours swam uncertainly through my mind. The gold was only incidental. The cards were something more.

The deck felt suddenly heavy in my shirt pocket, I stood in the face of Georges's threatening growl trying to think, trying to figure out whether the cards were worth a gamble. Georges brought the gun in closer.

The coat was hanging from my hands and I slowly bunched the waist into a grip. "Aren't you going to a lot of trouble for a goddamn pack of cards?" I said. "You sold them to me in that bar you run, for Christ's sake. Why didn't you hold onto them if you wanted them?"

He moved closer, a hulking form in the darkness. His hand reached out for my shirt and the cards. I caught my breath, stepped back, and swung the hanging shoulders of the trench coat. The gold slapped against his hand like a blackjack. The gun exploded wildly, skittering to the dock. I swung again, but Georges anticipated the blow. He raised his thick arm with a Gallic oath; he fenced off the blow and tore the coat out of my grip. His bearlike body thrust itself against me and his arms wrapped me up.

His breath came hot and nasty against my ear. I worked a hand up between us and caught his chin and lips in my fingers. I dug in, trying to force him away. He only squeezed harder. His hands locked behind my back and his elbows slowly closed in at my sides like a vise. My fingers clung to the thick flesh of his face and he jerked his head in an attempt to loosen my grip. But he wouldn't relax the strangling hold around my body, relentlessly narrowing the distance between his steel arms until I thought my ribs would crack. A ringing went up in my ears as my breath stopped coming and a split second before it happened I realized I was blacking out.

When I went limp he eased up and I became conscious of the ringing in my ears again. My head spun dizzily; I had lost consciousness for only a moment. He was breathing like a bull. Slowly he let me fall through his arms and I lay face down against the wooden planks. He looked for the gun. It had disappeared in the darkness.

I lay still, catching my breath in short, silent gasps. He had found the gun. He returned, dug a toe under my shoulder, and kicked me over on my back. Then I heard someone approach beside him. Georges bent down beside me and found the deck in my pocket. Then I heard his voice.

"Take him midstream and dump him. The pig won't come up for a week."

My eyes were open, but I couldn't gather any strength for a moment. The guy, a river coolie, picked up my arms and hoisted me across his wet back. It was now or never. I twisted and threw the coolie off balance. I lurched for Georges.

He was fast. The butt of the gun cracked my skull almost before I touched him. He knew how to do it; he'd already practiced a couple of hours earlier.

When I fell to the wood this time, I was through.

Chapter Five

I was stretched out on a bed. The room was dark and I was sweating beneath the blankets. I pulled off the covers and staggered around until I found the light switch on the wall.

I saw that I was stripped naked. My clothes were hung about the room to dry. It was a small room that had "cheap hotel" written all over it. My eyes picked out a woman's blue raincoat draped across the back of a wooden chair. I turned.

I was not alone.

Against the wall, fright clearly on her face, stood Ariadne. She watched my eyes as though somehow she expected me to be angry with her.

"Forgive me," she said with hesitation. "You were wet through and through."

"Of course," I said, feeling a little foolish. I went into the bathroom and wrapped a towel around my hips.

"Your head—it aches?"

"A little."

Her voice was warm and delicate and French, with its "r" sounded far back. I hadn't heard her speak before. In Haigmann's presence she had been the brooding, silent Oriental girl.

"I'm not very good at thanking people," I said. "I guess you saved my life. Thanks. Now, why don't you sit down and stop feeling scared? You're standing against that wall as though I were going to throw knives at you."

"Cloud," she said. "Alexander Cloud. That is a lovely name. Will you take me with you?"

It came just like that. And that, I knew, was why she was frightened—not of me, but that I might not say yes.

"No," I said. "I don't blame you for wanting to get out of this crazy city, but I'm not your ticket. For one thing, Haigmann would get a line on us, and that would finish our beautiful trip."

"You are afraid of him?"

"He's not my idea of a sweet guy."

"Take me with you."

I went over to her and caught her hand. It was soft, the fingers long and expressive. I pulled her to the chair she had apparently sat thinking in, waiting in the darkness for me to revive. I sat on the edge of the bed and looked at her.

"Look," I said. "You're a nice kid, but don't get balky."

"You must leave Shanghai," she whispered earnestly. "I will go with you. He will not find us."

I looked at her black hair, brushed severely to her shoulders. I looked at her breasts, full and breathing apprehensively. I liked what I saw and it made me angry. I didn't want any entanglements. I wanted a chance to live the last two years over again. I wanted to find Flame.

"You like me?" she asked softly.

"Of course. You're beautiful."

Her Oriental eyes clouded. "But I am a half-caste—that is why you will not take me with you."

She put her hands over her face, over the eyes that gave away her mixed blood, the cheekbones a little too high and heavy for a purely Western face. She began to sob.

"For Christ's sake," I said, getting up. "You're off base. I want to help you, but I can't take you with me. It would be suicide for both of us."

In my awkward way, I was beginning to feel like a heel.

"Of course," she said. "I'm sorry."

She straightened and I saw that hope was vanishing from her eyes. I pulled her to me and lifted her chin with my hand. Her lips withheld any response when I kissed them. I gave it up and turned away.

"How did you get away from Haigmann?"

She answered in a soft, unemotional voice. "He takes sleeping pills. When you left he went to bed. He will not awaken until noon."

"All hell will break loose if you're not there when he gets back."

"It does not frighten me."

I looked at her. "No." I smiled gently. "I don't think anything really frightens you."

"I was afraid Georges would hurt you. Haigmann trusts him, but I do not. I was right."

"Thanks again."

She avoided my eyes. "I heard them arranging to take you to Pootung from the lumber wharf. I waited until August was asleep and went there. I thought I must be too late. I hoped maybe you had got away from Georges. But then you came, and I heard the shot. I watched. When Georges left, the coolie carried you down to his sampan. I awoke the Chinese in a sampan nearby and he *yulowed* fast until we could catch up. Then I bought your body from the coolie and brought you here."

I smiled down at her. "Sounds like you own me. Hope I wasn't too expensive."

"You joke." She lay back in the chair, looking suddenly very tired.

"Georges got the coat—and the cards."

She showed no sign of surprise or alarm. All she said was: "That does not matter. You are alive."

"What about those cards? What do they mean?"

"It is best that Georges has taken them. He will be killed because of them. You would have been killed too."

I lit a cigarette and threw the match in the wastebasket. "What do you mean?"

"The gold in your coat," she said after a long pause, "was meant for your assassin. August has that type of mind. He is one who likes to do two things at once. It was to happen in Hong Kong, after the cards were taken from you."

I took a deep drag on that one. It was beginning to seem like a dream. Haigmann, with a touch of cunning, had come up with a self-liquidating device. I would have been handing a guy the fee for killing me when I handed over the coat. At least he would have been well paid. "Let's get back to the cards," I said. "What's the gimmick there?"

She twisted her head in a gesture of innocence. "Who knows? August has his hands in many things. While you lay unconscious, he and Georges did something to the cards—with glue. I could not see what."

"Could he be passing information of some sort?"

"Perhaps. It would not be the first time."

"I see. What about the gold?"

"He told you correctly. Certain Red officers pass it to him and he ships it with cargoes of margarine to Canton. From there it is smuggled to Hong Kong. But the past few weeks he has had something that is more important. Our place was searched once by the military. I don't know what they were looking for. It is better if we don't know."

I swung off the bed and started to walk around. I was intrigued and angry at the same time. I had stopped breaking my neck for stories, but this excited my old instincts. At the same time I didn't like being turned into an expendable chessman in somebody's private chess game. If Haigmann wanted me dead at the end of my errand, it could only be because alive I represented a threat—the threat that I would find out what he was up to and trace it back to him.

"How does this fit for size?" I muttered. "Haigmann told me Flame was dead because he didn't want me nosing around Shanghai looking for her. Whatever he did to those cards, he was anxious to get rid of them himself and yet know just where I was—stowed in the stinking bottom of some sampan and staying out of trouble."

She nodded. That fitted.

"I called the Cathay Hotel," I said. "Thanks for the pinpricks. But Flame had checked out."

Ariadne raised her eyes timidly. "You must love her very much to risk so much for her."

The remark irritated me. "Don't make me out a hero," I said. "I'm nobody's hero. I lost something when I lost Flame. I want to get it back. Maybe I'm only a fool."

"She must have hurt you."

"She was entitled to walk out on me. I wouldn't have any respect for her now if she hadn't. Want me to go on?"

"No, please don't. I'm sure you treated her badly."

"How did you know where she was staying?"

"I heard August mention it several times."

"What about Cottardo?"

"The name means nothing to me."

Ariadne sat there with her legs held apart, as Oriental women are apt to sit. The pale yellow Shantung skirt was split along the left side and I was having some difficulty staying on good behavior. I had been trying to hold back straying thoughts since that moment only a few hours ago when I had first seen her. She was at once tempting and desirable.

She said, "You will leave Shanghai soon?"

"Friday night."

"It is dangerous for you to go on the streets. This room, I think, will be safe. Until then I will stay with you. Perhaps you will grow to like me, and take me with you. I can be useful to you again. You will need me."

"You don't give up easily."

"I love you, Alexander Cloud."

She said my name very softly, as though it were poetry. Her expression was still and shy.

"You're a nice kid, but—"

"I am not a kid. I am a woman, can you not see?"

I could see, all right. The shantung gripped her legs. It would be too easy, too cruel. I told myself no.

"Do you really want to help me?" I asked. When I looked into her eyes, suddenly hopeful, I saw that this would be crueler still. But I had to go on. "You know the ropes. You could find Flame."

Her eyes fell and her response was easy and natural. "Of course." She got up. "Tomorrow I find her. Tonight you must sleep."

"It is morning already."

"But it is not yet light."

She put her hands softly against my face. She bent closer and kissed my lips. Her touch undercut my resolutions; I knew I wanted her as I always wanted anything lovely, but it raised an old hostility in me even as I pulled her to me, forcing her young, hard breasts against my chest. I had spent too many hours regretting the cheap passions that had cost me Flame's love. I wanted that sort of thing behind me and forgotten. I wanted Flame. But Ariadne wasn't cheap and I tried desperately to think my way out of it. I took her narrow shoulders in my arms and held her off. "You don't love me," I muttered. "Don't say it again."

"I want to love you. That is the same thing."

"You'd better get out of here."

Her body stiffened in my hands as I got to my feet. "I am half-caste," she whispered. "I can see that matters too much."

"That doesn't matter a goddamn," I said. She wrenched out of my hands, and the old confusions stirred in me. I stopped trying to reason with myself. I wanted her, and I let myself say to hell with everything else. "Come here."

"Please—"

I caught her hand and pulled her close. My arms tightened around her back, forcing her against my half-naked body. She turned her face aside, avoiding my kiss. She didn't relax until my hands traveled along her back, undoing the buttons. She didn't relax until the blouse slipped off her arms to the floor.

Then her lips found my neck in small kisses that sent my blood soaring. Her arms held me tight, and through her light perfume the clean, washed odor of her body came to me.

When she looked up, her long black lashes were wet. "You love me a little?"

"Sure," I mumbled. "I love you a little."

"I am satisfied—to be loved only a little."

I undid the clasp of her bra and she stepped back. She let it slip off her arms to the floor. The rebellious innocence was gone from her eyes, the hesitant self-reproach, and a subtle daring was there. Her Eurasian breasts stood out, small, almost immature, firm. "I am small," she said, concealing them with her cupped hands. "You do not mind?"

"No," I said. "I don't mind." I took her wrists and turned the hands back, baring the bright pink tips. "I don't mind at all. They're lovely."

I touched them gently, and she smiled. She edged me back until I was seated on the bed and stepped away, naked to the waist. She stripped off the stockings and then worked at the short zipper along the side of her skirt. When it fell to her ankles, she kicked it aside and asked me to close my eyes. She was very serious about that, and I closed them.

It was only a couple of seconds before she whispered for me to look. When I did, my blood went cold.

"Now you see," she said painfully.

It was a couple of seconds before I could bring myself to say anything. "The stinking bastard," I muttered finally. "The dirty, stinking bastard. He's living in the Dark Ages."

Around her narrow hips and looped across the threshold of her sex lay bands of arrogant brass. Haigmann had enforced her fidelity with a key.

She held out her hand. A small brass key lay in her palm. "I found this," she whispered.

I got up and walked to her and closed her hand around the key. A protective fury came over me as I wrapped my arms around her and kissed her. "Go in there," I said. "Get rid of it."

She went into the bathroom and I turned off the light. I got in bed. A moment later the bathroom door opened and for a second, before she flicked off the light, I saw her as she should always have been, free and smiling and natural. She slipped under the sheet and clung to me, eager and fresh. She wanted desperately to be mine and I liked that, and I wondered if maybe I did love her—a little.

When, finally, we lay back beside each other, she was very quiet for a long time. The mood passed and then she was kissing my ear and laughing playfully and asking me if I were tired. I told her I was, but not too tired, and she kept kissing my ear, and I found I wasn't tired at all. It was daylight before we got around to going to sleep.

When I awoke she was gone. I took a long shower and got into my clothes, dry but misshapen and dirty. I was unshaved, and my head felt raw in spots where Georges had twice been at work. I looked a mess. I felt a mess. But at least I was still alive.

I took a better look at the room. The wallpaper was yellow with age and blistered with heat. I looked out the window and tried to locate myself. The jagged Shanghai skyline stretched out to my right, and I knew I must be in the old Native City. Yesterday's wind and clouds had passed. The sun was almost overhead, bright and challenging.

Ariadne's raincoat was still hanging over the chair. That meant she would be back. I wasn't sure I wanted her back. I looked in the pasteboard wastebasket where I had thrown the chastity belt after beating it to ruins with my heel. She had wanted me to see that on her. She had wanted me to see the twisted sort of retribution Haigmann was taking out on her. To hell with it, I thought. I wanted her back.

My stomach was empty. I took a last dissatisfied look at myself in the mirror and went to the door. I turned the knob, but the door only rattled in its frame. I was locked in.

I goddamned everything that came to mind, including Ariadne, especially Ariadne, and shook the door again, but it wouldn't open. I looked for a phone to call the desk. No phone. I looked for a fire escape at the window. None. Did Ariadne think I was a child, locking me in for my own safety?

I was beginning to boil over when hurried footsteps sounded in the hall. When a key began to twist in the lock, I stepped back cautiously. It might be Ariadne, it might not. The door swung in, concealing me.

It was Ariadne, with bundles under her arms.

I stepped forward and wrapped my arms around her. "You're beautiful," I said. "Even when I'm angry at you, you're beautiful. Baby, you're beautiful."

She spun around in my arms and kissed me. She looked very pleased with herself and in a moment held up her packages. "First," she said, "you must eat. Then you must change clothes."

"You're a great little manager."

She smiled shyly. "You are angry?"

"Only a little," I said. "I like to look after myself. Thanks for taking over."

"I am only trying to protect you. It is not safe for you to be on the streets. August said the police are looking for you."

"He could be wrong."

"He is seldom wrong."

"I didn't kill that guy, and if the police are looking for me, they know that too."

"Perhaps they have other reasons." She tossed her head with passing resignation. "What does it matter?"

"That's right," I said. "What does it matter? I'm a dead pigeon either way."

She set the night table with paper napkins and laid out sandwiches and coffee. We ate together. She was happy.

Finally she got around to it. "I find out about your woman."

I tried not to seem overanxious. This was Ariadne's show.

"Does this Flame love you?" she asked.

I went on eating. I couldn't look at her. "I'll ask her when I see her," I said. "I don't know."

"I love you," she said.

"I know," I muttered. "I've made a note of it."

"You think of me only as a child."

"That was yesterday," I said. "Today I think of you as anything but."

We ate in silence for a few moments. She must have understood how desperately I wanted word of Flame, but she wasn't ready to unload.

"Tell me about you and Flame," she said after a moment. "Is she beautiful?"

I put down my coffee slowly. "She's beautiful."

"There was trouble between you?"

"Nothing serious," I muttered. "I was only playing around on the side. An old habit. It didn't appeal to her sense of humor."

Her eyes fell. "I see."

I lit a cigarette. "I didn't know I was in love with her at the time," I said. "It was the first time for me, the only time. And she was gone when I discovered that this affair was different from the others. Tough luck, eh?"

"You have been hurt."

"Don't feel sorry for me," I snapped. "I hurt myself."

"You smile about it. That is indecent."

"I think it's funny as hell. Now maybe she's a Red and I ought to break her neck when I find her."

She shook her head tensely. "You must not think badly of her."

"What are you getting at?"

"She is in trouble. Very bad trouble. The police last night raided an apartment on the Rue Corneille. It was a meeting place of underground workers. Flame was there."

The words brought me to my feet. Rue Corneille. I had followed little Picasso to an apartment on that street.

"Did they get her?"

"Justice at the hands of the secret police is instant. They executed six."

"Answer my question!"

"Flame escaped in time." Ariadne looked at me as though she were losing hope that after last night I might care a little less about Flame. "Your woman was prominent in the underground. She had been followed to the apartment. But when the secret police came, they found the agent unconscious in a doorway across the street."

My brain grabbed at it. I had thought all along that character was tailing me. It was Flame he was waiting for. She must have come there to wait for the artist. And Marie hadn't told her I was there.

"The police found a Chinese at a printing press in the attic. He was making resistance handbills. They killed him. Also a Frenchwoman and her husband. They kept girls in rooms and lured Red officers there. It is a crime for an officer to visit such places. There were cameras in the walls, and the officers were sometimes blackmailed for military information."

"What about the girls?"

"They were executed on the spot as an example to others."

I ran a hand through my hair. The Texan's troubles were over. She'd never see it rain in Dallas again. "The lousy sons-of-bitches," I muttered. "Where's Flame now?"

Ariadne threw back her head. "Who knows? She hides. Just as you hide."

I picked up my wrinkled coat hanging from the foot-post of the bed. It occurred to me that I had already got in a lick. If I hadn't clipped that guy in the doorway he would have followed Flame out of the apartment. Her number, obviously, was up. They would have picked her up at her next stop. It could have been only chance that she left prior to the time of the raid.

I started toward the door, but stopped and turned around to face Ariadne. "Wait for me, baby. We'll leave Shanghai together. The three of us."

"No," she said, getting up. "You were right. I would be an added danger. I will get along by myself."

I walked back to her and took her in my arms. "Don't be a fool," I said. "Haigmann will turn this town upside down for you."

"He will not find me. I shall be too smart for him."

I knew what was going through her mind, and there would be no answer for it. "Yes, I think you will."

"You mustn't go out until dark," she said firmly. "They will find you and kill you."

"I'll have to take my chances."

Her arms moved up to my back and held me close. "You stay," she whispered softly. "I will not let you go so soon."

There was desperation in the way she said it, and I knew she was right. With that drawing of me floating around, I ought to stay out of sight. She clung to me a long time, and then her hands moved quickly to the buttons on her blouse.

I threw aside my jacket.

I stayed until dark.

Chapter Six

I walked through the dim streets of the old walled city, past rice shops and dry-goods stores and small native restaurants. The sidewalks stirred with noises and Eastern odors and throbbed with life. In the distance a loud-speaker sent a singsong voice through the evening air from a radio shop. I stepped around a cross-legged coolie patting charcoal fibers into fuel balls. I walked.

I passed below the lights of the Willow Tea House, perched like a fantastic wooden nest in the weathered buildings on my right. When I crossed the Boulevard des Deux the streets broadened and the buildings became taller and the lights brighter. I followed the Rue Ningpo until it became Avenue Joffre and tried to avoid the gawking Red soldiers strolling along the sidewalks.

I stopped in at a pawnshop and tried to buy a gun. I would have felt better with a gun. The old woman running the shop made it clear to me that the Reds had cleaned out the loose firearms in the city. People without arms can't make trouble.

I moved on. When I got within a block of Georges's bar I slowed my pace. I paused just short of the familiar striped awning, lit a cigarette, and looked around me. A legless beggar moved down the sidewalk on his body, twisting over and over with an arm always outstretched and sobbing for money. The foot traffic stepped around him, Occidentals and Orientals who had learned not to notice. His eye caught mine, and I turned away. I didn't want to notice either.

I strolled past the doorway and glanced inside. Three or four figures sat at the bar and only one of the tables against the wall was occupied. I stood beyond the doorway uncertainly for a moment, then turned and walked in.

I picked up the drift of idle conversation at the bar as I passed to the end and got on a stool. The two men at the table, where I had sat for so many hours waiting over endless games of solitaire, were Chinese in Western dress, one round-faced and handsome, the other thin, both smoking English cigarettes. They ignored me.

Georges was not behind the bar. The cage of canaries was covered and quiet for the night. A middle-aged blonde moved toward me behind the bar as I laid out a bill. She might once have been pretty, but the East had obviously worn badly on her. She stood now opposite me, disheveled and wan, asking me with a tired movement of her eyes what I wanted. I told her I wanted a glass of beer and I wanted Georges.

Her frail wrist brushed back a strand of fallen hair and she straightened to peer at me. Her eyes were dark and cautious, nervous and hopelessly resigned. "I am Georges's wife. What do you want?"

"We have business together," I said. "Where is he?"

She touched the money with the back of her hand, pushing it toward me. "Get out," she said.

"That's no way to talk to a customer with money on the bar."

"I do not like the smell of your money."

"I don't like the smell of your bar. Why don't you take it easy? I don't make trouble unless I have to."

She stared at me a long time. The skin of her face was polished with perspiration, and her expression was taut with nervousness. It couldn't have been any fun being Georges's wife, and it was clear that something was churning up inside her. "He will not be back for a while," she said at last. "Maybe never."

I pushed the money back toward her. "Why don't you get me that beer?"

Her lips parted for an indecisive moment and I just looked at her as though I thought she still was pretty. She moved off toward the beer tap and her thin fingers upturned a glass and filled it.

When she got back I said, "You're used to his being gone for spells, I suppose?"

"Maybe."

"You look as though you think he has left for good."

"What business is it of yours?" She picked up a bar rag and began wiping up around me. "Who are you?"

"That's not important," I said. "You must have been very beautiful once. In France?"

"Belgium," she answered. "Twelve years ago we came here. What a twelve years!"

"Why did you leave Belgium?"

She turned steely eyes on me. "You ask many questions for a stranger."

"I want to find Georges," I said. "He tried to kill me."

The rag stopped a few inches from my glass. Then continued its jerky movements again. "You are making a joke," she snapped solemnly.

"I don't think it's very funny."

"He is not a killer," she said quickly. "Whatever he is, he does not kill. He does not have the courage."

"Never mind that," I said. "I'll forgive him for trying. I'll bring him back to you alive if that's the way you want it."

She straightened with a pitiful attempt at bravura. "This time when he comes back I will not be here, m'sieu. He thinks I do not know about his women. I know! I know where he keeps them, even his newest one!"

I began to grow tense as I watched her. I saw that her emotions had been bottled up for hours and I didn't want to pull the cork on them. "You need a drink," I said. "It's on me."

"These fancy pigs he sleeps with," she went on, "what do they see in him but the money in his purse! And what is he but a pig himself!"

"Get that drink," I said.

Her fingers ran nervously through her hair, and she got hold of herself. Her face became stolid. After a moment she said with a thin, apologetic, embarrassed smile, "I'm sorry, m'sieu. I didn't mean to—"

"Forget it."

"*Merci,* but I do not care to drink."

She moved off to the other end of the bar, where someone was clicking his glass for service; I looked across the bar to the wall mirrors and studied the reflection of the two Orientals at the table behind me. They spoke to each other in low, relaxed tones and appeared disinterested in the bar life about them.

Georges's wife was a long time coming back. She found a dozen things to do at the far end of the bar. I emptied my glass and waited. Three Chinese soldiers in seedy green uniforms looked in the door with curious smiles on their bony faces, then darted away. Farm boys on leave in the big city.

When Georges's wife came back she took my glass, and her soft voice, almost inaudible, carried a determination that surprised me. She had been thinking, deciding, sizing me up, and the disorder in her mind came up with what I wanted to know.

"He has a place," she muttered, "on Sinza Road near the Carter Road bridge."

"I know the area."

"Over a bicycle shop. Maybe he is there. That is where he keeps his fine pigs."

"I'll find it," I said. I became aware of movement behind me and looked into the mirror. The two Chinese were getting up from the table. They put out their cigarettes silently, left a tip, and walked unhurriedly to the door. My eyes followed them until they were out of sight on the sidewalk. Georges's wife was saying something to me.

"Tell him," she murmured coolly, "this is the last time. Next time he will not find me here to forgive him."

"I'll convince him of it," I said.

She stared at me curiously for a moment, and then asked what must have been on her mind for quite a while. "You are an American?"

"Yes."

"Then you must be careful."

"That's good advice. I'll take it. There's one thing I want to ask you. I'm looking for another American, a girl. Red hair. Very beautiful. She might have been in here looking for me within the last several hours. Have you seen a girl who might be an American sitting around as though she were waiting for someone?"

It didn't take her long to remember. "Yes."

My heart began to pound and I got off the stool. "When?"

"This afternoon. But she wasn't waiting for you. She was waiting for Georges. She is his newest one."

"Is her name Flame?"

Bitterness flared in her eyes. "I do not know." She turned away and left me standing there.

It wouldn't be Flame. It couldn't be Flame. Her taste in men didn't include anyone as gross as Georges. But the possibility revolted me. There were other American girls left in Shanghai. I let it go at that.

When I got outside the beggar had rolled his torturous way almost to the corner, but I could still hear his chilling wail. I flagged a pedicab and suddenly realized I should never have run the risk of returning to Georges's. As I stepped into the carriage the two well-dressed Chinese appeared on either side of me. They seemed to come out of nowhere.

"You will not mind joining us," the round-faced man smiled. "We have waited many hours for you."

"Sorry I kept you waiting," I said, stepping down. My mind began to heat up, but I knew I had better play it calm. The thin, wiry character began frisking me. He seemed disappointed that I carried no gun. Within seconds we were circled by curious faces, passers-by anxious for a moment's excitement.

"You will come with us."

I smiled. "Of course," I said.

They broke through the crowd and I walked between them, towering over their Oriental builds. They led me to a black Ford sedan parked around the corner on the Rue Bourgeat. Its license plate had a large, official red star on it. The throng followed at a cautious distance, chattering speculations behind us.

These guys were a smooth and confident intelligence team, and I knew they were deadly. The thin one opened the back door for me, and I spotted leg irons attached to the floor board. Once they got those on me, I was through.

The bony man helped me firmly into the back seat while the other slipped behind the wheel. I sat down and put my feet where hands guided them. The gleaming shackles were open and waiting. The thinner man stood on the pavement while his body bent into the car and his hands began fussing with the irons and my ankles.

And that's when I let him have it. With my foot.

The toe of my shoe clipped his chin and my other foot quickly rammed into his face. The breath came out of him in a heavy wail. His pal in the front seat spun and I catapulted a fist into his flat nose. Blood spurted instantly. I gave him another one as hard as I could. The guy at my feet began to grab at me in a daze. I kicked him, and he fell backward onto the sidewalk. The bloody face in the front seat was coming out as I hurtled myself over the guy I had kicked out of commission. He sprang out of the door as I did, and he was getting hold of his service revolver. I grabbed for it and pushed the flat of my hand into his face. I felt the blood smear all over.

But he held onto his gun with an iron grip. He tripped me, but I brought him down to the sidewalk with me. He twisted loose with the gun and I saw that the blood had momentarily blinded him. I sprang against him, cracked his wrist, and wrestled with the gun. I got it loose and brought the butt down on his head. I heard myself yelling every curse in the book. I brought the butt in again and again. In another moment he was through.

The chattering crowd had spread out from us in momentary fright, but now they held their positions. I was prepared to shoot, but their eyes were laughing. I stood watching, and realized they were not laughing at me. I started walking through the circle, a heavy pounding in my ears, holding my breath. There was an animated jabbering about me. Maybe it was political approval. They let me walk. Then I ran, and lost myself in the human traffic on a side street.

Within a few blocks of the Carter Road bridge, costumed figures moved along the sidewalks. They were mostly chattering teen-agers, some carrying banners, a few in fantastic parodies of Uncle Sam's striped trousers and top hat. As I drew closer to the bridge I saw a throng forming in the square created by the dead-end jog where broad Soochow Road stops and Connaught Road picks up the line of traffic. I stood a block away, in the shadow of a doorway, and it didn't take me long to figure out what was forming: a "Hate America" demonstration. I saw Chinese swarming over the bridge from Chapei to the collecting area, and heard a drummer now and then warming up. It was going to be a big time.

I turned off Carter Road at Sinza and there it was, three doors down. The bicycle shop. I approached and saw a dim light burning inside and a fleshy Chinese with shaved head sitting on a box in the doorway reading a paper. He looked up occasionally at the eager faces moving past to join the demonstration, but his squinting expression remained unchanged. Inside, under the hanging light, I saw a youngster of about seven laboring over a schoolbook and stroking characters with a pointed brush on brown wrapping paper. His father looked up as I passed, considered me with a squint, and returned to the news.

Sinza Road near the bridge and over the bicycle shop. This was Georges's place. I looked up at the darkened windows above and a flock of black pigeons fluttered down from the steep tile roof as though taking a look-see at me and climbed back to their perches.

There was a "No Vacancy" card behind the glass of the entry door. I walked up and looked over the name cards on the brass mailboxes. Georges wasn't fool enough to list himself. A mistress's name, perhaps, but not his own.

I looked over the cards again, hoping for some clue. One box carried no name. Apartment 3-C. It struck me as odd, since the sign said there were no vacancies in the building. It was worth a try.

The wooden stairway was narrow and uncarpeted. The odors of sweet pork and burned charcoal lingered on the second-floor landing. I climbed to the top, the third floor, and met an amah in black trousers coming out of the corner room. She ignored me and went down.

I flicked my cigarette out of an open window at the end of the hall and looked out for a moment on the rooftops to the end of the block. No breeze passed through the window. The hall was badly lit and the air was close.

Apartment 3-C. I knocked and waited. It was, I figured, a good guess. No answer. Maybe I was wrong. I tried again. No good.

I heard the chatter of a child being put to bed at the end of the hall. I walked over there and knocked on the half-open door.

A man in his thirties, blond and in tropical shorts, appeared. "Yes?"

"I'm trying to find a place to live," I said. "Three-C is vacant, isn't it?"

"The superintendent, second floor," he answered shortly in a middle-European accent. He started to close the door.

I stopped it with my hand. "He's watching the demonstration outside," I said. "Don't you know if anyone's got that room?"

He turned to a woman inside. "Mamma, iss there any openings on this floor?"

"*Nein,*" she called back.

I said thanks, thanks a lot.

I went back to 3-C and tried the knob hard. It wouldn't give. I returned to the street and walked into the bicycle shop. I bought a spoke from the old man and took a hammer to flatten the end into a thin chisel. The boy watched me with fascination, and I winked at him. Then I returned to 3-C.

It didn't take long to work the flattened end of the spoke against the thick iron hammer, forcing it back into the intestines of the lock. When I had it sprung I pushed against the door, but it opened only an inch and set a chair that had been hooked under the knob.

I stepped back and my heart picked up a few beats. Someone was in there. Someone had been frightened by my first knock and had barricaded the door while I was below.

Was that person unarmed?

I got out the service revolver I had taken from the Oriental, and shoved against the door with all my weight. I worked against it again until I heard the wood snap and splinter and the shoulder of the chair collapse. I pushed the door free and stepped aside.

No shot rang out.

"I'm unarmed," I lied. "I'm coming in."

Except for dim reflected light through a large window on the street, the room was dark. A live cigarette coal moved in a slow arc in the corner and I could make out a vague form behind it. My hand felt for the switch on the wall and I snapped it on. A pink table lamp ignited beside a rattan chair, and a woman was sitting there, nerveless and composed. A flickering column of smoke rose from her fingertips, and she sat there only looking at me, not reacting, just looking at me.

"Hello, Flame," I said.

Chapter Seven

She stared at me.

"You bastard," she breathed.

"You meddling idiot," she growled.

"You goddamn newspaperman," she spat.

I took another step into the room. "We were always two of a kind, baby." I smiled. I found a cigarette somewhere in my pocket and lit it slowly. "Did I ever tell you I loved you most when you were angry?"

"Stop being sentimental. I don't want to be sick."

"Stop being angry. I don't want to have to get rough."

She crossed her legs and took a resolute puff on her cigarette. "Please do me a favor," she snapped. "Go to hell."

"I'm just coming back," I said. "I've been there for two years."

"You must have met a lot of women you know."

Her eyes, large and green and chilly, touched every base as I approached. I felt suddenly conscious of my dirty suit, bagged and wrinkled, and my mud-caked shoes. I had refused to put on the change of clothes Ariadne had brought me.

"Maybe you were expecting Georges," I said. "Sorry to disappoint you. Nice place you've got here."

"Any place with a bed looks nice to you."

"I come well remembered. Thanks."

A wire bird cage, lacquered a foolish yellow, stood beside the window with a pair of canaries jumping around and making noise. They reminded me of Georges, and I didn't want to be reminded of Georges. I walked over, unhooked the cage, and opened the door of the closet to put them away. I saw a woman's slip hanging from the hook on the inside of the door, two dresses on hangers, and a pair of red mules on the floor. I put the cage away and tried to convince myself that the stuff belonged to someone else.

"I see this apartment came already furnished," I said.

"Let's get it over with," she snapped: "What do you want?"

"A couple of things," I said. "One of them is you."

"You found your way in the door. I wonder if you can find your way out."

"I generally get what I go after, baby."

"Bully for you."

She rose and walked to the window, her shoulders thrown back in that indomitable way that always angered me. A simple chartreuse dress with an Oriental collar tugged at her smooth hips and legs. She looked as fresh as if she had only a moment before stepped out of a shower. She always managed to look that way. I don't think her nose had been shiny since she was a copy girl on the *Herald Tribune*, where I had first met her. At the moment, she might have had a date at a cocktail party instead of one with a police coffin.

"I owe you an apology," I said. "I heard you had turned Red. I believed it for a while."

"Please shut up."

"Would you mind if I swatted your bottom?"

She turned, facing me. Her eyes were glacial. "I suppose it will please you that you couldn't have turned up at a nastier time. Your item in the press was interesting—to a lot of people."

"It didn't bring very good results, either. Your little artist died because of it."

She didn't say anything and I walked over and took her shoulders in my hands. They stiffened at my touch. "Look, Flame, I was a fool back in Rome. Sure, that's me admitting it."

"You're breaking my heart." She twisted out of my grip, and walked away from the window. "'Flame,'" she muttered. "'I'm alive and waiting for you at Georges's Bar.'"

"Maybe that was mean and scurvy," I said. "But what do you expect from a goddamn newspaperman?"

"Mean and scurvy devices," she remarked. "Two years haven't changed you."

"I was a louse. I told you I was sorry."

"We walked out of each other's lives once. I wanted you to keep walking. I still do."

I looked at the copperish sheen of her hair as it swept up her neck to a plateau of curls on top. "I came to Shanghai because I got the crazy idea you needed me," I said. "I also came because I need you. Now that I've found you, we're leaving together."

Hate America was getting under way a block away. Somewhere in the streets a loud cheer went off, and Flame recoiled slightly at the sound. I went to the window to close out the echoes of it.

I said, "Our kind doesn't seem to be very popular in this city. And I don't seem to be very popular in this room. I was sort of hoping you'd be a little glad to see me."

"I'm not."

"I understand the security police would be delighted to see you."

"I've stopped being afraid."

"You always had a lot of guts."

"You always had a lot of brass."

"I'm getting tired of this song and dance," I said. "Get your stuff out of the closet. We're leaving."

She turned her back. After a moment she said, "I am glad to see you, Alex. But I don't want to be glad." Her tone was tense but warm.

"That's a beginning."

She stood very straight. "I was at Marie's the night you came there. But I didn't want you to find me."

"You almost succeeded. I came here looking for Georges."

"So did I."

"The rumor is that you're sleeping with him."

"Do you believe it?"

"No."

"Can't you understand, Alex—I'm mixed up in something. I don't want you to get mixed up in it too."

"You're being thoughtful as hell."

The brittle edge came back into her voice. "I'm trying not to be a bitch."

"You must not be trying very hard."

She walked away from me. "You're wasting your time," she snapped. "Thanks for trying. The last train left Shanghai a long time ago for me."

"That's what I figured. We're sailing tomorrow night."

"I'm staying."

"Stop kidding yourself, Flame. You're in trouble right up to those pretty green earrings."

"I can't leave!"

I stood in the center of the room and anger enveloped me. I let myself accept what I didn't want to think. She was waiting in Shanghai for Cottardo. Alex Cloud was only in the way.

"How dumb can a guy be?" I muttered slowly, staring at her. "Until yesterday I thought Cottardo was dead. He's been in Shanghai. Maybe he's still here."

Her eyes flared up searchingly.

"Don't fake it, baby. Don't pretend you didn't know."

She took my arms in her hands. "Alex, I've got to find him!"

I peeled off her hands with contempt. "Cottardo was class, wasn't he? And you've been chasing him like a Paris chippy after a five-dollar bill. You never loved me. Why have I been kidding myself? When you caught me in bed with some drunken tramp, that was only a swell excuse to get rid of me. If Cottardo's in Shanghai, he's all yours, baby."

She took it standing up, without blinking an eye. I said a couple of things I knew weren't true and they must have hurt. But she didn't show it.

She turned calmly. "You're right," she said. "I'm waiting for Cottardo. I never loved you. I was only looking for an excuse to get rid of you."

I stood there with mixed-up feelings. I was angry and I was being a heel about it. I was cut up inside. It didn't seem to matter. I went on being a heel.

"I'm glad I found you," I said. "I'm glad to know was only chasing a dream. It was a nice dream, baby. Thanks."

"Have a nice voyage."

"Sorry I busted that chair getting in."

"Don't worry about it."

"See you around."

"Yes."

She wasn't crying. She never cried. She held it between her lips, clamped together. I looked at her and felt like wringing my neck. I walked over and took hold of her. "You crazy kid," I said. "Why don't you punch me in the nose?"

She clung to me for a moment. "I'm sorry if I'm being a bitch," she whispered. "I'm scared. I've never been scared like this before."

"I'll let you in on a secret, baby. I'm a little scared myself."

"Alex, I did love you. I loved you too much." She broke away from me and stopped at the window. I fished out a couple of cigarettes and lit them.

"I spoke out of turn," I said.

She took a long drag on her cigarette. "I tried awfully hard to get you out of my system. It wasn't easy being in love with you. I'm afraid to go through that again. I didn't want you to find me in Shanghai. I don't want to get hurt all over again."

"I told you to punch me in the nose."

She avoided my eyes. "I didn't want to fall in love with Cottardo. You did that to me, Alex. I wanted to stay in love with you. You wouldn't let me."

"You were the finest thing that ever came my way, Flame," I said softly. "I want you back. I don't make the same mistakes twice."

"Neither do I."

"Cottardo was a mistake, Flame."

"Cottardo was good to me. No fights, no terrible doubts, no lies; it was the kind of love that's meant to stick. I can't walk out on him. It would be cheap and monstrous."

"He's cheap and monstrous, and that's what tore me up so much. It drove me crazy that you were letting a guy like him make love to you."

"You never understood him."

"He's a phony, Flame. You've got to accept the truth about him."

"You're wrong about him, Alex. Terribly wrong."

I sat on the edge of the bed and bit at the end of my cigarette. "If I hadn't cared so much about you, in spite of the fights and lies and doubts, I wouldn't have bothered digging up that story on him."

"I've learned not to believe what I read in the papers."

"If he had any claim to a title, you can be sure it was phony. If there was any aristocratic blood in his veins, he could have got it only by transfusion."

"Please stop it."

I put out my cigarette and got up. "Wise up, sweetheart. He's a cheap, chiseling poser looking for the fast buck. He's been in and out of trouble all his life in Italy. He used to work in an olive-oil factory until he got big ideas. He should have stayed there. At least it was honest work."

She wasn't listening. Her eyes had a distant look. "He blamed me," she said. "He thought you had planted me next to him to get your story. It took me months to learn he had gone to China, that he hadn't been killed in Greece, as the papers said. I had to find him. I owed him an explanation."

"You don't owe him anything. He went for you because he was a climber. You could be influential as newspaperwoman. But you can be sure that since he came to China he has found other influential women to climb into bed with."

Her hand flashed smartly across my face. I let the sting die and took her roughly into my arms. I kissed her hard. Her fingernails dug into my back but I only pressed her closer. I kept my lips against hers, and then felt her thighs relax and pretty soon she wasn't fighting any more. Her arms came up behind my shoulders and she was kissing me. We stood there that way a long time. A hell of a long time.

Her eyes were wet. "Your nose is shiny," I said when I could see it.

"I don't care."

I kissed her again. Another hell of a long time. I had been waiting two years for this. I wasn't sorry.

"So."

The voice came from behind us, from the door. I turned. Georges stood there in a formless white suit, his heavy legs firmly planted, his eyes bulging, and a gun in his hand.

"So," I said. "So what?"

He came in, his face florid. He looked beyond me to Flame, who had broken out of my arms and stood now against the window. She looked very cool.

"Maybe you play only a game with Georges," he said to her. "You try to make a fool of me."

"You know why I am here," she said. "I keep my promises."

"And I keep mine," he said with a squint.

I glanced at Flame, and her eyes challenged me briefly. Georges turned to me, sweat rolling down his forehead. "So the American still lives."

"Maybe you'll have better luck next time."

"Next time, maybe will be now."

I glanced at the gun and it looked ready to wink. I made no move for the revolver in my pocket. I would never reach it alive. "I'll turn around so you can do it in character."

The perspiration dripped off his face. There was a moment's hesitation as he stood there, and I knew what it meant. Georges just wasn't a killer. He didn't have what it takes to pull the trigger himself. There was only one end of the gun he'd ever had courage enough to use.

"Put it way, Georges," I said.

I heard Flame catch her breath. "Don't move!" Georges snarled. He was talking to her, not to me. "So you deceive me so soon. Maybe I am not handsome enough for you, yes? Already you find someone else to use my bed."

His hand was trembling and I turned quickly to Flame. There was cold fear in her eyes. Guilt and fear. Guilt. My mind wanted to reject the idea that she had become Georges's mistress, but I saw now that it was true. My muscles went tight with revulsion. When I spun back to Georges his eyes had turned small and deadly. I understood why. I had made him show himself up as a coward before a woman he wanted.

I didn't take time to think clearly. I stepped back. The gun was going off because Flame no longer gave a damn about her sleeping companions. What a blind fool I had been! I grabbed her arm viciously and jerked her in front of me. If Georges wanted to pop that gull, let him pop it.

"Shoot, you greasy bastard!" I shouted. "Do me a favor and shoot!"

Georges stared at me dumbly, rivers of sweat streaking his fleshy face. I held Flame in front of me, tightening my hold on her in rage and wanting that gun to go off. My stomach was in a knot. I wanted her to die.

But the gun only shook in Georges's hand. His finger wouldn't tighten on the trigger. Suddenly his lips parted with a thick groan. It came from deep in his stomach. His gaze went wandering somewhere above us and his left hand reached out to steady his teetering weight against the wall. His legs were giving way. He went over on his stomach and the gun fell from his wet hand. The sounds that came from his throat chilled me. He curled with sudden great pain. I tossed Flame on the bed and walked over to him. When I saw what someone had done to his bearish back, I knew that his last moments before us had been heroic.

Blood had soaked the back of his sliced coat until it wasn't white any more. Blood had dripped down the backs of his legs to the cuffs, like wax inched along a candlestick. Someone had butchered him alive, and left the knife in the rolling fat and muscle.

Flame lay on her stomach across the bed, her hands over her face. She was crying. Really crying. Let her cry.

I bent down over the huge, curled body and went through Georges's pockets. He had a lot of things in his pockets. But he didn't have the cards. I straightened. He couldn't have come far in this condition. Had he got it along the stairway?

I went over to Flame. "Snap out of it," I growled. "You're going to live. Start talking, and make it good."

I pulled away her hands and looked into her eyes. They turned away, avoiding mine. "Leave me alone," she whispered.

"Your boy friend is nice and dead," I snapped. "I think I could have taken anything but you and Georges."

She shook her head with a tense, desperate effort.

"Where do you fit in?" I smoldered. "Do you think I don't know about that little package of dynamite floating around Shanghai? I had it, baby, and I lost it, but I'm going to get it back. Was Georges to bring it here?"

She looked at me with wet, miserable eyes. I got mad and slapped her face around, but she just took it. I got madder and took her wrists and twisted them. "Let's have it!"

"I—I had to play along with Georges. I despised him."

"I wish he had killed you."

"Alex—"

I let go of her wrists and got up. I glanced at Georges and saw that the blood had crept along his thick sides to the rug. A couple of black flies had found him and were beginning to explore the mess.

"He wanted me," she said in strained gasps. "I saw a chance to use him, and I took it. I had to. It was the only way. But I never would have gone through with—with *sleeping* with him."

I looked at the closet door. I didn't believe her.

"He knew where to get—something I was after. He was delivering tonight—here."

"And you were going to have to deliver for it. I didn't realize the market was so cheap."

"I couldn't have gone through with it. You've got to believe me, I couldn't have!" She rose to her elbows and watched my movements around the room with desperation in her eyes.

"He didn't have to bring you a damned thing," I said. "He knew the Reds were looking for you, and he knew where you were. He's the type that would have blackmailed you into coming across—and maybe he did. From what's in the closet I'd say you've already set up housekeeping."

She fell back on the bed. I was torturing her, and I liked it. I had been cut too suddenly and too deeply for words or tears to heal it over. I didn't want to see her again. I gave the place a last look and pulled out. I stepped over the formless mass on the floor and opened the door.

"Alex," Flame whispered, almost inaudibly.

I shut the door hard after me.

When I got to the end of the hall I was shaking, and the sweat was soaking into my clothes. Deep inside I knew I was being impulsive, but I couldn't help myself. I hated her with all I had to hate with.

I got down the first flight somehow, wanting to turn back, but not able to bring myself to do it. When I got to the bottom I transferred the revolver to a pocket of my trousers. I reached the glass of the entrance door and stopped.

A cap with a red star on it moved past the door. In a second he returned and stood there. I saw the tacky uniform and the rifle barrel pointing up over one shoulder.

I fell back, but he wasn't looking in. He was just standing there, as if someone had told him to. Then I saw movement beyond him, more red stars, and I realized what I had got into.

I got back up the stairs and I wasn't shaking any more. When I reached the third floor I moved swiftly down the hall and into the room. Flame was on her feet. She was trying to light a cigarette. I ignored her and walked past her to the window. I looked down. Two Red army jeeps had swung onto Sinza Road and were beginning to close off the street. I saw more green uniforms than looked healthy; this wasn't just the police. The military was taking over, and those boys didn't give a damn about catching a guy wanted for a fifth-rate murder like me. I saw a couple of soldiers ordered around back of the building, and the officer who appeared in charge pointed out our room to a couple of his *chan-shih*.

I stepped back from the window.

I looked at Flame. Her nose was very shiny and a few strands of hair wandered aimlessly across her forehead. "There's an army downstairs," I snapped. "Those boys are looking either for you or for Georges. How badly do the Reds want you?"

"They posted a price on my head this afternoon."

"Why?"

"Espionage."

"They're looking for blood. We'll leave them Georges."

"Alex—"

"Save it." I caught her wrist and pulled her after me out of the room. We moved down the hall to the fire escape on the left, but when I looked down I saw two soldiers at the bottom looking up. I jerked Flame after me on the run to the stairway at the other end of the hall. I took the gun out of my pocket. I had no plan. All I knew was that I had never been in a tighter spot, that this was no outfit to surrender to.

There were already footsteps coming up the stairway when we reached it. The window. "Climb through and drop," I said. "I'll follow."

Flame hesitated for only a moment. Then she reached down and ripped her skirt where buttons held it together along the side. She stepped through the window and dropped to the next rooftop, about six feet below.

The creaks on the stairway sounded painfully near. I had one leg out the window when red stars rose, two of them, around the turn and appeared before my eyes. I fired. I paused a split second and fired again. I couldn't have missed. I didn't. Some human noises sprang up behind them, and I dropped.

Flame caught my hand and we moved. The roof was flat with a tiled bank at the front. In the darkness we felt our way along. Our feet seemed to scratch up a hell of a racket on the dry gravel surface. A flashlight shot out from the window. We reached the next building and I catapulted Flame up the five feet or so with my hands. Almost at the same moment I heard the thud behind us as a soldier made the drop out of the apartment-house window. I kept the gun in my hand and got up to the next roof with Flame.

The beam of the flashlight weaved around looking for us. In a moment there were two, one of them on the roof itself. We raced to the far end of the wooden building we were on.

There was a six-foot gap to the next roof.

Flame's hand tightened in mine. It was no go for her.

"Alex—"

"Shut up."

I looked around desperately for something, anything. My eyes stopped at a wooden roof sign facing the street. I left Flame and hurried to it. It was braced up by two-by-fours. I looked back and spotted a form hoisting itself to the level of our roof. He must have been anxious to die. The lighted flash in his hand marked him. I held my aim until it was steady. He screamed like hell when he fell back.

The sign was shaped in the form of a bottle. Patent medicine, I thought. I knocked away at one of the supports until I got it loose. It came too easily, and I realized the damned thing was almost rotted by the weather. I hoped it would hold.

I dragged it to the side of the roof and connected it to the next roof. A two-by-four never seemed narrower. And the ground never seemed farther away.

Behind us, the noises of men carried in the motionless night air. Flame slipped off her shoes, but stopped when she got both feet in place on the two-by-four. She was scared stiff.

"They always say to look straight ahead," I said. "Don't look down."

I could almost hear her heart beat. I let go of her hand and she started across. Those few paralyzing seconds seemed interminable. She got halfway across and I thought she was going to stop. But she didn't. She reached the next roof and then I came across. The beam of a flashlight suddenly popped through the air. I pulled the plank after us. The light danced around. It didn't find us. I didn't shoot.

We moved to the back of the roof and almost walked into a wooden stair shed. I pulled at the door, but it was locked. At the same moment a shaft of light caught us. I pushed Flame down and the bastard started shooting. I blasted with my gun until the light tumbled wildly away and I kept shooting until all I got were dry clicks. I tossed the gun away. I cursed myself for wasting my shots. I had got him after the second one.

"Come on," I said.

"I've got to rest for a moment."

"Are you hit?"

"No."

"Come on."

I yanked on the rickety door until the whole business came loose, and led Flame quickly down the black stairwell into the building. We came into a short hall with rows of doors that made me think we were in a cheap office building, shabby, dirty, but at least apparently deserted for the night. We took the next flight to the ground floor, then worked our way to the back door. The window set in the upper half was broken and the space was partly boarded up. I twisted the knob, but the door, like the one above, was locked.

I tried to force the lock, but it wouldn't yield.

Flame slipped her shoes back on. "I suppose I ought to thank you while I have a chance." Her voice was strained. "You're risking your neck—for me."

"Yeah."

I ripped away the boards across the window and chipped at the raw edges of broken glass in the frame. I peeled off my coat and padded the serrations along the bottom. I picked up Flame in my arms and moved her feet first through the hole. Then I climbed out as gingerly as I could and got only a couple of scratches. I left the jacket there. We hurried on our way.

It was dark as hell behind the building. We crossed through what turned out to be a vegetable garden and I walked into the branches of a fig tree. I looked back once and saw flashlights dancing around on the rooftops. Sweat pumped out of my pores; I was drenched.

We came onto a small cobblestone lane that led between two buildings on Soochow Road, bordering the creek. The Hate America boys were making a. hell of a racket at the end of the broad street. Keeping in the shadow of the lane I spotted red-starred caps moving around beyond the sidewalk. I realized then that the Reds knew how to run these operations. The soldiers, a handful of serious-looking customers, were taking up positions with their rifles in their hands and not across their backs.

The block, obviously, was being surrounded.

Chapter Eight

A rasping Chinese voice was cutting the night air, haranguing the teeming Hate America throng at the corner intersection. He finished suddenly and a thousand ranting throats burst with approval. A calypso-like song with a jarring rhythm was struck up. Performers would now be going into the *yangko*, the Red street dance.

I stepped back into the lane and Flame stopped me with her hands. "They're not looking for you, Alex," she said firmly. "This is where we separate. I'll find my own way out of this."

I caught her arms and held her tight. "Forget it."

"They won't give you a second glance if you walk out there. Get away while you can."

"They haven't got us yet. Let's keep it that way."

A soldier moved up cautiously to the entrance of the lane, and I clamped a hand over Flame's mouth. He peered in cautiously and we hung there, hardly breathing, not fifteen feet away.

I don't know how long we stood there, but he didn't see us and he didn't enter the darkness of the lane. Then something must have happened out in the street, because he pulled back and I saw another soldier hurry past him toward the huge demonstration. The *yangko* rhythm ended and a deafening cheer went up. High-pitched drums began to rattle out a new beat and a few horns joined in. Within a few seconds the human dyke broke and the demonstrators swarmed like mice past the lane entrance. They carried banners and feverishly ignored the few soldiers who were trying to head off the march.

The street became thick with Chinese, some of them in tall paper hats with stars and stripes pasted around them: Uncle Sams with ridiculous false noses and dollar signs painted on their suits. Others pushed by with animal-like masks over their heads—"running dogs," the contemptuous characterization of Chinese friends of the United States. I'd seen this all before on a lesser scale in Hong Kong, where the police broke things up. It was a different story in Shanghai.

"Wait here," I said, and moved in the darkness to the entrance of the lane. I stiffened against the wall and waited in the shadows. A pair of "running dogs" finally crossed the narrow space and I pulled them both to me out of the surging procession.

It must have scared hell out of them. They were short and their bodies looked young; students, I thought. They began to jabber and I yanked off their papier-maché masks. I spun them around and pushed them back out into the torrent of bodies. The wave of yelling demonstrators carried them quickly out of sight. They probably felt lucky they were still alive. They were.

I wheeled and in the distance behind the lane I saw the exploratory beam of a flashlight. When I got to Flame I pushed a mask over her head and got into one myself. We hurried to the end of the lane, into dim light.

I clamped a hand on Flame's wrist. "Let's go."

We pierced the edge of the swarm and the nervous current of the procession carried us away.

My hand felt hot and moist and slippery on Flame's wrist. I forced our way to the left against the pressing bodies. The discord of singing and yelling was deafening. We reached the edge of the curb rand I pulled Flame into the street. My head seemed on fire under the close mask.

Flame tripped over something in the street and I almost broke her arm keeping her upright. We kept going. We cut across the torrent in a long diagonal. My mask got shoved out of place and for a moment my eyes lost the peepholes and I couldn't see. I swore loudly but in the din my voice went nowhere.

My feet finally felt the raised curb at the other side of the street. Someone struck playfully with a stick against the top of Flame's mask. I pulled her in tighter against the laughter at our ears. Her body was as tense and rigid as a frightened cat.

I pulled her with me up the curb and someone with a horn blared into our faces. I moved in front of three tall Uncle Sams with hands clasped and they carried us along with them. It was all I could do to keep my fists from tearing into them.

The embankment of Soochow Creek was somewhere on our near left. We forced ourselves away from the Uncle Sams and fell in behind a Chinese on short stilts who managed miraculously to stay upright. He was lighting small firecrackers and tossing them high in the air. The air cracked with a thousand different sounds.

Suddenly our movement swirled and there was an outcry ahead of us. A fight had broken out. In a moment we were almost upon it and I saw that someone had dragged in an Occidental, perhaps a Britisher. I saw arm after arm flail against the terrified man, who would do until an American came along. He cried out as he tumbled to his feet and they began kicking him. Flame grabbed me in a terror of her own. Everyone wanted to poke or kick the poor bastard, but all he could do was clamp his hands over his bleeding face. My blood felt frozen. The opening that had so suddenly developed around him now closed up with bodies and we were swept along over him. When he was under us there was no sound from him. Flame clung to me and we tried to avoid stepping on him. By the time the mob passed he would be pulp.

I pressed to the left, tangled with a guy waving a paper sign on a bamboo pole, and finally felt the hard rail of the embankment. We moved down until I felt a break in it and cut loose from the throng onto a dark loading platform jutting over the creek. Flame's body trembled and her breath was coming hard and fast. The yelling mob surged by without us. We hurried down a ramp and into the safer shadows of the concrete bank. Dark native houseboats nestled thickly about the jetty and the shore.

I stopped and Flame fell against my chest, her arms tight around my neck, catching her breath and not saying anything. I left it that way until the noises of the mob trailed off and disappeared in the sweep down Soochow Road. I pulled the mask up by its dog's nose and looked about us.

On the creek, families huddled under the cloth or bamboo canopies of their cluttered sampans and houseboats. You could hear them; you could smell them. Bamboo poles strung with skimpy washings jutted like flagpoles at crazy angles from bow or stern. It was a floating shantytown. The river Chinese seldom if ever touched their bare feet to the modern pavement only a stone's throw away. It seemed incredible. It was incredible.

We took off the masks and let them drop into the water.

"I've never been so terrified," Flame whispered.

"We aren't running dogs any more," I said. "Just running Americans, and maybe we'd better keep running."

She tightened up on me, and I bent down and found her lips. They were soft and yielding and anxious. I didn't think about anything but kissing her. We were two of a kind, despite Georges, despite Cottardo. I just kissed her hard and wanted to kiss her again, and did.

After a moment we moved to the water's edge and stepped onto the flat wooden stern of a narrow boat. There were people eating under the low shelter of a black tarpaulin hitched up on four poles. The family looked at us sullenly, and we moved on to the next boat and the next, until we reached the end. I saw an old woman nearby tying up a snub-nosed sampan at the edge of the shantytown. I whistled to her.

She went back to the hind oar and *yulowed* the craft around and up beside us.

The fumes that came with her were enough to turn us back, but I was already holding out some *jen min piao* and the old lady snapped it up. The money quickly disappeared somewhere in her black trousers while she kept a muscular hand on the oar to keep the sampan poised in the current.

I helped Flame onto the stern platform. We seated ourselves beside the calloused feet that flattened out like hands on the planks. I pointed out the direction I wanted her to taxi us, and she grinned broadly and began working the fishtail oar in sweeping, circular motions.

The boat reeked with human odors and when I looked forward into the well of the sampan I saw why. This old harpy was part of Shanghai's primitive sewer system. Her boat was half loaded with night collections from the city, a musky cargo that would bring her a price from the farmers upcreek on the outskirts of the city.

"What the hell," I said. "It's a living."

"Shut up," Flame muttered. She had the edge of her skirt pulled up to mask her nose. "I'm afraid I'm going to be sick."

But she held onto her dinner, if she had had any, and after a while we started to laugh. I hadn't laughed in a long time. It felt good.

We passed under arched concrete bridges every couple blocks down the creek and watched the city pass on both sides. We even got somewhat used to the odors of the cargo. The old gal handled her tub as if it were a matchstick, dodging sampans and lighters on the move along the center of the creek. Native craft bordered the banks all the way down, like wooden shadows, dark but alive.

After a few minutes I said, "The Reds didn't mind going to a lot of trouble to get you. They must have had an awful yen for you. Want to talk about it?"

"Where are you taking me?"

"To Hong Kong. Only part way on this barge."

She didn't say anything for a moment. I could see she didn't want to leave Shanghai—yet. I didn't press the issue. I didn't want to fight.

"The Reds are after a couple of million people in China," she said finally. "They are after me because they think I have what they want desperately to get back."

"A deck of cards?"

She looked up curiously, then shook her head. No. The deck of cards meant nothing to her. The old hag labored beside us, working the long oar like an automaton, ignoring us, her alert eyes leveled on the dimness ahead.

I had only one cigarette left and we started to trade puffs. She turned her eyes on me suddenly. "Alex, I've got to know. You *don't* believe I let Georges—"

I tightened up. I wasn't sure what I believed. I *had* believed it back in the apartment and I wanted him to kill her. I wanted to hurt her. I didn't want to hurt her any more. I just couldn't talk myself out of loving her.

"Forget it, baby," I said. "That stuff in the closet came with the apartment. Forget it."

She gave me back the cigarette. "That's the way it was. Period."

"Period," I said.

We sat silently for a while, drifting through the chocolate waters of the Soochow. Finally I tossed away the cigarette. "What did you have that the Reds wanted?"

She didn't answer.

"Look," I said. "We're playing against a big-league team. We're going to have to compare notes or we'll never win."

"I told you before I don't want you mixed up in it."

"Maybe I'm already mixed up in it."

She shrugged her shoulders. "It doesn't matter too much now. I got hold of something and I lost it. It's gone."

"What?"

"A roll of film. Microfilm."

I thought about that for a couple of minutes. And I thought of the deck of cards. Did the two fit together?

"What was on the film?"

"An espionage jackpot."

"Keep talking."

"Nothing but names. About seven hundred of them."

"Names of what?"

"Men and women, some American, some native, some everything. All of them key undercover Red agents at important posts in the West Pacific area. Their names, their addresses, and brief summaries of their dossiers in Moscow."

A whistle went off somewhere in my head and came out my lips. "And you lost it."

"I lost it."

"Nice going."

"It's a copy," she muttered. "The list came from Peiping. The government knows the copy was made and that it's floating around Shanghai. They've made a thousand raids and arrests, but it keeps slipping through their fingers. I had it until three weeks ago." She rubbed her cheeks bitterly. "It was hidden in a lipstick case. I woke up one night and there was a man in my apartment. He—he got it."

"How did you get hold of it originally?"

"I'd rather not say."

"Suit yourself."

"Don't be angry."

"Where did Georges fit in?"

Her voice was soft and spiritless. "A couple of days later he called at the apartment to see me. He knew exactly what had happened. He said he could get it back for a price, and on second thought, a favor."

"You weren't very smart."

"I was too desperate to be very smart."

A roll of microfilm and a common deck of cards. I was certain now that they fitted together. I began to understand something more of the deadly puppet show I had been cast in. If Haigmann was pulling the strings, it meant he was playing a performance down the middle. Once he got the film safely out of Red China, it might end up on the open spy market. It might be dangled from a distance before the eyes of Peiping and sold back, unless the Allied price was better. Anything could happen if the film—the deck of cards—was in the wrong hands.

"That's sweet," I muttered. "Seven hundred political hatchet men to stir up the right kind of trouble at the right time. And seven hundred bastards who wouldn't be worth a damn if Washington got hold of their names and made a lot of copies."

"It's lost to us now."

"Maybe."

"What do you mean?"

"I think I know where to lay hands on it."

She looked at me sharply. She looked at me as though she didn't believe me.

"What else do you know about it?" I asked.

She tossed her head back in a futile gesture. "The names came from Moscow. Peiping has that much influence in the Kremlin now."

"I'm not surprised. It controls twice as many Chinese as Moscow does Russians."

She looked out over the water. Garden Bridge was in the distance. "It means loss of face if Peiping doesn't kill that copy—if the Kremlin even finds out. I suspect they're already on it."

"We sail tomorrow," I muttered. "That doesn't give me much time."

She turned. "I wish I could believe you."

"Try."

We approached Garden Bridge and a streetcar was clanging over it to Hongkew. The river traffic thickened as we passed beneath the bridge and swept into the fast current of the Whangpoo. I made the old witch at our backs understand we wanted to cross the river to the Pootung side and work upstream.

It must have taken twenty minutes to reach the China Navigation Company wharf, where the Sassoon was tied up. Its black stern, scaling and rusted, rode low in the water. Sampans hovered along the flanks of the ship like filings drawn to a giant magnet. We moved in along the dock pilings until we found a ladder, and I sent Flame up. The woman began yakking for more dough, but I ignored her and climbed to the dock. She jabbered what must have been a curse as strong as her cargo and let the current sweep her barge downriver.

The forecastle of the ship stood under lights where coolies were loading barrels of hides into the single forward hold. It was a small ship, as freighters go, but hardy and pugnacious. We found a steep gangway leading to the quarterdeck, but Flame stopped me at the foot of it. "What are you going to do with me?"

"Put you on ice," I said.

She softened for a moment and put her hands on my chest. "I do appreciate your risking your neck for me, Alex. But remember I've got my newspaper instincts too. This is bigger than a story and I've got to see it through."

"I'll do the legwork for you. Get up there."

She flared up. "I'm not ready to leave Shanghai!"

"We'll discuss that in Hong Kong,"

Her hand cracked across my face. I spun her around and gave her a hell of a slap on the bottom and hustled her up the gangway. She was silent and glacial by the time our feet touched the deck. A brown sailor, half naked, was on the quarterdeck. He had been seated on his haunches with a rifle across his knees. He stood up at our approach and gave me a broad smile of recognition. This was Kish, who had been a student in Bombay and had attached himself to me on the voyage up from Hong Kong. The Sassoon's crew was largely native, Javanese, Filipinos, a couple of Indians, like Kish, with strong British accents.

Kish rested the stock of the rifle on the deck. "Where have you been, sahr? Captain's advanced the sailing. We didn't know where to fetch you."

I looked at his eager, friendly face. "When do we sail?"

"With the flood, sahr. About three hours, I believe."

"Maybe that's time enough," I muttered. "Where's O'Rafferty?"

"Captain's at the company office," he said. "Raisin' a bloody fuss over some passengers. Captain don't like that. He don't like strangers on his ship, he don't, sahr."

I took Flame's arm. "This is Miss Forrest," I said. "You'll like her if you don't get to know her too well. Don't let her off the ship until it gets to Hong Kong or I'll kill you."

Kish's white teeth flashed as big as his cheeks. "Got you, sahr."

Flame turned to me, "I'm going with you," she said firmly.

"You bet you are," I said. "Right down the passageway to my cabin."

Kish laughed and I forced her through the hatch and she stopped fighting. All she said was: "Goddamn it, goddamn it, goddamn it!"

"Remind me to teach you a larger vocabulary on the trip south."

"Goddamn it!"

We reached the mahogany door of the cabin I had used coming up. It was unlocked. She walked in and, looked around.

"What a miserable hole!"

"Our first home together," I said. "You'll grow to love it."

I found the key hanging from a nail over the washbasin. "Get some sleep," I said. "You need it."

"Please get out."

"Always glad to oblige a lady."

I think she was smiling a little when I locked the door after me. I gave the key to Kish.

Haigmann's place was dark. I stood on the porch upstairs and all I heard was the growl of the police dog from inside the apartment. I waited. If Haigmann were asleep, the dog would rouse him, but nothing happened. The dog only kept snarling. I tried the door.

It opened at my touch.

I stood there uncertainly for a moment. The dog kept warning me. I opened the door a few more inches and held it firm. He should have come tearing over to the door, but he didn't. His snarls within the apartment came like twists on a Fourth of July ratchet. I opened the door a little more and began whispering to him. It wasn't doing any good, but I stayed with it.

"Easy, boy, easy," I said more firmly.

I got my answer. It was a woman's voice, thin and frightened.

"Alex?"

The muscles in my back relaxed. "Alex," I said.

It was Ariadne in there.

I stepped through the door and found the light switch. She was crouched in the corner by the bed, her hand on the dog's collar, holding him back.

"You frightened me," she muttered softly.

"We're even," I said.

She told the dog to lie down. He gave me a distrustful look, a final growl, and leaped on the bed.

"What are you doing here?" I asked. "Did Haigmann bring you back?"

She shook her head. "I waited outside in the garden until he left. I had to come back and get a few of my belongings." Her dark eyes darted around anxiously. "Turn out the light. If he comes back too soon, it will warn him.

"Let him be warned," I said.

"You found—Flame?"

I nodded. "There's room for you with us, Ariadne. You could start a new life in Hong Kong."

She turned away. "No. I am going to Hangchow. It is a big city, and I will lose myself. He will not find me. My mother was born in Hangchow.

I will be happy there."

I didn't argue with her. She'd be happy in Hangchow. I hoped so.

I said finally, "I came back for the deck of cards. Georges returned them to Haigmann—a little against his will. Where would he hide something like that around here? Downstairs in the plant?"

"No. Only the gold he keeps there."

She suggested a couple of places, a false bookend with a compartment built in the base, the jar of pipe tobacco, under the sink. We found nothing. I began looking into everything, behind everything, while Ariadne got together a few dresses and trinkets.

I found a half-empty pack of cigarettes, lit one, and pocketed the rest. I went on poking through things, realizing all the while that the cards might not be in the apartment at all. I might have to wait for Haigmann to find out.

I turned suddenly and Ariadne was standing against the door, her clothes tied up in a bundle like washing and a good-by look on her face. I walked over slowly, slipped my fingers through her black hair, and kissed her.

"Maybe I'll find you someday in Hangchow," I said.

"Please, no," she whispered. "I don't want to see you again."

I kissed her again softly. She walked to the bed, brushed a hand over the dog's expressive face, and left me alone in the apartment.

I felt like a heel.

Chapter Nine

The dog, his tawny body poised sphinxlike on the bed, followed my movements with alert brown eyes. I would wait for Haigmann to return. Whether he had held the knife that carved up Georges's back, or merely bought the hand that held the knife, I wasn't sure and didn't care. I felt certain of only one thing: It had been Haigmann's work one way or the other. That meant he had the cards. He had the film.

My eyes stopped at the mantel clock. It was almost eleven. If Kish were right, the Sassoon would be pulling out sharply after one o'clock.

Two hours. I went into the pantry and started a pot of coffee. I walked about aimlessly waiting for it to perk. I had cut my teeth on deadlines; this one wasn't close enough yet to bother me. Two hours. Time enough.

I poured a cup of coffee and sat at the table smoking a cigarette. The clock stroked out its mechanical seconds. The dog dropped his head sleepily between his paws, but kept watch. I muttered to him now and then, but he wouldn't thaw. I looked at a couple of framed photographs on the walls of Haigmann as a cavalryman, probably taken in Austria.

I passed forty-five minutes.

A thread of anxiety came alive in me. I couldn't sit still any longer. I walked about, peeking out the window, poking into things I'd already poked into a dozen times. I was doing my thinking out loud now, telling Haigmann to come on, come on, while the dog picked up his ears at my voice.

The small voice of the clock began to intimidate me. After another ten minutes I wanted to break out of there, to move just for the satisfaction of movement.

The phone rang.

I wheeled and walked to the wall where it hung. I hesitated with my hand on the receiver. After the third ring I took the gamble.

"Yes?" I muttered. Maybe that's how Haigmann would answer his phone. I didn't remember.

The reply came quickly, a throaty voice. "Haigmann? I'm going aboard now. We sail in maybe an hour. Your American hasn't shown up yet."

The connection was scratchy and the voice sounded distant and small. But the words loomed large and they filled me with anger. Haigmann knew I expected to leave on the Sassoon. Was he planting one of his men aboard to keep an eye on me?

I muttered thickly, "My plans have changed. Leave the ship, eh? Let it go without you."

There was a long pause at the other end of the line. Then the voice snapped, "Who is this?"

"I told you I have changed my plans. I will explain later."

But it was no go. The other party listened for another few seconds and hung up.

I jammed the receiver in place and stood swearing at it. The dog's ears picked up at my words, but even when I quieted down the ears stayed up.

A low growl started in his throat, and then I heard what he was hearing. Noises under our feet, in the margarine plant below.

I started toward the door of the inside stairway and the dog leaped off the bed. His growl became heavier as he nosed at the crack under the door. Suddenly he was snarling.

No. It wasn't Haigmann down there.

I checked the clock, turned off the light, and walked to the window. I saw no activity on the badly lit street below. It was after midnight.

I wanted no part of this little party. I slipped out the door to the back porch and moved down the steps.

When I got to the bottom, I saw I wasn't going anywhere. A shadow came alive in the doorway and it had a gun in its hand.

"Going somewhere, *t'ung-chih?*"

I stopped in my tracks. "Going your way," I said. *T'ung-chih.* Comrade. He had used it contemptuously as a European might. My eyes picked out a thin face, heavily lined, with incredible pince-nez glasses. He looked like a bookkeeper, but he didn't operate like one.

He patted over my pockets with an expert's touch. He removed my wallet and my cigarettes and drew back to a safe distance. Then he told me where we were going. Not far.

A ricksha stood against the curb half a block below Haigmann's plant. A rangy man in a Panama hat sat in the carriage, hunched forward, leaning his bony chin thoughtfully on an upright walking stick. He could have been from anywhere along the underbelly of Europe. Even at first glance a dim familiarity nagged at my mind. A nose pinched high at the bridge. Dark eyes set wide apart. Had I seen him somewhere before?

The bookkeeper handed over my wallet and cigarettes and explained where he had found me. The ricksha coolie sat on the curb with complete disinterest. Panama Hat looked me over patiently, then nerveless fingers explored the wallet.

His voice, nasal, came out with an aloof smile. "Ha, no name."

"No name," I said. "Ha."

"You have a name, perhaps?"

"Perhaps," I replied. "I was never good at remembering names:"

"Yours is not important. We will let it pass." He extracted the thick wad of Chinese bank notes and tossed my wallet into the street. He took the cigarettes next, tore the entire top off the pack, and emptied the half-dozen cigarettes into his spidery hand. With great care he tore each cigarette in two, then crumbled the pieces between his thumb and forefinger.

When he had finished, he pursed his sunburned lips and dusted the tobacco off his fingers.

"Ha."' He smiled brackishly. "That would have been too easy. But what I hunt—what we hunt, perhaps—is easy to conceal. So easy, and there are so many on the trail. Forgive me, I come late into the game. I do not recognize you."

It struck me then. I remembered that birdlike face, the Panama hat. He was sitting across the table from Cottardo in the picture I had got from the scrapbook!

"You also hunt the trifle?" he asked.

"I'm hunting for Cottardo."

That stopped him. His eyes re-examined me. "Indeed. Do you expect to find him in Shanghai?"

"Can you suggest a better place?"

He laughed through his nose. "I am not in the habit of being a fool. I suspect I would be a fool to tell you."

"I wonder if you're working for him."

The amusement died away and I saw that I had hit a touchy spot. "You underestimate me. It was I who introduced him to the proper persons in China. I work for no one but myself. So you know Cottardo. That interests me."

"So I see."

"Why do you search for him?"

"I have a long overdue punch in the nose to deliver."

"Indeed! If you find him, you must add a blow with my compliments. He will understand."

"I'll be delighted."

"Thank you. Meanwhile, you also hunt our trifle, do you not?"

"Don't let the competition worry you."

"In this business," he grinned, "it is always best to eliminate the competition."

"I'll do you a favor," I said. "I'll eliminate myself."

I took a testing step, and his walking stick thrashed out across my path. The bookkeeper brought himself up and made me feel the cold nose of his gun at my back.

The river, two blocks away, sent occasional noises along the deserted streets. A ship's winch clacked, a whistle sounded far upriver. I couldn't have more than an hour left. Maybe only forty-five minutes.

"Ha, you have courage." The stick swung back into the carriage. "Kitchigin too has courage as long as he has the gun. It is quite a beautiful gun. Have you looked at it?"

"You're wasting your time," I snapped. "I'm not looking for trifles."

"I have plenty of time. One must always be patient in this profession." He clamped the heavy stick between his knees and snapped open a penknife. "I am curious to discuss the matter with you. One can always learn from his enemies." He took an apple from a sack beside him in the carriage, carved a slice, and ate it with elaborate delicacy from the blade. "What did you say your name was?"

"I didn't."

"My name is Peric. Perhaps you know where the Austrian *taipan* hides the film. Perhaps you will think it wise to tell me."

"Your boys are going over his place. Ask them."

"Ha."

"Look," I said shortly. "I don't know what side you're pitching for and I don't give a damn. You've got a guy with a beautiful gun and I'm supposed to be scared, but I'm only getting mad. I wish you luck. I'm sure if you find the film you'll make excellent use of it. I'm walking away from here. My advice is not to try to interfere."

"You speak like a brave fool."

I took the step, but this time when his cane flashed out my hands caught it. I yanked it out of his grip, wheeled, and plowed the end of it across Kitchigin's face. The glasses flew off their perch and the gun exploded—wild. He stumbled into the ricksha as I spun around. Peric had got to his feet, his face contorted with rage. I saw the knife blade standing from his fingertips, ready to fly. His wrist flicked as I struck at it.

The blade spun. I jerked and clipped the stick back in a second blow, this time across his face. The knife found flesh, but not mine. A cry of pain and terror shot out behind me and when I twisted I saw the handle quivering from Kitchigin's neck. The blade was sunk half its length in his throat. The coolie was making off in fright down the street.

I whacked the stick again, and blood was flowing freely from Peric's face. He stood there in a daze. His eyes stared beyond me—to Kitchigin. He must have really liked the guy. I worked the stick against that angular, stolid face in a frenzy, but Peric no longer flailed his arms to protect himself. He was accepting my blows with a sickening eagerness. He seemed to want the beating, and I couldn't go on. I broke the stick across my knee and tossed the splintered parts to the street.

"Next time I see you," I muttered, "I'll finish you."

Peric turned his bleeding head slowly, but his eyes were expressionless when they found me. He said nothing. Kitchigin's fingernails clutched stiffly at the sidewalk, making a small scratching sound. I wheeled around the ricksha and crossed the street. I was running.

The sampan coolie, a misshapen gray fedora pulled on his head, wanted money in advance, but I growled loudly enough to establish my credit. I got under the canopy and felt my pockets absently for a cigarette. Spray came in thin gusts with the rocking of the boat as the coolie moved into the stream. No money. No cigarettes. Peric had relieved me of everything but my life.

When we were midstream I climbed forward to the bow and stood up. A tall, faded junk was tacking at a slow angle across my line of sight.

When it passed, I looked upriver and made out the familiar iron hide of the Sassoon, a couple of open portholes spilling light onto the brown water. A thin, dirty cloud trailed in the breeze from its single low stack. It was a happy sight and it sent my heart racing. I pointed out the ship to the coolie and he worked toward it. It seemed to take forever and I kept staring ahead, half expecting to see the ship part from the dock before I got there. When we finally rode in along the pilings, I climbed up and told the coolie to wait.

The wharf was almost deserted. A couple of Chinese dock hands, stripped to the hips, waited at the cleats to throw off the lines. A lonely black ricksha stood opposite the gangway, which some sailors were beginning to raise. I had a feeling about the ricksha, and I approached it.

"Sorry I kept you waiting," I said.

Haigmann turned his leathery face; the wrinkles at the ends of his eyes grouped up in an easy smile. "Patience," he declared, "is a virtue I have learned well after twelve years in China. But, Herr Journalist, I had almost given you up."

"Come to wish me *bon voyage*, of course."

"It is the civilized thing to do, I believe." The bowl of his pipe flared red as he sucked a slow breath.

"I was detained by a friend of yours," I said. "A guy named Peric."

His eyes examined me with passing surprise. "I hadn't heard he was back in Shanghai. I must look him up. I'm sure you dealt with him properly, eh?"

"He seemed to be looking for you," I said. "He doesn't seem to favor competition in his profession."

"Peric is a scamp." Haigmann chuckled. "We shall not worry about him, eh? He picks up a few coppers by buying and selling, and when he cannot buy, he steals. The Orient is full of his type. A man of no principle. No honor. He will end up with a knife in his back."

"Perhaps you'll arrange it."

He laughed. "Perhaps."

I kept my eye on the Sassoon. I knew I had only a couple of minutes left, but I would have to take time to play my cards right. I could be useful to him so long as he considered me still innocent enough to trust. I could see that he was re-evaluating me as I stood before him.

"I waited for you at your apartment," I said. "But I see you knew where to find me. Is there anything you don't know?"

A small, vain grin appeared on his face. "It is a principle with me to know everything about my business partners."

"Have we business together?" For the first time I spotted my raincoat rolled up beside him on the seat. His leggings smelled strongly of wax, as though recently polished.

"I came to wish you *bon voyage*, as you guessed."

"I thought I had kept my method of departure a dark secret."

"Your ship is the only one that has put in here from Hong Kong in ten days. Even a fool could have figured it out, eh?"

"Remind me never to underestimate you."

"I will keep you reminded." He laughed deeply, and I understood the meaning of the laugh. His agent was aboard. He continued, "I must, of course, apologize for my late friend Georges. Have you heard that he is with us no longer? The Orient makes fools ambitious. But I am glad to see you have survived his ambitions."

"Lately I have made it an ambition just to survive."

"Excellent. The girl Flame. You have found her?"

Was he trying to trap me? He had uncanny sources of information. I thought before I answered. "Flame's dead," I said. "You told me."

"Of course." He smiled. "As I told you. My own woman, half-caste, she has disappeared."

"You treated her badly. I am not surprised." Didn't he know that it was Ariadne who had helped me?

"It is no matter. She will be back." He said it as though he meant it. No, I thought, he didn't know.

"Do you mind if I say I hope not?"

He laughed warmly. "I forgot. You would treat her like a princess, eh? It does not matter. I shall find another woman. Perhaps a full-blooded Chinese. Yes, I am ready for a Chinese."

The chief mate at the rail was calling down to the dock hands. It was now or never. "I'm going aboard," I said. "Good-by, Herr Journalist."

My heart stood still, but I turned. I started to walk, with no intention of going very far. I sensed he would make the final move. He did.

"You are forgetting your raincoat, Herr Cloud."

I turned and he was holding it out. I had passed muster. "Of course."

His face was sardonic. "Have a good trip."

I took the coat and felt the weight of the gold in the shoulders. "Thanks." I wanted to dig a hand in the pockets to see if the cards were there. I held back. It would tell him that I knew too much. I heard his pipe thud against his legging as he emptied the bowl. "Herr Cloud," he called as I started away again.

I stopped.

"Your 'passport' is there too, in a pocket. It will be useful to you. Take special care. You will understand when you reach Hong Kong."

I held my emotional reaction to a breath. I nodded briefly and walked to the edge of the dock. I had won! I had the microfilm! The Sassoon sent up a warning whistle to the sampans that swarmed its outer side. The gangway was gone and the dock hands threw off the lines from the cleats. I approached the edge and called up for Kish. I had eight hundred miles ahead of me, now. Four days if the ship ran into no trouble. When Kish's brown head appeared over the side I told him to throw me a line.

"Yes, sahr!"

When the line dropped Kish made it fast and I pulled myself up, the trench coat thrown over my shoulder. He gave me a hand over the side. "I knew you'd make it, sahr," he grinned. "I wasn't worried."

"I was," I said. "Got the key to my cabin?"

He dug it out and I asked him to toss some money to the sampan that had taken me across the river. The metal plates under my feet vibrated with the engines, and from the wheelhouse O'Rafferty was barking to the deck hands. The ship slowly detached itself from the wharf. I stood at the side for a moment, and in the ricksha Haigmann was waving his hand in a gesture that seemed to say, "So long, fool journalist."

Chapter Ten

The upper section of the cabin door was louvered and I could see no light within. A small fear started in me. I shifted the trench coat and unlocked the door. The bulkhead light worked from a chain and I pulled it.

Flame was there.

She stood at the porthole watching the lighted Shanghai skyline drift behind us. She turned. "Welcome to our happy home."

"You never saw a happier guy."

"You never saw an unhappier girl."

"Stop pretending."

She returned to the passing sights.

"Beautiful city—from a distance," I muttered.

"A horrible city. I hated it."

"A million people across the river would like to be where we are. Getting out. After a couple of days at sea, stowaways will turn up like lice aboard this tub."

She walked away and sat on her bunk. "Do you realize I haven't a stitch of clothes except what I'm wearing?"

"Don't worry about it. That's the fashionable way to travel out of

China these days."

"I'd rather be out of fashion, then." Her green eyes narrowed on me. "This is a double tier of bunks. It has nowhere entered your mind seriously that we're going to share this cabin?"

I smiled self-consciously. "I'm told I don't snore and I'll be happy enough to take the upper bunk."

"You might be a gentleman and offer to sleep on deck."

"I'd rather be a perfect bastard. I don't want to wake up out there with a knife in my back."

"In case it has escaped your notice, you're more in danger of getting one in here."

"I'll enjoy running that risk."

"Must you be completely hateful?"

"Must you be angry?"

"Where did you go?"

"Like I said, legwork. And speaking of legs, one of yours is showing where you ripped the side of your skirt."

She tightened up her skirt. "There, now don't let it bother you."

"I ought to warn you," I said. "I plan to make ardent love to you on this voyage."

"I wish you luck."

"I expect to have it, with a little co-operation."

"Will you please wipe that grin off your face?"

"Get comfortable," I said. "I've got something to show you."

I checked the door to make sure I had locked it and went to the porthole. I looked along the deck and saw a couple of sailors off duty leaning over the side, watching the shoreline pass. I dogged down the port, fixed the blackout shield over it, and returned to the bunk.

Flame had worn out her headstrong pretense at anger. She hadn't believed I knew where to lay hands on the film, but now she considered it and her eyes were alert.

I went through the pockets of the coat and found the pack of cards. Her eyes caught mine expectantly. I think that for a sudden moment she respected me, the way she once had.

The wooden bulkheads of the cabin were creaking gently with the strain of the ship's movement. I tossed the cards into Flame's lap.

"Alex—"

"That's what everyone in Shanghai was scratching around for," I said. "You spoke of microfilm. I spoke of cards. We were talking about the same thing."

She seemed afraid to open the case, afraid the soaring hope would explode. I took the case out of her hand and sat on the bunk beside her. I emptied the cards in my palm and examined the case itself first, uncertain where we would find the black roll.

The case was empty and I thumbed through the cards. They weren't glued together as I had imagined they would be. When Flame first mentioned the film to me, I had pictured a pocket cut out of a solid group of cards where the roll could be cached. Every card was separate and I felt the first sting of fear.

I picked up a card, a joker, and felt the body of it. My fingers told me nothing. The biting thought came to me that Haigmann may have known far more than I credited him with. Had he put me aboard the Sassoon with a phony pack in order to get me out of Shanghai without any trouble?

"The film *could* be cut into pieces," I said a little desperately.

Flame looked at me with growing doubt in her eyes. I tapped the edge of the joker against the wood of the bunk to soften the layers of pasteboard at the corner. I got a small grip on the edge of the card and peeled the blue back off the body of it.

The gray inner layer looked back at us, fuzzy and innocent.

Anger hit me. "If that slick son-of-a-bitch tricked me, I'll get off with the pilot and tear him apart."

I picked up another card and split the layers nervously. When the back was stripped only part way off my anger left me.

"Alex—that's it!"

Two narrow strips of film, gray-black, lay against the inner layer of the card.

I breathed for the first time in several seconds. "So it is. I'll be goddamned."

Her hands clasped my arm. She gave me a long apology with her eyes.

I extracted a piece of film and held it up to the light. It was impossible to see anything but the great reduction in size of the copy, the names, the dossiers. The strip was three frames long.

I cased the cards and got up. I was smiling. "I'll send Haigmann a box of cigars."

When I said his name, she started. The dancing in her eyes slowed down until there was only an oblique fear in them. "Haigmann?" she said softly. "Did you get this from him?"

"You know the guy?"

"Yes."

"As I recall, he tried to make me believe you were dead. Didn't want me mixed up with women."

"He's dangerous, Alex. Does he know I'm aboard?"

"I don't think so. Maybe. Don't let it worry you, baby."

The cabin was not large enough to pace comfortably, but she made a stab at it. The ship's engines breathed heat through the deck and bulkheads. I stopped her and held her in my arms. I wasn't feeling sorry for her. I was feeling irked.

"Haigmann's dangerous, but so are a lot of guys who are after this film. You don't scare easily. I don't think you're scared. I think you're hiding something."

She broke away and stood against the door. A few rust-colored tendrils had come loose from the pile on top of her head and stuck with the heat along her neck. "Alex, do you know what Cottardo was doing in China?"

"Making shady deals with shady people and probably making a fortune. Guys like him don't change."

"He worked with Haigmann."

I stared at her. She knew plenty that she hadn't told me. "They must have made a happy couple."

"I worked for Haigmann too."

That stopped me cold. "What?"

Her hand moved nervously at a wrist. "There's a lot you don't understand, Alex."

"Make it good."

She walked away from the door and kept moving around. "Could you bear it from the beginning?"

"That's generally a good place to start."

"Well, I got to Shanghai a year ago last May. I told you I had followed Cottardo to China. It wasn't exactly that. I only wanted to get out of Europe and a friend got me a job on the *Post and Mercury* in Shanghai. That's how I got introduced to underground work. It was a new experience for me, and I could put my heart into it. For once I was actually doing something, instead of only reporting what someone else had done. The Reds folded the paper soon after I joined the staff.

"They herded those of us who remained in Shanghai to 're-education' classes. I graduated with honors. It seemed an ideal way to stay alive and active, and I pretended to be a good little American Red. But I couldn't find another newspaper job and ended up as a cashier in a cabaret in Hongkew."

"The Viennese Club?"

She nodded, surprised that I could guess it. "That's where I met Haigmann. He had plenty of pull and was able to keep it running until three weeks ago. They had closed him up once before because he ran raw floor shows."

"Where does Cottardo fit in?"

"I thought I had got over him—just as I thought I had got over you. When I saw him again I knew I still loved him."

"Tough break."

"He had been living in Peiping all the while. But about five weeks ago I walked into Haigmann's office to turn in the night's receipts and Cottardo was there talking to him.

"He pretended not to recognize me. When I left for the night he was waiting outside and took me home."

"It must have been a hell of a reunion."

"He told me he had got into trouble with the Reds and Haigmann was trying to help him out of Shanghai."

"What sort of trouble?"

"He was the one who had made the microfilm copy of the Moscow list."

"Did he tell you all that?"

"No. The underground had already got wind of it. But that night Cottardo gave me a lipstick and asked me to hold onto it until he could safely pick it up. He wanted to turn it over to the Allied authorities, but Haigmann wanted to put it up for sale. That was the first Cottardo knew Haigmann's motives were financial."

"I'll bet."

"When Cottardo didn't come back after a week, I got curious about the lipstick and found the film. I knew immediately what it was. Everyone was looking for it."

"Why didn't you turn it over to the underground?"

"The Reds were stepping up their purges so fast I was afraid to. I waited in Shanghai for Cottardo to come back. He would get it out of China. But he didn't come back."

"Chances are Haigmann fixed him up the way he fixed up Georges. He doesn't like ambitious guys."

"He's alive. I know it."

"Then Haigmann must have discovered Cottardo had turned the film over to you for safekeeping and had it stolen. End of story."

"I didn't know it was Haigmann."

"He probably didn't know you understood what the film was, or he would have killed you. He doesn't leave loose ends."

I didn't say that I knew Haigmann had planted someone aboard the ship. Flame came up to me and put her hands on my arms. "I still love

Cottardo," she said softly. "I don't deserve any kindness from you. I would have waited forever for him in Shanghai."

"I'll try not to be too kind."

A feeling came to me suddenly that there was someone at the door. I put my fingers to Flame's lips and listened. The noise was largely my heartbeat; then a definable rustle. I pushed Flame aside, snapped the key over, and swung in the door. When I stepped into the corridor I heard a scrape beyond the hatch onto the open deck. I ran, but when I got out of the deckhouse there was no sign of life. I wheeled around from one place to another, but I had lost him. I swore and walked back to the cabin. Maybe my ears had only played a trick on me. Maybe I was too jumpy.

"Get some sleep," I said. I threw my trench coat to the upper bunk. I picked the cards up off her bunk and slipped them in the pocket of my shirt where I might have kept a pack of cigarettes if I had had a pack of cigarettes. I'd have to learn to treat the cards casually. To do anything else would make them suspect to a perceptive mind.

"Am I a stowaway, or are you going to square me with the captain?"

"I'll do that in the morning. He's probably on the bridge with the pilot and not much concerned with one stowaway more or less. I suspect Kish has already informed him there's a lady aboard."

I opened the port and looked out. We were moving past Kiangwan airfield, and close upon us a lighter stacked with cotton bales was drifting toward the Shanghai docks. Except for the distant whine of the engine below, there was only the soft splash of water rolling back from the flanks of the ship.

I turned back to Flame. She stood watching me, the crestline of her breasts rising and falling in a small movement with her breathing. "If you're going to bunk in here," she muttered, "the least you can do is go for a walk while I get ready for bed."

I didn't say anything. I left the key in the lock and closed the door after me. I tried to force Cottardo out of my mind. I had four days to force him out of hers.

The pilothouse was unlit except for the small greens and reds of the instruments. The quartermaster was standing for a moment at the radarscope. Against the windows, in a dim outline, the helmsman, a native boy in shorts, shifted the wheel with easy movements to the calm commands of the Chinese pilot. The captain, O'Rafferty, sat puffing a cigarette in a tall sport-fishing chair mounted on a pipe from the deck. I could sense his ill humor even before I heard his voice. It couldn't have been easy for him to step aside while a stranger took over his iron baby to pilot the fifty treacherous river miles to the open sea.

"Evening, Captain," I said.

O'Rafferty was staring straight ahead. "Look-see, I'll be thanking you to stay out of the pilothouse, Mr. Cloud. 'Tis no place for spectators."

"I wanted to find out if there's a spare bunk on this luxury liner of yours."

"You've been issued a cabin to yourself. Perhaps you'd prefer an entire suite?"

"Something with a view, if it's available."

O'Rafferty cleared his throat and rubbed the end of his nose. "You're fortunate to have a bunk, Mr. Cloud. My second and third mates are sleeping with the crew. Rushed out of their cabin by our guests."

"I'll try the crew's quarters."

"If your accommodations fail to suit your noble tastes, Mr. Cloud, I can arrange to put you off with the pilot. Perhaps the Queen Mary will happen by to give you passage." He twisted in the chair and looked at me. "I would advise you to stay clear of the crew. A few of the native chaps play politics with knives, and your native land may not be popular with some."

"I'll take your advice." I had tried, after a fashion, to get another bunk. I owed that much to Flame.

"I doubt that you've ever taken any man's advice. Else you'd never have made this trip with me."

"I'm out of cigarettes."

He tossed me his pack, freshly opened. "Keep them if it will keep you out of my sight."

The pilot turned his head and his rimless glasses picked up a twist of green light in passing. I could make out a dark English suit on a wiry body; he looked more like a Chinese merchant than a river pilot. There was something about him that told you at once he felt uncomfortable in the presence of O'Rafferty, sensitive in his role of usurper.

I took a few cigarettes from the pack and handed the rest back. As my eyes accustomed themselves to the interior dimness I looked over the fuzzy mat of O'Rafferty's lazy brown beard, the long hanging ears, the bearish shoulders in a short-sleeved khaki shirt. Seated there, he seemed a larger man than I knew he was. I found a box of matches and started to leave. O'Rafferty's coarse voice stopped me.

"Mr. Cloud, you are bringing back what you came for, I believe."

"Yes."

"Protect your cargo. I do not like the looks of the voyage."

"How many passengers did you take aboard?"

"That's a question I cannot yet answer. The stowaways I do not mind. They stay clear of my sight. The others I deeply detest. Passengers that I know of—five, not counting yourself."

"I'd like to look over the list."

"You'll meet them soon enough. I'd be much surprised if they signed their born names, anyway. A miserable rabble they are."

"I'm sure you'll manage to make them even more miserable."

"I'll do my best, Mr. Cloud."

He may have been smiling a little when I left. I stood for a moment on the wing of the bridge; we were in the broad Yangtze. The open air, touching gently against my body, was an almost inaudible whisper off the mud flats of the delta. A high-pooped Ningpo junk approached as a silent shadow, moving sharply out of our way. A dog barked, as though to intimidate our moving iron shadow, until the creaking sails were far behind us.

I ambled down the companionway to the main deck and entered the passageway to the cabin. I wondered why O'Rafferty had thought to put me on guard. Was it only a way of dramatizing himself, or did he know something more? But I knew he had grown to like me, in his gruff way, on the trip up, and he would be a valuable guy in my corner if trouble came.

I ran a finger along the jalousies of the door. "Are you proper? I'm coming in."

"It's your stateroom."

Flame was in the lower bunk. Her only dress hung from a hook beside the door. She lay on her back, looking up, an unironed sheet pulled over her. The cloth fell in idle flounces from the shape of her body. She was obviously self-conscious of her prone figure, separated from my sights by a thin sheet, the air too still and warm for blankets.

I felt awkward and embarrassed. I had destroyed any right I might once have felt to see her this way. "I got some cigarettes," I said.

"Congratulations."

"I tried to get myself another bunk. The place is loaded."

"It was swell of you to try."

"I thought you'd appreciate it. Want a cigarette?"

"No."

I lit one and moved absently about the cabin. I had come almost eight hundred miles to get Flame and she still seemed eight hundred miles away. After a moment I settled in the chair and looked at her. "Your nose is shiny."

It was a brilliant remark. It brought a brilliant answer. "You need a shave.”

"You never looked more beautiful."

"Your bunk is way up there. Remember? I *would* like a cigarette."

Her arm came out from under the sheet, disclosing a stretch of shoulder strap against her clear, fresh skin. I put a cigarette between her lips and lit it.

"I wasn't the smartest guy in the world two years ago," I said. "Maybe I'm still not very smart. I think we can pick up the pieces and start over again."

She replied through a cloud of smoke, "Alex, a girl doesn't have to be a virgin to have a few principles even about sex. When I stopped trusting you, I stopped loving you."

"You can start doing both any time now."

"You were foolish to come looking for me in Shanghai."

"Are you sorry?"

She took a thoughtful drag on the cigarette. "Angry at first. Then confused—maybe even happy. I don't know. All I know is that I don't want you to make love to me."

"Thanks," I said, "for being afraid that I would try. You ought to know there are plenty of occupational hazards in the foreign-correspondent racket. One of them is too many women on the make. I didn't have sense enough then to play fair with you. A guy was never more anxious to do a rewrite."

"What a pretty bedtime story! But I've heard it before."

"Maybe you'll get to believing it."

I got up, checked the lock, and turned off the light. I got out of my shirt, slipped the cards under my pillow, and climbed up. I finished undressing and pulled the sheet over me.

"Alex?"

"What?"

"Won't there be some shipboard scandal about the two of us sharing this cabin?"

"You can tell people anything you want."

She laughed. "I'll tell them you're my grandfather."

I smiled. If there were any scandal I knew she'd love it.

Chapter Eleven

When I awoke daylight peered at me from the open porthole and a fresh breeze scurried through the cabin. I found my sheet bunched around me as though I had been chilly in the early-morning hours and needed its thin warmth. The ship was virtually without side motion; you could hear only the hushed throb of the screws twisting slowly through water. I leaned on my elbows and looked around. Flame's dress still hung from the hook, a bright stretch of color against the pale green bulkhead. I felt under the pillow for the cards. They were there. I slipped into my trousers and came down ready for breakfast. I was hungry as hell.

When I glanced at Flame's bunk it was empty.

I looked back at her only dress hanging beside the door. I stood there groggily, half asleep, trying to figure it out. She was either walking around the ship almost naked or she was in trouble. My skin felt prickly. I jammed the deck of cards into my trousers pocket, didn't stop to put on a shirt, and left the cabin in my bare feet.

I saw Kish immediately. He stood two doors along the passageway with a lettering brush in his hand. His instant smile annoyed me. I cut off his greeting.

"Have you seen Miss Forrest?"

Kish waved the brush through the air in an outline of curves. "She's something to see indeed, sahr."

"You idiot! Something has happened to her. Where did you see her last?"

"Only a few minutes ago, sahr. On the afterdeck taking the sun."

I stood there foolishly, staring blankly at him. "What did she have on?"

"Not very much." He was grinning like hell and I felt like knocking the expression off his face. He turned back to his work, and I realized for the first time that we were standing before the lavatory door. He was lettering "Women" on it.

"Woman singular, women plural," he beamed. "We have two women aboard, sahr, and both—" He repeated the motion with the brush.

I calmed down. "Am I too late for breakfast?"

"I shall bring you something to eat."

"I'll be on the afterdeck."

I went back to the cabin feeling like an idiot, washed, and finished dressing.

Flame was stretched out on a deck chair on the isolated afterdeck. She was wearing a bathing suit that should never have properly left Cannes. My blood churned up as my eyes traveled over the rust hair, the splendid figure, the long legs crossed at the ankles under the warm sun.

"I was afraid I'd find you half naked," I said.

"Like it?"

"Splendid."

"I'd forgotten," she smiled. "You do snore."

"Only when I sleep alone."

"Really I'll be hearing lots of it, then."

I sat on the deck at her feet. "I see you managed to get a few threads together. Very few, at that."

She was obviously pleased with the ensemble. "There's another woman aboard. She offered to share her wardrobe with me."

"Excellent."

"Maybe you'll be able to stop snoring, at that. Have you seen her?"

"Not yet."

"Some stuff, as the saying goes. Says she's a White Russian. Her husband has been transferred to Canton. Engineer."

"That sounds suspicious. I'll keep an eye on her."

"I'm sure you will."

"Then maybe you'd better keep an eye on me."

Kish came up the ladder with a napkin-covered plate in his hand and a mug of steaming coffee. His dark brown eyes checked Flame over slyly, approvingly. If he had dared, I think he would have winked at me. His coffee-colored skin took on a golden sheen under the hot sun; his black hair, thick and straight, hugged his scalp from a fresh wetting and combing. He wore tropical shorts and a reasonably clean pair of tennis shoes without socks. By his standards he was dressed up. With ladies aboard, he could hardly run around barefooted, as he normally did.

I unfolded the napkin and found a plate of buttered toast. I thanked Kish, but when he hung there still I sent him for some cigarettes.

"Take your time," I added. "Say, three or four days."

He slipped down the ladder and we were alone on the raised deck of the poop. The screws kicked up a lazy simmer of brown water in the wake. The Yangtze, emptying its cargo of silt in to the sea, discolored the shallow waters for miles. The spar of a sunken ship on our left stood out of the surface like a rotting finger pointing the way to heaven. The Sassoon followed a course of sharp turns, as though the pilot were guiding her along a submerged channel. We were, I judged, still threading our way out of the expansive mouth of the Yangtze.

"I can't believe someone really was listening outside the door last night," Flame muttered. "Seems too melodramatic to be real."

"Yeah." I took a sip of coffee. There was no sense in alarming her with the news that one of Haigmann's eyes was aboard.

My eyes had drifted to the forward part of the ship when a man stepped out of the deckhouse. He was tall with a slight stoop to his shoulders. Wings of gray hair stood out from a glistening bald head, high-domed, like the rounded end of an egg. He was immaculate in a suit of whites, his feet thrust in brown sandals. He gripped the flared ends of three Indian clubs, decorated with painted bands of bright orange. He seemed not to see us, strolled to a clearing between the two afterhatches, and began juggling the clubs with a monotonous pattern of movement.

"All this and vaudeville too," I said. "Do you know who he is?"

"I met him at breakfast. He says he was a Shanghai attorney, but a Mexican national. Calls himself Bejarano. Couldn't take the Reds any longer and decided to pull out."

"I wonder if he also juggles knives."

"He has charming manners. I like him." She settled back and watched the wake dissolve in the distance behind us. The sun had baked out the tensions of the night before. Her skin gleamed in the fresh sea air and she looked innocently adventurous, like a white-collar girl on a two-week cruise. Bright color shimmered around her breasts and hips.

A short while later a motor launch came toward us on the starboard side and the Sassoon cut speed. When the boat was almost alongside we stopped and poised in the current. A couple of sailors threw a jack ladder over the side.

Almost at the same time I saw that Bejarano had deserted his spot on the main deck, and then his head appeared before us as he came up the ladder. He moved slowly, but with balanced steps.

"Forgive me for intruding," he said when his sandals reached deck. "Is something wrong? The ship has stopped."

"They're taking the pilot back to shore," I remarked. "From now on out we're on our own."

"Oh, I see." His face broke into a shy, apologetic smile. "It was foolish of me to be alarmed. I am so anxious to leave Shanghai behind me I was very thoughtless. I should have guessed." His voice had a light ring to it. He nodded politely to Flame. "Yes, I see I have intruded. I will return to my practice."

"This is Mr. Cloud," Flame remarked. "Mr. Bejarano."

"Felix Bejarano." He smiled, picking up the opportunity to hang around for a minute and giving us his first name. "Bejarano—pronounced like an h and spelled with a j. It is always either mispronounced or misspelled. One has a right to be vain about his name, you must agree."

"Bejarano," I said. "Spelled with a j. I'll try to remember."

His face darkened diffidently. "Yes, I intrude."

"You're mighty handy with those clubs. I'm a sucker for jugglers."

His features came loose in an eager smile. "The clubs are my passion, my only exercise. I do six, you know, but I could only find space to take three with me." He offered us English cigarettes and we lit up. "Fortunately it is an exercise that can be enjoyed alone."

"Mr. Cloud enjoys only one exercise too," Flame put in with a half-smile. "Unfortunately, it takes more than one."

"Yeah—tennis," I said sarcastically. "Where are you bound for?"

"Who knows?" Bejarano replied with a shrug of his stooped shoulders. "At my age—I am fifty-six, you know—it is difficult to start practice over again. I was twenty years in Shanghai, except, of course, for the Japanese occupation."

"Maybe you'll be able to go back someday."

He smiled at me benignly, as though I were only a college boy and not to be expected to understand the affairs of the world. "Meanwhile, I have my clubs. They are a challenge to the mind, the muscles, the spirit. I never exhibit, of course. I shall be glad to instruct you, Mr. Cloud."

"Thanks anyway. I don't attempt things I can't expect to excel at."

"You can teach me," Flame put in. "It would be fun to learn."

"Splendid." His long, angular face beamed. "Tomorrow morning after breakfast, we start."

"Splendid," she said.

"Splendid," I added.

When he was gone I asked myself if his was the voice I had heard over the phone at Haigmann's. The connection had been faulty and there were the metallic alterations in sound the telephone itself had worked. Was Bejarano, a Mexican gentleman with no tag ends of his native language in his speech, the man Haigmann had put aboard? I couldn't decide. There had been too much unnatural politeness in Bejarano's voice to know what it really might sound like.

The ship got under way again.

"Kish told me you wanted to see me," I said.

The Captain was in his stateroom on the starboard side off the bridge, an airy compartment about the size and shape of a small hotel room. Thin static from the adjoining radio shack pierced the bulkhead. O'Rafferty sat at his writing desk, plucking at his wiry whiskers. His face was at once handsome if somewhat fleshy, distinguished if somewhat unkempt, sharp-nosed, alert. "Sit down," he said.

He looked at me as though he wished I would drop dead. I told him so.

"I shall not be that demanding," he replied. "When I agreed to give you passage to Shanghai I believed not for a moment, Mr. Cloud, the cock-and-bull tale you spun. Look-see, any man who would go to that much trouble for a woman would be a lunatic."

A brass-cased chronometer over the desk read four-thirty. The ship, having moved into the East China Sea, rocked slowly; the horizon line crawled back and forth across the portholes. O'Rafferty's weathered black cap, the gold turned moldy green from the sea air, sat on a half-empty book cabinet beside the desk.

"Apparently you were not satisfied to be a common lunatic," he sputtered. "You must be at least the greatest lunatic that ever was born."

I leaned forward in the chair. "What are you trying to say?"

"I have seen the woman"—he cleared his throat—"and, may I say, rather more of her than proper. During the last hour, Mr. Cloud, we received this message from the Chinese authorities in Shanghai."

He passed me a sheet of the ship's paper on which the radioman had taken down the communication: "Our information you have aboard American woman, Paula (Flame) Forrest, red hair, green eyes, 5' 3", 118 pounds. Wanted by People's Government for underground banditry. Reward. Confirm. Gen. Lwai Kin, Shanghai Military Commission."

I handed it back. "Have you confirmed?"

"No."

"Are you going to?"

"What do you propose, Mr. Cloud?"

I tried not to show my alarm. I looked at him coolly. "It's my impression that you're running cargo to the Reds for only one reason. It's the fastest buck in the Orient. If you also happen to approve their political point of view, I'd say you won't be able to sleep nights if you don't confirm and collect that reward."

His face was glacial. "My politics are my own business. I have been able to purchase most of the stock in this ship, Mr. Cloud. I shall own it in another six months, unless I have been a fool and a lunatic like yourself." He handed me another message, one he had written himself. A grin stretched his whiskers.

It denied that Flame was aboard.

I looked at him respectfully. "I guess I spoke out of turn."

"You generally do."

"We thank you, both of us."

He shifted, and his eyes darkened again. "The cunning Chinese general is not so easily satisfied. This came over the wireless just before you walked in."

The message: "Put in at Ningpo immediately for inspection."

My heart pounded. "Are you changing course?"

"They can make business difficult for me if I fail to co-operate."

"How far is Ningpo?"

"We could reach it tonight."

I got up and started walking around the cabin. "They don't want her," I explained. "They want something they think she has. I have it, and if you're the softhearted bastard I take you for, you won't throw her to the wolves."

He cocked an eyebrow. "I allow her to share a cabin with you. Perhaps that is infinitely worse."

"I haven't touched her."

"Look-see, you are a lunatic indeed, Mr. Cloud."

"Is it Ningpo?"

He rubbed his beard thoughtfully. "I have yet to make up my mind. You say you have brought something highly dangerous aboard. That interests me, somewhat."

"Let's let it go, somewhat."

"You don't trust me, then, Mr. Cloud."

"I don't know you well enough to involve you in my mischiefs."

"You are thoughtful, indeed." His eyes, small and gray, kindled with the vexations of the moment. "As you know, Mr. Cloud, it is not my policy to accept passengers aboard this ship. Not only do I detest their company, for they disturb the peace of my ship and demand I entertain them at my table, which I will not do, but they are dangerous to have aboard as well. Say we have trouble with the Free Chinese vessels operating off Formosa, or the pirates that are even more of a nuisance south from there; can I trust my passengers? Especially wealthy passengers, such as our Mr. Wei. Have you met him?"

"Not yet."

"The pirates could get a good ransom from him if they captured him, and these Chinese sea bandits have an excellent information service. The point being, Mr. Cloud, that I am at least forewarned. Whatever it is you possess, I should like also to be forewarned."

"You don't have to take orders from the Chinese. They'll forgive you as long as you bring rubber and more rubber."

"You are evading the point."

"I was hoping to lose it entirely."

"As captain, I have the right to insist."

"As a gentleman, you won't."

His fingers began drumming against the surface of the desk. He was angry and I didn't blame him. But couldn't tell him about the film. It could be too risky.

Almost at once we heard steps outside the door and then a firm knock. O'Rafferty growled something and I sat back impatiently in the chair.

The Chinese wore a gray silk gown, black shoes well shined, and a gray felt hat, uncreased. He carried a book in the crook of his arm, like a scholar, and I suspected at once we were in the presence of the wealthy Mr. Wei. O'Rafferty confirmed it by introducing us.

"I ask a favor," the Oriental said in a voice that told you he generally got what he asked. "The officer sharing my cabin is drunk."

It was clear O'Rafferty didn't harbor any affection for Mr. Wei. "Poor chap probably has reason enough to be drunk, bless his soul."

"You will, perhaps, find me other quarters." His flat face, almost white-skinned, was aloof and its expression unchanging. It seemed an expression out of touch with the upheaval of his China, the sort of face you saw often enough along Shanghai's streets before the Reds came; the wealthy Oriental able to stroll past hungry coolies curled in doorways, seeing but feeling nothing, worried only about where his next million yuan was coming from.

O'Rafferty's voice was crisp. "You will have to put up with the good and the bad. This ship does not have passenger accommodations. If you prefer, you may sleep on deck."

Mr. Wei's thin eyebrows raised confidently. "May I remind you, *laota*, I have paid two hundred British pounds for passage. That is a great sum for bad accommodations. You can do better."

"If you want your money back, I can arrange to put you off at Ningpo."

O'Rafferty's eyes flashed at me. I detected a twinkle and my pulse stopped shooting. He had made up his mind. He would not change course.

Wei dismissed him with a final glance, turned in a silent rage, and left the stateroom.

"Him and his two hundred pounds," O'Rafferty glowered. "He's lucky I don't put him to chipping paint."

"Who's he bunking with?"

"A black Irishman like myself. Says he's a professional soldier. Fought with the Reds, the rascal, but couldn't put up with their guff any longer. Name's Cork."

I lit one of O'Rafferty's cigarettes. "Did he desert?"

"Not yet. He's to be transferred to the Indo-China border. Got a lieutenant's commission, the bugger. Hopes to slip away in Hong Kong."

I didn't like the sound of it, despite O'Rafferty's easy sympathy for a countryman. I didn't like the idea of having a Red officer aboard, despite his self-avowed intentions. "It strikes me as odd," I said, "that the military didn't provide the man's transportation south."

O'Rafferty glanced up without replying. He lost his fingers in his beard and I realized he had thought of that too. We let it go.

Night crept over us slowly. The Sassoon was doing full speed, a miserable nine knots, and the plates vibrated with the effort. The bolder stars pierced the indigo twilight, and then, when it was dark, the sky blazed with flickering lights. I had left the wardoom immediately after dinner and stood smoking a cigarette at the bow.

How, I wondered, could the Shanghai authorities have learned Flame was aboard? Even if Haigmann somehow knew, and I reminded myself not to underestimate him, he wouldn't have tipped off the military. He wanted the Sassoon to reach Hong Kong without delay. I touched the cards reassuringly in my pocket and tried to dismiss the matter from my mind.

"You are Mr. Cloud, of course." A voice with a smile.

I turned and saw a pair of white slacks, beautifully filled, a sleeveless blouse, beautifully filled, and blonde hair trimmed short.

"Who are you—a dream walking?"

"Call me Helena." She laughed. Her voice was throaty, torchy. "It's not my real name, you understand, but it has a nice sound. May I have a cigarette?"

I fixed her up. "I was beginning to think you'd never leave your cabin," I said.

"It takes me about a day to get my sea legs."

"I missed seeing your legs at dinner. I'm always curious about White Russian girls traveling alone aboard a tramp steamer."

"I'm never alone for long."

"I can see why. Feeling better?"

"Much."

A perfume, heavy and languorous, hung about her despite the breeze that snapped the silk fabric of her blouse. A golden belt hugged her narrow waist, and I saw she was wearing golden sandals as well. Her breasts were incredible. You wanted to touch them to discover if they could he real. I merely speculated.

"The woman—she is your wife?"

"Does it matter?"

She smiled wisely. "Not at all—to me."

"You don't waste any time."

"It is a short trip. Four days pass quickly. One must make the most of them—Alex." She blew a puff of smoke. "She is, of course, quite lovely. We are well matched, yes?"

"May I ask an impertinent question?"

"Please do."

"Are those things entirely real?"

Her chuckle had a cocktail-bar throatiness to it. "Before we reach Hong Kong I expect you'll be able to answer that question for yourself, yes?"

I tossed away my cigarette and gave her my best cocktail-bar smile. "I'm going to shock you," I said. "No."

"Men don't say no to Helena," she said gaily. "You will see."

"As you say, it's a short trip. I don't want you to kill valuable time. No kidding, you're wasting it, baby. I'm not interested. But thanks for asking."

She leered with amusement and flicked away her cigarette. "You charming fool," she laughed, and strolled away.

I stood there feeling uncomfortable about the whole thing. I had met Helenas before, in Paris, in Rome, in San Francisco, in Hong Kong. We had had fun. But I wanted all that behind me. I had found something better and I'd have to fight to get it again. I pressed my lips together and made a resolute decision to do no research in the field of Helena's intimate upholstery.

When I returned to the cabin I found Flame sitting in the only chair; she was smoking a cigarette, looking pale and all nerves.

"You'd better lock the door," she whispered.

"You didn't have to wait up for me."

"Please don't joke. I think the cabin has been searched."

I locked the door. I glanced quickly around the cabin. Nothing seemed out of place. Reflex brought my hand to my pocket to check on the cards. My trench coat still lay on my bunk and I examined it. The shoulders still weighed heavy with gold.

"You're just jumpy," I said. "No one could tear around in here and leave things so orderly."

"Maybe." She was wearing a gray slack suit from Helena's wardrobe; Flame's own dress was thrown across her bunk. She put out her cigarette, got up, and showed me the shoulder pads of the dress. "If someone was in here, maybe he didn't want to put us on guard by messing the place up. I was going to wash out my dress and discovered this."

I looked closely at the shoulder pads she held out. A slit, about an inch long, was cut in the seam of each one. It looked as though a knife had sliced the threads to allow a finger to probe around inside.

"You're sure the rips weren't there before?"

"Yes."

"Why didn't you call me sooner?"

"I couldn't make up my mind if it really meant anything."

"How long ago did you leave the wardroom?"

"About twenty minutes."

"Who was in there with you?"

"No one. I was reading."

I threw the dress down on the bunk. "I think it's a good guess someone's been in here. But we won't worry about it. He must have been scared off before he had time to give the place a real going-over. Whoever it is knows what he's looking for."

"It's not like me," she said, "but I think I'm really beginning to be frightened."

"I haven't seen anyone on this ship yet I couldn't lick," I said. "Forget it."

What I didn't say was that whoever had entered the cabin had apparently made a beeline for the only thing of Flame's around, as though under the impression she had the film. That meant that Haigmann's plant was watching me, and another party was watching Flame as well.

What the hell, I went on thinking, at least we're evenly matched. Two against two.

Chapter Twelve

Breakfast was almost over when Cork, the professional soldier, showed up. He wore wrinkled army trousers, no jacket, and a clean white T shirt. He had thick, alcoholic features and a bad skin. His hair was dark and coarse and rebellious looking. He seemed to be in his late twenties. His sullen expression told you he had been fighting his way through life since kindergarten and that he had a trigger temper. He smoked a cigarette broodingly and found a place at the end of the table. The frigid eyes of his cabinmate, Mr. Wei, studiously avoided him. Helena glanced speculatively at his raw-boned body, his cold, moody face, and tentatively rejected him.

There were a few silent nods of good morning and the table banter resumed. He said nothing.

The man beside him, Henri Dufour, I had met at dinner the night before. He shared Bejarano's cabin and completed the list of passengers. He was a bouncy little man in shell-rimmed glasses who talked incessantly—generally about Henri Dufour. He claimed to be a motion-picture director who had spent the last five years in China making documentaries.

"Hollywood will never, *never* get Dufour," he was rambling on now, fluttering his hands above his plate. "*Certainement*, I have had the offers. Six, seven, eight—I do not count any more. *Alors*, Dufour is not interested in wasting his time with love stories." He turned to me and hammered home his point. "You Americans are children. In these times there are other things to be put on film."

He was looking squarely into my eyes when he struck the word "film," and it was all I could do to hold my expression, which was one of boredom. I looked at Flame. She snubbed out her cigarette nervously.

The moment passed and Dufour let his blood pressure get away from him. "What a fool was this man Freud! A charlatan, of course, a mountebank, a witch doctor. He tried to make us believe that sex is the fulcrum of life. Marx, *mes amis*, knew better! It is the community of spirit, yes? That is the real fulcrum. That is the truth we must put on film. The Russians understand, the Chinese too, but we of the Western world, *mes idiots*, sex and cinema remain inseparable."

He paused, glowing, but before he could get back on the sound track Flame got up and nodded to Bejarano.

"It's after breakfast," she said. "My lesson, remember?"

"I have not forgotten." He smiled, getting up.

The others detached themselves from the table to go on deck. As she passed, Helena patted my cheek. "Have a good night's sleep, charming fool?"

"I snored all night."

When she was gone, I was left alone with Cork. He ignored me. I lit a cigarette and watched him finish his breakfast.

In three or four minutes, however, my silent presence must have begun to work on him. He gulped the dregs of his coffee and got up to leave.

"Rushing off to catch a streetcar?" I remarked.

He stopped, one foot over the hatch combing. "What do you want, Yank?"

"I thought we might discuss Irish plays. Or can you suggest a better subject? What you're doing aboard this ship, for instance."

"That's my business."

"That's *our* business."

"Who says so?"

"I said so. Just now."

He pinched the coal off his cigarette with his fingertips, ground it dead on the deck, and slipped the butt in his pocket. "Want to stay out of trouble, Yank?"

"Not particularly."

"Stay out of my way."

"You're scaring hell out of me, *t'ung-chih*."

He spit malevolently and disappeared along the passageway.

I got up smiling, I had wanted to hear his voice and I had heard it. Haigmann's man? The voice I had heard over the phone? I played with the idea for a couple of moments and finally went on deck to watch Flame tangle with the Indian clubs.

Later in the morning, two Chinese stowaways were discovered in barrels that were thought to contain hides. Both of them had submachine guns with them.

I was in the pilothouse when the news came to O'Rafferty over the intercom. "Keep them below," he snarled. "I'm coming down."

He turned to me, his cheeks quivering with rage. "We are a marked ship, Mr. Cloud. But we shall outwit the devils."

I followed him down the ladder and forward to the hold. "Pirates," he sputtered. "That's what we must contend with now. I've been pirated twice. I know their slimy tricks. Invented the fifth column, they did. Plant a few men aboard to take over the bridge when their armed junk comes alongside."

The chief mate, a blond man with the build of a Welsh coal miner, was waiting for O'Rafferty. He held a machine gun on the two sallow-faced stowaways.

O'Rafferty picked up the second gun. His bare cheeks, above the line of the beard, shone red as apple skin. The storage hold was dim and the air hot.

O'Rafferty acted with a directness that caught me by surprise. He picked out the more husky of the two Chinese and, pausing only long enough to relieve himself of a solid curse, pulled the trigger. The muzzle coughed and flamed, and the startled Chinese went rigid on his feet like a guy being electrocuted. Then he lay on the deck. O'Rafferty turned to the other, a flat-nosed Oriental who stood with a cool expression.

"Now, you son of the devil himself," O'Rafferty glowered, "you'll be telling me where your junk hopes to intercept my ship or you'll get what's left in this gun."

The guy obviously didn't understand English, although he might have guessed. O'Rafferty put it to him again, but when he got no response he ordered one of the crew nearby to get Mr. Wei. Wei would translate.

When the wealthy Chinese arrived, his brown eyes absorbed the scene in a small, noble glance. O'Rafferty turned on him at once.

"This is what your evil two hundred pounds brings me," he thundered. "Not my silks and hides and cottons are they after, but a fat ransom. If you want to save your skin, you'll be asking him where his fellows wait for us."

Mr. Wei, far from intimidated, questioned the stowaway in calm tones. The stowaway turned aside without answering.

"Tell him he'll get what his partner got!"

The stowaway answered then—with a spit. Mr. Wei translated. "He wishes to remind you that he will be shot even if he talks."

"That he will!" O'Rafferty snarled.

"You might as well shoot him," Mr. Wei remarked. "He will never talk. It is a trait of my countrymen."

I looked at our Chinese passenger. "Ask the guy," I said, "if there are any more of his friends aboard ship."

Mr. Wei raised a contemptuous eyebrow my way and left.

There was nothing to do but clean the affair up. The chief mate used the gun on him and a short while later the two bodies were given the deep six.

O'Rafferty ordered an immediate inspection of the ship. Six additional Chinese, including one woman, and two Eurasians were turned up, none of them armed, all of them scared stiff. O'Rafferty had them locked up in the paint compartment and established a twenty-four-hour guard outside the door. "I ought to shoot every man of them, and some of the passengers as well," he glowered,

He spent the rest of the afternoon in the pilothouse boiling over with oaths. Rage did not die easily within him.

Flame had found a battered volume of Chaucer in modern English, with all the naughty passages marked, and she curled up with it in her bunk during the evening.

"That's not recommended reading," I said, "on a sea voyage."

"I'm skipping the marked passages."

"If you get lonely, just whistle. A wolf whistle will do."

I felt her eyes on me as I left. During the day she had lost her tenseness and we had even had a few pleasant words together. No gossip had sprung up about us; no one seemed to care.

Earlier, I had borrowed a tube of glue from the chartroom and fixed up the card I had split looking for the film. The deck appeared perfect. And it was still in my pocket.

O'Rafferty was sitting in his tall chair in the pilothouse, smoking a cigarette and thoughtfully watching the bow struggle through the sea, beginning to run heavier.

"My guess," he said at once, as though I had entered upon a train of thought he was anxious to make vocal, "is that we'll see our pirates off Amoy. The scum, they know we'll be hugging the mainland through the straits."

I lit a cigarette. This was the only corner of the world where pirating was alive, and I had to be in it. "It must be slim pickings for them," I said, "thanks to the Nationalist blockade."

"I suspect the blockade bothers them little more than it does me." He twisted in the chair. "When there are none of us bigger fellows around, they go plundering the fishing boats. The Reds will have a jolly time trying to reform them as long as anything of value floats through these waters, Mr. Cloud."

"The blockade doesn't seem to be very effective. Maybe we ought to hug the Formosa coast."

"I can do without your advice, Mr. Cloud," he remarked. "For your information, I prefer to deal with pirates if I must."

The Free Chinese navy, I knew, consisted of about thirty combat ships afloat, the rest rotting for lack of repair on the Formosa coast. It was a navy almost without oil for its tanks and a hell of a stretch of water to patrol.

"Pirates are good newspaper copy," I said. "Let me know if you see any."

"We'll reach Hong Kong if only for the pleasure of putting you ashore and getting you out of my sight."

The wardroom was deserted except for Helena and Dufour when I entered. Unless I missed my guess, he was trying to talk her into a movie career.

"Ah, the American newspaperman," Dufour interrupted himself. "You must make us all famous if we are attacked by pirates. *Sacrebleu,* a living anachronism. Pirates in our time, imagine it!"

"I can hardly wait," I said.

Helena was smoking a cigarette in an ivory holder. "Henri is trying to talk me into making a picture with him. Do you think he is only saying it?"

"Probably wants you to start at the bottom and work up."

"He teases, *ma chèrie*." Dufour beamed through the lenses of his shell-rimmed glasses. "The Americans think only of sex. That *also*, is a living anachronism."

Helena smiled. "But so charming, eh?"

"Careful," I said. "I'm a Freud man. Your fulcrum of life is showing."

Dufour turned sour. "You joke, you two. These are not things to joke about."

"You may go now," Helena interrupted him.

He stood for a moment, like a guy suspended in midair, and then stormed out of the compartment.

"He is a delightful fool." Helena smiled, running a hand languorously through the short, wind-blown hair. "I believe he is in love with me."

"Splendid."

"You must not be jealous."

"I'll face it like a gentleman."

"Would you like to kiss me?"

I poured myself a cup of coffee. "Not if I can help it."

"You prefer coffee to a kiss? What a child you are, darling."

"You must try to hate me. I'll try to make it easy for you."

She extracted the white holder from her lips, poised with expression. "You love the other woman?"

"I knew you'd catch on if I were patient."

"You are making me angry."

"I'm trying to play hard to get." I smiled. "It's a hell of an experience. You ought to try it sometime."

"Life is too short," she replied in a surly voice. She killed the cigarette and put the holder away. "Helena is hungry. Be a darling and get me something to eat."

"The pantry is in there."

"You are insufferable!"

"I'll despise myself in the morning."

She rose and moved behind me. Suddenly I felt her arms snaking around me. Her perfume enveloped me, thick and persuasive. I wasn't kidding myself; she was tempting as hell, but I had a feeling she was going after me with too much purpose. Was her motive strictly amorous? Could she be after the film? "I'm going to my cabin," she whispered. "The door will remain unlocked. Do not be a fool."

The compartment seemed warm as hell; my pulse was stirring. I tried to say something foolish to get off the hook. "Thought you were hungry. Stick around and get something to eat."

"Helena has a different appetite now."

"I never sleep on an empty stomach," I said heroically. "See you in the morning."

Her hand left my chest and slapped my face. Playfully. She disentangled her arms and moved slowly to the hatch.

I made myself sit there. I hadn't touched my coffee and had lost any appetite for it. Point one: What the hell, I was only human. Point two: I hadn't had any practice resisting desirable women. Point three: I loved Flame.

I got up. I knew what I had to do, but I wasn't sure I'd be able to keep my head. How close could you get to a fire without getting burned?

The cabin door was unlocked, all right. There was a derisive smile on her face as I shut the door behind me. She came to me without a word. Her arms pulled me close against her soft, yielding body. She kissed me hard. The palms of her hands stroked my chest lustfully; they stopped when one of them fell over the cards in my shirt pocket. I pushed her away and leaned my back against the door.

"Now let's see what you've got to brag about," I said.

"You make it sound so businesslike, darling."

"I'm always suspicious of free passes."

"Turn off the light, yes?" She kicked off her sandals.

"No. I can't see in the dark."

"You have no sense of touch, perhaps?"

"Start with the blouse."

"I will start with you." She came toward me, smiling, and undid a couple of the buttons of my shirt. She slipped her arms inside the shirt and around me and held me close. Then she pulled my shirt apart and kissed my chest softly and dartingly. I managed to stand there like a wooden Indian, though I didn't feel like one. I pushed her away and she laughed. "Helena will show you about love," she said. She moved across the cabin to the porthole and the red tips of her fingers danced about the buttons of her blouse, undoing them. Her shoulders stood out rawboned under the dim light from the bulkhead. Her breathing came faster and her eyes narrowed on me darkly.

She faced me as the bra fell away. Her breasts, pendent now, moved gently with their freedom. She wrapped her arms under them and raised them up. She held them that way as though they were pets.

"I'll be damned," I said. "They're real."

"You like?"

"What else have you got?"

She laughed throatily and began unbuckling the golden belt. "Is that a deck of cards in your shirt pocket?" she asked suddenly.

"I'm really a card shark in disguise."

Her long legs appeared as she stepped out of the slacks. She kicked them to a corner of the cabin and moved toward a small steamer trunk, open at an angle. I watched her as she walked, her buttocks flat under the tight black lacework. I might have expected her to wear black. She opened a small drawer and at first I couldn't see what she removed. When she turned, facing me again, I saw that she held a small pair of scissors.

"Men expect love trophies from Helena." She smiled—from experience. "This will be yours, my Alex. But I will fix them so you can never give them to another girl, yes?"

She started snipping carefully down the front of the lace. Her navel appeared and I held my jaws tight as I watched. The black came apart slowly to her legs.

"I see you're not a natural blonde," I said. "You had me fooled."

"That is a woman's privilege."

The lace fell away and she put down the scissors.

"Love that birthday suit," I said grimly. "Many happy returns."

She threw the panties to me, and a heavy perfume came with them. It was a perfume I knew, expensive but cheap, and the memories it evoked disgusted me. It reminded me of too many Helenas. I let the lace lie at my feet, but even then she didn't catch on.

"Not bad," I managed to say. "You'd have been great in vaudeville." I was still glued to the door, watching her, trying desperately to play it flip.

"I am naked," she muttered, touching fresh perfume over herself. "Do not be so cruel as to joke about it."

"They're not very good jokes."

She put the perfume bottle aside and started toward me slowly. "Still you wait?"

"I'm torturing myself."

She stopped and her dark eyes began to smolder. "So?"

"So this is where I walk out, baby."

"You *can't!*"

But I was going to if it killed me, and it nearly did. "Pin a medal on me for heroism."

"Pig!"

"I told you before to mark me off your list. If I haven't made myself clear now, I'll engrave the rest on the head of a pin."

"Shut up!" She scooped up some clothing in a rage and clasped it to her body. "How cleverly the girl Paula allows you to chase her! You think I have no eyes to see? I offer to share my cabin, but she prefers yours. Does her body compare with mine? What does she know about love? Get out!"

"What she's got she doesn't throw around, baby. It makes a difference."

Her eyes were flaming. She rattled off something in Russian and spat out a few bastards in translation. She swept up her shoes.

"By the way, Lady Godiva," I said, stepping out the door, "those're mighty pretty earrings."

The door was closed when the shoes struck. I felt like a heel.

I was.

Chapter Thirteen

The running lights had been out all evening. O'Rafferty had ordered blackout shields in place over the portholes and that hatches he kept closed so that no light would escape into the night. We had entered the Formosa Straits shortly after dinner.

The result was that the passengers felt jittery.

The island of Formosa, shaped like a stubby feather, lay one hundred miles off the China mainland. O'Rafferty had ordered flank speed in order to run the straits under darkness. The ship whined and jarred against the sea as though it would spit out the rivets that held its black skin together.

O'Rafferty stood before the dark windows of the pilothouse. I looked at the clock. It was only a little after ten. It seemed much later. A native boy was stationed at the radarscope watching the continual sweep of the green line. O'Rafferty turned to me. "You can be of no assistance up here, Mr. Cloud." He was in a dark mood, but so was I. Pretty soon he was talking again.

"We hug the mainland," he mumbled sullenly. "Perhaps it is an evil choice. We tempt the pirate fleet. They are well armed, Mr. Cloud, make no mistake about that. Cunning as well, and daring. To port, the Free Chinese wait, like Napoleon, on their Elba. I think sometimes I would best hug the Formosa coast."

I was only half listening. My mind was below, in Helena's cabin, the sight of her naked skin dancing before my eyes. What a pious fool I had made of myself!

Yet, as I turned the affair over in my mind, I considered that she and Dufour might be a pair. It was only a vague feeling; maybe I was becoming overly sensitive to symptoms of danger. They had been together in the wardroom. That was slim evidence, except that he had left us together too readily once I walked in on them. The only thing I felt certain of was that I didn't want to be softened up by a nice pair of legs. I had to walk out on her. I would have been a fool to let her come between Flame and me. It was the toughest walk I had ever taken in my life, and I couldn't believe it was anything but a crazy dream. It wasn't like me—pin a medal on me.

Then I remembered what she said. Flame had turned down an invitation to share her cabin. My pulse picked up the meaning.

"... found two guns. One can never be sure of passengers in these waters."

"What?" I muttered.

O'Rafferty turned angrily. "I was saying, Mr. Cloud, my chief mate inspected the cabins during dinner. He found two guns in the Mexican's bags."

"Bejarano. Maybe he juggles guns, too."

"I don't like the look of it, Mr. Cloud."

"How about the others?"

"Nothing of interest to us. We unloaded the guns and took the spare cartridges. Left the guns, so as not to arouse his suspicions too soon."

"What are you thinking? Bejarano came aboard to run this end of the piracy?"

"Who knows? It's the way they work. Paralyze the bridge at a given signal, they do, and then the junk unloads men on us like mice. Seagoing junks. Machine guns and whatnot. I was ready for them off Foochow. We're beyond Foochow now. I suspect it'll be Amoy."

"When do we pass Amoy?"

He grunted. "Dawn, perhaps. Unless that mist turns to fog and I'm forced to cut speed."

I stayed on the bridge until almost midnight. O'Rafferty was unable to sit still in his sport chair, and I warmed it while he paced before the windows. We passed through waters patched with fog and O'Rafferty cursed it feelingly. Before long the open stretches of night vanished altogether, and a gray, wet blur closed in.

O'Rafferty plowed through the solid fog for fifteen minutes before he could bring himself to give the order. "Cut speed to four knots," he growled angrily.

The ships vibrations disappeared and we began to plod through the water.

"At least," O'Rafferty grunted, "the Free Chinese won't be bothering us on a night such as this. But Lord help any floating thing that gets in our way. I'll not turn the running lights back on."

He stood watching the radar screen. I stuck around a while longer and then went below.

The wardroom had come to life. The blackout shields were in place, the lights were on, and the air was filled with smoke. Only Cork was missing. The others sat around smoking, bantering, but there was a definable tenseness in their smiles. Apparently no one but Cork had been able to fall asleep. Dufour had found a gray life jacket and was wearing it. He reminded me of a puffed-up frog.

Helena, fully dressed, sat beside him. Her eyes steadied on me. They had the gift of speech.

Flame greeted me with a fresh smile as I walked in. Her hair was nicely done up. Somehow, I felt I was making progress with her.

"Ah, the newspaperman," Dufour announced with exaggerated emphasis. "We were considering that you may have jumped overboard."

"Sorry to disappoint you. Hello, Flame."

She pulled me down to the chair beside her. "I was about to send a Saint Bernard after you. Where do you hide?"

"Frightened?"

"Having a wonderful time. Chaucer began to bore me. Thought I'd come out to see how our pilgrimage to Hong Kong was getting along."

"Some bunch of pilgrims. Chaucer never had it so good."

She slipped her arm through mine and wrinkled her nose. "Neither did I."

"I thought you hated me, sort of."

"I do, sort of."

Mr. Wei sat in a corner chair reading. He looked about, pressed his lips together distastefully, and returned to his book.

"Imagine," Dufour was chattering. "We've virtually on a desert island, *mes idiots*. Stranded on the sea. Castaways on a steel island, perhaps, our different lives suddenly brought into the same focus. You must write the screenplay, M'sieu Cloud. I shall direct. Have you never seen any of my films?"

I considered what he might really mean by that remark. "Do me a favor," I said. "See if that life jacket really floats."

"Ah, the American is in a bad mood."

The cards felt suddenly very heavy in my pocket.

"Please," Bejarano cut in. "We have enough trouble on this voyage without adding to it ourselves." He turned to me. "Miss Forrest is an excellent student with the clubs. Her co-ordination is rare."

"He's joking," Flame said. "I was a miserable student. I dropped a club on his foot."

"Only an accident," he replied. "My foot has already forgiven you."

Helena sat through the conversation eating cigarettes.

The mess boy brought in a fresh pot of coffee and we stepped to the side table to fill our mugs. Within a few minutes Cork walked in, his green jacket unbuttoned, the red-starred cap far back on his head. He looked as though he had been standing on deck for a long time. The fog had dampened him, but his morose face had turned friendly.

"A hell of a night," he muttered to one and all.

Flame's arm tightened against me. The familiar sight of his *yenan* green uniform stiffened her nerves.

He poured himself some coffee, stood around awkwardly for a moment, and then found a seat at the table.

Half an hour passed and the coffee grew cold in the pot. Conversation began to ebb.

"*Sacrebleu*," Dufour sputtered suddenly. "We must find something to amuse us. It invites madness, sitting around waiting for the inevitable. Either the Nationalists or the pirates, one of them will strike."

"We have a good captain," Bejarano put in. "He could outwit the devil."

"Ah, the Captain. He would as soon we swim to Hong Kong. He is the devil himself! He does not like his fellow man, our captain. But— he is serving his purpose, *mes idiots*. The Reds need his kind. He is robbing them, of course, but that is to be expected. He is also a pirate, filling his chests with gold like the others."

Bejarano puffed his cigarette slowly. His eyes sparkled contemptuously. "The Captain's motive is perhaps the fairest of all. Profit. China was opened up like a melon one hundred years ago for the profit of our world. Now she closes the melon, picked and rotted. But a few remain, like flies. I was one of them, but I could no longer find a profit. I could not win a case. So I am flying away. The Captain too will fly away in time. Meanwhile, let him make his profit."

"A handsome speech." Dufour laughed, applauding. "I must use it in my next picture. Meanwhile, what do you suggest we do to pass time?" He threw up his hands. "One would expect at least a checkerboard on this ship. The Captain provides nothing, not even a deck of cards for the passengers. Is he a religious man? I don't believe it!"

My heart began to pound as I watched Helena. She jabbed out her cigarette and gave me a flash of eyes. "Mr. Cloud has cards," she said. "He is a card shark traveling in disguise. He told me so himself."

Dufour beamed. "*Bien*, we will watch his fingers. I prefer poker." He held out his hand. "The cards, eh?"

It was a nice squeeze. "I lost them overboard," I snapped. The shape of the deck was obvious in my shirt pocket, the flap buttoned down. It was a foolish thing to say, and Helena corrected me quickly. I felt trapped. I wanted to break her neck. Maybe I would.

I sat there perspiring, my mind spinning. If the deck were not already suspect, it would be if I refused to come across. If I followed through, there was the chance the cards would escape detection. I'd have to take the chance.

"Poker's fine," I heard myself say. "But we're broke."

I hoped that would discourage the whole idea, but it didn't. "I shall be glad to loan you money," Bejarano put in with a smile. I looked at him curiously. His benign face seemed almost too friendly.

"Thanks," I muttered.

Flame put out her cigarette thoughtfully. I unbuttoned my pocket and threw the deck on the table. Flame's eyes caught mine briefly.

Dufour sent the mess boy for some matches for chips, picked up the cards, and began shuffling. My heart was beating so loudly I was surprised no one heard it.

"Stud?" Dufour asked.

Helena raised an eyebrow significantly. "Strip poker would be more to Mr. Cloud's taste," she snapped.

Mr. Wei refused to join in. The matches were distributed and we assembled, clockwise, Flame, Dufour, Helena, Cork, Bejarano, me.

Bejarano won the cut for deal, and in a moment the cards scaled low from his fingers around the table.

"We must watch M'sieu Cloud carefully, *mes idiots*," Dufour said. "'We must not let him forget it is the top of the pack one deals from."

Helena picked up her cards as they came. The rest waited until they were dealt, blue against the white tablecloth.

I collected my cards. Somewhere around the table sat the outsider, on the trail of the film. Whoever Haigmann had put aboard would be interested only in keeping me on the straight and narrow path to the Imperial Hotel in Hong Kong. The outsider was the one to worry about now.

The discards began.

"An excellent hand." Bejarano smiled, filling out his cards. "I'm embarrassed I dealt it to myself. Forgive me if I win."

"*Sacrebleu!*" Dufour pouted. "If this is the best you can do off the top, I would prefer M'sieu Cloud dealt me off the bottom."

Matchsticks collected at the center of the table. Flame was steady. She was a good actress.

Cork won the pot and it was my deal. I picked up the cards. I shuffled as casually as I could. As I passed out the cards my eyes skimmed over them, afraid some flaw would disclose the pastings.

"M'sieu, you give us a card too many."

I stopped dealing and swore under my breath. Small blunders could give me away. "Sorry." I retrieved the last cards dealt, returned them to the pack, and laid it aside.

"Mr. Cloud's mind is elsewhere," Helena put in.

A half hour passed somehow. Then another. The ship swayed with an easy, predictable motion. Mr. Wei remained at his book. It was hard to remember he was even there.

Helena began to win steadily, and her eyes danced with victory. When she dealt, she flung the cards out like dollar bills.

"I deal you a special hand, Mr. Cloud," she said. "All jokers."

"I prefer something with legs," I said. "Make it queens."

"Did you know," Dufour cut in, "that the Reds have outlawed mah-jongg? What a pity. It is a good game."

Cork looked up sarcastically. Dufour had been getting on his nerves with his constant chatter. "The Reds are apt to outlaw movie directors next," he said.

"Ah, the silent lieutenant has found his tongue," Dufour chortled. "I liked it better where it was."

"You talk too much," Helena put in.

"You are a poor winner. I am almost wiped out, *mes idiots*." He helped himself to some of Helena's matches and stayed in the game.

Another hour passed. Flame sat looking miraculously composed. She shared the fears churning through my mind, but none of it showed in her manner. She neither won nor lost. She merely played.

My eyes burned. I wanted desperately for the game to end, but it dragged on. By three o'clock talk had almost left us. We did nothing but deal cards, toss matches, and reshuffle for another deal.

Dufour, at last, was cleaned out, and even Helena was losing. She refused to stake him any further.

"Fine," he muttered. "Pirates would be more entertaining than this."

He got up and stretched, the bulky life jacket rising with the effort.

The game was over.

"I'm going to bed," Flame said. "I've been asleep for an hour anyway."

"I shall stay up," Dufour declared. "*Sacrebleu*, the experience of a life-time. I could not sleep. I would die rather than miss our pirates."

Bejarano gathered up the cards and put them in the case. I didn't want to appear in too much of a hurry to get them back. I let them lie on the table as long as I could stand it. Then I got them back into my pocket. My joints ached with the strain of sitting tensed and expectant. Now it was over, and Flame and I traded glances. We hadn't been discovered.

Mr. Wei was nodding sleepily in the chair, the skirt of his gown tight between the outward slant of his knees.

"I too shall go to bed," Helena announced. "Alone."

Flame picked up the remark with a cutting smile. "I'm sure that will be a novelty—for you."

Dufour laughed.

I looked in at the pilothouse before returning to the cabin. O'Rafferty was still there, now resigned to his sport chair, the fog beyond the windows blinding.

"Can't you sleep, Mr. Cloud?"

"I haven't tried. We've picked up speed, haven't we?"

"Aye, against my best judgment. We're doing seven knots."

"When do we pass Amoy?"

"Perhaps nine or ten o'clock. And may the fog hold."

The second mate was on duty and I asked him to have me awakened at eight A.M. by whoever was on duty then. On the way back to the cabin I passed through the wardroom. Mr. Wei was alone in there now. He was reading again.

Flame was in bed, but she wasn't asleep.

"You ought to get an Oscar," I said, "for the smoothest acting of the year."

"I was scared stiff."

I slipped the cards out of my pocket and put them under the pillow. I got out of my shirt. Flame turned on her side, facing me. "I was just thinking," she said. "We could name our own figure if we wanted to put the film on the spy market ourselves."

"Are you suggesting it?"

"I was only wondering what it would feel like to own a fantastic sum of money. It might bring a half-million dollars if you found someone who wanted it badly enough."

"I could never count over two hundred a week and expenses. It's been coming in every week on a nice, clean pay check. I have a hard time spending it alone."

"Two hundred a week and expenses," she said playfully. "I'm impressed.”

"Keep your eye on it, baby. Unless I've been fired and don't know it yet, it'll keep coming in regularly, week after week, fifty-two weeks every year...."

My heart turned over. Fifty-two. My hand darted under the pillow and brought out the deck. I emptied the case and began counting the cards rapidly.

"What's the matter?"

"Shut up."

The packet in my hand lightened as I thumbed off the cards. Perspiration began to stand out all over me when I got to the final cards. "...forty-four, forty-five, forty-six—*forty-seven!*"

My hand was empty.

"Alex!"

"We've been taken, sweetheart, like babes in the woods."

Her face went white. "Are you sure it was a full deck when we started?"

"It was when I played solitaire a few nights ago."

"My God, that means—"

"Yeah. One of our smiling tablemates held out a hand of cards. The film has probably been discovered by now. It means the son-of-a-bitch knows right where to go for the rest of it."

Chapter Fourteen

Flame threw back the sheet, disregarding the lingerie she had gone to bed in, and slipped into the slack suit Helena had fitted her out with earlier. It took us an hour to peel the cards with care and remove the film. Some of the cards were blanks. When we finished we had sixty-four strips of film, three frames to a strip. There was a small chance that the missing cards held no film. Very small and not worth betting on.

My mind returned to the game. Bejarano had been the last to touch the deck. He had gathered the cards and put them in the case. He could have used that opportunity to palm off the five missing cards.

Yet, Henri Dufour had broken up the game. Was he anxious to get himself alone in order to examine the cards?

Mr. Wei, at least, was eliminated. He hadn't touched the cards.

Where had Cork gone from the game? His might have been the voice I heard over the phone. I couldn't be sure. If he were playing on Haigmann's team I felt certain his job would begin when we docked. And he wouldn't know about the film. Haigmann wouldn't be fool enough to entrust that information to a hireling.

I sent Flame to the chartroom for glue, and then we repaired the cards. It was a messy job, but it didn't matter now. I put my shirt back on and buttoned the deck in my pocket. Our pursuer, the outsider, wouldn't wait long to strike. We would be ready.

I tore a piece of cloth out of the sheet and rolled the numerous strips of film into a tight tube, wrapping it in the fabric. "For the time being," I said, "slip this film you know where. For Christ's sake, don't let any-one make love to you. Stay locked in the cabin. I'll let you know when I want in."

"How about you?"

"Me what?"

"Making love to me."

"When I want the film I'll be a perfect gentleman. I'll take it."

She stepped closer and kissed me. It was for luck, I think.

"No one will bother you as long as he thinks the cards still have the film in them," I said.

"Or she. I don't trust her."

"You're just jealous. Stay that way, baby."

Flame locked the door after me. With the hatches closed, the pas-sageway seemed airless under the dim light in the bulkhead. It was de-serted. I rolled Kish out of his sack below and told him to stick around the cabins as a precaution.

On the way up to the bridge I stopped in the wardroom. Mr. Wei looked up. A fresh cigarette smoldered from his parchment fingertips. He nodded politely. I nodded politely and left.

I had a funny feeling about him.

Through the windows of the pilothouse dawn was brightening the fog and turning it white. The wheel creaked gently under the hands of the helmsman. O'Rafferty stood beside the boy at the radarscope, his own alert eyes following the sharp line sweeping a continuous circle on the face of the tube, lighting up pale green lacework that was the coast of China fifteen miles on our starboard side.

Dufour was standing beside a mounted searchlight on the open wing of the bridge, the life jacket bulky under his short arms. Bejarano was in the pilothouse, standing against the windows, looking out into noth-ing. He turned to me with a half-smile. "It is a suitable farewell for me," he said. "China bids me good-by with a shroud of fog. I leave a lifetime's work behind."

"It could have been worse," I remarked. "You might have left your life."

"Of course. We are lucky, those of us who stayed too long, to get out at all."

Coffee was brought up from the galley and the warm fragrance brought Dufour in from the bridge. "Ah, I am afraid our pirates will never find us in this weather," he said.

I watched them both intently; their faces and their words told me nothing. It was as though the card game had never been played. But as long as I made myself available, with the shape of the deck in my pocket, I knew I would not have to wait long.

O'Rafferty left the scope and the native boy resumed the watch. O'Rafferty got up into his chair, brushed his beard with the flats of his hands, and glowered at the three of us. Then he drank his coffee.

By seven o'clock everything blazed white around us. Looking forward you could see the charcoal lines that were the booms. The bow was invisible beyond.

The captain's breakfast came up on a metal tray and Bejarano and Dufour went below to the wardroom to eat. I decided this would be the best opportunity I'd have to ditch the film properly. I went below and awoke Kish, who was dozing on his haunches against the bulkhead of the passageway.

"You're a lot of help," I said sarcastically. "Can you get me a passkey to these cabins?"

He said he could, got up, and went away.

Flame let me in.

"Go to breakfast," I said. "I'll take the film."

"Are you going to be a gentleman about it?"

"Not if I have to ask again."

She turned around and got the film. For a moment it was hard to keep my mind on anything as inanimate as film.

I took it from her hand. "Keep Bejarano and Dufour at breakfast as long as you can. I'm going into their cabin."

"I hope you know what you're doing, Alex," she said seriously.

"Just keep them at breakfast."

Kish came up as she left. I got the key and told him to get lost. Then I moved down the passageway to the starboard side, to the door across from Helena's.

I let myself in. The cabin was identical to ours in size, but it was jammed with the luggage of the two men. I gave the place a fast search on the off chance I might discover the missing cards. I didn't expect to find any sign of them, and I didn't.

The Indian clubs stood in a canvas bag specially made to carry them. I unzipped the top, removed a club, and wrapped it in a hand towel.

As I stepped out of the door, Helena's door opposite opened and there she was.

She stood startled for a moment. So did I. Then her oval face burst into a sneer.

"You were, perhaps, looking for me? Your sense of direction is bad."

I closed the door after me, stepped across the passage, and clapped a hand over her mouth. I pushed her inside her cabin and got the door closed. The club slipped out of my grip and clattered to the deck.

Her eyes swelled with rage, but I kept my hand over her mouth. I owed her an explanation and I gave it to her.

"You might be aboard this ship just for the ride," I whispered firmly, "or you might be here because it's open season on a half-million dollars. I'm sorry you saw me coming out of that cabin just now, because I'm going to have to keep you boxed up for a while."

She tried to bite my palm. Her breath came hot and strained.

"If you make any noise I'll kill you," I muttered. I pulled her toward the bunk, where I saw a pair of stockings. I forced her face down on the pillow and almost smothered her. I wanted to scare hell out of her, and I did. When I let up she didn't fight any more. She just lay there.

I pulled her arms around back and bound the wrists with a stocking. The other I slipped twice around her head, gagging her mouth. I found a belt to use around her ankles.

"If you're just a sex-happy kid with nothing more serious on your mind, I apologize. I can't take any chances and I don't trust you, sweetheart. Sorry."

I left her there that way, prone on her stomach, her head turned to one side.

I found the woodshop below deck in the afterpart of the ship. It was the size of a large closet; no machine tools, just a workbench, a wooden vise, and hand tools.

I padded the body of the Indian club with the towel so that the vise wouldn't mark it. I tightened a drill about the size of a thick pencil in the brace and bored a hole in the base of the club.

About half an inch down, yellow metal began to curl out with the shavings, That stopped me.

My fingers picked up a sample.

It was gold.

Questions began spinning in my mind. Was Bejacano, after all, Haigmann's man? Or was he merely getting out of Shanghai with as much as he could salvage? With the exchange at Hong Kong bringing $56 an ounce, the clubs were literally worth their weight in gold. Was he only a shabby professional smuggler?

I went on drilling. When I was a couple of inches down I extracted the bit and forced the film, wrapped in sheeting, into the cavity. I found a can of plastic wood and plugged the hole. I snapped on the electric unit under the glue pot, force-dried the plug over heat, then sanded it carefully until only the freshness of the repair gave it away. I dirtied it. When I was finished it wasn't an invisible job, but it would pass as the clubs spun in the air. It would pass unless Bejarano found reason to examine the base of his plaything.

I wrapped the club in the towel again, returned to the outside of Bejarano's cabin, and looked through the porthole. The room was empty. I entered the passageway and let myself back in. I returned the club to the zipper case and got out of there. Helena was quiet in her cabin. Tough break. But I couldn't run the risk of her dropping any remarks about my fussing around the Bejarano-Dufour cabin.

I went into the wardroom and started breakfast as the others were finishing theirs. Later, I brought Helena something to eat. She was a good girl when I removed the gag. I told her I'd kill her if she weren't. She believed me. I bound her up again, good and tight, and left.

Mr. Wei had returned to the wardroom when I looked in. He was alone in there, and he was reading. I started for the bridge and met Flame coming down the companionway.

"There's something wrong up there," she said at once. "I was coming to find you. The radar's out."

I pushed past her and stopped, turning. "If anyone asks about it, the White Russian is seasick. She's resting in her cabin. You stick in the wardroom. Wei is there. The moment he leaves, grab the phone and buzz the pilothouse."

"Did you—"

"Yes. Everything's O.K. Get going."

I could hear the echo of O'Rafferty's temper even before I stepped into the pilothouse. Dufour stood at the door, his face livid and his hands fluttering about like the wings of a hummingbird.

"*C'est terrible!* We will all be killed!"

"Get out!" O'Rafferty raged from the radar apparatus. "I'll be fit to kill you myself in another moment!" Dufour stepped away, startled, but he didn't go below. He moved into the foggy air of the starboard wing of the bridge, muttering and pacing nervously.

"Anything I can do?" I asked. It was a foolish question.

"You can get out as well! It's an evil day when you take passengers on a voyage like this. One of them has fixed us up right smartly—jammed the antenna, he did!" I looked into the scope. The line of light that normally sweeps around the screen stood burning like the beam of a searchlight that has stopped.

"Bastard waited until we safely reached the waters outside Amoy," O'Rafferty blustered, striking the apparatus with the palm of his hand. Almost at once Bejarano came in from the port side. He had apparently been standing there in the fog. He stood silently at the window now, looking forward and looking calmly fatalistic about the whole thing. O'Rafferty dismissed his presence with a growl.

The buzzer sounded and I went for the phone. "It's for me," I snapped when O'Rafferty began to explode.

"Wei wasn't in the wardroom when I came in," Flame told me.

"Lock yourself in your cabin," I said firmly. "Don't give me any argument and don't waste any time about it." I hung up, turning to O'Rafferty.

"I'd shoot our friend Wei on sight," I said.

"Fortunately you're not the master of this ship. He's the one they want, a ransom Chink, he is. He's worth twice my silks and cottons and hides to the pirating scum. Well, we'll give them a bellyful of trouble, that we will. My gun crews are ready fore and aft." He moved to the windows and peered into the white fog. "It's Cork that's in league with them, I'm sorry to admit. The others were standing here when the radar went out— unless, Mr. Cloud, it was you who did the dirty work. My chief mate's searching the ship for Cork at this minute. His pirate friends are waiting out there somewhere for us, you can be sure of that."

My jaws were tight. I could be wrong about Wei, and O'Rafferty could be right about Cork. But I had to say what I thought: "If you ask me, you're going after the wrong man."

"I don't recall asking you, Mr. Cloud!"

"Mr. Wei may be a wealthy Chinese, but I'm willing to bet he didn't make his yuan in Shanghai real estate. I've wanted to have a look under that gown he wears. A guy could conceal an armory along his legs if he wanted to. Remember, he didn't want to share a cabin. He needed privacy."

"Your astute observations come too late."

We turned. Appearing as though conjured out of the boiling white fog, Mr. Wei stood outside on the companion of the open port wing. Gripped loosely in his spidery hands was a lightweight submachine gun, painted in jungle camouflage, a simple but deadly apparatus that the Aussies used to carry in the Pacific.

O'Rafferty instantly dove for the bulkhead to set off the klaxons in a general quarters alarm. The gun sputtered fire ahead of him, cutting him off with a warning. O'Rafferty's face turned purple with self-contained rage.

"I shall be obliged to kill if anyone moves," Mr. Wei declared calmly. Dufour poked his head in to see what was going on, and the Chinese ordered him forward. "All of you, line up facing the windows."

Mr. Wei stepped inside the compartment, taking up a position in the corner where he commanded both entrances to the pilothouse. Bejarano's face was ashen. He turned his stooped back to the Chinese as ordered. I fell in line at the far end. O'Rafferty held back. Mr. Wei smiled. "You give commands, you must also learn to take them, *laota*."

"I'll be thanking you to get it over with quickly."

"Of course. It is my wish also. But first we must catch the flies who are attracted by my unfortunate noise. With the others, please."

O'Rafferty moved up bleakly, his eyes almost hidden under eyebrows that pressed downward like wings. It was less than a minute when the chief mate brought Cork in, and both fell into the trap. The helmsman stayed at the wheel, keeping the ship on its course.

Two or three minutes may have passed; no more flies. Mr. Wei ordered O'Rafferty out of line.

His command: "Order gun crews below."

O'Rafferty, resigned now, gave the order.

"Stop the ship."

O'Rafferty signaled the command to the engine room. "Turn on running lights. Searchlights."

He was brightening us up like a gambling ship. He was going to make us easy to find in the morning fog.

"That I'll not do," O'Rafferty whispered hoarsely, straightening and looking suddenly regal.

"Chief mate," Mr. Wei snapped. "Stand in the doorway."

The officer moved slowly. The gun instantly spat into him. He spun and fell against the windows, his face tense with sudden pain. He slipped to the deck. In the silence that followed, drifts of cordite pinched our nostrils.

"You see, *laota*," Mr. Wei said solemnly, "you robbed me of my men. I return the favor. My job is not easy to perform alone. I am forced to be deadly."

O'Rafferty gave the order. We lit up. "Where will you take my ship?"

"Bias Bay. We can safely strip you there. If you give us no trouble, your command will be returned."

"Aye, so you can hijack me on my next voyage, I suppose."

"Of course, *laota*. There are few enough ships in these waters now. We must preserve the ships."

"I'll not sail these waters again," O'Rafferty said bitterly. "I've had my stomachful of you and your countrymen."

The ship had stopped and bright fog pressed against the windows like cold steam. The thought skittered through my mind that any newspaperman would give a month's pay to eyewitness a story like this. The thought turned to nausea. There was the film. The story would come later.

The third mate, curious no doubt about the ship's stopping, walked into Mr. Wei's gallery of victims, and later the steward. We stood for a long time, and my back began to ache. The booms swayed in the fog as we drifted with the current. How clever I had planned to be! The passing remembrance rankled. I was going to find a moment to play possum— stretch myself as though unconscious in a passageway. Whoever found me would give himself away. If hands went for the cards, I would have him. If not, I could mark that person off the list.

"*Voilà!*" Dufour sputtered suddenly. "There it is!"

A dark shape, at first only a shadow in the fog, appeared to starboard. As it bore down on us the shadow burgeoned with black, spined sails, like a giant sea bird. I stared, fascinated. Within seconds the huge, malevolent eyes of the junk, set under the blunt bowsprit, peered at us through the mist. The junk was tacking and slowly rode in alongside, its wooden fenders scraping us.

Mr. Wei moved quietly to the starboard side. He was smiling. The tall sails, like bat wings, seemed close enough to touch.

From somewhere on the Sassoon's decks I heard a sailor yell an alarm.

I looked at our Chinese, at the other end of the pilothouse from me. He couldn't resist brief glances at the junk. I stood about six feet from the open door to the port wing. It was now or never.

I watched until his eyes left us again. I ran.

It seemed a mile to the door and the gun chattered as I reached it. The helmsman chose that wild moment to spin the wheel. He must have wanted to die a hero, separating the two ships in the current. Mr. Wei instantly diverted his aim, which was close as hell to me, and cut the native boy down. I was outside, behind the bulkhead, when lead began perforating it. I dropped to my feet and slipped down the ladder to the main deck. I didn't turn around to see if the Chinese had crossed the pilothouse to follow me down with slugs. I just ran.

The crews had got to the antiaircraft mounts fore and aft and the rapid *pow-pow-pow* ripped the air. I picked my way to the starboard side and saw that ship and junk were dividing at the bows, like the jaws of an animal, answering the helmsman's twist on the wheel. If the junk had been too close in before for the Sassoon's gun crews to do more than rip the sails, the separation of the two vessels gave the forward crew an opportunity to scatter Chinese along the decks. The gap slowly closed up again, and the junk began firing back with high-pitched old machine guns hastily mounted on tripods. They hadn't expected a fight.

I spotted Mr. Wei on the starboard wing of the bridge, machine gun poised, waiting for his men to crawl aboard. His job was to paralyze the brains of the ship and he had done it expertly. His eyes were alert to the men in the pilothouse. One of the Sassoon's crew pushed by me in confused alarm, as though looking for something to fight with. There was a mixture of yells and commands and gunfire from both ships that was deafening. I knew what I had to do.

I crossed through the ship. A native boy was on his knees in the passageway praying. My temper shot out of control. I knew how he felt, but the time for praying was past. I shuffled him to his feet and ordered him out on deck to fight.

I climbed up the superstructure on the port side, staying out of sight of the bridge as best I could on the ladders. When I was behind the pilothouse I got out of my shoes and climbed to the roof. The only danger I felt was the chance that Wei would return inside the compartment and hear me close above him.

I paused, hugging the roof with my body, about two feet from the edge. Below, on the wing, stood the deadly Mr. Wei.

The junk had now secured itself to us and pandemonium broke loose on the deck far below as the Chinese began a tumultuous flow over the rail.

I jumped.

I heard the breath escape him when I hit. My weight, striking like a wet rag, threw him against the spotlight. The machine gun jammed in the crook of his arm went off, dancing wildly and sending jarring vibrations through his body. He sunk under me to the deck and I managed to strike the gun out of its perch. It went skittering down the ladder, firing intermittently, and fell silent.

He spun under me and dug his sharp-nailed fingers into my face, yelling defiantly. I landed a smack into his face and then I felt O'Rafferty pulling me away.

"Don't hurt him, Mr. Cloud," he stammered with rage.

I rammed an elbow into the side of Wei's face, just to get it out of my system, and let O'Rafferty go to work. I leaped down the ladder for the machine gun. I moved onto the boat deck, found a good spot, and began to blast. I must have been yelling, but I couldn't hear my own voice against the gunfire.

I began having a lovely time.

A Chinese machine gunner spotted my fire and began whistling slugs my way. I let him have it and almost immediately my gun went dead—empty.

He kept firing but he must have been blind. I tossed the gun away and drew back to safety. The ships began to part as someone in the pilothouse got on the wheel. Lead was still coming my way and I got out of there.

The screws began to kick up a wake and we were beginning to move forward. I threaded my way to the main deck, where several hand-to-hand fights had broken out. I got in one.

Brown bodies still clung to our side, left there as the ships parted. I got a flash of Kish, a rifle butt in his hands, beating against the clinging fingers until the bodies dropped from the rail into the sea.

A seaman beside me let out a chilling scream and when I turned I saw the Chinese who had ripped a knife along his chest. I let fly with my fist, fell against him, and brought him off his feet over the rail. He crashed into the water.

As we drifted apart from the junk, our gun crews found solid target and began tearing the wooden hull apart. The Chinese answered with scattered firing of their own. They didn't give up easily.

But on deck there was no one left to fight.

Kish came over and we traded smiles. I started up the ladder to the bridge and was halfway there when a burst of machine-gun fire chipped around me. I dove.

I must have landed on my head.

When I came around, I saw at once I was in Flame's bunk. She was seated in the chair watching me. I said the first thing that came into my head. "What hit me?"

"According to reports, you dove headfirst."

"It seemed a good idea at the time."

The ship's steady motion rocked itself into my consciousness, and then everything else came back to me. My hand went to my shirt pocket, and my head went flying.

"Don't bother to look," Flame said. "The cards are gone."

Chapter Fifteen

I muttered something suitable and unprintable. I had chosen a hell of a time to take a nap; I had fouled up the chance to trap our fellow passenger into exposing himself. "Who found me?"

"I did."

"I told you to lock yourself in the cabin."

"You *couldn't* have expected me to, darling," Flame said.

"Someone got to me before you did." I felt my head. "You might at least have been first."

"I'll remember next time."

"How long have I been napping?"

"About half an hour. It was a great show. The junk caught fire at the end. Too bad you didn't see it."

"Yeah."

"We picked up a few survivors—one is a white man."

I jerked up. "Who is he?"

"Wouldn't give his name. The Captain's got the whole bunch of them locked up like sardines." She put her cool palm on my forehead. "Feel good?"

"No."

"Sorry."

I got up and rubbed my neck. The throbbing in my head was rapid fire. "Whoever got to those cards knows now we've got the film hidden somewhere else."

She turned, looking suddenly very tired, weary of the prolonged crisis that had started in Shanghai and would end only when we tied up in Hong Kong. "Where have we got them hidden?"

"I'll let you know when we get to port."

"Don't you trust me?"

"Get me a cup of coffee. No cream or sugar."

The Sassoon lost three men, and there were plenty of bandaged arms and heads working around the ship. The guy I had found praying had turned in a masterful performance, according to the gossip, and I decided maybe he had been praying for victims. O'Rafferty chose not to bury the men at sea, since we would be in Hong Kong next day, and the bodies could be shipped home from there. By noon the fog had thinned and disappeared, but sea and sky turned dark and it began to rain. It was an easy rain, without much wind, mottling the surface of the sea and striking the decks and superstructures with a small voice. The Sassoon was churning a rolling wake at flank speed, and the steady strain of the ship to reach Hong Kong must have given us all a feeling of affection for it.

None of us had had any sleep, unless you count my short siesta, and we all looked it at lunch. Nevertheless, there was lively table talk. While the crew may have felt mixed emotions at winning a fight but losing three of its number, the passengers were as excited as if they had won the daily double at Caliente.

Mr. Wei was, as the saying goes, conspicuous by his absence. So was Helena, but Flame made apologies for her and there were suitable wishes for a speedy recovery.

"*Mon Dieu,*" Dufour chattered, pausing with soup spoon in hand, "I was right there, *mes idiots*, seeing the whole thing, as it were, from the gallery. Had I been directing, I couldn't have handled the boarding scene better—although I would have preferred a bit more hand-to-hand fighting at the rail, of course."

"You were free to join us," I said.

"Ah, but I am a director. I do not act. And the Captain, *sacrebleu*, he performed like a madman." Dufour dipped into his soup, pausing only long enough to swallow. "He personally, with his own hands, twisted the neck of our former passenger like the neck of a chicken. I shall never forget that scene. And then—over the side. It is a suitable end, of course, for a pirate."

Bejarano ate quietly.

The ship lurched suddenly and all of us went for our plates. In a moment the ship steadied at its regular pitch. "O'Rafferty must be breaking in a new helmsman," I said darkly.

Cork, who had gone into the hand-to-hand fighting the moment the bridge had been cleared, seemed to want to make friends now. The closer we drew to Hong Kong, the better his disposition had become. "You were right, Yank," he said, turning to me. "The Chink had leather holsters on his legs. The gun was broken down and carried in parts."

"Alex knows everything," Flame put in—a little proudly, it seemed to me.

"It was only a good guess," I said defensively. "I did a story on a magician once, a Chinese who would produce a small boy from an empty cloth. The boy rode in harness between the magician's legs, under the gown. Since then, I don't trust those gowns they wear."

"What a charming secret," Dufour said, apparently just to be saying something. He had chucked his life jacket at last.

Later I rustled up some chow from the galley and brought Helena some lunch. I felt like a miserable heel. But I'd have to keep feeling like a miserable heel.

"Call me a lousy son-of-a-bitch," I said when I had her untied. "Maybe it'll help."

But she wouldn't talk to me. Not even to call me names.

As I watched her eat, I knew I'd never be able to tie her up again. "Want to make a deal?" I asked finally. She raised her eyes suspiciously.

"I'll let you have the freedom of the cabin," I said. "But if you make any noise or try to attract attention to yourself—"

"No stockings?"

"No stockings. You'll be O.K. unless you try to get out or try to talk to anyone. Just act like you're seasick."

"I promise."

When I got back to the wardroom only Flame was there. She sat smoking a cigarette with a final cup of coffee. Rain fell outside the portholes in gray streaks and the slow rolling field of the sea came and went.

"Everything O.K. with Helena of Joy?"

"I like puns. But not that one."

"You're getting a little touchy about her, aren't you?"

"Forget it. Where're the others?"

"Bedtime, darling. It's raining out. No one slept last night. Ergo, it's bedtime."

She poured me a cup of coffee and I lit a cigarette. Except for the impersonal creaks and strains, the ship was oddly still. Our cigarettes burned silently. We were both thinking—perhaps about the same things.

"We'll be in Hong Kong tomorrow," I said suddenly. "You'll be a free agent once we reach shore. There were no strings when I put you aboard this ship. All I wanted was to get you to safety."

"I thought you also wanted me to fall back in love with you."

"I guess I haven't had much time to work on it. How am I doing?"

"I find you resistible."

"Well, that's something. You use to find me detestable."

"How's your head?"

"It aches."

"Bad?"

"No worse than a third-rate hangover. I've written my best stories with hangovers."

"You're a great guy, Alex. I mean that."

I grimaced. I recalled a city editor once who told me, "You're a great newspaperman, Alex. You're fired."

"Thanks," I said.

She wrinkled up her nose that impish way that always did things to me, and got up. "I'm going to bed."

"If you can't sleep, just whistle."

"I'll be old-fashioned, darling, and count sheep. Or blondes you have known."

"That'll take you all night."

"Speaking of blondes, Helena—"

"She's not really a blonde."

"I was afraid you'd investigate."

"Jealous?"

"Certainly not, darling. I'm sure it was fun."

She gave me a mildly angry look and left. She was, I decided, at least a little jealous.

I sat there alone, finishing the cigarette. A lot of old memories flickered through my mind. Most of them hurt. I had existed in a happy little triangle in Rome: the nearest bar, the hottest story, and the nearest hottest girl in the corner pockets. When I woke up to the fact that I wanted Flame there as a permanent part of the geometry, she got tired of the traffic in her corner. I couldn't blame her for pulling out. I deserved that. But some of the memories were happy, like the week end we had gone off to Capri and Flame's new Mr. John, a funny straw hat, was knocked off and ruined in the grotto. And the first time...

I wondered for a moment whether I'd have a job when we got back to Hong Kong. I had taken an unauthorized leave and they'd have a perfect right to can me for it. I was already on good behavior. They couldn't know I was being an angel. They couldn't know I would never be worth a damn again without Flame.

And I didn't seem to be fighting to get her back, now that I had found her. What was I waiting for? She had turned down Helena's invitation to share another cabin. What was I waiting for Flame to do—carve our initials in the bunk post?

I got up, poked out my cigarette with resolute jabs, and followed the passageway to our cabin. I began to smile. I must have been blind.

When I got inside the door, the only light came through the porthole in shifting afternoon rays. The chartreuse dress, swaying from the hook, touched me as I stood there for a moment.

"I thought I heard you whistle," I said.

Flame looked at me from her bunk. "Really?"

"Hello, beautiful."

She cocked a hostile eyebrow and just looked at me that way. I started to feel a little sheepish; she wasn't going to make it easy.

"I think we've met somewhere before," I went on. "Indiscreetly, as I recall."

She spoke. "Your bunk's up there, darling, remember?"

"Is this the time to say I love you?"

"I suppose it's customary with what's on your mind."

"I love you."

"You're terribly sweet when you're on the make, darling." She smiled like an old friend.

"You're beginning to sound like you spent the last two years knitting eyebrows." I came closer, looking down at the full lines under the sheet, and then into her eyes. "I want you for keeps, baby."

"That has a familiar ring."

"This time I mean it."

Her green eyes held me for a long time and her voice softened. "Don't say anything you don't mean. Not now, Alex."

"I've tried to change, Flame. Nothing much matters to me any more except you."

"I wish I could believe you'd changed."

"You might start by trying."

Her face had turned thoughtfully serious. "I don't want to fall into the same trap twice, Alex. Maybe I've loved you all along. I don't know— I can't help being afraid of you."

The gentle pitch of the ship set a steady rhythm. "Maybe I'd better go out and come in again."

"The fresh air might do you some good."

"Let's forget the whole thing."

"Don't be angry."

"I'm not angry. I'm just in love with you, that's all."

"Please, darling—"

"I thought maybe you were getting Cottardo out of your system."

"Maybe I'm trying."

"But I frighten you."

"I didn't say that, darling. I said I was afraid. You're just not a one-woman guy. Remember, it's an occupational hazard?"

"That's history. Let's forget it."

She wasn't looking at me now, and she didn't say anything. I stood for a few seconds, then bent down beside her. I picked up her chin and looked into her eyes, and she must have seen that I wasn't just a guy on the make. I kissed her, and pretty soon her arms came up around my neck and she was kissing me.

"Maybe I've been a fool," she whispered tensely.

I didn't want to talk any more and I didn't say anything. We clung together, and then when I pulled back I saw that the sheet had worked below her breasts. Her bra was clear nylon, concealing nothing, her dark pink tips projecting firmly with excitement. Her tips were large, and they always embarrassed her, but she wasn't embarrassed now. I got up and turned off the light and when I started back I met her in the dark. She had got up. Her arms went around me, as we stood together, and she was naked now. Her body trembled with emotions past due, and this seemed right; this was what we wanted.

I took it from there.

Chapter Sixteen

When I awoke in the morning, sunlight streamed through the porthole. I disentangled myself from Flame's arms without waking her. Her nose was shiny. I watched her sleep for a couple of minutes and then went out to shower.

She awoke when I came back and we talked for a while. After breakfast I got some food in to Helena and then went looking for O'Rafferty. I found him in his stateroom.

"It was an evil voyage, this one," he reminded me. "I suppose Hong Kong will look good to us all. We'll be there in perhaps six hours."

"Where are you keeping those survivors from the junk? I want to have a look at the white man."

O'Rafferty rubbed his beard as though he would pluck the guy out of the brown fuzzy hair like a magician. "Scum," he muttered. "Let him be, with my thanks. There's plenty of white scum in these waters and, I expect, always will be."

"I've got a hunch about him."

"So you have a hunch, Mr. Cloud. May I express a hunch? Your woman, and the 'trifle' you brought aboard, have marked this ship for trouble. I have been a fool to give you passage." He bore down on me with his eyes. "What is your game?"

"Don't overrate me," I said. "I have no game. I'm just a seedy foreign correspondent who went overboard for a dame. The trifle has got to remain top secret. When it's been declassified you'll read about it in the papers. Look for my by-line."

He pursed his lips and gave me a dissatisfied look. "I've a naturally curious nature and I don't believe a word of what you say."

"Then fill in your own answers. What about the white man?"

"Let's have a talk with him, indeed."

I sensed then that O'Rafferty had already interviewed the guy. He called the third mate and sent him to bring up the stranger. He drummed his fingers on his desk while we waited.

When the door opened, I saw a familiar face. The guy had everything but the Panama hat; high-pinched nose, bony chin, the nerveless manner. Peric, the man who had tangled with me outside Haigmann's apartment; Peric, the man who appeared with Cottardo in the photograph I had picked up from the prostitute.

"You never give up, do you?" I smiled faintly.

"It is a necessary trait," Peric declared, "in our business."

O'Rafferty looked at me. "So you *do* know each other."

"We're buddies," I said sarcastically. "I was hoping I had seen the last of him."

"Sorry to disappoint," Peric said coolly. "Haigmann was generous enough to tell me where you had gone with the prize."

"Put that in basic English," I snapped.

Peric's rangy body loosened and I saw that he had been waiting for this moment. "The competition has narrowed now. Perhaps the three of us can be the survivors—a noble sum to be divided into princely portions."

"What about Haigmann?"

"Oh, he's quite dead."

The words rocked me. I had come to think of Haigmann as invincible. Was Peric lying? Yet, how else could he have got a line on me unless it were beaten out of Haigmann?

"Has this gentleman, Captain, offered you what I offer for my freedom now? Has he told you what he brought aboard in a deck of cards?"

O'Rafferty turned dark, angry eyes on me. "I wonder if you have made a fool of me, Mr. Cloud."

"You haven't been made a fool of yet," I snapped. "This guy has nothing to offer but an eventual knife in the back."

"A roll of film, Captain, and name your own sum. He has it. He could share it with us. I could dispose of it."

My fist shot out, but O'Rafferty got on my arm and ruined my strike. "Allow our visitor to make his proposition, if you please, Mr. Cloud." He pushed me aside firmly.

"Don't be an idiot," I said hotly. "Don't you realize he's just trying to talk his way to freedom?"

"Produce the cards," Peric smiled, "and the captain will see that I am not only using empty words."

"Well, Mr. Cloud?"

"They've been stolen from me," I answered between clenched teeth.

"Come now," Peric laughed. "That is too convenient. This is my proposition, Captain. I have gone to great trouble to board this ship, as you must realize. I have sufficient contact—even with the pirate gentlemen—to have arranged my passage on the junk, though only as a passenger. I have more powerful contacts. Once we reach port, keep me, the headstrong American, and the film aboard. I will arrange for one of my friends to visit us with more Hong Kong dollars than you are apt to earn by plying this foolish coast for years to come. You will be rich overnight, Captain—*overnight!*

I watched O'Rafferty carefully. Peric was speaking the language he best understood: money. I could see what was tumbling through O'Rafferty's mind. He'd be able to purchase the remaining stock in the Sassoon. The ship would be his.

"O'Rafferty, don't be a sucker," I said slowly. "The friends he'll invite aboard won't bring a cent with them. They'll be gunmen. Do you suppose he's the type that buys anything when he can take it at the point of a gun?"

"My proposition stands in good faith, gentlemen."

I turned on Peric. "Is Cottardo in this game with you?"

"We have had dealings in the past. This is not one of them."

"I wonder."

O'Rafferty was pulling at his beard, his brow wrinkled with thought. "You must admit, Mr. Cloud, he paints a pretty picture."

I started talking and talking fast. "Look. By Eastern standards no one blames you for chasing a fast buck in these waters. The cash registers in Hong Kong haven't stopped tinkling, because cash registers have no politics. But if you've got a conscience tucked away in some corner of your brain, you'll tell this con artist to cut his throat before the authorities do it for him. I'll tell you what's on that film—names, a whole mess of names."

Peric straightened suddenly and his hawkface telegraphed me a warning: Don't talk.

O'Rafferty smiled. "Names, Mr. Cloud?"

"Names. Red undercover agents waiting for the whistle to blow all over this part of the world. When they get through there won't be any water out here that your ship would stay afloat in. Because the Reds will own it all."

"The American is an idealistic fool," Peric growled. "The film will reach American or British hands, perhaps. But where he would give it away, we would put a price on it. Legitimate trade. That is something you can understand, Captain."

O'Rafferty turned lively eyes on me. "I like the jingle of money in the man's proposition, Mr. Cloud."

"Do me a favor, both of you," I said. "Drop dead."

Peric smiled victoriously. "It is arranged, then."

I started toward the door, then swung around when the thought hit me. "No Allied government would see that film if it fell into the hands of a powerhouse blackmail outfit, O'Rafferty. Seven or eight hundred bastards would pay through their Red noses to keep from being exposed. Think about it, O'Rafferty."

I left.

I went into the wardroom, got a cup of coffee, and tried to steady myself. I wondered for a moment if O'Rafferty's name could be on that film. I preferred to think not. I couldn't have misjudged him that badly. But I began to consider every possibility and to prepare for it.

Later, I went looking for Flame. The day was a clear one, intensely bright and blue, and the swells in the sea were very mild. I might have been talking to myself as I strode along. I don't know. But I felt tense and angry.

I spotted Flame and almost blew up.

She was standing with Bejarano between the afterhatches, talking a final juggling lesson.

My heart was in my throat as I hurried over. I should have warned Flame!

"Good morning, Mr. Cloud," Bejarano said. "Our student is doing excellently."

Flame had three clubs going, wobbling swaths of orange and wood in the air, her expression taut. I looked to the sides of the ship and tried to get hold of myself. The ship had a small pitch, but I realized now that even if she spilled the clubs they'd have at least twenty feet to roll over the side.

Flame's eyes followed the clubs fearfully. "Go away, darling," she said. "You're making me nervous."

"Flame, will you put those down? I want to talk to you."

"I'll be through in a minute."

Bejarano was all smiles as he watched her. "I have never had such a quick student to learn. She is remarkable."

"Flame!" I said demandingly. Maybe it was safe enough, but I couldn't stand those clubs being juggled by inexperienced hands.

"I'll never learn if you're going to stand there razzing me."

"I'm not razzing you."

The clubs flipped and began weaving in irregular orbits and I saw that she was beginning to lose control. I kept my mouth shut. But she corrected herself nicely and they began spinning regularly. I breathed again.

That's when it happened.

The ship lurched to starboard very suddenly, as it had when the new helmsman had caught us by surprise at lunch the day before. The ship rolled with a swell and I clutched the hatch for support. At the same instant Flame was thrown off balance with the clubs still dancing in the air. Her hand gripped one of them as she fell to a knee and the others clattered to the deck and began to roll. My heart was in my mouth. I hurled myself along the deck and fell on top of one of the clubs. The other was loose, and from the level of the deck I watched petrified as the orange bands revolved out of reach; the club twisted and rolled like a pin ball toward the port side. It struck a cleat, teetered for a crazy second, and disappeared. In that moment of stretched tension, a small splash echoed. The ship gradually righted itself.

I lay there on the deck, the club under me. "*Dios,*" I heard Bejarano mutter, releasing his grip on the hatch.

Flame picked herself up and turned to him apologetically. "I *am* sorry," she said.

He shrugged his shoulders with a breath. "It was not your fault. Let us forget it. It was nothing. Only a bit of wood."

Only a bit of wood. I got up. Bejarano had lost a small cache of gold. I was almost afraid to turn up the club in my hands. Maybe we had lost the film!

"The sea appeared so calm." Flame returned the single club she had held onto, which Bejarano accepted with apparent eagerness.

I looked at the base of the club I had saved. It was a blank.

My heart skipped a beat. There was only the club remaining in Bejarano's hands. If the scars of the gimmicking weren't in the base of that club, it meant the film was now settling to the sea bottom in the third Indian club.

"You'll want this," I said, handing him the club I had saved.

"Thank you."

He wanted to leave, but I held him in conversation. I had to get a glance at the base of the other club. And finally, as he held them nervously, I did.

I was immediately impressed with the near invisibility of it. But the faint telltale marks of the plug I had made over the hidden film were there.

Blood began to flow through my veins again.

Flame, innocent of what had really happened, tossed the whole thing off with a smile. "Two are easier to juggle than three, anyway," she said, as though that would help.

"Yes," Bejarano said. "If you'll excuse me now..."

After he was gone I explained to Flame why the two of us had turned white when the clubs began to scatter. She turned pretty pale herself.

When we returned to the cabin we found it torn part. The two mattresses had been pulled to the deck, slit open, and the cotton scattered over the place like dirty snow. The chair was on end, the drainpipe of the washbowl unscrewed. Dufour hadn't missed a lick.

"Dufour?" Flame echoed.

"That's the way it stacks up to me," I said, picking up my trench coat. He had slit part of the collar. He must have seen the gold, but since that wasn't what he was after, he apparently let it go without further damage. He realized I wouldn't have been fool enough to hide the film with something so immediately valuable. "Bejarano's been tied down giving you a juggling lesson, Helena's locked in her cabin, Cork's got too strong a right arm to pull slinky stuff like this. Dufour's afraid. He doesn't want to show himself unless he has to."

"Dufour! Then he has the missing frames of film."

"Providing there was film between the cards he palmed off."

"There must have been, or he wouldn't have gone after the deck."

"That's right." I started righting stuff in the cabin. "But I doubt that he would do anything but destroy the film he got. I have a notion he's a guy with a Red streak down his back. My guess is he's a phony, and his name's on the list itself."

I heaved the mattresses back in place. The wreckage in the cabin would throw O'Rafferty in a fit. O'Rafferty ...

I froze. O'Rafferty and Peric. It was an ugly thought, but I tore after it. Maybe this wasn't Dufour's work.

"See you later," I snapped.

By the time I reached O'Rafferty's stateroom I had decided to play it innocent and give O'Rafferty the benefit of the doubt. Had he really been taken in by Peric, or had he only been amusing himself at my expense? I knocked.

He told me to come in, and I found him seated at his writing desk, hands neatly folded across his ample belly.

"There's the smell of Hong Kong in the air, Mr. Cloud," he said. "It puts me in a meditative mood."

I closed the door quietly. "What have you done about Peric?"

His brown eyebrows fell. "Your Mr. Peric offers an attractive proposition to a poor man such as myself."

"He's white scum, if you'll allow me to quote you."

"Perhaps I am of the same stuff, Mr. Cloud. Look-see, a man of principle would not run cargoes of rubber to the Chinese Reds, now, would he?"

"You've made up your mind, then?"

"Yes, Mr. Cloud."

My suspicions turned to anger. "Then that's the way it is," I muttered, holding myself back. "I didn't think Peric was that slick. At least I know how the cards are stacked against me. You needn't have ransacked my cabin. I would have told you the film is not there."

"I have made up my mind, Mr. Cloud, to turn Peric over to the authorities as a pirate. Did you think I considered doing otherwise for more than a moment? Now, what's this about your cabin?"

I looked at him blankly, and then started to laugh. At myself.

"Never mind the cabin," I said finally. "I owe you an apology. I guess I'm not very good at playing cat and mouse—when I'm the mouse."

"You've lost your sense of humor, Mr. Cloud," he said. "When that happens to a man, he'd best get out of the Orient."

Maybe it was good advice. I told him I'd consider it. "I'm not a man without an occasional childhood impulse," he muttered. "You understand?"

"Of course. You're a nice guy in sea wolf's clothing."

"A man must balance his conscience from time to time. Good day, Mr. Cloud."

Chapter Seventeen

Lunch was a nervous affair. Hong Kong was only a short two hours off; anticipation became something tangible around the table. Although he had scrupulously avoided dining with the passengers during the voyage, O'Rafferty ate this final meal with us. I had released Helena from her cabin; if she had been working with Dufour he wouldn't have accepted news of her sudden "illness" without suspicion and investigation. But my warning to her still held, and she promised to keep her lovely mouth shut about my visit to the Bejarano-Dufour cabin.

Bejarano, I saw, picked at his food without appetite, while Cork ate ravenously. Dufour, if my conviction about him was right, smoothly concealed the workings of his mind with a flood of idle conversation, and

O'Rafferty glowered impatiently at him.

Midway through lunch O'Rafferty could contain himself no longer and turned on him. "Must you jabber like a monkey? My stomach's turning for the first time in thirty-five years at sea!"

"Ah, *mon capitaine*, you are in an ill humor. What a pity. But soon enough you shall see the last of us."

"It can't be soon enough," O'Rafferty growled, throwing down his napkin and storming out.

Dufour, undaunted, turned to me. "How fortunate," he said in grand tones, "to have the American newspaperman with us. His story will make us all *très célèbres, mes idiots!* M'sieu Cloud, you will remember to spell my name right, yes?"

"I might even go so far as to spell your *right* name," I muttered.

"Dufour—D-u-f-o-u-r." He passed my implication off as though he hadn't heard it at all. I looked around the table. Haigmann's agent was still among us, careful not to tip his hand prematurely. I had checked up on Cork. He had stood most of the morning alone at the bow, as though peering out for first sight of Hong Kong. Each day, as white territory drew that much closer, his disposition improved.

Helena was her old outspoken self again.

"You are all so happy to reach Hong Kong," she said smiling. "Helena? She is sad. My husband in Canton, it is only a few miles up the Pearl River to him. He is such a dull one to go back to."

Flame had borrowed needle and thread and repaired her chartreuse dress, which she had ironed and was now wearing and looking most beautiful in. It was her color, setting off her eyes.

Bejarano lit a cigarette for her, and she asked him a question I had hoped to ask more privately. "Where will you be staying in Hong Kong?"

"I think the Imperial Hotel. I have stopped there before on visits to Hong Kong. I recommend it."

My suspicions stirred again. Was it only coincidence that Bejarano should mention the Imperial? That was the hotel Haigmann had made my destination. Was Bejarano, after all, Haigmann's man?

An idea crossed my mind. I would find out right now. "Flame, honey," I said, "I've been keeping some news from you—I didn't want to upset you. But you'd find out when we landed, so I'd better tell you now. Haigmann is dead."

Flame looked up and her expression froze. I looked quickly at Bejarano. If the information startled him, he didn't show a thing. Cork went on eating. Dufour lit a cigarette.

Helena, I saw, like Flame, froze.

It lasted for only a second, like something caught in a photographer's flash.

She thawed quickly, finding something to say. "A close friend? I am sorry. There is too much death in the Orient now, yes?"

I listened to the throaty voice. Was that the voice I had heard over Haigmann's phone—thinking it a man's voice?

"Maybe not enough," I said, staring at her.

Innocence flickered uncertainly across her face. "Perhaps the Americans have a joke between them."

"Let's all laugh," I said.

Dufour, watching us, looked like a man viewing a game of tennis without understanding the rules. Bejarano too was puzzled. Cork wasn't interested.

Helena!

She was part of the web Haigmann had so ingeniously spun around me. "Shall we talk it over here, or would you prefer the privacy of your cabin?" I asked.

But Helena was still pretending. "Are you making a proposition? That should indeed be done in private."

"Wake up, sweetheart."

A hardness to match her voice finally came into her dark eyes. She got up, gave the others an aloof glance, and walked out. I followed.

When we got inside her cabin, I locked the door and told her to sit down.

Her crimson lips were sarcastic. "Wouldn't you rather I lie down?"

"Congratulations, baby. You had me beautifully fooled."

"You are a child."

"I'm surprised he trusted a woman. You must have special qualifications. Want to tell me about it?"

"Don't be a bore." She began moving about the cabin nervously.

"Haigmann's dead, baby. Get that through your pretty head. Did he tell you *why* you were to tag me?"

Her eyes flashed hatefully.

"No," I said. "I don't think he would. He wouldn't trust you that far."

"Shut up."

"Maybe I can figure out some of the answers myself. Haigmann figured if you could keep me in the sack you could keep me out of trouble."

She laughed icily. "Yes. He knew your weakness for a pair of pretty legs. That was his way, to play on weaknesses."

"Your legs came well qualified."

"My legs," she muttered bitterly, "are my weakness too. I was a dancer once. Ballet."

"You must tell me about it sometime, but not now."

"So he is dead."

"Yes. I want to know what your job was to be when we reached Hong Kong."

She turned and stood looking out the porthole. Then she shrugged her shoulders as though she were telling herself. "What difference does it make now?"

"If anything happened to you aboard ship, I was to take the pack of cards from you and bring them to Hong Kong. If you tried to slip away in Hong Kong, I was to make you take me with you."

"You might have got away with it, baby. I've fallen for less attractive bait. Haigmann doesn't miss a lick. Do you know what the cards represented?"

"No."

"What would you have done if we'd slipped away?"

"I would have called one of Haigmann's men here and told him where you had taken me. He would have come for you and killed you."

"Wouldn't that have mattered to you?"

She looked at me balefully. "I didn't expect to fall in love with you."

"I'm sure you haven't. Who were you to call?"

"I know only the number."

"Want to tell it to me?"

"I won't be using it," she answered softly. I memorized it as she gave it. I realized she might only be making up a number out of her head, but I'd check.

"O.K., baby, you're free to go back to your husband in Canton now."

"I have no husband in Canton."

I started toward the door. "It shouldn't take you long to find one."

"Alex—"

"What did you say that phone number was again?"

She repeated it without hesitation.

"What were you to get if you delivered me all tied up in love knots?"

"I work for money. But I am sick of it." Her eyes turned soft. "Alex—"

"Don't make a play for me, baby. It won't work."

We entered the bright blue waters of Tathong Channel a few minutes before two o'clock. I stood at the forecastle alone, listening to the water wash back along the flanks of the ship. It was like entering a different world. There were civilian pleasure cruisers out for fishing and here and there racing sloops tacking, sails crisp, in the fresh wind. Hong Kong hung out the same old sign: Business as Usual. It was all familiar, but it didn't seem real to me now.

On the port side the serrated profile of Dragon's Back, a spine of hills I had climbed often enough, stood out against a dazzling blue sky. The wind snapped at the trench coat in my arm. I considered for a moment tossing it overboard, but I knew I would have to see the business through to the end. The single bar of gold Dufour had come upon and left I now carried in my trousers pocket. We passed Junk Island and rode through the narrow, swirling waters of Lyemun Pass—a graceful curve— and then the waterfront skyscrapers of Victoria and Kowloon rose from the hills.

I went up to the pilothouse.

O'Rafferty was swearing and his beard trembled with a fresh rage. We had moved to the far end of Victoria now and he snapped an order to set the anchor detail.

"Lord, will there be no end to the evil luck on this voyage!" He turned to me suddenly, seeing me for the first time. "I told you once before the pilothouse is no place for spectators."

"I thought I'd like to thank you for everything and wish you good-by."

"There's time enough for that, Mr. Cloud. We're not going anywhere for a bit. We're anchoring in the stream for half an hour or so."

My mind snapped up the possibility of getting a head start. "What?"

"Look-see, another ship's moored to our dock. The captain was off drunk somewhere, they tell me. Should have sailed before noon. They've only just laid hands on him."

The anchor chain ripped from the bow. I grabbed O'Rafferty's thick hand in an impatient clasp and got moving. Even as I reached the main deck, sampans were beginning to collect along the sides of the ship. I checked at the cabin and found Flame. I told her to come on.

When we got on deck I tumbled a coiled jack ladder over the side and started down. Flame knew this was no time to ask questions, and she didn't. She followed.

I set foot on the sampan that had nosed in as the coolie saw us coming down, and gave Flame a hand.

"Get this piece of driftwood moving," I shouted to the old Chinese, who was all smiles and no teeth.

We settled under the canopy and I looked back at the wet, black sides of the Sassoon. We were moving away. But we hadn't gone twenty feet when Dufour's startled face appeared over the rail. For once, his mouth was shut.

"Here comes trouble," I said.

Dufour came over the side like a fat lizard. A sampan was under his feet before he reached the bottom of the ladder. He pointed us out excitedly to his coolie.

I looked up at the half-naked Chinese at the *yulow*. "Chop-chop!" I snapped. He gave me his number one grin again, but I saw at once I was wasting my time. He was strictly slow motion. He was ancient. "Never mind," I muttered with resignation. "We're going to have company. It has been ordained." I settled back on the bench across from Flame.

Within a couple of minutes Dufour was alongside. He boarded our sampan clumsily, a hand in his pocket, and joined us under the canopy. He was wearing a plaid jacket with lots of red and green in it.

"You're just in time for cocktails," I said.

"I trust I am intruding," he remarked. His ruddy face, his perpetual smile were transformed into a pale, icy grin. His hand came out of his pocket. It gripped a Jap Nambu automatic.

"Put it away," I said. "You might blow a hole in the bottom and sink the boat."

"*Alors*, it's a chance we must take."

"Bejarano's gun?"

A thin smile fluttered across his face. "He had a pair. He will not miss this one."

Flame, sitting across the narrow passage, braced herself against the rocking of the sampan. She would not be intimidated by the gun. She looked at me as though to say, "This is your department."

I remembered that O'Rafferty had taken the precaution of unloading Bejarano's guns. Had Dufour checked? Had he reloaded?

"Now that you have us cornered like rats," I said academically, "what do you want?"

"The film, m'sieu."

"What will you pay?"

Flame looked up, startled.

"What will you pay?" I repeated.

Dufour grinned. "A cash transaction is out of order, M'sieu Cloud. You forget, I have the gun."

"Who are you, Dufour?"

"Does it matter?"

"I'd like to guess."

"Give me the film. I have no time for games."

I glanced forward. The water front stood some distance off. Maybe five minutes before we would pull up. I started guessing. "I think you're a Red, and whatever your real name might be, I'll bet it's on that microfilm list. You're a dead duck if it gets into Allied hands."

"Do you know, *mon idiot*, you are talking yourself to death?"

"Sitting through one of your pictures must be a worse death—or maybe you're not a film director at all."

"You make jokes in the face of a gun?" Behind his glasses, Dufour stared at me with withering scorn.

"It is one of my major talents."

He held the gun nervously. "You are mistaken," he snapped. "I was a director in France, but today it is different. I hold a menial government post in Indo-China." He stood rigid against the steady rocking of the boat. "There are many of us who see that the old world is dead, and we must only bury it. China, new China, offers the intelligent ones tomorrow's world. *Entendu?*"

"Sure." I grimaced. "I understand. The misfits and the failures have a way of ending up in China. What a lousy director you must have been, Dufour."

Bitterness swept his face. "I was ahead of my time. France did not understand me."

"I'll bet the Chinese do. You're cut right out of a pattern. The Western crackpot running a Red fever who can be useful to them. How do you say traitor in French, Dufour?"

A storm gathered on his round, perspiring face. "Give me the film!"

"We haven't got it."

"I am not so easily fooled, m'sieu."

"I tell you you're out of luck. You can see we have no baggage."

"It could easily be hidden in your clothes."

"I'll make a bargain with you," I said, as an idea began developing in my mind. "And I don't see that you'll have much choice. If you want to search the clothes on our backs you'll have to shoot us first, and this is no spot for executions. I'm having the film brought ashore. Drum up some money and it's yours."

He steadied himself and weaved the gun between us. Thought came through to his forehead in wrinkles. Either he knew the gun was unloaded and he'd have to bluff, or it was loaded but the busy Victoria waterfront was no place to pull the trigger.

"Agreed," he said finally.

The sampan was coming in. It scraped along a landing and Dufour pocketed the gun, keeping his hand in the pocket. I told him to pay the coolie; we were broke.

We stood for a moment on the landing, looking at the white buildings sprawled along the slope to Victoria Peak, a city grown up on a hillside. It seemed a century ago that I had left Hong Kong. It had been only a couple of weeks.

Dufour walked behind us until we reached a taxi, an old dusty Cadillac. He took the jump seat so as to face the two of us, and brought the gun in sight again. I told the Portuguese driver to take us to the Imperial Hotel, and settled back beside Flame. She passed Dufour a loathsome glance and gave her attention to the shifting sights along the water front. I had to hand it to her. She was cool as hell.

It bothered Dufour, who felt his gun deserved more respect than it was getting. "Miss Forrest seems bored," he said. "Perhaps she is a poor loser. I almost made a serious mistake. I believed she had the film, not you, M'sieu Cloud."

I shifted the trench coat in my arms. "You're forgiven."

"One of our agents, a dock worker, recognized her when she came aboard with you in Shanghai. That was unfortunate for you, yes? Many of us have been in the field hunting the microfilm, *entendu?* We traced it to her, then, poof, she disappeared. But only for a moment."

"Were you the bastard who notified the authorities in Shanghai she was aboard?"

He tossed his head impatiently. "When I was able to verify that the woman was indeed the underground worker we searched, I put a few Hong Kong dollars in the hands of the radio operator."

Flame opened her mouth. "Clever," she said.

"You know," Dufour smiled, "I am on vacation from my job. But I have never worked harder."

The Imperial was an ornate hotel facing Victoria Bay. A long wooden veranda traveled the width of the front, and drinks were served there at polished black-wood tables. A few Britishers were sitting around in spotless whites as we walked through to the lobby. Inside, several fans flicked their wooden blades through the air without much effect, and here and there a Hong Kong gentleman sat behind his delayed copy of the *London Times* and dropped expensive cigar ashes amid the potted palms.

It was an old hotel, something that had sprung up a century ago with the opium trade when the British turned Hong Kong from a pirate's lair into an Oriental cash register with a view.

"Cloud," I said to the desk clerk. "You have the reservation."

He turned to his records to check, put a key on the counter, and punched the bell. "Room seven-twelve," he said.

"Never mind the bellboy. We have no luggage."

That seemed irregular, but he didn't let it bother him. "Oh, Mr. Cloud," he muttered as we turned away. "This envelope has been left for you."

I wheeled. He handed me a manila envelope. I ripped off the sealed flap and extracted a folded sheet of drawing paper. It was the sketch the little artist had made of me back in Georges's Bar.

The room had pink walls. The windows were up and a gentle breeze off the bay stirred the crisp white curtains. Dufour took the liberty of locking the door after us and stood behind his gun again. An old four-poster bed jutted from a wall, a telephone stood on a small rattan table beside it.

I had jammed the sketch in my pocket. Flame had given me curious glances; Dufour dismissed it. His mind was on a single track: the film.

"Well, m'sieu?" he said impatiently.

"How much money can you raise?"

"First the film. Then we will discuss money."

"Did you destroy the strips of film you got from palming off those cards?"

"Of course." He smiled. "The rest must be destroyed also. Well?"

"I don't trust you to pay up, Dufour."

"You have no choice but to trust me, m'sieu."

I looked at the gun as though it frightened me. "O.K.," I sighed. "A seaman's bringing the film ashore for me. I'm to meet him under the grandstand at the Happy Valley Race Track. As you discovered when you tore through our cabin, I've got a lot of gold in the shoulders of this coat. I promised it to him if he'd keep his mouth shut and get over there as soon as the Sassoon docks."

The gun must have felt good in Dufour's hand. He smiled.

"We will meet him together," I said firmly.

"No," Dufour corrected me. "I shall meet him alone."

"What about the pay-off to me?"

"You will need no funds where you are going. May I have the coat, please?"

I lowered my eyes on him. "You won't get away with a double cross."

"I am being charitable," he remarked. "I could kill you both now. But I shall instruct my comrades with more stomach for killing to do the job for me."

I swore at him as though I meant it. There was no question in my mind now. The gun was unloaded.

He came in closer, pulled the trench coat from my arm, and returned to the door. His hand trembled on the doorknob. He had won. He locked us in and got on his way to the Happy Valley Race Track.

Flame gave me a look that asked if I had gone completely crazy. "He's going to stand in for me at a shooting," I said, motioning her over to the phone. "Can you drop your voice to Helena's level?"

"Do you mind cutting me in on all this cloak-and-dagger stuff?"

"Give me time. I'm going to call a number and I want you to tell whoever answers that Alexander Cloud jumped ship and is hiding out around the grandstand at the race track."

"I hope you know what you're doing, darling." "Keep your fingers crossed."

I called the hotel operator and put through the number Helena had given to me. I handed the phone to Flame when the connection began to ring.

In a moment she began to talk. She put on a good little act. I held my breath.

"You did fine," I said when it was all over.

"I think you've gone completely mad."

I told her then that Haigmann had had a representative aboard the Sassoon, that Helena's job was to tip off his Hong Kong end if I attempted to get away. And that was the Hong Kong end she had called.

"But the man who answered said it was the Chu Wah Drug Company."

"That could be a front," I said hopefully. "Remember, I was marked for killing down here. That trench coat has death written all over it. When Haigmann's rub-out artist spots it on Dufour, he'll go to work. That gold is the pay-off for his chores. But I figure he'll also have instructions to pick up the deck of cards from the body. When he doesn't find that, he'll check here looking for trouble." I started pacing around as I anticipated how to handle what was coming. "And he'll get plenty of trouble."

I dug out the sketch and looked at it. I hadn't counted on having that turn up in Hong Kong. They might have got my name from Haigmann. I didn't enjoy the possibility that they knew what I looked like. That could ruin it.

When I showed it to Flame, she understood at once it was the drawing she had sent little Picasso out to get of me. "For Christ's sake," she said. "Let's get out of here."

The phone rang.

We both stared at it, and then at each other. I paused with my hand on the receiver, then picked it up. "Hello?"

I winked to Flame then. It was Bejarano's voice at the other end. I breathed easier. And I realized that the film was now ashore.

"Checked in about five minutes ago," he was saying. "You two haven't forgotten we're having dinner together this evening?"

"I had forgotten," I said. "But thanks for reminding me. What room are you in?"

"Just a moment. There's someone at the door."

I heard the receiver scrape as he laid it down, and I waited. Distantly, voices came to me from Bejarano's room. I lit a cigarette and Flame kept her eyes on me. Then, over the receiver, I heard a sudden shuffling and finally Bejarano's voice in very firm terms: "Get out of this room, sir!"

I pressed the receiver hard against my ear and my heart began skipping beats. A high-pitched groan came to me, and then a heavy thud close to the phone.

I broke the connection immediately and called the desk.

"What's the matter?" Flame asked, sensing my alarm.

"Someone's onto those Indian clubs," I snapped. The desk clerk finally got around to taking the call, and I asked Bejarano's room number. Room 301.

I banged down the phone and made for the door. Dufour had locked it from the outside, and as I struggled with it I wondered if it would save time to call down for a chambermaid. But I saw that it wasn't going to be much of a challenge. I threw myself against it until it gave way.

I high-tailed it to the stairway and Flame followed. Bejarano's room was four long flights below, and it seemed to take forever to get there. When I reached the third floor I ran into a startled chambermaid and finally swung around to room 301. The door was ajar.

I pushed through. Bejarano lay on the floor near the phone, blood trickling from the back of his head.

On the dresser stood one Indian club. The other was gone.

Chapter Eighteen

I checked Bejarano's pulse. He was still alive. I told Flame to call the hotel doctor, and poked through Bejarano's things for the Nambu automatic, the twin of the one Dufour had taken from him. I found it in a pigskin overnight bag, and a box of shells. O'Rafferty must have returned the cartridges as Bejarano left the ship.

I loaded the magazine and snapped up the phone book. I found the address of the Chu Wah Drug Company on Jervois Street in the Chinese quarter.

"Bejarano's coming to," Flame said.

I bent down to him and gradually got the story out of him. The guy was tall, gray at the temples. He had struck Bejarano with the butt of a gun.

The doctor strode in as I started to leave. Flame caught my arm. She looked a little shaken, but game. "You're not going without me."

"Come on."

We threaded our way by foot through the narrow, crowded streets of the Chinese quarter. It was faster than going by ricksha, and I knew I wouldn't have been able to sit still for the ride. We moved down a block lined with sidewalk beauty parlors, and farther along a Chinese street dentist rattled a necklace of human teeth at us as we passed. Flame held my hand, and I moved at a trot.

We finally reached Jervois Street and worked along it as the numbers decreased. And then the Chu Wah Drug Company stood across the street, its vertical cloth signs motionless in the hot sun. We stopped to catch our breaths. If Helena had deceived me, this was a wild-goose chase.

I checked the gun in my pocket. We crossed the street and started into the store.

It was a native shop, long and narrow and badly lit. The walls were lined to the low ceiling with jars and colored packages of herbs and patent medicines. Displayed on the parallel counters running the length of the store were large glass pens of live baby lizards and a dozen varieties of snakes. I felt Flame tighten against me. Toward the back of the shop at a small butcher's table a thin attendant held down a writhing snake and slit open its stomach. A Chinese woman beside him, a customer, watched him remove an organ and drop it in a nearby glass of amber liquid. She immediately drank the remedy for God knows what. Flame turned white.

An older Chinese approached us, nodding politely, his hands buried in the cuffs of his sleeves. I looked beyond him to the back of the shop, to a closed door.

"August Haigmann sent us," I said. "Are you the boss around here?"

"Who I say calling?"

I pulled the gun out of my pocket, holding it in close so as not to attract attention. "We'll announce ourselves," I muttered.

The Chinese glanced at the gun and smiled pleasantly. I decided at once this wasn't a wild-goose chase. He turned and led us to the back of the store. Flame walked very close to me; the place terrified her. We passed an aquarium thick with swimming leeches and a jar of dried centipedes. Sitting with strange majesty at the very end of the counter was a glass cage containing a golden king cobra. What its use in Chinese medicine was I couldn't guess. Maybe it was only meant to give you the willies. If so, it worked.

The Chinese paused at the back door, looked at the gun again, and grinned. "Upstairs," he said softly.

I motioned the Chinese through the door with us. It led to an old stairway. I closed the door, spun our guest around, and cracked him quickly with the butt of my gun. Flame gasped, but that was more than he did. He just crumbled with a thin moan to the floor.

We entered upon the stairway. Flame stopped me halfway up.

"Alex, I'm scared stiff."

"Don't give out on me now, baby."

She took a breath and got a grip on herself. We climbed softly to the top, and found a single door across the landing. My hand was sweating around the handle of the gun.

I turned the knob and pushed open the door.

It was a large room, furnished as an office. The open windows looked out on a good view of the bay. The rug was a rich Chinese yellow, the chairs new leather, and the desk a polished natural mahogany.

There was a man, facing us now with surprise, sitting at the desk. The Indian club lay in his long, manicured fingers, and he had been probing it with a penknife.

The face was familiar.

"Cottardo!" Flame whispered.

I don't know how many seconds passed as we stood looking at each other. There wasn't a sound during those taut moments. Cottardo's eyes fell on the gun in my hand, and finally his expression changed. He smiled. "Come in. I love reunions."

"We'll stick around and sing 'Auld Lang Syne,'" I said. I felt as if I were talking in a dream. I closed the door after us.

"Hello, Flame, my sweet," he said, ignoring me. "You're looking perfectly grand."

His white teeth gleamed. He had been in tight spots before, and it was clear his thoughts were not so Rotarian as his smile. Since I had last seen him, he had picked up a distinguished touch of gray at the temples. His tall body was neatly clothed in an expensive white suit, and a blue polka-dot tie was cinched up in a loose Windsor knot. He had always reminded me of a foppish perfume salesman, and even now there was the starched handkerchief at casual half-mast from his breast pocket.

"Cottardo," Flame whispered again in a tense little voice. "I can't believe—"

"Really, Alex." He cut her off. "That's no way to greet an old friend—with a gun in your hand."

"You'd be surprised how friendly it makes me feel." I looked at the chips of plastic wood in a small area on the desk; he had apparently all but cleaned out the plug. The club still lay in his hands. "When did you take up juggling?"

"Just today," he said, very relaxed. "Just now, to tell the truth."

He was going to play it calm, very calm.

Flame stared, as though disbelieving the scene before her. "I waited for you," she muttered, as though that made any difference now. "In Shanghai. You didn't come back."

"Flame, my sweet, you must forgive me."

The pretense was over with him, but Flame seemed unable to face the reality that Cottardo was Haigmann's alter ego in Hong Kong. That was too shattering, too painful. But after a moment she could no longer ignore it and humiliation appeared in her shocked green eyes. "You never planned to come back to me."

"You were a convenience." He seemed almost eager to explain. "The film was too hot for us to hold for a few days. You kept it cool for us."

"I see."

"Really, you can be very silly and innocent, Flame, my sweet. That is remarkable—for a newspaperwoman."

He wanted to hurt her, and he was succeeding. My fist developed a quick yen for the touch of his fine Italian nose, yet I wanted him to keep talking. Flame had finally come face to face with the Cottardo she refused to believe existed, the man without his mask.

And slowly, hostility came into her eyes. "What a complete fool I've been! It was nowhere in your mind to turn the film over to the authorities!"

"You always were too idealistic to be practical. I found it charming for a while."

"You're contemptible!"

He leaned back in his chair, in what passed for excellent humor, and laughed. "Flame, my sweet, I'm flattered that you always saw me as a fine gentleman, but I really fancy myself as a scoundrel. One must be frank with himself. Actually, I had planned to come back to you—for the film. But I had to leave Shanghai unexpectedly. The Reds, you know. I like Hong Kong much better than Peiping." He toyed with the club almost absently. "Haigmann, of course, saw to it that you were relieved of the film. All we needed then was a safe courier to take it out of Shanghai. Alex generously made his services available."

"Glad to oblige," I said, keeping an eye on the club. At the moment he was outmatched as to weapons. Helena, I felt certain, had tipped him off to the club, and I swore at myself for having trusted her at all. It had dropped out of my hand in her cabin, and she must have suspected more than I gave her credit for. I felt just as certain that Cottardo would pay her well for the tip. "I suppose congratulations are in order," I said. "With Haigmann dead, you are no doubt taking over his organization."

He laughed. "I have a way of reaching the top in a short time. It is one of my talents."

"It was thoughtful of Haigmann to send you that sketch of me."

"He was always thoughtful. You know, Alex, that was a foolish thing you did. It was Georges, poor fellow, who saw your bit in the paper and thought it wise to intercept the sketch. He called Haigmann, and of course it was taken care of. We have a most efficient organization. So of course you will put away that gun. You would not live to reach the sidewalk if you're thinking of making use of it."

"Did the gunman sent out to get me at the race track know what I looked like?"

Laughter came back to him again. "You put us to some trouble there, Alex. I don't quite know what to make of it. But unfortunately it struck my sense of humor to return the sketch to you at the hotel. I hadn't anticipated the slightest trouble with you. That was my mistake."

"Your only mistake," I said, "will be to underestimate this gun. I'm taking the film, Cottardo. Lay the club on the desk."

He remained, leaning back in the chair, still laughing softly. "You'd be insane to imagine you could leave this building with that film in your pocket."

"Then consider me crazy as hell."

His blue eyes held me curiously for a long time. "All right," he said. He leaned forward and slowly set the club upright at the center of the desk. A breeze skittered in through the open windows. He was standing now, and moved out from behind the desk as though to say. "You see, we won't fight over it."

I approached, the gun leveled on him. My left hand reached for the club.

He did it so smoothly I couldn't pull the trigger fast enough to miss firing into Flame. His hand lashed out, caught her wrist, and yanked her to his body as a shield. As I wheeled he rushed her into me and got his fingers on the barrel of the gun. I couldn't shoot. He was turning it in on her.

I shot a hand over her shoulder into his face. Flame did the smart thing; she let herself go limp and slid down between us. Cottardo's right hand came in against my cheek with what felt like enough force to snap my neck. I held tightly to the gun as my head kicked back with the blow, and he spun me, getting on my arm, and dug his fingers through my hand for the gun. It went off in the wall and then his pressure opened my fingers and the gun clattered to the floor.

He shoved me against the desk as he dove. My hand found the Indian club and I hurled it. It struck his shoulder with a thud and his fingers kicked the gun that was almost in their reach several inches along the floor. I sprang on him.

Flame had pulled herself away from us and got the door open. Cottardo reached the gun as I reached him. The club rolled away from us and I wrestled the hand with the gun. "Get out of here," I yelled to Flame.

The gun went off again. I got a grip on it and twisted. I must have knotted up his shoulder with the club and it was giving him trouble. I got the gun free and brought the butt in for a blow that dazed him badly.

I went for the club and struck it against a leather chair until the film, tightly wrapped in cloth, shook out. I got it in my pocket and made for the door.

I saw Flame give Cottardo a backward glance, her face pale, and she followed me down the stairs.

The door at the bottom opened almost as we reached it. The Chinese had got over my sleeping pill and was coming back with a gun. When I caught the gleam I didn't wait. I shot only once.

Almost at once I heard Cottardo stumbling at the head of the stairs. "Stop!" he shouted desperately. "We'll make a deal! I'll pay you!"

"Go to hell!"

He came down after us as we stepped over the bleeding body in the doorway. The gunshots had emptied the shop, and we were halfway to the front door when a fresh shot rang out and I realized Cottardo had got the Oriental's gun.

I couldn't have killed him upstairs in cold blood. Now I pushed Flame in the space between two counters and fired fast. He dove behind the far end of the opposite row of counters at the back of the store. I chipped wood.

Outside the front windows of the store a cautious crowd began to form. For a moment Cottardo was out of sight. He rose suddenly and let go a wild shot. I held my fire. But his slug shattered a glass jar of small striped snakes that stood directly above us on the counter. When the snakes began dropping off the counter beside us Flame gasped and went rigid with fear.

"They're harmless," I snapped. "Crawl behind the counter to the front."

I thought I saw Cottardo beginning to rise and fired impulsively. It was a miss. I thought to count my shots now. I had loaded seven; five were gone.

I brushed off a snake that had fallen to my shoulder and moved behind the counter to the back of the store. Cottardo seemed to be staying put. I figured I was almost opposite him now. I couldn't afford to miss.

I rose slightly to look, ready to fire. He was down. Near him, on the counter, the cobra was nervous in its glass pen, alerted by the shooting. It moved in a growing rage, its shingled skin a brilliant gold.

A shot whistled above me. I moved, around the end of the counter and steadied my aim where I expected him to appear. When he showed himself he was a few feet off. I fired.

I missed him. The air rang with breaking glass and I saw what I had hit.

The cobra rose up from the ruins of the pen, its hood flaring. Hidden behind the counter, Cottardo crouched almost directly below it. A burning silence stretched between us. Only the snake moved, weaving, picking out its target. I heard Cottardo's gun go off. But he wasn't firing at me—and he missed the swaying golden head.

The cobra hissed and struck. I saw nothing for the next seconds until Cottardo came up with bulging, frantic eyes. The snake was clinging with its fangs at his neck, its body writhing. Cottardo stumbled out desperate in panic, his mouth wide, and fell in the aisle in a paralysis of agony.

He lay there pitifully for a moment, his hands pawing desperately at the snake. Then laughter burst from his open mouth. Violent, convulsive laughter, shrill and completely mad.

I stood trying to shut the sound of it out of my ears. After a moment the cobra disengaged itself and began a slow, curious slither across the floor. I shot its head off.

We sat looking at each other across a glass-topped table in a quiet bar I knew on Queen's Road. Flame was wearing a large straw hat and something cool and white and summery.

"Hello, beautiful," I said.

"Hello, newspaperman. When are you leaving?"

"End of the week, maybe. Soon as my relief shows up."

"I'll pay you back for these clothes."

"Of course you will," I said.

"As soon as I find a job, I'll pay you back."

"Fine."

She played with the fine stem of her glass. "I can't expect you to forgive me, darling, for being such an idiot about Cottardo."

"Naturally not."

"I can't forgive myself." She grimaced. "What a horrible way to die!"

"What the hell," I said. "He died laughing."

The Chinese boy came over to empty our ash tray, something he was doing more often than necessary.

"You'll have fun in San Francisco," she went on. "Bureau chief and all that sort of thing."

"Hell, I had them over a barrel."

I recalled the cable I had found on my desk when I got back to my office. A relief man was on his way, it notified me crisply. Consider myself fired when he showed up. I tossed the cable in the wastebasket, sat down angrily, and wrote it out—the Hate America demonstration, a news story on gold smuggling, conditions I had witnessed within Red China, an I-was-there piracy yarn. But I kept the biggest story of all on ice—the film, which was immediately classified when I turned it over to the authorities. I would have to wait until the arrests were over before I could write that story. The arrests had already begun.

Then I got the chief in New York on the phone and made him listen to a few excerpts from my typewriter. I hinted at the beat I was sitting on and almost provoked a long-distance heart attack.

It just happened, he remembered suddenly, that Ragan, San Francisco bureau chief, was retiring, and how would I like a tour of duty back in the States? Be a sport, ol' man, and put those stories on the cable. You've been with us a long time, best in the business when you can keep your mind on news, ol' man, knew you'd snap out of it...

Flame was smiling up at me. "You know, darling, I've been watching a perfectly lovely pair of legs at the bar. You've hardly given them a passing glance."

"I've taken the cure."

"I'm beginning to believe you."

Her glass was empty and I ordered another drink.

We talked about Bejarano, who was leaving by plane for Mexico City within a few days. I had sent him anonymously the gold bar that Dufour had half ripped out of the coat when he searched our cabin. I hoped it would repay Bejarano for the gold he had lost when the Indian club went over the side.

Flame's eyes lowered coyly on me. "It just occurred to me, darling, you'll be able to hire and fire people when you're bureau chief. Maybe I ought to ask you for a job."

"Maybe I ought to ask you to marry me."

"Give me a couple of seconds to think it over."

I waited.

THE END

Counterspy Express

By A. S. Fleischman

Chapter One

She was watching me.

A chill draft swept through the unheated room. I clamped my jaws and moved around on the stone floor, trying to keep my feet warm. The room smelled of the wet, cobbled street and the Genoa harbor. I could hear the cries of a tug moving a ship along the channel. Raw afternoon light pressed through the windows, streaked with the winter's grime. It was Wednesday. It was March and this was sunny Italy and I was standing around in cold storage.

I wished the customs men would get started. I didn't like the way the girl was watching me.

I turned and our eyes met. She looked away quickly. I kept watching her and tried to shrug off my suspicions.

There were seven of us waiting in the customs house, passengers off a Spanish freighter returning to Barcelona. I had picked it up two days before in Athens. My instructions were to slip into Italy as quietly as possible, but somewhere between Washington and Athens there could have been a leak.

The girl was traveling alone. I had seen her come aboard, in a rush, half an hour before the ship sailed from Athens. She had drawn the stateroom next to mine, and I had heard her through the thin walls being seasick. She hadn't taken any meals with the rest of us in the officers' saloon. Instead, she had stuck to her cabin and lived on crackers. Hearing her nibbling on them had gotten on my nerves.

A newspaper blew in from the street and rustled around one of the square pillars of the room. Maybe they've put someone on your tail, I thought. Maybe there's been a leak and she's been assigned to you. Maybe she's been watching you for two days.

I stuck a cigarette between my lips and hesitated on the match, glancing at the cluster of 'No Smoking' signs. To hell with them. I lit up.

The girl had taken a paperback novel out of her bag and stood, pretending to read. I rolled the cigarette between my chapped lips and took a good look. She had nice ankles. She wore a black sealskin coat and a toque to match. Her skin was clear and pale, and her eyes had a dark intensity. She wore large, gold earrings. I liked what I saw, but reminded myself that was beside the point.

A truck rumbled to a stop outside the doors and a porter in blue smock and a faded beret began carrying in our luggage. He lined it up on a splintery wooden platform and I spotted my only bag, an old G-4 with bulging canvas sides.

She was looking at it too.

What the hell, I thought. Our eyes met, and this time they held. She closed her book and started toward me. By the time she reached me there was a cigarette between her fingers.

"May I have a light, m'sieu?"

"Do your fingers always shake that way?"

"In customs I am always nervous."

I held up my cigarette and she pressed hers against it. She picked up the light with a sort of raw sensuality and stepped back.

"*Merci.* You are Victor Welles, yes?"

"No," I said. I stared at her. I was Victor Welles, yes, but I was entering Italy under another name. My suspicions crystallized. She had made a disastrous approach and she knew it. Her cheeks reddened and the cigarette twitched as she puffed on it. If she hadn't been seasick she might have checked the name I was traveling under with the purser.

"I'm sorry," she said. Her voice picked up the intensity of her eyes. "I thought you were Victor Welles—the resemblance is striking."

"My name is Jim Cabot."

"Of course—it is my mistake." She might have smiled, but she didn't. Her eyes hung onto me, and I could see her mind racing to repair the damage she had already done. "I thought I had seen you at the Grande Bretagne Hotel in Athens."

"Did you?" I had to admit to myself that was possible. I had been registered there under my own name. I had gotten my new assignment, my new passport and my new name after I checked out.

"I am Alexandrine Duvivier."

"I know," I said. "I checked with the purser."

I didn't think she was French. As I looked at her I thought she could be Rumanian or Hungarian, a bright kid with a talent for languages and a degree from the Moscow Spy School. Her French name and French accent could be phony, and she could be on my tail.

She seemed to get a grip on herself, and tried a smile. "I am a bad sailor. Next time I go by train. I have had nothing to eat but crackers for two days."

"It was a rough trip."

"You will be staying in Genoa long?"

"I haven't decided."

"You know the town, M'sieu Cabot?"

"I get around in it."

"Perhaps you can tell me a good hotel to stay."

She was asking all the right questions, and I felt annoyed. What kind of fool did she take me for? "Try the Bristol Palazzo," I said.

"You will be staying there?" Brightly.

She was incredible. "No," I said.

That's when she got to the point fast. "M'sieu Cabot, I have a confession to make. I have hidden something in your bag."

"*What?*"

"Please—it is some money I did not want to declare. With Americans, they hardly look at your things. But I have a French passport. He will go over every inch of my bag."

I looked past her black, furry shoulder. A customs inspector was walking toward the luggage platform. He scanned the line-up of bags with an expression of bored contempt. He was a little guy in a baggy coat and he needed a shave. After a moment he tapped a suitcase to start with. It wasn't mine, and I turned back to Duvivier.

"Do you always take Americans for granted?"

"I hope you are not too angry."

"Hell yes, I'm angry."

All I needed was trouble with customs. I hadn't even tried bringing a gun in with me. I stared into those dark, nervous eyes of hers. What was she trying to do to me? I ought to break her neck.

I glanced at my bag sitting almost at the inspector's elbow. It was too late to pull her bankroll out of there without attracting attention. I'd better risk leaving it. I had to risk it.

"I will meet you at the Bristol Palazzo," she said.

"I expect to be leaving town."

"Please, it will only take a moment. I felt I could trust you."

"Don't hand me that, baby. I don't like being played for a sucker."

"You don't understand, m'sieu."

"Don't bother to explain."

"I'm sorry, M'sieu Cabot. Perhaps it will be best if we aren't seen too much together here." She stepped on her cigarette and walked away. A moment later she had her book out and was again pretending to read.

I glanced impatiently at the customs inspector pawing through the open suitcase. His hands looked cold, but some sort of professional dignity must have kept him from blowing on them. He wore a heavy ruby ring and it darted like a beacon as he worked. He finally made a chalk mark and glued clearance stamps along one side of the bag, straightened and tapped another suitcase. It wasn't mine. I looked at Duvivier. It wasn't hers. I killed my cigarette.

Maybe I had her wrong, I thought, but maybe I had her right. I stood there, my hands jammed in my overcoat pockets, and tried to dope it out. It could be a gag. A trick. A device to keep a string on me once we left customs. She didn't want to lose me in town. We'd meet at the Bristol Palazzo.

That's nice, I thought. That's lovely. I've picked up a tail. A dark-eyed bitch with a nervous cigarette and me—she must think I'm a Central Intelligence agent with my brains knocked out.

Then I reminded myself it didn't really matter what she thought of me. She wasn't that important. Max Becker was important, but Max was dead. He'd gotten close to something big in Genoa and had asked Washington for me, but just before I'd left Athens he got himself killed. Killed the crazy way, in an automobile accident on the Brenner Pass. And he died in bad company—there were a couple of Italian Communists in the car with him. All I had to do was pick up the pieces. *Imperative you recover loss,* Washington had crackled. *Friend covering until you reach Genoa. Will fill you in. Good luck.*

Duvivier glanced up from her book and I turned away irritably. She had waltzed me into a nice little trap and there was nothing to do now but sweat it out.

The trouble was, I couldn't be sure of her. She might only be involved in a currency smuggling racket. Either way, I wanted no part of her. And I didn't like those big gold earrings.

My feet were ice and I started moving again. How had she sized you up, Vic? *His eyes are hard blue and beginning to bag*—yes, she'd start with my eyes, I thought. *They have seen too much and need sleep. Years of sleep. The nose is undistinguished and seems to shift its profile each time you look at him. Perhaps it has been broken once and well set. The shoulders are good, like an amateur boxer's, and he is tall. The bow tie needs straightening—his taste in clothes is utterly bourgeois: the tie, the gray herring-bone tweed overcoat, the polished black shoes. His lips are thin and self-possessed. The eyes and the lips worry me. It is not a face that smiles easily. He smoked a cigarette despite the signs—typical bourgeois American. But an experienced espionage agent, this Victor Welles, alias Jim Cabot, and I must not underestimate him. I almost gave myself away when I called him by his real name. I must be more careful. I must not lose him.*

The customs man struck another bag with his knuckles, and I turned. It belonged to Duvivier. She closed her book. Her eyes breezed past me with a faint touch of victory as she got out her keys and moved to the platform. What the hell, I thought. Had she been worrying that I would be cleared first and leave her behind?

Either she was worried about losing the money she had planted in my bag, or she was worried about losing me. How much dough? What kind? All I needed was to get tied up in Italian red tape over a chunk of folding money that wasn't mine. Or pinned down on someone else's smuggling rap. I ought to break her neck. I really ought to break her neck.

She had a leather suitcase with a lot of straps. I stuck a cigarette between my lips, left it unlit, and wandered closer to the baggage platform. The inspector finally got all the straps unbuckled and opened the suitcase. I decided I wanted a look inside and I got it. Most of what I saw was lingerie, but as he dug down I caught a glimpse of spare shoes, a couple of skirts, three or four gaudy belts and a black box camera. He took the camera apart. She had hidden nothing inside.

But she was right. The inspector didn't miss a lick. He finished the job by testing the thickness of the leather sides, and she helped him buckle the thing up again. He thumbed on clearance stamps and directed her to a counter at the far end of the room where she could declare her money.

I watched her walk away, her shoulders straight, the sealskin on her back catching the gray afternoon light like satin. Her suitcase told me nothing I hadn't already assumed. She had packed in a hurry because she had left Athens in a hurry. A woman doesn't travel with a single bag if she can help it. She hadn't even brought along a spare hat.

The inspector was tapping my canvas bag, looking up impatiently for the owner.

"Mine," I said, walking over.

"Open it, *signore*."

I found my key and opened it.

"*Grazie*."

I stood back and my palms began to sweat. I'd been a fool for letting myself be maneuvered into a spot like this. Where had she hidden the money? She'd better be right about the easy inspection for Americans. But this guy looked dedicated to his job, and I watched the quick motions of his hands and the flash of the ring as he went through my shirts and socks and underwear.

"Cigarette?"

He stopped and eyed my pack. His spidery fingers withdrew a cigarette and he put it in his pocket. "I save it for later."

Then he went back to my things, and I wondered if I ought to give him the whole pack to put a damned stop to the inspection. He tumbled things around and I kept watching for money to rise up in the explosion of movement. My lips clamped the dry cigarette between them. He was going through my stuff as though he had a score to settle with Americans.

I found myself holding my breath. She'd done a good job of hiding the dough, but this little bastard was tearing my stuff apart. I threw down my pack and it slowed him down. He put it in his pocket without a word and looked up at me.

"*Buonissimo*. Any coffee, sugar—"

"No."

"A radio?"

"No radio. Only what's in my bag."

"How many cigarettes?"

"Just that broken carton."

"*Grazie*." He turned for his glue and stamps, and I got out a fresh pack and closed up my bag. Out of the corner of my eye I saw that Duvivier was leaving the room. The porter, carrying her leather suitcase, led her out the door to a waiting taxi.

The inspector moved on to the next bag and I walked to the end of the room and declared my money and travelers' checks. My passport was given a brief glance, my face compared to the picture on page four, and the visa pages checked for the smudged black entrance stamp put there before I left the freighter. I signed a form and they were through with me.

I felt as though I had been walking a tight rope and finally made it to the end. At least Duvivier had done a good job of hiding the dough. She had planted it so well, I wondered suddenly if it had been in my bag at all.

Her taxi pulled away from the curb and I watched it go.

The idea began to buzz through my head.

The porter picked up my bag and I followed him to the narrow sidewalk. A drizzle had begun to fall. A character stood outside the doors who looked like a money-changer and he was. I got rid of the Greek drachmas I had left and picked up a fistful of soiled lire. The porter put my bag in a taxi, and I gave him a fifty-lire note. He began to protest, but I shut the door on him and told the driver to take me to the Piazza Acquaverde. I had spent too many years in Europe to overtip.

As soon as I was in a taxi, I broke open my bag and began pawing through my stuff. It only took a couple of minutes, and then I was sure. There was no money in my bag.

I closed it up and lit a cigarette. I saw it now, and it made me angry that I hadn't seen it before. I settled back against the cold leather seat and played with the idea. She hadn't planted any dough. She had only tried to put a hook into me. It was a hook. And there was a line on it and she had almost reeled me in.

Well, that was that. There had been a leak, and the Reds had put Duvivier on my tail. I swore and tried to stretch out my legs. This was a hell of a way to start an assignment. I was spotted before I even began. On the other hand, I thought, to hell with her.

I looked at my watch. It was almost five. I didn't have to make contact until eleven-thirty and that gave me a few hours of velvet. Tonight I would eat at Perelli's. How long had it been—two years? I would order a bottle of Orvieto and try not to think about Duvivier cooling her heels in the lobby of the Bristol Palazzo.

We came to the dock gate and a soldier in a heavy green overcoat bent down to look at me through the taxi window. Then he passed us through with a grin and we made a sharp turn up a steep road that connected to the busy Via Milano.

And then I saw her: Duvivier. She was waiting in her taxi at the curb. We had hardly gotten into the stream of traffic before the green and black Fiat began to follow. Anger shot through me and I pulled the cigarette out of my lips. I bent forward and told the driver to swing around to the *Stazione Principe* when we reached the piazza. I glanced behind us. Okay, baby, I thought, now we'll play things my way.

The tires began to hiss against the wet cobbles as we picked up speed. She must have noticed the inspector giving my bag a hell of a fine going over, I decided, and then assumed I had caught on. Now she wasn't even trying to be subtle, but the Russians had too much ego to be subtle. She was on my tail and she meant to stay there. Maybe she thought they'd hang her by her earrings in Red Square if she lost me.

We reached the crest of the hill and came into the Piazza Acquaverde. My taxi swung through the piazza and pulled in behind the others at the station. As I got out I saw Duvivier following at a crawl. I paid my driver and grabbed my bag.

I walked along the arcaded sidewalk, past the station entrance, and into the small *Compagnia Italiana Tourismo* on the far side. Once I dropped Duvivier, I decided, I'd check into the Hotel Columbia-Excelsior across the way, clean up and start feeling human again.

A bleached blonde in a smart blue uniform met me at the counter.

"When is the next train leaving the station?" I asked.

"To where, *signore?*"

"To anywhere."

Her eyes hardened a little, as though to say she'd never catch on to Americans. "In twelve minutes there is a train for Firenze. Perhaps if you hurry—"

"Like mad."

"First class, of course, *signore.*"

"Make it third." If Duvivier took the bait let her sit on a hard wooden seat all the way to Florence, or at least until she got wise.

The blonde passed a ticket across the counter and I paid. I picked up my bag and entered the station proper. I stopped to buy the Paris edition of the *Herald Tribune,* and glanced back to the sidewalk. A porter had picked up Duvivier's suitcase and she was entering the CIT office.

I shrugged and folded the paper under my arm. "*Sessanta lire, signore.*"

I paid and didn't wait for the change. It was a long walk through the underground concourse to the train platforms, and I hoped Duvivier had sense enough to hurry.

I got my ticket checked at the gate and went down a broad flight of stairs. I passed a few offices at the bottom and turned right into the drafty concourse. It was a cold, dimly-lit walk—there seemed to be miles of passage. I finally checked my watch. The train was due to leave in four minutes.

I thought I could hear the click of Duvivier's heels far behind, but I didn't bother to check. I reached daylight and the train sheds. I stopped at the first third-class car I came to and paused on the steps. I glanced back and saw Duvivier just coming out of the concourse with her porter, and she was running.

I hesitated long enough on the steps to make sure she saw me and got up into the vestibule. I went down the aisle and entered the next car, which was a combination first, second and third. I found an empty compartment and tried the window. It opened easily.

I sat down and lit a cigarette. Plenty of time now. Duvivier would get aboard. The thin train whistle came after I'd had four or five puffs. I could hear the clank of metal as the car doors were being shut. I took a couple more puffs and killed the cigarette. The train was beginning to move.

I dropped my bag out the window, climbed over and let myself down to the gravel. Staying in a crouch, I watched the carriages glide by. Even if Duvivier had gotten a window seat and was looking out, she couldn't have seen me.

The last car went by and I stood up. There were still handkerchiefs waving from the raised platform across from me and a couple of Austrians in leather shorts and halters were yelling, "*Auf Wiedersehen,* Zoë!"

I walked back for my bag, got up on the concrete platform, and began thinking about Perelli's. I was going to be hungry and it had been a long time since I had looked at a bottle of Orvieto.

Chapter Two

I left Perelli's at eleven-twenty and hoped my contact would be on time. The sky had cleared, but the streets were still wet and the night air was crisp. I walked out of the dark Vico Falamonica and entered the Piazza de Ferrari, the hub of the city. Then I hoped he wouldn't be on time. I hoped he wouldn't even show up. I'd go back to the bar in Perelli's and pretend I was just another American in Italy.

Night traffic swirled fitfully around the large fountain in the center of the square. BORSA glowed in the darkness from the Bank of Italy building across the way, and on the arcaded sidewalk below a waiter was taking in the wire tables and chairs from the café terrace. Only a couple of customers sat drinking their *cappuccinos* in the chill air.

I lit a cigarette and crossed the cobbles to the broad sidewalk that ringed the fountain pool, an island in the square. I leaned against the massive pool embankment and began to wait. The newspaper was under my right arm, the alternate buttons on my overcoat were undone. He would ask the time and we would exchange a few lines of crazy dialogue. I always felt ridiculous making a contact. Routine precaution. Routine assignment, I thought, routine death. But they pay you for it.

Behind me the fountain waters splashed. I could look down the wide Via Venti Settembre, its theaters and smart shops deserted for the night. I looked at my wrist watch in the glow of my cigarette. If he was going to show, he had three minutes.

I glanced around the piazza. Lights flickered like stars from the hills behind town. A moment later I saw a figure rise from one of the remaining sidewalk tables under the arcade. He paid the waiter and sauntered to the corner. An empty truck shouldered by, filling the piazza with rattling sounds. He waited and I watched. Then he stepped into the street, swinging a cane like a middle-aged boulevardier.

I checked my watch. Less than a minute to eleven-thirty. If that was my man he was going to be on time—to the second.

He was little more than a shadow on the cobbles. I rolled the cigarette between my lips, trying to make him out. He reached the fountain sidewalk and paused for a moment as though undecided which direction to take. Then he came my way.

He stopped suddenly, looking at his wrist watch. He shook it and turned to me with a gesture of annoyance.

"I say, have you the time? Big Ben here is on the blink."

He was a spare figure with a heavy muffler wrapped around his neck. His hat was European with a short brim and his tailored overcoat was partly unbuttoned, like mine.

"It's time for Beany," I answered.

"Look here, I think your watch must be wrong, old chap."

The British accent, I thought, must be just for laughs. "No," I said, shrugging impatiently at the lines they'd written for me in Washington. "My watch is right, but I never learned to read time."

He stepped on his cigarette and his voice changed. "Backward child, eh? Welcome to sunny Italy." He leaned beside me at the rim of the pool. "Am I on time?"

"To the split second."

"I'm a perfectionist. Been in the business a long time. It pays off. Got a gun?"

"No."

"Here." He reached into one of the pockets of his overcoat, and a moment later our hands met. From the feel of the thing I knew it was a Beretta. I put it away.

"Thanks," I said. "Am I going to need it?"

"You can count on that. These boys are mad. Any chance that you've been spotted?"

"I carried a tail all the way from Athens. Female. Put her on a train for Florence. I'm clean."

"Good. I'm to work under you. The word is you're tops."

There seemed to be a trace of resentment in his voice despite the easy camaraderie of his manner. I found myself wondering if I were going to like him. He seemed to me close to fifty, and maybe he felt seniority should have reversed our positions. He'd no doubt been in the game when I was still playing cops and robbers with rubber guns.

"Want to go somewhere to talk?"

"We can't be overheard here. The square's deserted. We're safe enough, unless you didn't shake that tail the way you said."

"I shook her," I replied. "Let's get on with it."

"Want to take notes?"

"I'll remember."

He shrugged his narrow shoulders as though to suggest a man was a fool to trust to memory, and then contradicted the gesture with a smile. "It's going to be fine working with you. Call me Jackson."

I wished he'd stop trying to flatter me. "Cabot," I said.

He nodded, and got a small notebook into his gloved hands. "Did Washington tell you what Max was working on when he got killed up north?"

"No. You're supposed to fill me in."

"You knew him, didn't you, Cabot?"

"We worked together once in Rome. I haven't seen him in a couple of years."

"Too bad he had to get killed that way."

"One way's as good as another."

"Check. But it's tough to see your friends go."

"We weren't friends."

He chuckled. "I see."

"You don't see. Let's not stand here all night."

"Check." He straightened the ends of the muffler inside his overcoat, even though they were already faultlessly in place. His tan shoes were ripe with polish; he must spend an hour a day on them, I thought. The hat was set at a precise and jaunty angle and he wore gloves. I wondered how many total hours he had spent fussing with his wardrobe for this rendezvous, as though I had to be impressed—and as if it mattered. There was a heavy scent of licorice on his breath. He'd been drinking anisette.

The light was bad but I could see a mobile face that shifted expressions as he spoke, like a silent accompaniment. It would be exhausting to spend an evening watching that face, I decided. I would try to avoid it.

"We'll start with Evgeni Borsilov," he said. "Does that name mean anything to you?"

I shook my head.

"Crusty old Russian who got himself smuggled out of Russia before they could purge him. One of their big atomic brains. He's got a head full of beautiful secrets, and he's running around loose somewhere in Europe. Washington wants to pick his brains before the Russians blow them out. All we've got to do—you and I—is find him. Preferably before the MVD gets to him."

"Any leads?"

"I've done some legwork," he said, his face tightening, "...while waiting for you to get here."

I glanced at his polished shoes. "Good."

"It's pretty certain Borsilov was here in Genoa—maybe about ten days ago. It's even possible that Max had him on ice. What happened next is anyone's guess."

"What's yours?"

A trace of pomposity crept into his voice. "I'd say Borsilov and Max got parted somehow. The Russian went north and Max went after him. And that's when the accident happened. Tough break." There was a flutter of resentment in his voice, as though it had been poor sportsmanship for Max to get himself killed and leave us holding the bag. "Of course, we can go on the assumption that Borsilov is in central or northern Europe. That's a beginning, Cabot."

I clamped my jaws. All this was conjecture and no legwork. You could sit at a bar drinking anisette and dream up theories like this by the hour. "What about the two Italian Reds in the car with Max when the accident happened? I doubt if he'd go chasing after Borsilov with that kind of company."

"You're right, of course, Cabot." A horse and carriage entered the square, the hooves clacking through the still, cold night. "We can assume they muscled their way along. They got what they deserved. All dead—the three of them." I didn't say it, but I thought it: *You've got it too pat, mister.* Max wouldn't have led them to Borsilov, even with a gun in his back. "Did you go up to the Brenner Pass and have a look at the car?"

He shook his head with a smile. "No need of that. Waste effort. I have friends with the *polizia* and got a full report. Anyway, Cabot, the car was a complete wreck. Went over an embankment. You know those Alpine roads."

"Max may have tried to conceal some information for us—"

"Look, Cabot, the Russians are gunning for Borsilov and they're also gunning for anyone interested in Borsilov. This town is loaded with Soviet agents. Don't you see, if I went nosing around that wreck up north it would tip our hand. We've got to play this one close to our chest."

I let it pass. Spray from the fountain behind us brushed my neck in a gust of wind. "What else have you?"

He thumbed through his black book. "Here are the names and addresses of the two Commies in the car with him."

He had a pencil flashlight with the bulb painted red to cut the glow. He read off the names. Both men had Genoa addresses.

"Who was the car registered to?" I asked.

"A woman. She's a singer at the Florentine Club, just off the Via Venti Settembre. Not far from here. She claims the car was stolen."

"What's her name?"

"Pia Brindisi."

"Are you satisfied she was telling the truth?"

He shrugged, and his face gave me a yes-and-no answer. I doubted that he'd even bothered to talk to her. Maybe he was afraid that would tip his hand too. I was sure now he'd done nothing more than read the police report on the accident.

"About the car," he went on, glancing at notes in his book. "There was a fourth passenger. The only survivor—identity and whereabouts unknown at present. I suggest we work on that angle. Passenger X. I think that's our real lead."

He watched for some sign of approval, but I didn't respond.

"Male or female?"

"Male."

"What's the evidence?"

"One of the ash trays in the back seat was jammed with cigarette butts—Baltos."

"French brand."

"Yes. The two Reds we know about carried Italian cigarettes. Max didn't smoke. Passenger X smoked French cigarettes. No lipstick on the butts. Ergo, Passenger X is male."

"That's all?"

"That's all."

"Where did Max stay in Genoa?"

"He rented an apartment on the Via Garibaldi. One of those old reconverted *palazzo's*—very chi-chi and expensive. Number 29."

"Did you go over his stuff?"

Exasperation hastened his answer. What kind of punk was I? Couldn't I get the situation through my skull? "Look, Cabot, you're *finished* the moment you put your foot in the door." He italicized the word with a gesture. "The Reds have the place staked out. They're just waiting— just waiting for someone like you or me to show up."

"My God!" I snapped. "You mean you've let his stuff sit up there all this time without taking a look? What the hell's wrong with you?"

"Take it easy, Cabot. I've been in this business a long time. We'll get our man Borsilov. I've got plenty of ideas. Look—"

"Sure, sure, you've got plenty of ideas." I pushed myself away from the embankment and tried to hold my temper in. It wouldn't do any good to tell him off. There was nothing wrong with Jackson except that he was too damned scared to do his job.

He did the little things with an iron discipline, but he hadn't gone up north to look over the wreck, or talked to Pia Brindisi or examined Max's apartment. He was afraid to tip his hand. Afraid. He was afraid of getting killed. He'd been worried that I might have been followed and would contaminate him.

"Is there anything else?" I said. I lit a cigarette and threw the match in the pool.

"Look, Cabot, you mustn't think—look, I've got a lifetime of experience at this work."

"Sure." I wanted to feel sorry for him, but I couldn't. He should have gotten out of espionage when the stuffings came out of him, but instead he was bluffing and blundering his way along. And I hated him for it.

He got away from the embankment and faced me. "You want me to do the legwork on this Passenger X angle? Say the word and I'll get right on it."

"Don't do anything," I said. "Just go to your hotel and stay there until I get in touch with you."

He disregarded my anger with a smile. "We're in this together, Cabot. Don't forget that."

"Beat it."

I'd work alone. This guy was too damned anxious to get on that missing passenger, if there was one. It could be something he dreamed up, an excuse for some waste motion, nice and safe. The trouble was I couldn't be sure. I'd have to check. Why hadn't the CIA put this guy out to pasture long ago? Didn't they know?

"Look, what do you say I come by here at midnight tomorrow?" he said in an aggressive tone. "You're angry now, but you'll cool off tomorrow when you've had time to think over the facts. Get some sleep. You'll find I'm a good man to work with."

A taxi began swerving toward the fountain. Instinct warned me before I really saw what was going to happen. It appeared too suddenly and it was going too fast.

"Get down!"

The quick burst of fire cut my words in two. I flattened against the sidewalk as jets of flame leaped from the taxi window. For a flashing second it lit up the side of the car. The tires screeched and the taxi careened around the fountain and off in the direction of the cathedral. Long after the shooting died the echo rattled around the walls of the piazza.

"Cabot—"

The rest of it was choked off. I heard a scraping thud beside me, and then he began to cough as though there was no wind in his lungs. I lifted my face from the wet sidewalk and turned my head. I few inches from my eyes, his fingernails grated against the sidewalk as if searching for a hold.

"Hit bad?" I whispered hoarsely. I got over to him.

"...bad."

In the distance a police whistle began to shrill.

"I'll give you a hand."

"No. Run. My number's been up... a long time. Let me alone."

"Here—"

"Get going." He seemed almost relieved that the long waiting was over. "Italian cops... tie you up in red tape."

And then he gave up trying to cough. I could hear excited voices from the edges of the square, and the police whistle screamed. I knew he was right. I'd feel like a bastard running out on him now, but there was no choice. He'd be rushed to a hospital without me. Or the morgue. I saw the black book on the sidewalk where it had fallen from his hand and I snapped it up.

I touched his shoulder. He'd been afraid I might have been followed, but it looked like someone had been on his tail. That gunman had meant to get both of us.

"Cabot..."

"Yes?"

I could see figures coming my way from the cafe terrace and the bus stop in front of the dark columns of the opera house.

"Don't get... mixed up with a woman. My mistake..."

"Sure."

I left him lying there and hurried into the street. A bus swung in from the Via Felice. Its headlights spread over me like a searchlight. I kept running.

There were two police whistles, then three. I heard the sharp thud of boots on the cobbles behind me.

"*Fermate!*"

I didn't stop and a shot broke the night air. I reached the sidewalk and raced down the narrow Via San Matteo, its cluttered shops closed and black.

I kept running.

Chapter Three

I sat until past one in the New York Bar near the harbor. A vintage juke box against the back wall played American records. The waiter spoke Berlitz English, and all you needed to think you were back in the States was a load on. The bar was empty except for a bleached blonde with a heavy Latin face, who sat perched on a stool like a piece of bad statuary. She had lifted her skirt around her knees when I walked in, but I let them get cold and she had pulled the skirt back in place.

I thumbed through Jackson's little black book again. The perfectionist had kept windy notes and I was glad the book hadn't fallen into the hands of the *carabinieri*. I would destroy it; digest it and get rid of it.

I remembered him lying there in his own dark blood, his immaculate fingernails scraping the sidewalk. I tried to wash away the picture with a mouthful of brandy. You fall in love and you no longer want to take the risks. Was that what he was trying to tell me? I shrugged off the idea. The pitiful bastard. He was probably dead now. And he'd been my only contact in Europe. Well, that left me on my own.

His notes were full of theories, each once contradicted by a fresh notion on the next page. He was a bear for question marks. Only one of them meant anything to me, because it got under my skin. He asked himself if Max might have been a double agent, drawing his pay both from Washington and Moscow. *"How else explain,"* he wrote, *"two Red in the car??????"* Six question marks. Count them. Six.

I snapped the book shut and damned the man under my breath. I had worked with Max for over a year. I had never warmed up to the guy, but I trusted him. I remembered the tall, lanky figure and the easy, New Orleans smile. Max was sharp and ambitious and he'd been around. But he wouldn't have sold out to the Russians for all the oil in Louisiana.

Max had liked me. He liked working with me and he liked doing things for me. He'd asked Washington for my help. If I hadn't warmed up to him my reason was personal. He was an intellectual machine; the kind of guy who could figure out a chess game from the first move. I had never thought of him as being entirely human. But he was a hell of a good agent.

I put the book away and finished my drink. Double agent. I bristled at the idea, because I couldn't overlook it now. Double agents happen. I hated Jackson for planting the thought in my head. Any agent could turn sour. Even Max. Even me. I knew I wouldn't be able to rid my mind of Jackson's six question marks until I discovered what two Reds were doing in the accident car with Max. Still, I resented the theory because it was insidious and treacherous. I reminded myself that the important job was to find Borsilov. Before his own people got their hands on him.

I caught the bartender's eye and nodded. He refilled my glass and I paid up. I swallowed the brandy while he got my change. I would look up the singer, Pia Brindisi, I decided. She might have been lying to the police about her car. Max's apartment could wait. If the Reds had the place under surveillance they would already have taken a crack at his belongings. Chances weren't good that they had missed anything, but eventually I'd have to check it out. Pia. I liked the name.

I left a tip and walked into the toilet. I ripped the pages out of the book, tore them up and flushed them into the Genoa sewer. I started on the cover and stopped abruptly. Jackson had hidden something inside the lining, and I had almost ripped it in two. I removed it gingerly. *G. Barabino & Figlio, Via Ravecca 83.* It was a pawnticket.

I thought about it for a moment and put it away in my billfold. Then I got rid of the rest of the book. When I came back into the bar the blonde decided to give me a second chance. She hitched the skirt above her knees again.

"Buona sera, signore. You are alone?"

I nodded and followed the headwaiter through the crowded room to a table near the bandstand. The Florentine Club was small but brassy and full of tourists. A colored jazz band had the dance floor jammed, and long-legged cigarette girls in black mesh stockings strolled between the tables. The place had the contrived atmosphere of a plush speakeasy, and the girls made you feel naked.

"When is the next show?"

"Only a few minutes, *signore.* Sit down—enjoy yourself."

The few minutes dragged out to half-an-hour. I drank Courvoisier and tried to forget my impatience. The pawn-ticket would have to wait until the place opened tomorrow. And it would be no use trying to talk to Pia Brindisi before she went on. She'd be in a hurry and brush me off. I'd have to wait.

The show finally broke with a fanfare. A dance team did the tarantella. There was a female ventriloquist with a Lesbian haircut whose dummy told off-color jokes in Italian. A gypsy did a strip tease. There were a couple of other acts jammed into about twenty minutes of show, but no Pia Brindisi.

Twenty-year-old jazz filled the floor with tourists and I called a waiter.

"Pia Brindisi singing here anymore?"

"Not for two days, *signore.* It is a pity, yes? Ah, that one had style. I, personally, am very sorry she is no longer with us."

"She quit, then?"

"Ah, no. It is quite mysterious. She was dismissed. Imagine, *signore,* such a rare talent. I, personally, was in love with her."

"How long had she been working here?"

"More than a year, *signore.*"

"And suddenly fired."'

"Exactly so."

"Have you any idea where she lives?"

"Me?" He shrugged briskly. "I do not know these things, *signore.* Perhaps if you talk to the *ufficio*—you are a friend of the *signorina?*"

"I, personally, am in love with her," I said. *"Favorisca, il conto."*

He nodded and added up my bill. I covered it with a good tip. "Where is the manager's office?"

He pointed to a door on the far side of the bandstand, and picked up the money. "*Grazie, signore.*"

"*Prego.*"

I cut across the dance floor and decided my first suspicions about Pia Brindisi were paying off. I knocked at the door marked *Privato*. A few days after Max got killed in her car, she got canned from her job after having worked a year. It looked like a connection. I wondered how many question marks that would have rated in Jackson's little black book.

"*Avanti.*"

I opened the door and walked in. It was a long, narrow room with stone walls. There was no heat in the room, and it was like stepping into a different world. When I shut the door behind me the noises of the club vanished. The room ended in a Gothic arch with a small, high window, and a tall man sat there behind a massive antique desk.

I walked toward him on the uncarpeted floor and my heels echoed against the walls. There was a towel around his neck and shoulders, and a barber was shaving him with a straight razor. There was a black leather neck brace on the desk, and nearby stood a small, filled glass of creme de menthe. The overhead light turned it into a green glow. Like his eyes, I thought.

My glance swept across the name plate on the desk—MAGGIORE C. RICASOLI. Aside from the one he sat on there were no chairs. You had to stand before Major Ricasoli.

I nodded.

The little barber didn't interrupt himself and the major watched each flight of the straight razor in a hand mirror. His eyes, deep in a square, strong face, checked me over when the barber paused to wipe his razor.

"If I can be of service, *signore*." His neck remained rigid as he spoke, and I glanced at the leather brace on the desk. It looked polished with wear, and I wondered if he'd broken his neck during the war.

"You can," I said.

"You think you have been overcharged? *Maledetto!* Always you Americans think you have been overcharged."

"It hadn't occurred to me to check my bill," I said. "Maybe I should have."

He took his eyes off the hand mirror and looked me over a second time. He laughed. "One gets weary of the same complaint, eh? It is better to strike first. Well?"

I decided to make an oblique approach. "I'm throwing a party in Rapallo. I'd like to raid some of your floor-show talent."

He said nothing, his eyes returning to the mirror. "Your gypsy stripper, for one," I said.

"I'm not a booking agent, *signore*. If you need talent there are men who make a business of supplying it."

"I want your gypsy."

"I'm sorry, *signore*. I know about these parties you Americans throw. You will keep my gypsy drunk for a week. No. I will keep her here."

I hoped he was sufficiently misdirected. "That's final?"

"You can see I am busy, *signore*."

"What about that girl you had singing for you? The last time I dropped in here she stopped the show. I might be able to use her. Is she still in town?"

His eyes slid off the mirror and stared at me, green catlike eyes. For a moment there was only the scraping of the razor over his skin. "Pia Brindisi is no longer working for me."

"You must have been crazy to let her go. She has class."

"I do not recommend her, *signore*."

"I'll take a chance on her. Do you know if she's working around Genoa anywhere?"

The barber finished with the razor and began massaging the full, hard face. There was nothing to do but wait. I wondered if I was being at all convincing. I wanted more than Pia Brindisi's address; I wanted a line on why he'd fired her, but he didn't look that talkative. I lit a cigarette and let my eyes wander around the room. There was nothing but stone walls, the desk and Major Ricasoli.

The waste basket stopped my eye. Some sort of stringed musical instrument, maybe a lute, smashed and in pieces, lay there as so much junk. It made me think that this cold potato had a hot temper, but I couldn't envision Major Ricasoli at a music rack. He'd beaten hell out of that instrument. A lute? Maybe it had come with the antique desk.

"Is there anything else, *signore*?"

The barber was snapping the towel to dry the perfumed astringent he had rubbed into the major's skin. My interview was clearly over, but I wasn't ready to go.

"Pia Brindisi," I said. "What's the last address you have for her?"

"She will not want to perform at your party."

"Do you do her thinking for her?"

He picked up the creme de menthe and began to sip it, as though it had been waiting on the desk as a reward for going through the torture of being shaved. "There are many other performers at liberty, *signore*. I cannot understand your interest in acts of mine."

"Class acts are hard to find—you know that. If Pia Brindisi doesn't want to take me up, that's her business. You must have her last address, for God's sake. What are you trying to hand me?"

The barber fitted the leather brace around Major Ricasoli's neck and began lacing it up in back.

"She is at Via Garibaldi 29," he said with sudden indifference.

I stepped on my cigarette to cover my surprise. Max's address! "Thanks."

"One moment, *signore*."

The little barber had packed up his instruments and nodded to the major without smiling. When the barber had closed the door after him, the green eyes steadied on me.

"The truth is, *signore*, I'm trying only to do you a favor. I dismissed *Signorina* Brindisi only two days ago. It was very difficult—she had a big following here at the Florentine Club."

"I'm not surprised."

"I received word that the *signorina* is a Communist. It is a principle with me. I fired her at once."

"I see."

"The Communists are everywhere in Italy—but there are none working at the Florentine Club." For the first time I saw a suggestion of emotion in that refrigerated face. "They are pigs—even the beautiful ones. *Maledetto!* I know them! I fought side by side with them in the *partigiani*. I—"

"Are you positive about her?"

"My information is accurate." He stared at me, his head resting on the brace, like a man waiting for his photograph to be taken. "I do not believe, *signore*, you would wish to take home to Rapallo one of the *comunista* pigs."

I nodded. "Thanks for the tip."

"Ah, in your ear they whisper *pace, pace*—behind your back they make war. I have had enough of war, *signore*."

It seemed to me he was protesting too much. There was a suggestion of the unreconstructed fascist about him, and I wondered if he'd really fought with the partisans. "It looks like I struck out twice," I said. "*Grazie*."

"*Prego, signore*."

I walked back across the cold floor, and I could feel his eyes on my

back. I wondered if he were really an ex-major. I didn't even feel sure he
was an Italian. Whatever he was, he seemed a weird character to be running a tourist trap.

Before I reached the door a rapid knocking struck and echoed through
the room.

"*Avanti.*" His voice was loud and impatient.

The door opened as my hand touched the knob, and a woman swept
past me. I saw black. The black sealskin coat. My eyes took in a nice pair
of legs and the flash of large earrings. It was Alexandrine Duvivier.

She had breezed past me into the room before recognition struck her.
She stopped and turned and caught her breath. Her dark eyes were startled and disbelieving. What was *I* doing here?

I didn't hang around to give her any answers. I went through the door
and shut it after me.

I got out fast, not stopping for my hat and coat. I hopped into a taxi.
As we pulled away I looked back and saw two men hurrying out of the
club entrance. One of them, thick and short in a black leather coat,
pointed toward my taxi. Major Ricasoli hadn't lost any time getting a
couple of his muscle men on me. Before we turned the corner I saw them
pile into a cab.

He would send someone later for Pia Brindisi, I thought—or go himself. I hadn't done her any good opening my mouth, but I was going to
get to her first. Whatever he fired her for, I thought, it wasn't because
he had no use for Reds. Max's address—Pia Brindisi's address. It was a
connection and it might lead me to a headful of Russian science: Evgeni
Borsilov.

I glanced behind and saw the pair of headlights bearing down. We
turned right along the darkened hulk of the opera house. I knew it was-
n't far to the Via Garibaldi and got out a couple of thousand lire notes.
Jackson had said Max's place was staked out, and I wondered if I could
get to Pia Brindisi without picking up a Soviet agent. Hell, I'd face that
when I came to it.

I saw that the taxi door hinged beside the front seat. I leaned forward
and told the driver not to stop when he got to Number 29.

"Slow down at the turn and I'll jump," I said. "Here's your money.
Once I'm gone, take off. There's another car on your tail. Try to lose it.
Do you understand?"

He examined the money under the dash light as he drove. He turned
his face and nodded silently. He'd do a lot more than that for two thousand lire. I opened the door as we crossed a small piazza, and he began
the sweep onto Via Garibaldi.

The street was badly lit and black shadows fell against the old *palazzos* that lined it. I got my feet on the running board and when the taxi straightened out I pushed the door all the way open.

"*Grazie!*"

I dropped off and the driver accelerated. My feet hit stone and I rolled on the wet cobbles. The jerk of the car slammed the door after me. I sprang up and headed across the sidewalk and into the nearest doorway. I watched the taillight fly through the darkness. The other car squealed at the corner and I watched it flash by.

I stood for a moment catching my breath. Then I got out the Beretta and checked it over. Loaded. I slipped it under my belt and snapped up the collar of my jacket against the cold. The street lay silent again. I looked up at the door number and figured out that the place I wanted was down a few doors on the other side of the street.

If Major Ricasoli had a man anywhere, I decided, he would be inside the building. It would be impossible to keep track of the goings and comings of an apartment house from the street. Inside. The concierge, maybe. I decided to act on that theory if I saw trouble.

The great façades of old palaces lined both sides of the street. I walked along, past high walls studded with cheval-de-frise and dour buildings from other centuries. I stopped and watched the doorway of Number 29. There was no one around. I crossed.

I paused at the massive wooden doors, weathered and tall, as though they had been built for a race of giants. I turned the handful of knob... locked for the night. I found the metal knocker and pounded for the concierge. The great doors boomed like a drum, breaking the silence like thunder. I waited. I tried again.

It was a long time before I heard anyone on the other side of the doors. They opened with a crack of light. A thin, gray-haired Italian appeared, his eyes heavy with sleep.

"*Che cosa desidera Lei?*"

"Let me in," I said. I decided to risk my guess. "Major Ricasoli sent me to—"

"*Sì...*"

He opened the door as though I had used an incantation. The concierge may not be out of Moscow, I thought, but at least the major had put him on the payroll. He was already set up to report anyone who might show an interest in Max's apartment.

He closed the door after me. He had turned on a light in the entry and it splashed out into an open courtyard overgrown with vines. Statuary long at rest looked like objects sketched in charcoal.

"Which apartment is Pia Brindisi's?"

He pointed to a marble stairway on my right. "Upstairs. Number Six, at the front."

"If anyone else knocks," I said, "ignore it. Don't let anyone in until we go. Is that clear?"

"The *signorina* is in trouble too?"

"She's in trouble. Go back to bed."

He turned away, and I sensed he was losing sleep over what was going on in the apartment house. Maybe he was thinking he should never have gotten himself involved with Major Ricasoli. These things he didn't understand, but now he had to do what he was told. He went through a small open door and shut it silently.

I took the stairway by twos. A dim night light burned in the hall and I hurried along. One of these doors might have been Max's, I thought. I wondered if there'd be time to go through his stuff. If he'd known he was taking an outside risk before he left, he might have tried to stow some information.

I found Pia Brindisi's door and knocked. She'd be in bed, I thought—I knocked harder.

I heard a shuffling inside the room and the murmur of voices. A man began to swear excitedly in Italian. And then a woman quieted him angrily.

I waited and she finally spoke to me from the other side of the door. "I'm drunk," she announced. "Beautifully, beautifully drunk. Please go away."

I pounded on the door. "Open up!"

She laughed, and I heard her walk away. Then the man laughed.

I stood there feeling like a fool.

But I had to find Borsilov. Drunk or sober, Pia Brindisi shaped up as a lead.

Chapter Four

I got a skeleton key from the concierge, turned it in the lock and swung the door open. They had left all the lights burning in the living room. It was a big room with a gilt ceiling and terrazzo floor. The walls were lined with old, plum-colored silk. Maybe Lorenzo the Magnificent had slept in the joint once, I thought. Pia Brindisi must have pulled down a good salary from the Florentine Club to afford this lashup. I looked around at the wild litter of Cinzano bottles and cigarette butts.

The bedroom door was shut. I crossed the polished floor and threw the door open. The living room light fell across the bed. Pia Brindisi lay on her stomach. She didn't stir; she must have passed out. All I could see was her short titian hair on the pillow. The man beside her in the canopied bed was a dark Latin type, and he began to blink his eyes in the sudden light.

"*Per Dio!*" he whispered, crossing himself as he lay there. "She has a husband."

I walked over to him, the gun in my hand.

"Get out."

"*Sì*—I only—"

"Fast."

"*Subito, signore.*"

A pickup, I thought. How long has she been drinking—a week? The apartment reeked of vermouth. Valentino tumbled out of bed and picked up his shirt and trousers from a chair.

"Put the gun away—see, I am hurrying."

I ignored him and checked the street from a window. There was no sign of Major Ricasoli yet, but it still worried me. I lit a cigarette and turned.

"What's your name?"

"Piero, *signore*. I am innocent. She said she was afraid to stay alone—so I come here." He left his shirt unbuttoned and put on his hat.

"Just a dull evening."

"She paid me 5000 lire—but I will give it back. *Sì*. I meant no harm. She wouldn't let me touch her."

"Keep the dough—just get out."

"Already done, *signore*." He started for the door in his bare feet.

"Your shoes."

He stopped and turned. "*Sì*."

"Put them on when you get home."

"*Buonissimo.*" He picked them up, half expecting my gun to go off in his back. His wrists were running with sweat. He was big and slick-haired and scared stiff. His type grew on street corners. Well, he was Pia Brindisi's business, I thought, and it was nothing to me.

"I apologize, *signore*," he said at the door. "Sincerely, I—"

"Get out."

When he was gone I returned to the bed. Pia Brindisi was out cold. I grabbed her shoulder and shook. She roused slightly, but not enough to matter. I pulled her over on her back.

"Come on, baby. Snap out of it."

I switched on the table lamp, wondering if I were wasting my time. I really saw her then for the first time, and for a moment all I could do was look at her.

Even with vermouth strong on her breath, there was a deep loveliness and intelligence in Pia Brindisi's face. Her skin was clear and very pale and fresh-looking. Long, dark lashes closed her eyes. Her nose was fine with a small mole at one side of the bridge. Her red lips were slightly apart, calm and reposed. Maybe she needed Cinzano and Piero for that, I thought.

Hell, she couldn't have been more than 22.

I was sorry I had had to find her this way. She didn't look the type, and I felt suddenly indecent breaking in.

I slapped her cheeks a couple of times, but I saw that she wasn't coming around. I went into the kitchen, ground some coffee beans and got a pot going. I found a silver soup tureen and filled it with cold water. I checked the street again from the window, but saw no one. I hoped I was wrong. I hoped that Major Ricasoli wasn't interested in this kid. But I swore at her for being stiff when I had to talk to her, and I felt nervous at the delay. I had to get her out of here.

I found a towel and carried the tureen into the bedroom. I splashed the calmness and repose off her lips. Her breath caught and her eyelashes fought the water.

"Get up," I snapped.

I pulled the wet quilt down, hoping she hadn't gone to bed in her fine Italian skin. I got hold of her ankles and swung them around. She had gone to bed in some smoky silk that piled up around the slim oval of her hips and evaporated into lace at the fullness of her exquisite breasts. She had the pale skin of the north and she was taller than I'd expected. Her feet touched the floor and she raised herself to her elbows and blinked at me in pure amazement.

"How dare you—" She stopped. Her voice was soft, her Italian pure. "Who—you're not—"

I waited, but she couldn't remember his name.

"I'm not Piero," I said.

"No?"

"No."

Then she turned phony, as though she didn't want to be herself. "Truly, *signore?*"

"Truly."

She lay back, thinking it over hazily. "*Buonissimo,*" she smiled. "I didn't like Piero. He smelled of olive oil."

"Get up."

She had a throaty laugh and she used it. Something was funny. Something was very funny, but I didn't bother to find out what it was. I caught her wrists again and pulled her to a sitting position on the edge of the bed. The laughter vanished and she closed her eyes, as if the throbbing in her head had just begun. Then she tried to get me in focus. She stared. She blinked and she began to smile again. What a beautiful kid, I thought, and what a mess I had walked into.

"You're not very handsome," she said, cocking her head and running a hand through her wet hair. "Whoever you are, you're not very handsome."

"Here, dry your face."

She took the towel and buried her head in it. Then she began to rub it slowly through her hair.

"How soon can you get sober?" I asked.

She looked up from the towel, and the alcoholic caprice left her manner. "Get out," she said crisply. "I'm tired of you already. Get out."

"Get dressed."

"*Madonna mia*, leave me alone."

"Start moving, baby. I've got some coffee working."

"I despise coffee."

"I want to talk to you. I don't think this is a good place to talk. Sober up."

"I don't want to sober up."

I slapped her and it stopped the merry-go-round. I had an impulse to walk out, but I couldn't walk out. She felt her face and it must have stung. Or maybe she'd never been struck before. She got to her feet and I left her standing. I felt like a punk, but I didn't let it worry me. She was beautiful, but she was going to be a pain in the neck. I went into the kitchen. The coffee wasn't strong enough to do much good, but it would help and I didn't want to wait any longer.

When I brought it into the bedroom, she was standing in front of the bed the way I'd left her, except that she had a stiletto in her hand. She was exquisite, but she was Latin and she might be dangerous with a knife.

"Who sent you?" she whispered.

"You're sobering up fast. Put it away. No one sent me."

"Don't think you can fool me, *signore*." Her legs were unsteady and it could only have been colossal determination that kept her upright at all. The bed light behind her poured through the silk gown, defining her long, fine legs. She was stacked, but I tried not to give a damn.

"What do you think you're going to do with the knife? Sharpen a pencil?"

"I told you to get out."

"We're leaving together. Who are you afraid of, baby? Major Ricasoli?"

"He sent you, didn't he?"

She was scared. Plenty scared. "No one sent me," I said. "Get it through your head. Does the major have any reason to kill you?"

"Ask him."

I set down the coffee and walked toward her. "If we hang around here long enough maybe I'll have the chance. I thought I told you to put away that knife."

"If you take another step I will kill you!" She spat it out and she meant it.

I stopped. "I hope you're sober enough to understand," I said, "I don't really give a damn what happens to you, baby, but it will have to happen after I'm through with you. Major Ricasoli may be on his way over now. Or maybe he'll just send over one of his punks. Now either put on some clothes or you'll come as you are."

There was a loud squeak of tire at the curb below and even she heard it. I went for the window. I looked down and a moment later a man stepped out of a dark Alfa Romeo. There was no mistaking the stiffness of his movements, the neck in a brace. I motioned Pia Brindisi toward the window. "There he is—in person."

She stared at me, confusion in her eyes. Maybe she thought I was only trying to trick her, but an inner fear overwhelmed her.

"Get away from the window!"

I stepped away and watched her advance. She looked down and I saw a tremor go through her.

I lashed out for her wrist and knocked the stiletto out of her hand. It dropped to the floor and I snapped it up. I heaved it upward and it stuck in the ceiling with a thud. She hardly realized what had happened. "He won't be able to get in the door," I said. "Is there a back way out?"

"Yes." She was fighting now for her senses. She knew she had to get out of there, and she forgot about me. She opened a closet and tore down a suit. She started to strip off the nightgown, and then she remembered I was standing there. She hesitated for only a second, and pulled the thing off. I turned. I went back to the window. I saw Major Ricasoli below at the door. Well, the concierge wouldn't answer his knock.

But what I saw then I didn't want to believe. The door opened for the Italian at his touch. It was crazy. He didn't even have to knock.

That bastard Piero, I thought suddenly. He'd lit out in such a hurry he hadn't bothered to shut the street doors after him.

I turned back to Pia, already in a slip and zipping up the skirt of a beige suit. "Time's against us," I snapped. "Is Max's apartment close by?"

She looked up. I think she was ready to deny knowing him, but there wasn't time for her to think it out. "Next door... is his."

"You have a key."

She stepped into shoes, and I could trace the doubts racing through her head. But she nodded. "In the drawer of the bed table."

I walked over and got it. I glanced at her and wondered if Max had been playing around with Pia Brindisi. Well, that was Max's business, and Max was dead.

"Connecting door?"

"Yes..." She pointed through the living room to a far door. She buttoned her jacket over her slip, took down a coat and snapped up a cashmere sweater she hadn't taken time to put on.

"Let's go," I said.

I picked up the pot of hot coffee and emptied it in the sink. I'd just as soon Major Ricasoli think she was out and had been out for hours. We crossed the living room and I saw a half-filled bottle of Cinzano sitting on a wire recording machine. I could have used a drink.

"Why the machine?" I said quickly, turning the key in the connecting door.

"To improve my style. I can hear my faults. It was a gift."

"From Max?"

"Yes... from Max."

We could hear footsteps in the hall. We moved into the darkness of Max's apartment and I locked the connecting door. I would want to talk to Major Ricasoli, but not now and not here. Not until I was ready. I needed more to go on and a session with Pia might give it to me. I was certain of one thing—Borsilov was still loose somewhere in Europe. Major Ricasoli wouldn't have reacted to me, once Duvivier walked into his office, if Borsilov was a dead issue.

We had hardly collected ourselves within Max's apartment when the place flooded with light. I heard Pia's voice catch.

We looked across the room to the concierge with an old army revolver in his gnarled fist. He wore a knee-length serge coat with the crossed keys of his station in the lapels.

"*Non s'incomodi!*" he ordered bitterly. "It will pain me to shoot, *signore.*"

From the hall there was the sound of Major Ricasoli tapping at Pia's door.

Chapter Five

The concierge walked slowly away from the light switch. He had stiff gray hair and a heavy, sculptured nose. The gun looked like something that hadn't been cleaned since the war. But it was a gun and it was probably loaded and I stood still in the face of it.

"You get around," I muttered quickly, keeping my voice low. "I suppose you were glued to the keyhole. Hell, if I'd known I had an audience I'd have put on a better show."

"You did well enough, *signore*. I'm tired of the *maggiore* and his friends such as you. I'm through—you can tell him that."

Pia's expressive eyes flicked up to me. Fear was sobering her fast. Maybe she hadn't been as drunk as she'd wanted to be, but now a fresh suspicion caught her. Anger spread over her face. "You—"

"No."

"Ricasoli did send you!"

"The concierge's got it wrong. I lied to get in the building."

"*Signorina*—over by me," the concierge snapped. "I will call the police for this creature of a man. These things I do not understand—but you I know are good, *signorina*. The police will know what to do."

"Listen," I whispered firmly, "and listen fast—"

But I didn't go on with it. Pia walked away from me, going quietly toward him, looking very thankful for his help. "You're a good man, Vito. But perhaps this time—"

"Pia!" I muttered.

She grabbed viciously for his gun and I leaped. He was astonished and tried to draw back from her. Somewhere in the back of my mind I registered the click of a door opening. Major Ricasoli next door. I got hold of the concierge's gun and Pia slipped aside as though she were ready to collapse.

His fingers wouldn't give up the weapon. I felt for my own gun, spun to one side of him and let him have the butt. I struck on the side of the head and hoped I wouldn't give him anything more serious than a headache. I hated to do it, he deserved a better break, but there was no time to argue. He clung to me as his legs gave out, and then he dropped to the floor.

The room stood still and I listened for Major Ricasoli. He must have heard something going on in here. Pia was pressing her face in her hands. I picked up her coat where she'd let it drop on the floor and put it over her shoulders.

"Thanks for believing me," I said. "You've got guts, kid."

She turned, and maybe she was hating herself. "Did you have to strike him?"

"He'll be all right. But next time, don't stick your neck out for me."

"I don't even know your name."

"I'll think up one. If it helps any, I'm a friend of Max's. We can talk later. Let's get out of here."

The porcelain knob in the connecting door squeaked faintly, and we both glanced at it. At least I'd had time to turn the key before the concierge surprised us. I still had the key to Pia's hall door in my pocket and decided to use it. "Wait here."

"What?"

"I'll be right back. Look in Max's closet and see if you can turn up an overcoat for me."

I opened Max's door a crack and looked down the hall. Clear. I hurried to Pia's door, fit the key in place and turned it. Almost at once I heard a burst of Italian from inside. He caught on fast. He was locked in.

Pia was waiting with a trenchcoat. "There is only this."

"It'll help."

I took a quick look around the apartment, and it registered for the first time that the place was torn apart. Someone had searched it and he must have gotten desperate. I remembered the pawnticket in my pocket. Maybe. I snapped off the light, locked the door and saved the key. If the pawnticket was a dud, I'd want to come back.

"Let's go, baby."

"Don't call me baby."

I took her hand and pulled her along. Her high heels tapped quickly against the marble floor, and I growled to myself. We'd wake the whole neighborhood.

We reached bottom and I pushed open the huge wooden doors. It had begun to rain again and I flipped up the collar of the trenchcoat. There was no traffic on the street, only Major Ricasoli's parked Alfa Romeo.

"There might be a taxi in the piazza," I said. "We'll have to walk."

"Where are you taking me?"

"To my hotel."

"I see."

"You don't see. All I care about is keeping you alive for few more hours. After that, you're on your own. You pulled a hell of a time to get drunk."

"Suddenly, I was never more sober, Signore—"

"Cabot. Jim Cabot."

"American?"

"Yes."

"You speak Italian very well. But there is something in the accent."

We reached the end of the street, but there were no taxis in the square. A bus rumbled in as I stood wondering what to do next. It was marked for the nearby Piazza Acquaverde and the *Stazione Principe*. We went up through the middle doors and I paid the conductor 70 lire.

We came to the end of the line beside wet palm trees in the center of the square. We crossed over toward the Hotel Columbia-Excelsior.

"You loathe me, don't you?" she muttered suddenly.

"It's raining. Let's hurry across."

"I must know."

"Look, I don't have any feelings one way or the other. Let's leave it at that."

"But I must know what you're thinking."

"It's not important."

"To me—it's important."

We reached the small driveway arcade that fronted the hotel and entered the lobby. The elevator was just inside the entry doors and I dropped her off there. "Wait a minute."

"You might at least register me."

"It's better this way. You won't be staying long."

"I see." There was frost in her voice.

I crossed to the mail desk. The concierge was typing a letter below the level of the counter and he didn't hear me come up. I touched the bell and he looked up in surprise.

"*Scusi, signore.*"

"Is my passport back from the police?" I asked. "Cabot—Room Three B."

"*Sì, sì...*" He turned for my key and withdrew the green passport with it. The Italian police hadn't given up the routine of checking every move foreigners made, and I always felt better with the passport back in my hands. "Also," he said, "there is a letter for you."

"I'm not expecting any mail here. There must be a mistake."

"It is possible."

He laid it on the desk together with the key and passport. The envelope was unstamped, but it had the right name written across it: *James Cabot, Esq.* The handwriting was large and free and expansive.

"Who left this?" I asked.

He shrugged. "It was in your box when I came on duty. A mistake?"

"No mistake."

"*Buona notte, signore.*"

I put the letter in my pocket and started back for the elevator. Pia was waiting. I wondered who the hell knew I was in Genoa. And staying at the Columbia-Excelsior. I looked around for the elevator boy, but he wasn't around.

"*Ascensore!*"

He appeared from somewhere in the pillared lobby, coming at a trot, his white gloves flying. When we reached my floor, he bustled out the doors ahead of us and bowed his good night. Then he trotted back into the glassed car, like a man trying to do the mile in a fish bowl.

I had a nice room with a little stone balcony that overlooked the piazza. An antique mirror, black with age, reached from floor to ceiling, and the bed was a period piece with innerspring mattress. The night maid had turned back the covers. My bag lay on the bed. That was the first thing I noticed when I turned on the light.

My bag. I hadn't left it there. And I hadn't left it open. My stuff was flung on the floor like dirty wash.

Chapter Six

"Don't mind the mess," I said. "I'm not very tidy."

Pia held back near the door, her eyes taking in the details of the room. I tried not to let my astonishment show. What could anyone have been looking for in my bag? Had I somehow been followed earlier when I shook Duvivier and checked into the hotel?

"Something's wrong, isn't it, *signore?*" Pia muttered.

"Usually, something's wrong," I said. "Don't let it worry you."

"Mr. Cabot—"

"Jim."

"You're terribly sure of me, aren't you, Mr. Cabot?"

Raindrops glistened on the shoulders of her fur coat. I glanced at her face, the lips slightly apart—a face without makeup and still exquisite. The cold air had braced her, and her eyes had a fresh, challenging brightness.

"No," I said. "I'm not." I became conscious of a pounding inside me. You could tell she was used to thinking for herself. She could also take care of herself and she felt out of character tagging along with me.

I didn't think she was especially embarrassed that I had found her not-so-beautifully drunk in bed with 5000 lire's worth of male. She'd been around—and what the hell, it was none of my business. But my zero reaction left her uncertain of herself, and it showed. I turned away. It was none of my business, sure, but I couldn't shake the scene out of my head. I hated Piero's guts.

"You look good in the doorway," I said.

"I'm trying to make up my mind. I don't usually have this much trouble."

"Look, I have some questions to ask and I hope you'll answer them. You don't have to stay if you don't want to."

"Is that how you got your nose broken, Jim?"

"What?"

"Asking questions people didn't want to answer."

"It was the other way around."

She smiled a little and shut the door. Maybe she squared me away with a snap judgement. "I've changed my mind, Jim. I would like some coffee."

I got room service on the phone and put in the order. I watched her reflection in the smoky mirror as she slipped off her coat and straightened the slim skirt of her suit. Her clothes looked like money, more money than she could have been getting out of the Florentine Club. The alcoholic edges vanished in the mirror and I saw more than a singer in a tourist trap. She looked at her reflection and seemed to be asking herself what was happening to Pia Brindisi, as though she'd come a long way... down. She lit a cigarette and glanced at me on the phone.

Then she went into the bathroom. I hung up and threw my stuff back in the bag. A moment later I heard the shower hiss. I glanced thoughtfully at the door. I wasn't sure I liked having her make herself that much at home. She was stacked, sure, and her hair was titian and she'd be nice to have along for a weekend at Eden Roc. But don't get involved, Cabot. You haven't time.

Hell, I thought. Maybe she only wanted to get the smell of olive oil out of her mind.

I fished the letter out of my pocket, sat down and threw my feet on the edge of the bed. The envelope was hotel stock. I ripped it open.

"*My dear Cabot,*" I read. "*Please forgive my leaving your things in such a frightful mess, but I was quite annoyed at finding so little of interest. By the by, your shirts are shamefully frayed at the cuffs—you must change laundries. I shall be happy to recommend a good one in Genoa when we meet.*

"*Since time is of the essence in this matter that interests us both, may I suggest tiffin tomorrow? Do you know the Righi? The food there is excellent and the view magnificent. I shall introduce myself, providing you come alone. About one o'clock? In haste—"*

There was no signature. I crumpled the letter in my fist—I had missed a trick somewhere. This guy was way ahead of me. I couldn't help noticing the cuff of my shirt. It was frayed, and I let off some steam. I broke into a laugh. This bastard, at least, had been able to keep his sense of humor.

A blind meeting. A trap. I turned the possibility over in my mind. No, I decided, the odds were against it. A public *ristorante* in broad daylight was an unlikely spot for anyone to cut my throat. An Englishman—the letter made that clear. I remembered the mess someone had made of Max's place and wondered if that too was the work of my recent caller. What was he looking for? The pawnticket?

I burned the letter, walked out on the balcony and emptied the ashes over the side. The *Stazione Principe* across the square was deserted, the lights flickering in the rain. A streetcar went by below, rattling like an old boxcar. I hoped the weather would be clear tomorrow; it seemed a year since I had felt the sun warm on my face.

When I returned to the room, Pia had turned off the shower and someone was knocking at the door. It was the floor waiter with a pot of steaming coffee.

I lit a cigarette and waited for Pia. I decided I had made a mistake bringing her here. All I wanted was a safe place to talk to her alone, but I wasn't sure my room was safe anymore. I looked at my watch. It was past three and I wished I could grab some sleep.

She came out of the bathroom in her suit skirt and the cashmere sweater she'd brought along. It was short-sleeved and dark blue and high at the neck. If I didn't know before she'd been too rushed for a bra, I knew it now. She looked refreshed and her short red hair, turned a darker shade by the rain and the shower, was parted on one side—giving her face a casual, boyish look.

"I hate entrances," she said.

"You look fine."

"I suppose I ought to thank you for turning me out of my apartment in time. I dimly remember insulting you."

"Don't worry about it. It didn't take."

She picked up the coffee pot and began to fill the cups. *Caffé latte?"*

"Black."

A fragile smile parted her lips. "Italian coffee isn't meant to be taken—"

"Black."

She nodded and handed me the cup. She put an ash tray on the bed where she could reach it, sat down and lit a cigarette. Maybe she was used to adjusting herself to strangers. She looked entirely relaxed now.

"I didn't expect Pia Brindisi to be so beautiful," I said.

"You didn't bring me here to tell me that."

"No."

"Well?"

"Are you a Red, Pia?"

She breathed deeply on her cigarette. She looked at me, but she didn't answer.

"I thought you'd like to know what they're saying about you," I went on.

"Who?"

I sipped the coffee. It was strong and bitter, but it warmed me. "Major Ricasoli."

"Do you believe it?"

"He could have been lying. He was trying to warn me away from you."

"And if he was telling the truth?"

"I suppose I'd rather you weren't a Communist."

She looked into her coffee cup, and I saw that she wasn't really relaxed at all. "You're lying, Jim."

"Am I?"

"You're hoping I am a Communist. Then you could despise me—quite automatically. I'm in trouble and you don't wish to involve yourself. It makes a difference if I am a Communist—you can abandon me when you're finished with me. That's really what you would like, isn't it?"

"I didn't think it showed."

She put aside her coffee and reached for her bag. After a moment a card fluttered to my lap. It was made out to Pia Brindisi and it said she was a member of the Communist Party of Italy. "That ought to make things easier for you, Mr. Cabot. Shall I go now?"

I tossed it back. She had enough pride to want to offer me an easy out, but suddenly I wasn't sure that I really wanted out. A Communist card was easy to come by in Italy, and I wasn't convinced. "Stick around," I said. "And stop trying to read my mind."

"Your hospitality bores me already."

"Why are you afraid of Major Ricasoli?"

"Isn't that obvious? He intends to kill me."

"How long have you known that?"

"Two days."

"Why didn't you run away?"

"What was the use? He would only find me again. You can't escape from them."

"So you got drunk instead."

"That's not why I got drunk."

"Max?"

"Yes."

"Were you in love with him?"

"Is this important, Mr. Cabot?"

"It might be," I said seriously.

Her eyes fell and her voice softened, as though her emotions had long ago been shredded and there was nothing left but words. "He was killed because of me. I made it possible. And I loved him."

I felt moved and suddenly embarrassed, as though I'd stumbled onto a page of someone else's diary that I didn't really want to read at all. "Tough break," I said. "I'm sorry."

"I loathe pity," she muttered quickly. "I'm sure I must be boring you."

"Was Max in love with you?"

She looked up and she had an emotional chip on her shoulder. "Do you find that so hard to believe?"

"I find that very easy to believe, Pia."

"He was in love with me. We were going to be married. When he was killed, I stopped caring what happened to me. Does that answer all your questions, Mr. Cabot?"

"I liked myself better when you called me Jim," I said. "You haven't stopped caring. You came here with me."

"I was frightened. And you said you were his friend."

"Are you still frightened?"

"No. There's something about you—"

"Like Max?"

"Like Max."

Why tell her, I thought. Max had never been in love with her; he could only have been making a fool of her. His past was studded with Pia Brindisis. A woman in love with him could be useful, providing she were the right woman. He must have put on a great performance for Pia; she couldn't have been easy to break down. Well, she'd fallen for him, and I was sorry.

Jackson's little black book nagged at me like a toothache. I'd often thought that espionage might only be a passing interest for Max, like newspaper reporting and acting and gold prospecting. Had he taken the long step and begun working for the Russians too? On what side would that place Pia? I wondered how much of what she was telling me I could safely believe.

I put aside my coffee and tried to shrug off any doubts about Max. "Does the name Borsilov mean anything to you?"

She lit a fresh cigarette with the stub of the old. There was caution in her eyes. "You're an American agent, aren't you? I sensed that from the beginning."

"You're entitled to your opinions."

"Funny," she said. "I didn't know Max was from your government until after he was dead. When Major Ricasoli fired me he told me about Max."

"I see."

"And he was sure Max had made a spy of me... and perhaps he did. I don't know."

"What else did Major Ricasoli tell you?"

"That I'd better tell him everything or he'd kill me. I told him I didn't know anything and he could go ahead and kill me."

"You were more useful to him alive. But I don't think he intends to keep you waiting any longer."

"That's a comforting thought." She got to her feet, rubbing her arms as though the room had turned suddenly cold.

He knew Washington would send out another man and had left Pia around as bait, I thought. Well, he needn't have bothered. Duvivier had spotted me for him. Once I walked out of his office, Pia lost her usefulness and he would finally be getting around to killing her.

She had turned toward the balcony doors, but she faced me suddenly. Her voice was soft, but it carried a punch. "I don't want to die, Jim. Yesterday I didn't care. It was the moment of death I dreaded, the pain. But suddenly—I want to fight. Suddenly, I just don't want to be killed."

"You're doing fine, Pia."

I found myself on my feet, and we stared at each other. Her eyes moistened and I began to feel like a fool. Something feminine and instinctive inside her had fixed itself on me—Max's friend, her friend. She needed me and wanted me, but my manner had been cold and mocking. Well, she'd offered me a way out, but I hadn't taken it.

I reached out for her wrist and pulled her to me. The touch of her skin was warm and alive. I kissed her lips, kissed them hard and stopped thinking about Max and the CIA and Borsilov. Why kid myself? This was what I wanted. I would have to find time.

After a moment she looked up from my arms. "You were afraid of me, weren't you, Jim?"

"I don't know you well enough to be afraid of you."

"I'm glad you kissed me."

"You're too damned beautiful, Pia."

Her arms tightened around me. "Help me, Jim. I'm terribly alone."

Chapter Seven

The coffee was cold in the pot.

"Borsilov," I said wearily. "Tell me everything you know about him."

Pia took a deep drag on the cigarette, her cheeks hollowing, her eyes on me. She shook her head as she exhaled. "Nothing, Jim."

"But you've heard the name."

"Yes."

"From Max?"

"No. Max didn't confide in me about his work here. I imagined he was in the black markets, but I was truly in love with him and I didn't care."

"Major Ricasoli?"

"Yes. He flung questions at me for hours—Borsilov, Borsilov, Borsilov! I hate the name!"

"All right. How could you have prevented Max from getting himself killed?"

"I could have refused to help him. He would never have gone on that trip."

"What help?"

She hesitated, as though the immediate past was too confused in her mind to find a starting point. But she found it. "There was another man in love with me," she said broodingly. "A young Austrian. I think he worked for Major Ricasoli."

"What was his name?"

"Kurt Schindler. He was handsome, you know, blond and athletic. But I was never in love with him. No, he frightened me. That kind of man. He always wore sun glasses, as though he'd just been skiing in the Alps and was going back on the next train."

"Where is he now?"

"I don't know. Max insisted I keep leading Kurt on—it made me angry, but Max had a way about him." She gave a small shrug. "I always ended up doing what he wanted."

"Go on."

"The day before the accident—last Thursday night—I found Kurt in my apartment when I came home. He was terribly drunk. He talked a lot, but none of it made any sense to me. I couldn't get rid of him."

"Did he mention Borsilov's name?"

"No. He boasted that he knew one of the biggest secrets in Europe. He kept snapping his fingers, as though he were on top of the world. If only he could sell in time, he would be rich. He would marry me. We would buy a villa in Monte Carlo—he'd already picked it out. What did I say to that? I told him he was drunk and to get out and leave me alone."

"Go on."

"Then he stopped snapping his fingers. He couldn't find a buyer. And he had only until tomorrow. After tomorrow his information would be worthless."

My jaws clamped. After tomorrow, Kurt was warning her, Borsilov would be dead. They had found him and were going to kill him. "Are you sure Kurt was drunk?"

"At the time I was convinced of it."

"Did he set a price for his information?"

"He raved about a quarter-of-a-million American dollars, and what a fine time we would have with it. Bottom price. He kept saying that. Bottom price. He began snapping his fingers again—he'd had an offer for less, but he had laughed at it. It was going to be all or nothing."

"Big operator."

"Kurt was ambitious—and reckless."

"But not drunk. He was counting on you to pass the conversation on to Max."

"I finally got Kurt to leave, and about twenty minutes later Max came home. We had a nightcap together. I almost didn't tell him about Kurt; I didn't think it was that important." She dropped her eyes. "But I thought it might make Max jealous if I told him Kurt was promising me a villa in Monte Carlo. If I hadn't tried to make Max jealous, he'd still be alive."

"I think you're wrong," I said. "Keep talking."

"Max became aroused. He made me repeat every word Kurt had said. Then he warned me Kurt would come back and I had to help him. I was to say I could get Kurt ten thousand dollars for his information—top price. And Kurt did come back... in the morning. To apologize for coming to my place drunk."

"Sure."

"I told him about the ten thousand dollars, but he pretended not to know what I was talking about. But before he left he let me know he'd be stopping for gas near Bolzano, late that afternoon. Friends of his ran an Esso station—he said he always stopped there on northern trips. He mentioned the name of the place, but I've forgotten it." She looked up.

"It was only a few miles from there the accident happened and Max and the two others were killed."

I remembered the names Jackson had given me of the two Reds. Neither of them was Kurt Schindler. I began to see light, a glimmer of what had happened, the outline of Max's hasty and desperate *modus operandi*.

"Anything else?"

"Nothing else. If I had said nothing to Max, none of it would have happened."

"Look, Pia, if Kurt couldn't have reached Max through you, he'd have found another way. He couldn't risk a direct meeting with Max in Genoa and so he used you. You worked for Major Ricasoli, and there was no danger in it if he was discovered in your apartment. You were a convenience for both of them. When Kurt let you know where he'd be stopping in Bolzano, he was asking Max for a last-minute, face-to-face rendezvous. He was willing to gamble that Max would feel the pressure and come across with some big cash. Maybe not a quarter of a million, but big."

"Kurt was too ambitious."

"Max must have met him in the gas station." I got up and began moving around. But it would have practically taken an Act of Congress for Max to lay hands on any real dough. I doubted suddenly that he had planned to come across with a dime. I looked at Pia. "You haven't had any word of Kurt since the accident?"

"No."

"Tell me about him. What are his habits?"

"I know only a little."

"It's important, Pia. Believe me."

"He always needed money. He even borrowed from me a few times. He had a system at the casinos, and it kept him penniless."

"Where did he gamble?"

"Once or twice a week he would go to San Remo and work on his system. He had many women—he was the type, you understand? But I didn't mind. I only wanted him to leave me alone."

"Did he always gamble at San Remo?"

"If he had enough money he would try the casinos at Monte Carlo or Nice. He liked to be around the rich. But mostly he liked to gamble. It was his nature. The croupiers all knew him. I don't know any more to tell you, Jim."

"Maybe that's enough. How come it was your car that Ricasoli's boys were driving?"

"The car wasn't mine."

"Then why did you tell the police it was stolen?"

"Major Ricasoli put the words in my mouth."

"Am I supposed to believe that?"

"I was confused. The car was registered in my name. I didn't know any-thing about the car until the accident. I suppose it really belonged to Major Ricasoli. It didn't seem to matter. I said what he told me to say."

I lit a fresh cigarette. "But it was registered in your name." Maybe that was just a device to keep himself covered, I thought. When Major Ricasoli needed a car for risky work, there was always one waiting in his garage—legally owned by a fall guy, in case it should be traced. Well, sending three trigger men to kill Borsilov had been risky, and it had back-fired. But the car had been traced to Pia, not Major Ricasoli.

Kurt. Okay, he had ambitions of his own, I thought, and wanted to sell out. He knew where Borsilov was holed up; he was one of three Red agents going there the next day to murder him. I turned to Pia.

"Do you know what brand of cigarettes Kurt smoked?"

"I never noticed."

"I'll tell you," I said. "A French brand—Baltos. An ash tray in the car was stuffed with them."

"Does it matter?"

"It matters." I had the pieces and they fell into place. I liked the pic-ture, because it took Max out from under the shadow of Jackson's lit-tle black book. I knew now why he was traveling with two Reds. I knew he hadn't been playing a double game. That removed any doubts I might have about Pia. He had trusted her and I could trust her.

And hell, there *had* been a Passenger X. Jackson hadn't imagined him. There had been another guy in the accident car, and he'd smoked French cigarettes all the way from Genoa to Bolzano. Kurt Schindler? He was still alive; he had to be. He was shrewd and money hungry and ambitious and probably the only man in Europe who could tell you where to find Evgeni Borsilov.

"Jim—"

"Listen to me, baby. Max never intended to pay off your friend Kurt. Even the offer of ten thousand must have been a stall. But Max drove to Bolzano and pulled in at that gas station. He waited for Kurt to show up. Maybe he hung around the lavatory. Sure enough, Kurt breezes in. Outside, the car is being gassed up and Kurt's innocent buddies wait. They're all on their way to murder Borsilov—never mind why. But Max knows he's got to get there first. Following them in his car is out—they'd spot a tail for sure. Max was good in the pinches and he used his head."

"I don't want to hear it, Jim."

Outside, a burst of rain struck the glass doors of the balcony. "Look, baby, you've got to get over Max. And you might as well get used to the idea that you couldn't have stopped anything from happening."

"I'm trying, Jim."

"Bolzano. Kurt walks into the rest room, and there's Max. No time for much talk. The guys in the car don't know Kurt is trying to pull a double cross for cash. Well, Max isn't parting with any. He all but breaks Kurt's neck—Max is good at things like that, take it from me. With Kurt unconscious, Max trades overcoat and hat. And sunglasses—you said he always wore sunglasses."

"Yes."

"All right, Max returns to the car as Kurt. It's risky, but Max has plenty of crust. The other two men are in the front seat. Max piles in back. All he has to do is pretend to go to sleep—to avoid talk—and wait for them to chauffeur him to Borsilov. He's got a gun, and he could have handled the situation beautifully."

"But the accident—"

"Yes. They all lost—Moscow as well as Washington. Maybe it was just an accident, or maybe one of the others got wise and Max had to pull his gun too soon. There could have been a struggle and the car went out of control."

She seemed to shiver.

I went on. "That leaves Kurt back at the gas station. He picks himself up off the floor finally, and he's hopping mad. He let a fortune get away from him. Maybe he hooks a ride. A couple of miles up the road cars are stopping along the embankment. Your car has gone down the ravine. He discovers his two buddies—and Max—have been killed. The breaks have come Kurt's way after all. But for Max, he might have been killed in that accident. Max sat in for him on a death ride."

"Don't make me think about it, Jim."

"Well, Kurt is very much alive and he knows where to find Borsilov. He also knows Major Ricasoli will send out another killer party once he reads the papers. Okay. Major Ricasoli must have tried again, but Borsilov was no longer on the spot. Kurt had moved in on him and put him on ice somewhere else. Borsilov is worth money to him alive. Half a dozen governments and twice as many fast-buck syndicates would pay through the nose to get Borsilov alive. All Kurt has to do is keep him under wraps until he can find a buyer."

"Why are you telling me this, Jim?"

"I want you to help me, baby. You know Kurt by sight. That might save me time and waste effort."

"Yes, I will help you."

Find Kurt, find Borsilov—he knew that. "Tomorrow we'll try the casinos. You'd better grab a couple of hours sleep. It'll be light soon."

"So you want me to stay after all."

"I want you to stay."

Her eyes brightened a little, as if the shadow of her fear had passed. "Will it be so bad having me around, Jim?"

"No," I said. "Not bad at all."

Pia undressed in the dark. I stretched out on the chaise longue with a blanket, and I could hear the rustle of her skirt as she stepped out of it. I didn't make a pass at her. I didn't intend to touch her. I wasn't sure I wanted to get that much involved.

There was the thin swish of sheets and I knew she was getting into bed. I would rather she weren't going to sleep in my room, but I didn't trust her to sleep anywhere else. If there was going to be trouble, I wanted to be around.

"*Buona notte*, Jim."

"Good night, baby."

It would have been useless moving to another hotel. I had only the one passport and I would have to register again as James Cabot, and if Major Ricasoli had men out checking hotels he'd find James Cabot wherever I went.

Pia turned in bed, and I glanced her way through the darkness. I didn't need her. I could find Kurt without her. But I couldn't abandon her, period.

Without Pia's story, I doubted that Major Ricasoli would have understood the switch inside the car. He could assume that Max had stormed the car and Kurt had gotten away and would turn up. Or that Max had killed Kurt and the body hadn't yet come to light. He'd be puzzled, sure, but he wouldn't have sent Kurt on the job if he hadn't trusted him. Without Pia to tip him off, he wouldn't be likely to start his thinking on the premise that Kurt was attempting a double cross.

Even if I wanted to wipe my hands of Pia, I realized, it would be idiotic. I had to hold onto her. I couldn't risk her falling back into Major Ricasoli's hands. Since I had appeared on the scene, his suspicions about her would have crystallized. This time he would find ways to make her talk.

A sudden fury of rain beat against the balcony doors, like a thousand fingertips trying to scratch their way into the room. I fell asleep with the sound in my ears.

Chapter Eight

I let Pia sleep in the morning. She might not rouse before noon, I thought, and that would be fine. I showered and shaved and changed into clean clothes. I glanced at her form under the blankets as I buttoned my shirt. She slept in a tight ball, as if for her own protection, the blankets almost pulled over her head. There were only a few tendrils of red hair showing on the pillow, and I could hear the faint, intimate sounds of her breathing.

I wrote out a note, telling her to keep the doors locked and not to let anyone in but me, not even the chambermaid, and I would be right back. Her slip lay across the foot of the bed and I left the note in its folds. I took my shoes in from outside the hall door. The night porter had put a crisp shine on them, and I had to remember to tip him before I checked out.

I examined the pawnticket once more! *G. Barabino & Figlio, Via Ravecca 83*. It wasn't far; I'd be back in less than an hour. Pia should still be asleep.

I stopped at the reception desk in the lobby, cashed a couple of traveler's checks and asked the clerk to arrange for a rented car. I showed him my international driver's license, he took down the number, and I left him a deposit. He said it would take a couple of hours. I asked him to speed it up.

I went down the steps into the driveway arcade. A Chrysler with U.S. occupation force license plates was unloading baggage. A young-looking captain and a girl who had the look of *fräulein* about her stood around directing the porter. Down from Germany for a holiday, I thought, and not a worry in the world.

I walked out of the arcade to flag a taxi, and I was no longer alone. A man came up on either side of me.

"Keep walking, comrade."

A chill spread along my back. They both had nondescript faces, one clearly Italian, the other possibly Russian. The Italian was bare-headed. His companion had a blanched skin and the loose knot in his necktie was almost as large as a pack of cigarettes. They had one thing in common. They looked tough—tough and professional.

"Sorry to keep you waiting," I muttered.

"We're used to waiting." It was the Russian who spoke, and he was obviously in command. "The car is over here."

The rain had passed and the sun was already bright in the square. Across from the hotel toward the hill a cop stood in a booth directing traffic, but we weren't walking that way. I wished desperately I could catch his attention, but I knew these guys would shoot and run if they had to.

Our shoes thudded on the cobbles; they walked with their hands in their overcoat pockets. We reached a parking area and they lead me to a taxi. I wondered if it was the same one that had come swerving around the fountain in the Piazza de Ferrari the night before, flashing gunfire.

The driver nodded recognition and started the engine. The Italian opened the back door and went in first. The Russian nudged my shoulder.

"Get in, comrade."

My impulse was to swing on him, but now that the Italian was in the car he showed his gun.

I got in.

The Russian sat on my left and slammed the door. The driver backed out and a moment later we were stopped by the light at the cross walk. The cop in the booth swung his whistle from a chain and his eyes flicked over us. He wasn't interested. The light turned green and we rolled into the Via Balbi.

The Italian pressed his gun in my side and the Russian fanned my pockets. He found the Beretta, gave it a contemptuous glance and slipped it in his own pocket.

"You guys have quite an act," I said. "Shows practice."

The Russian ignored me. My palms began to sweat; these bastards were cool and efficient and they didn't go in for patter. I made up my mind not to give them the satisfaction of seeing my growing alarm.

"I've been taken for rides before," I said. "I always get back."

"This time you won't come back, *signore*." It was the Italian who spoke. He wasn't boasting. It was a mere statement, something I might as well begin to believe.

I lit a cigarette. The Via Balbi lay in morning shadows. My eyes caught a faded 'Out of Bounds' sign stenciled along a bombed wall at an alleyway from the street below. The U.S. had left its marks all over Europe, but the U.S. seemed vague and remote to me now. These guys were real and they meant to kill me.

I'd been a fool to hope Major Ricasoli wouldn't have bothered to check the hotels for me. I wondered about Pia. Did he know I'd taken her to my room?

I stared at the driver's neck. I felt trapped.

They'd kill me mechanically and with supreme indifference. They didn't know any more about me than my name, and it wasn't even my real one, but they'd kill me with the purest of logic. They'd been ordered to.

We worked down through the narrow streets to the windy corso along the sea and began to pick up speed. I glanced out over the Mediterranean, the surface nervous with whitecaps. A scattering of masts cut the air from the small yacht harbor. Beyond, an American freighter was being coaxed inside the stone breakwater by a couple of coughing blue tugs.

I'd be crazy to try anything inside the car.

Wait.

We passed the Lido and the beach villas and pulled off the highway on a road leading down the cliffs. We came to the bombed shell of an old pavilion with a broken pier and stopped. The place was deserted except for sea gulls standing one-legged in the wind, as if waiting for something to happen.

We walked. They led me through the ruins to the littered beach. On my left the Portofino promontory stood in the sea like a poised arm. We walked into the chill shade under the pier.

"*Benone.*"

They separated themselves from me and left me standing. When I turned the Russian had my Beretta in his hand. It would amuse him to kill me with my own gun.

"You are satisfied with this place, comrade? One can die here in peace. There is no one to bother you but the sea gulls."

The birds squawked and wheeled in the air above us, their fluttering shadows gliding along the beach. I was dripping sweat and my throat was dry. Waves cracked and tumbled in, jarring the pier, and expired with a gravelly roll on the beach shingles.

"Shall I turn my back? You bastards might as well do this in character."

"*Non importa, signore. Buon divertimento.*"

I didn't wait for him to finish. I ran.

I reached the shield of a pile before the Beretta began to explode. Wood splintered at my hand.

"*Imbecille!*"

I was a fool, but I wasn't going to watch myself be murdered. My eyes flicked over the incoming surf. I'd have to try for the water.

The Russian barked an order. I zig-zagged between the tarred piles and the slugs kept coming. They had separated. My feet were in water and a breaker was rushing in. I dove into the churning white foam. I stayed under until the backwash carried me to a pile in deeper water. I came up for air behind it, amazed that I hadn't already been hit.

A wave broke over my head, but I hung on. The icy water numbed me, and I wouldn't last long unless I could get rid of the drag of my clothes. I looked toward shore. Only the Italian stood there, knee deep in water. He began to fire. I ducked back for cover.

I moved out to the next pile, shaggy with seaweed. The Russian must have gone up on the pier, I thought. I'd never be able to leave the protection of the planks above without getting plugged.

I got out of the trenchcoat and let a wave tear it away. I heard the heavy thud of footsteps above me and I let the current drag me out to the next pile. I looked up and in the gaps between the pier planks I could make him out. He wasn't going to wait for me to try to swim away. Suddenly peering down, he saw me. A moment later he was directly over me, and I saw the black nose of the Beretta lower between the planks.

I dropped under the surface and pushed away from the pile. I heard the growl of the slug. I was fighting a losing game, but I had to keep fighting. I came up and got hold of a crosspiece. The pier had caught a stray bomb near its end and there wasn't any further to go. I hung on, trying to catch my breath. There was nothing beyond me but the open sea, and he couldn't miss.

When I looked back, the Italian was on his knees trying to drag himself out of the water. I wiped the water out of my eyes, but couldn't figure out what the hell had happened. A dying wave swept over him and he gave in to it. On the backwash, he lay prone in the sand.

I looked up and the nose of the Beretta had found me again. I heard three rapid shots from the direction of the pavilion, and the barrel of the Beretta swung in an arc. There was a quick moan and clatter on the planks above.

I scanned the shore and saw a squarish man approaching the foot of the pier. All I could make out was a dark blue topcoat.

Chapter Nine

I climbed up the pilings to the level of the pier and saw the Russian trying to pick himself up off the planks. He had taken at least one slug, and it must have hurt plenty. Our eyes met, but he made no move for the Beretta wedged between the planks a few feet from where he'd fallen.

Instead, his hand groped inside his coat and I jumped all over him before he could get out his own gun. There wasn't much fight left in him. His face was stretched with pain; the slug must have hurt like hell.

I took away his gun and stood up. I saw then that he'd been hit twice. His shoulder was bleeding and, he held one leg out stiffly. He'd taken the second slug in the thigh. Well, he was going to live. His type was hard to kill.

I was dripping and the wind cut through me. I looked toward shore again. The man in the blue topcoat was waiting for me. He was a hell of a good shot.

I looked at the gun in my hand. It was a Tokarev automatic. I'd been up against Soviet weapons before and recognized it on sight. Their model 30. I checked the magazine. It was fully loaded, and I slipped the gun in my pocket. Then I pulled the Beretta from between the planks and tossed it over the side. It couldn't have had more than one or two shells in it.

"Comrade..."

I looked down at the Russian, his face in the sun. I had an impulse to put another hole in him, but I let it go. I didn't like to kill that much. If he wanted to live badly enough he could crawl back to the corso on his hands and knees. To hell with him.

I wiped the water off my face and started down the pier toward shore. The heavy-set man watched my approach, and when I was close enough I saw a whimsical, florid face. He nodded, grinning.

"These gentlemen were a bit unfriendly, eh? I took it upon myself to interfere, Cabot. No offense."

"You're a crack shot," I said. "Thanks."

"Life is cheap in Italy, sir."

I glanced at the Italian lying at the edge of the surf like a piece of water-soaked driftwood. I felt nothing. "Sure," I said.

He chuckled, a heavy man who must have been nearing fifty. His skin was pink and he had curly blond eyebrows and a clipped beard that gave his face a round, golden look. Under other circumstances I might have taken him for an English country doctor. He wore rubber overshoes and leaned on his umbrella. "May I introduce myself, sir? Jardine. Sydney Jardine."

I nodded. "You seem to know my name."

"Indeed. Both of them, sir. My car is waiting. I suggest we leave your former companions to their own devices, if any, and get you into some dry clothing."

We stopped sizing each other up and began walking. He might be British Intelligence, I thought. The English were sure to have men on the

Borsilov assignment. And yet there was something about Sydney Jardine that didn't ring quite true. The beard gave his face a piratical vanity and the humor in his gray eyes was bluff. I felt certain this was the man who had searched my room the night before and left me the note.

We skirted the debris of the pavilion, and the sea gulls were wheeling back to the pier now that the noise was over. Jardine had the brisk step of a man who enjoyed walking. The open topcoat flapped in the wind and he swung the black, furled umbrella jauntily.

I felt a vague annoyance that he knew my real name as well as the one Washington had assigned to me. But I was getting used to it. Everyone in Genoa seemed to have been briefed on me.

I looked back once: the Russian was already dragging himself back along the pier. I felt no sense of victory over what had happened. It had been too close and I had been too lucky.

Sydney Jardine pointed with his umbrella as we approached the taxi I had come out in. I saw the driver lying unconscious near the running board, but he was already beginning to stir. "Tried to put up a bit of resistance, he did. I had to hit him. A very foolish fellow, eh?"

"I'm impressed," I said.

"I don't mind a bit of violence now and then. Good for the spirit."

We walked up the road and came upon an Alvis Saloon parked halfway down the cliff. A couple of minutes later we were back on the corso heading for town, and Jardine was running an amber comb through his beard with quick, practiced strokes.

"You must have followed us out from the hotel," I said.

He nodded with a purring chuckle. "Shall I call you Cabot or Welles?"

"Cabot appeals to me at the moment."

"Good, sir. Cabot it is." He put away the comb and adjusted his shoulders. He was a hulk of a man behind the wheel. "You got my note?"

"I got it."

"Would you have kept our appointment at the Righi?"

"I doubt it."

He glanced my way, his eyes a merry squint. "You doubt it, sir. Ah, I doubted it too. I decided to pay you a private visit in your hotel room this morning. We have business to discuss, you and I, and it won't wait. But now I can't make up my mind whether you are merely a fool or a talented idiot."

"I won't argue the point."

"But at least you showed courage once you fell into their hands. Courage and patience. I admire courage, sir. And patience is a rare quality. I can use a man of your metal."

"My metal's rusting," I said. "Let's forget the whole thing."

He blasted the horn and swung around a flock of bicycles. "We shall see. At any rate, I was approaching the hotel—thinking surely you'd be still asleep at that hour. Instead, I saw you walked out into the company of the good major's patrol. I wasn't quite sure what you were up to and decided to tag along and see."

I wanted to thank him, but my pride got in the way. I was indebted to him for my life and I didn't like being indebted to anyone. He was already beginning to talk as though he owned me.

"I keep asking myself," I said, "how you recognized me."

"I recognized Major Ricasoli's staff. But even without them I'd have known you on sight. Max left me a detailed description of you. You remember Max Becker, sir."

"I remember him."

"Good man. I hated to lose him."

"Who are you, Jardine?"

"Ah, I'm getting under your skin, am I? Good. It's time you came to grips with reality. You prefer to believe Max was faithful to your government, but the truth is he was working for me. And you shall be working for me shortly. Let me outline my proposition."

"Never mind Max," I said. I hated to be plunged back into my earlier doubts about him, and Jardine could be lying. I decided not to let him get under my skin. "What's your business?"

"Poultry."

"Sure."

He worked on the horn and chuckled. "Eggs, sir. Eggs are my business. There's a fortune to be made in it, Cabot."

"I wasn't cut out to be a chicken farmer. Thanks anyway."

He gave me a fleshy wink. "Golden eggs, sir. Follow me?"

"We're going in different directions."

"Golden eggs, for a fact. The latest Russian exports. Scientific. Beautiful. Pure gold." He slapped the horn and cut around a gasoline truck. We were nearing the city and the hills of Genoa warmed themselves in the sun, the villas and apartment houses serrating the mid-morning sky.

"Golden eggs," I muttered.

"That presumes a goose, sir. I don't have to tell you the name of the goose that's laying these golden eggs. Every government in Europe, as well as your own, is anxious to lay hands on him. The Russians are equally anxious to slaughter him. We can't have that, can we, Cabot?"

"Where do you fit in, Jardine?"

"I have a proprietary interest in Borsilov, sir."

"No kidding."

"I arranged his escape from the Russian Zone in Vienna. I and my organization."

"You have an organization."

"Top-flight."

"But the goose is gone."

"Temporarily. I brought him to my villa here in Genoa and gave him every comfort a man could ask, if not more."

"And he laid golden eggs for you."

"Under the mistaken impression that they would buy him asylum in America."

"I see."

"Ah, you're beginning to anticipate me, eh? Now consider—we could have sold our charmed fowl outright. Lump sum. But there's more money in the eggs, and no one in his right mind would dispose of a goose laying golden eggs. I don't have to tell you there's a lively market for this sort of thing. Lively indeed."

"What are you trying to say? You've been selling the same stuff to several governments at once?"

"Exactly. The financial horizon is unlimited. All one needs is a fertile goose, sir. And we had him. We shall get him back." He smacked his lips and made a sharp turn off the torso. We left the Mediterranean behind us and the victory arch in the Piazza Della Vittoria loomed up ahead.

"You've got it all figured out," I muttered.

"I'm building up a syndicate, Cabot. Very smart. Very industrious. And we can be very dangerous. Dangerous, sir."

"You're scaring hell out of me."

"I'm offering you a chance to come in with us, sir. The profits are vast, and you shall have a share of them."

"You sized me up for a fool. Put it down to that and let me off at my hotel."

He took his hands from the wheels and spread them in an expansive gesture. "Look at me, Cabot. A picture of robust health, eh? Money does that, sir. I have a villa in the hills and a yacht in the harbor. This superb Genoa is my paradise. I live in the sun, I drink the best wines and eat the finest foods. I am reborn, sir. Three years ago I was a mere naval draftsman with a grubby flat in Soho. Then—ah, then—opportunity knocked."

"You don't have to spell it out." He'd discovered there was money in naval blueprints and begun to cash in. With a taste of financial blood, his ambitions had burgeoned. And here he was driving a sporty Alvis Saloon, he had a villa in the hills and a yacht in the harbor. Did he expect me to pat him on the back?

"In no time at all you too will have a tidy fortune salted away. Tidy, indeed. Women? My dear sir, they'll flock about you. You've no idea what a difference money makes. The best tailors will cut your clothes. You shall drive the most expensive cars. The finest families in Europe will welcome you. A tidy fortune, sir, and time enough to spend it. I promise you all that. Max would tell you I don't exaggerate."

"Max again." The muscles of my jaw were working.

"Fine lad, he was. You know he asked to have you transferred here?"

"I know." We left the broad, tree-planted *viale* and came into the thicker traffic of the Via Venti Settembre. Sunlight flashed off the tops of cars and the wide, arcaded sidewalk was doing a brisk trade in foot traffic. I slumped in the seat, wet from head to toe, and wished the ride would end.

A tap on the horn. "Max it was who promised to recruit you for my syndicate. I need men of your specialized skills, sir, and they are hard to find. He gave you the highest recommendation—the highest—or I wouldn't be wasting my time on you."

I straightened impatiently. "You're a liar, Jardine."

He threw back his bushy chin and laughed. "Call me all the names in the bloody book if it'll make you feel any better. A liar, am I? A liar I am on occasion, sir, but on this occasion I happen to be telling you the shocking truth. Max joined up with me shortly after he was transferred to Genoa more than a year ago. I spread before him the picture of immediate riches, and of course he accepted. There was a lad with his eye out for the main chance."

"You're bluffing."

Jardine snorted. "I'm a perfect scoundrel, eh? Don't be an ass, sir. The truth is the truth. Max used his good offices to plan Borsilov's escape from the Russians. He was with me one hundred percent."

"Go to hell." Did he think I'd be more easily persuaded if Max had tumbled before me? Maybe Max had been dazzled by promises of great wealth—he wouldn't have been the first agent who had been corrupted. Still, I rebelled at accepting Jardine's word for it. It was too easy dragging Max's name into his camp, now that Max was dead. No, Jardine was bluffing. He had to be. Max knew me well enough to be sure I was the wrong guy to attempt to recruit. It had been tried before.

And yet, Jardine had been given a description of me. He knew Max had asked for my transfer to Genoa, and he knew my name. To save me he'd killed one man and shot up another. And he'd spoken freely of his operations, as if there was no doubt that I was already firmly hooked. His openness was unnatural and it bothered me.

"Consider," Jardine went on, "if in your good luck you should beat me to Borsilov—why, it's just a matter of keeping things confidential. Between us."

"I have an impulse to break your neck."

"Of course you have." He broke into a chuckle. "But you owe me your very life, sir."

"I know. It keeps getting in my way. I'm trying to hang onto my temper."

We had reached the narrow Via Balbi, streaming with traffic. I felt as though I were sitting beside a leper, a disease carrier anxious to corrupt me as he doubtless had corrupted agents of other governments. He'd gone to a lot of trouble to save my neck. I owed him something for that, even if it was only restraining my impulses. I hadn't joined the CIA because I expected to get in the chips.

"Well, sir, there is my proposition."

"You can let me off at the American Express. I'll walk across to the hotel."

"Don't be a fool, Cabot. There is money to be made, huge sums, a fortune. Borsilov escaped us, but we shall have him back. And there will be other geese laying other golden eggs."

"What did you expect to find when you went through my bag last night?"

"A matter of no importance."

"After this, make it a point to stay out of my things. I have a quick temper. I'm funny that way."

"You have spirit, sir. I like a man of spirit. Think over my proposition. Nothing stands in your way but a bit of pride, I can see that. All right, sir! Take a few hours. I shall manage to contact you sometime later in the day."

He passed up the American Express, but he wouldn't risk having me seen in his car at the hotel entrance and turned up the hill above the piazza. He pulled over to the curb and I got out. "Thanks again for the lift."

"Ah, Cabot. Perhaps I should warn you, in all fairness, sir, that I shouldn't turn down my proposition if I were you. If you are not with me, you are against me. It is my practice to be generous with friends and ruthless with competition. Good morning, sir."

I slammed the door on that merry squint, the piratical face and the parting threat. The Alvis Saloon continued up the hill and I stood for a moment feeling as though I'd let him make a fool of me. He'd spoken as though he had an ace up his sleeve—one he wouldn't pull unless I forced him to. Turn down his proposition and the squint in his eyes would turn mean, and he'd play his hidden card. Well, I'd have to risk it.

I started walking back down the hill toward the hotel. For a moment I felt unnerved. He had information about me that pointed to Max. And he'd felt confident enough of my joining his syndicate that he'd killed in cold blood to save me.

I got some curious stares in the lobby. I'd been half-drowned and looked it. There were a few people waiting for the elevator and I decided to pass it by. I'd walk up. I felt no danger about the hotel now—Major Ricasoli would presume I was dead. It would be hours before he learned the truth. I took the stairway to my floor. I hadn't handed my key in at the desk when I left earlier and I used it on the door. When I walked into the room, Pia was no longer in the bed.

The bathroom door was open. I glanced quickly around the room, thinking of Major Ricasoli, and broke into a sweat. Pia was gone.

Chapter Ten

I showered quickly, put on dry clothes and packed my bag. Pia was gone, but I hadn't been sent to Genoa to chase after a red-headed Italian girl. I tried to put her out of my mind. I had started out an hour-and-a-half earlier for the pawnshop, but I hadn't gotten there. I had already lost too much time, and I couldn't risk losing more. At the rate I was going, Borsilov would die of old age before I picked up his trail.

I settled my bill at the reception desk and found that the rented car was waiting in the hotel driveway. I signed the *carnet* that would pass the car over European frontiers, and the porter picked up my bag and led the way.

It was a new Fiat, dark blue, and it looked like it had plenty of power. The porter placed my bag in the trunk compartment and handed me the keys. I tipped him and he touched his cap. "*Grazie, signore.*"

"*Prego.*"

I threw the *carnet* in the glove compartment and started the engine. I'd redeem the pawnticket and take off for the casinos and Kurt. I'd find him without Pia. I hated to think what might have happened to her. Forget it, Cabot, I thought bitterly. Don't think about it. Kurt will show you the way to Borsilov and nothing else matters.

Within a few minutes I was in the Piazza de Ferrari, and a dozen men were sitting around the fountain warming their faces in the sun. Water sprayed high into the morning air, and the scene struck me as unbelievably peaceful after the sudden gunning of the night before. In the arcade a waiter was setting out tables again.

I pulled up beside a parked taxi and got my directions to the Via Ravecca. The tires thudded on the uneven cobbles, but the Fiat handled nicely. I lit a cigarette and a moment later saw the sign. *G. Barabino & Figlio.*

The pawnbroker was an old man. He took the ticket and disappeared in the back.

He returned with the ticket still in his hand. "What was it you left with me, *signore?*"

"I'd been drinking. I don't remember what I pawned. But you must have it around here somewhere."

"It is strange I don't remember you. There was an American in perhaps a week ago, but you are a different man." He shrugged, peering at me.

"What did this other American pawn?"

"It has been redeemed."

"What was it?"

"An old musical instrument, something like a violin. All but worthless."

"A lute?"

"Perhaps it was a lute, *signore.*"

"Was it the American who redeemed it?"

"No. He sent an Italian friend."

"What Italian?"

He shrugged. "I didn't ask his name. He offered me an extra five thousand lire because the ticket was lost. Naturally I accepted. It was more than the instrument was worth, if you want the truth."

"Was the American who pawned it tall and light-haired?"

He nodded.

"What about the Italian?"

He lifted his hand in an explosive gesture. "Why do you bother me with these questions?"

"Did he wear a neck brace?"

"*Sì,*" he nodded briskly.

Max had pawned the lute and Major Ricasoli had redeemed it. I had seen the shambles he had made of it the night before in the waste basket of his office.

"When did the Italian come in here?"

"But only yesterday. I was—"

"*Arrivederci.*"

I walked out. Max had obviously concealed information of some sort in the lute, pawned it for safety, and Major Ricasoli had only found out about it yesterday. The ticket must have been found on Max after the accident, I thought, and Jackson had somehow wheedled it from the police.

I got in the car and started the engine. Major Ricasoli had obviously gone over every inch of the lute, taking it apart piece by piece. But still, I had to look for myself. There was almost no chance he had missed Max's gimmick; I was a day late. But he *might* have missed it, and I had to try.

I looked at my watch. It was almost eleven. There was a chance that the Florentine Club except for the cleaning crew would be deserted at this hour. I made a U-turn. If Max had left some information around, I couldn't leave Genoa without taking a quick stab at it. Sydney Jardine had obviously been looking for the *biglietto* when he searched my bag.

I parked around the corner from the Florentine Club. In daylight the place looked worn and disenchanted. The neon signs were dead. Through the glass entrance doors I looked in at the unlit foyer and I could hear the whine of a vacuum cleaner inside. I tried one of the doors and it opened.

It was a long shot, but I crossed the foyer and entered the club. I might have to go through the trash bin looking for parts of the lute and the task seemed hopeless. If Major Ricasoli walked in and found me on the premises he'd retire me from business in nothing flat. I had an impulse to forget the whole thing and turn back. But I had to have a look at the remains of that lute.

I wrapped my hand around the Tokarev in my pocket. It felt good. The stale odor of last night's liquor lay in the air like a hangover. I saw a middle-aged Italian woman working the vacuum cleaner between the tables, and a barrel-chested porter was waxing the dance floor.

I approached him. "*Buon giorno.* Is Major Ricasoli around?"

The porter got off his knees and wiped his perspiring face in the crook of his arm. "You are too early, *signore.* He seldom comes in before noon."

That gave me almost an hour. "I'll wait," I said. "Is his office unlocked?"

"*Favorisca*, his office is not cleaned up. Perhaps you would like to come back."

I felt a throb of relief. The waste basket would be untouched. I wouldn't have to go pawing through a lot of trash. "No," I said. "I'll wait."

"*Come Le piaccia, signore,*" he muttered indifferently. "I will unlock it for you."

I followed him to the door marked *Privato*. He found the key, pushed the door open for me and walked back to the dance floor. A high, barred window at the end of the office let in a shaft of light. I closed the door and strode toward the waste basket beside the desk. The head of the lute, bordered with tuning screws, still hung over the edge, the strings curled free like watch springs.

I emptied the waste basket on the floor and quickly examined the splintered wood, the pegs, the broken fingerboard. I was wasting my time and risking my neck. I tried not to think about Pia, but if he had gotten hold of her he might have beaten the Kurt angle out of her. He might even now be putting out a dragnet to find Kurt. And Kurt equaled Borsilov—I was sure of it.

I went over the pieces of the lute a second time. Major Ricasoli had examined every square inch of it, inside and out. It was hopeless. Whatever Max had concealed, the Italian had found.

I got up and tried to think. Still, something was wrong. The lute didn't look as though it had been carefully taken apart. It looked as though it had been smashed in anger or disgust. I felt that I ought to walk away from the thing while my luck still held, but I couldn't. Outside the office, the vacuum cleaner hummed.

I stared at the bits and pieces of the lute on the tile floor. The curled strings caught my eye again. And it hit. Pia's wire recorder!

I went down on my knees again and began separating the strings. That was why Max had chosen to pawn a stringed instrument, an antique that might have come with the apartment. He'd recorded something and strung it on the lute!

I felt sure of myself now and my heart vaulted. I worked quickly, disentangling the strings and comparing them. Within a few moments I knew I had the right one.

I stretched it out against the light and stared at it. The pawnticket hadn't been a blind alley even though Major Ricasoli must have decided Max had pawned the lute only to scare up a few bucks, and broken it to bits. I wondered what information Max had recorded on the long, shining strand of wire in my hands and felt a sharp impatience to get it on a machine. There must be a music store somewhere along the Via Vend Settembre selling recorders.

I coiled it up carefully, put it in my pocket and started for the door. The phone began to ring. I didn't hesitate. I didn't want the porter coming in to see that I'd been pawing through the waste basket, and picked up the receiver.

"*Sì.*"

"Ugo," a man's voice came back at me.

I pitched my voice a little higher, speaking crisply, and hoped I would pass for Major Ricasoli. "*Che cosy desidera Lei?*"

"I have found the girl, my major. I called your home first—I didn't think you'd be at the office so early."

Pia!

"Where are you?" I snapped.

"She came back to her apartment. I am holding her here. What do you wish me to do with her, my major?"

The little fool, I thought bitterly. Why did she go back? But at least she was still alive. "I am no longer interested in her, idiot. Leave her and come at once. There is trouble and I need you here."

There was a pause at the other end. "Who—"

"Don't argue with me. Come at once."

But it was no good. There was a longer pause at Ugo's end, and then he hung up. He had caught on, and I'd better hurry. I banged down the receiver. Borsilov came first, but I couldn't abandon Pia a second time. I started for the door.

But I didn't get there. A sharp knock stopped me.

Chapter Eleven

The vacuum cleaner moaned far off in the club. I looked quickly around the office. The only window was barred; there was no way out.

The knocking came again, more insistent this time.

I would have to bluff and hope for better luck than I'd had with Ugo. It might only be the porter after all.

"*Che è?*" I snapped.

But it wasn't the porter who answered. It was a woman.

"Alexandrine Duvivier, my major."

There was a tight pause. She didn't know Major Ricasoli's voice as well as Ugo, and I thought I might get away with it. I didn't want Duvivier or anyone else to find me. There was a measure of safety in letting Major Ricasoli believe I was dead and the longer he was under that illusion the better. I doubted if the porter would be able to give much of a description of me—the dance floor had been in shadows when I talked to him.

"I have information for you," Duvivier said in a forced whisper. "The

American—"

"What about him?"

"He has rented a car. I think he is going to leave Genoa."

"Your information is obsolete. The American is dead."

There was a pause. "I see, my major."

"Come back in twenty minutes. I am busy now."

She seemed to hesitate, and then I heard her move off without another word. She was used to taking orders.

I sweated out two or three minutes behind the door. I couldn't be sure she hadn't tumbled. She might only be playing it smart, but I had to take the risk. Every moment that slipped away from me gave Ugo time to phone around for Major Ricasoli, or take matters into his own hands with Pia.

Damning her for returning to her apartment, I opened the door a crack. The porter was almost as I had left him on his knees, waxing the floor by hand. The cleaning woman was vacuuming on the far side of the bandstand. Duvivier was nowhere in sight.

I walked out into the club. The porter looked up.

"*Ripasserò più tardi*," I shrugged, as if I were only going out for a cup of coffee.

He nodded and I kept walking. I stopped in the foyer long enough to pick up the hat and coat I'd left the night before. Then I got out of there.

I parked several doors past Via Garibaldi 29. There was a good view of the street from Pia's apartment, and I didn't want to take the chance that Ugo might be watching for trouble. It was more likely that he had hustled someplace else. I moved quickly with a growing sense of desperation. I must already be too late.

There was a scattering of foot traffic on the sidewalk and I all but ran. The big doors at Number 29 were ajar. I hurried up the marble stairway and strode along the hall. I got out the Tokarev. I had the feeling that I was going to burst into a deserted room, but I had to try.

I stopped at Max's door. I had taken the key with me the night before and I now let myself in. I'd enter Pia's living room through the connecting door: It might give me the advantage of surprise.

No one had made any effort to clean up the shambles that someone had made of Max's things. Sydney Jardine, I thought. I moved quickly to the connecting door and listened. I heard nothing, no voices, no sounds of movement and my heart sank. I twisted the key and flung open the door. I had the gun in my hand and felt impulsive enough to shoot.

Ugo was there. He lay in a heap on the polished floor, a Cinzano bottle near his head. He'd been hit hard. But Pia was gone.

I glanced around the room with a mixture of relief and exasperation. I had acted like a fool. Pia could take care of herself, but I had rushed over like a two-bit hero. She had taken care of Ugo without my help. The kid had guts. She was beautiful and she had guts and she'd be easy as hell to fall in love with.

I hurried to the recording machine and cleared the old bottles and glasses off it. Pia had probably gone back to the hotel to wait for me. Even though I had checked out I hoped she'd wait. Hell, she had nowhere else to go. Wait for me, baby, I thought. Wait.

I plugged in the machine and fed the wire through the gimmicks. My heart began to beat a little faster as I snapped on the machine and the spindles revolved. I hoped the recording would give me a short cut to Borsilov.

The volume was up loud and a voice suddenly sprang out of the speaker. I stopped breathing as I listened.

The voice didn't tell me a thing. It was a man speaking, but he was speaking Russian.

The message was brief and the strip ended. I stared at the spinning parts. Jardine had been after this and so had Major Ricasoli. That made it important. I snapped on the rewind. I got the hunch I'd been listening to the voice of Evgeni Borsilov. I played with the idea and it seemed to fit. This could be one of Jardine's golden eggs: Borsilov himself revealing brief, scientific data of some sort. It was only a hunch, but I believed in playing my hunches.

I began playing the strip through again. I had to get the wire to Washington. There wasn't much length, but I had a feeling it was choice. It could only be a fragment of what Borsilov was carrying around in his head, but Washington would want to take it apart word by word. I still had to find Borsilov in the flesh; meanwhile I'd get the wire out of circulation. If I was right about this, Jardine hadn't been lying. He was in the golden egg business.

The Russian voice blared in the room and I watched the wheels spin. I felt a certain excitement at having beat out both Jardine and Major Ricasoli on the recording. Then there was another sound, a rustle behind me, a quick swish of air. And it struck before I could turn. My head seemed to split open and a shattering incandescence leaped into my eyes. I don't even remember hitting the floor.

Perfume. I smelled a light, fresh scent of mimosa, and someone's fingers were digging into my shoulder. The floor was cold against my face. I tried to shrug off the fingers. There was a throbbing in my head and a singing in my ears. I wanted to lie there.

"*Presto*, Jim. Get up. We must hurry!"

I turned my head and forced my eyes open. I saw a shimmer of blue.

"Hold still, damn you," I sputtered. I felt light-headed and once re-moved from reality. I felt at peace and I wanted to stay that way. But then the singing in my ears began to fade and the wavering blue settled into focus and the immediate past came crashing in on me.

"Let me help you, *caro*."

I saw Pia.

Her red hair was carefully brushed, her dark eyes troubled. She was bent over me, her sharp nails in my flesh, the perfume close and lovely. A quick bitterness overwhelmed me. I rose to my knees, grimaced and tore her hands off me.

I snapped, "Next time I'll know better than to turn my back on you."

"Jim, what are you saying...?"

Pia. It had to be Pia. I rubbed my neck and tried to shrug off the crush of disappointment. And I'd even begun to wonder if I were falling in love with her. I looked up, smarting. She had changed clothes. A blue knit-ted dress hugged her hips and a double strand of pearls gleamed from her neck. She was wearing fresh lipstick, but her lips were apart in as-tonished alarm as she stared down at me.

I shook my head and tried to think straight. My eyes flicked over the recording machine. *The wire!* I had to get it back. What was her game?

I got up and held onto a chair until the whirling in my head passed and my balance came back. "I want it, Pia. Give it to me."

"Jim, you can't believe I did this to you."

I caught her wrists and snapped her closer. "The wire, Pia."

"You're hurting me."

"I'll kill you."

"Jim, *caro*—"

"Let's cut the act, baby. Where were you? In the bedroom? I should have looked in the bedroom."

"Jim, I came back and you were on the floor."

"Sure."

"Listen to me, Jim."

Her face was lined with pain, but I kept hurting her. I'd let her make a sucker of me all along, but she'd finally knocked some sense into me. Now she'd gotten her hands on the wire. Was she a Communist after all? Hell, she must be out hustling information for Major Ricasoli—

Then I saw that Ugo was gone. He wasn't unconscious on the floor. He was gone. I saw it and my thinking fogged. I suddenly let go of her wrists. The scent of mimosa burrowed into my brain and I knew I had made a mistake. Ugo. My God—

"Why don't you walk out on me, Pia. I don't deserve you."

"Jim, you've been hurt."

"I keep hurting myself. The medics must have a word for it. And I keep hurting you, that's the worst of it. I'm sorry, baby."

"It doesn't matter about me."

It hadn't been Pia. She hadn't struck me and she hadn't taken the wire. I looked at her and felt cheap. I'd started out feeling like a two-bit hero and now I felt like a two-bit bastard.

"You must have a headache, Jim. I'll get you aspirin. But it's not safe for us here."

She left me standing and I watched the movement of her hips as she walked into the bathroom, her heels clicking on the terrazzo floor. The kid had class and I was a punk.

I rubbed my neck and tried not to think about the recording. It was gone. Ugo was gone. Pia returned with a glass of water and a tin of American aspirin. "Hurry, Jim. Take this, it will help you."

"Why did you leave the hotel?" I said. "You were safe there."

"I had to come here for my passport so I could cross the frontier with you. So early in the morning I thought it would be safe."

"But Ugo was around."

"I didn't ask his name."

"You managed to hit him with a Cinzano bottle."

"Yes, Jim. We must leave now."

"Tell me. I've got to know. Tell me everything."

She handed me the glass of water and I washed down a couple of aspirins.

"We can talk later. Someone may come." Pia picked up her coat.

"What did you do after Ugo was laid out on your floor."

"I thought I had killed him. I changed clothes and packed a bag and left quickly. I was already in a taxi when I saw you walk up. I called to you, but you didn't hear. I thought you would come out in a few minutes and waited. My taxi still waits across the street. But a few minutes later, it was Ugo who came out."

My head was splitting. The recording was gone, and I might as well get used to the idea. I could lose hours trying to find Ugo, but the recording wasn't the big game. If I had doped it out right it was important, a golden egg, but I'd better get my hands on the goose.

Ugo must have come to while I was listening to the machine. He'd thought fast and moved silently and I had a headache to show for it. Well, he'd pass the wire on to Major Ricasoli and the information would go back where it came from—behind the Iron Curtain.

"Something has happened to you, Jim," Pia said, staring at me. "You're terribly upset."

"Let's go."

We'd head west, we'd go after Kurt. I couldn't afford to be sidetracked, valuable as the recorded secret might be. There was more where that came from. Borsilov. I had to find him before Major Ricasoli killed him. The wire had been a minor break, but I'd fumbled it. I'd better do better next time.

We left. Daylight hurt my eyes. Pia pointed out her cab across the street and I got her bag out of the back seat. There were a few tourists on the sidewalk, guidebooks in and, looking over the old palaces that lined both sides of the street. I paid off Pia's driver for waiting, and we walked to my parked Fiat.

"But Jim, it's a lovely car!" she said, brightening. "Blue, like my dress."

"Get in."

I threw her bag in the trunk beside mine. She had a lit cigarette waiting for me when I got behind the wheel.

"Pia, did Max ever borrow your recording machine?"

"No."

"Are you sure?"

"Of course I'm sure. No—wait, Jim. Once he took it to have it fixed. But that's not what you mean."

"I think it is."

"But really, I don't think it needed fixing. It was missing from my apartment one day and when I asked him about it, he said he'd taken it to be fixed."

"How long was it out of your apartment?"

"Only a couple of days. And it sounded the same when he brought it back."

I started the engine. Max had made that recording while Jardine had Borsilov under wraps at his villa, I thought. And there must have been more recordings made here in Genoa before Borsilov got wise and got loose again. Well, that was water under the bridge. What the hell had Max been up to? His job was to get Borsilov safely to Washington—it wasn't to pump him for scientific information.

"What are you waiting for, Jim?"

"Nothing," I said, looking at her. "Not a damned thing." The brooding fear was gone from her eyes and there was a quick eagerness on her face. You'd have thought we were starting out on a vacation.

I struck off for the Piazza Acquaverde and cut down the Via Milano for the harbor. We finally left the industrial section of Genoa behind us, traffic thinned and I followed the two-laned Via Aurelia. It would take us all the way to the French border. And it had better take us to Kurt Schindler.

There was a line-up at the French border and I had to fight bicycles and traffic through Mentone. It was almost five when we passed the small blue sign that introduced the Principality of Monaco. We had stopped at a number of casinos already. No one of Kurt Schindler's description had been seen. At least Kurt had had sense enough to try to change his appearance, I thought, and that meant he realized he was in danger. I felt sure we were on the right track.

I turned off the Boulevard d'Italie and followed the lower road cut in the cliffs along the bay. In a few moments we swept around the Monte Carlo promontory and the Moorish, stone facade of the casino rose above us, catching the last warmth of the sun.

I cut up the hill and found a parking place.

"Can't we go to a hotel, Jim? I would like to freshen up."

"We might not be staying that long."

"Kurt wouldn't be playing this time of day."

"Let's give it a check."

We checked and Pia was right. Kurt wasn't playing this time of day. I had an impulse to start asking around the hotels, but there must be a hundred of them in Monaco, and he might have gone to a pension. The search would take forever.

I decided to stay out of the big hotels, on the off chance that anyone might be trying to trace us, and checked into a pension on the Avenue de Rocqueville. It was early enough in the season that we got our pick of rooms, with a connecting bath, a pair of iron balconies and a view of the small square harbor below.

"We don't need two rooms," Pia smiled when we were alone again. "It was agreed—I am to be your *amante*."

"Was it?"

"*Santa Maria*, I will never learn to understand you, Jim."

"Go in and take your shower. You'd better grab a couple of hours sleep while you can."

She left me on the balcony and I sat with a cigarette watching the Mediterranean darken, and thinking about Pia. I had never fallen in love with a woman so suddenly and so desperately. Earlier in the day I had believed Major Ricasoli had gotten his hands on her and that he must already have killed her, and I had tried to wipe her out of my mind. Beautiful water under the bridge. But when I saw her alive, something happened. I knew I didn't want to lose her again. I knew I was in love with her.

When I got out of the shower the door to Pia's room was open. The tag end of twilight pressed through the closed shutters and fell across her bed in shadowy streaks. She was sitting up in bed having a cigarette and our eyes met.

She'd brushed her hair so that it almost shone even in the dying light of the room, and she had the sheet pulled over her breasts. It was obvious that she had slipped into bed nude, and she'd been waiting with troubled expectancy. I was so hard to understand.

I hesitated, glancing into my own room, the shutters open, lights beginning to come on across the harbor. Then I stopped being hard to understand. I took the cigarette out of Pia's fingers and her eyes softened with a smile. Our lips met and the sheet slipped down.

Chapter Twelve

We walked to the casino and played roulette until three in the morning. Finally the ornate, golden Salle Schmidt took on a deserted look except for the ragged, stubborn ranks of the *systémiers*, and I began to feel depressed. Kurt Schindler hadn't shown up. I wasn't sure what to make of it.

"Let's go, baby."

I tossed the croupier a *pourboire* chip. We stopped for a nightcap in the bar, and then walked back to the pension.

"What next, *caro?*"

"I start checking hotels in the morning."

"Is Kurt so important?"

"Not Kurt. But Borsilov is."

"I hate that name." She flicked her hands in an angry gesture. "He interferes with my life, and I don't even know what he looks like. It's maddening."

I kissed her, and it helped force Kurt and Borsilov out of my mind. I'd start worrying about them in the morning.

The morning was dazzling blue with still a touch of March in the air. I started with the luxury spots, working down to the Hotel de Paris on the Place du Casino. It was going to be a long haul, but I didn't want to sit around the Salle Schmidt another long night waiting for Kurt to walk in. If he's made a minor killing in San Remo, I figured he'd put up at one of the classier hotels in Monte Carlo. I kept trying.

When I left the lobby of another hotel, word was beginning to spread out over the square. It was visual. The gardeners left their flowers and even the *carabiniere* looked ready to abandon his post. I picked it up from a bell boy coming in off the street.

A body had just been found off Suicide Point. One of the *habitues* who'd been wiped out last night in the casino.

You get a feeling. I ran. It was Kurt Schindler.

They had him stretched out near the small train depot below the casino. Even wet his black hair had a dull, dyed tone. He was muscular and his closed eyes were bugged. There was no doubt about it. This was Kurt. My pipeline to Borsilov was dead.

I could hear the wail of an ambulance. A crowd was beginning to build up and a tourist was unslinging his camera. A pair of *carabinieri* in dark helmets and white belts were already on hand and I introduced myself as a doctor.

"But he is already dead, m'sieu. There is nothing you can do. *C'est affreux!* Such things are bad for the casino."

I bent down to the body and thumbed back one of Kurt's eyelids as if I knew what I was doing. I saw raw pocks on the backs of his hands. Cigarette burns, I thought, and a throb of desperation hit me. He'd been tortured and then stabbed in the heart. He hadn't committed suicide; he'd been murdered. Someone else had caught onto Kurt and made him talk. The body didn't look battered and that meant he couldn't have been in the surf very long. They'd dumped him and hoped he'd pass for a casino suicide. Not more than an hour ago, I decided. That gave someone at least an hour's head start getting to Borsilov, and whoever it was knew where to go to find him! I didn't.

I looked at the dark conservative suit hanging now on his stiffening body. It wasn't keeping his old style of dress. Even dripping wet the cloth looked new and unworn. I turned back the coat and read the label on the inside pocket. He'd bought the suit at Innsbruck, Austria.

All I could do now was play my hunches and play them fast.

"He's dead, all right," I said, straightening.

"*Merci, monsieur le docteur,*" the cop said with a touch of sarcasm. The ambulance was rolling in and I mixed with the chattering crowd and then took off. Borsilov could be under wraps in Innsbruck or one of the villages close by. I had to act on that possibility, but it looked fairly strong.

Kurt had managed to put Borsilov on ice, bought himself a new suit of clothes that lacked his usual flamboyant taste, dyed his hair and come south. You could always turn up a fast-buck artist around Monte Carlo and Nice, and Kurt knew he stood a good chance of making a contact, someone willing to invest in his information. Borsilov was something to be sold, like a prize head of beef. Meanwhile, Kurt could kill time at his favorite wheels.

I cut past the Sporting-Club International and worked up to the Avenue de Rocqueville and the pension.

Pia was sitting on her balcony having coffee and *brioches*.

"I've got to leave," I said quickly. "You might as well stick here on the Riviera. I'll come back for you."

"You're joking, *caro*."

"I want you to be safe. You'll be safe here."

"I won't let you run out on me."

"I'm not running out."

"See—I'm ready before you."

I smiled and cinched up my bag. Hell, it was a long way to Innsbruck and she'd be nice to have along. Within another ten minutes I'd paid our bill and was studying a map while giving the Fiat a few seconds to warm. The quickest route would be back along the Riviera and north from Genoa.

We made Genoa by twelve-thirty and I tried a hunch. I stopped near the entrance ramp of the autostrade and put in a phone call to Major Ricasoli. He wasn't at the Florentine Club, but I picked up his home number from the cleaning woman when I told her it was urgent that I reach him. Either his wife or his mistress answered my second call. She was sorry, the major was out of town and couldn't be reached.

That's all I wanted to know. I had played with the idea that Sydney Jardine may have gotten to Kurt, but now I felt sure it was Major Ricasoli. Kurt may have made the mistake of trying to sell to someone who passed the word on to Major Ricasoli, and the Italian had hurried to Monte Carlo personally.

But he'd had plenty of time to beat me to Genoa. If he weren't yet in town I assumed he'd dumped Kurt and started out directly for Borsilov. He'd kill the Russian with his own hands to make sure the job got done. There had been too many foul-ups trusting the assignment to underlings like Kurt. He had at least an hour's head start and maybe more.

Pia had bought a sack of butter cookies to eat in the car. She stuck one between my teeth and I turned up the long ramp to the autostrade, a fifty-mile stretch of high-speed highway. I stopped for the toll and got underway again behind a gasoline truck.

"Jim, what if you are wrong about Innsbruck?"

"Don't think about it. I've got to be right, baby."

Pia had her window rolled down and let the wind play with her hair. She sat with her dress pulled up at her knees for comfort; an easy intimacy had sprung up between us and she seemed relaxed and happy. I glanced at her legs and wished I didn't have to watch the road. I was glad she had come along.

"You're not a Genovese," I said.

"No. I grew up in Florence. My family has a villa in Fiésole."

"I've never heard of anyone leaving home when it was Florence."

"I'll go back someday, Jim."

"With money."

She lit a cigarette and ignored the barb. "From my bedroom when I woke up I could see the sun come over the pink rooftops of the big city below. It was nice. The day the Germans blew up the three bridges across the Arno, I was watching. I saw the explosions. It was grotesque."

We entered a tunnel and I switched on the lights. The long ceiling dripped water and the tires hummed on the wet macadam. I'd be glad when we got out of the mountains and could make some speed.

We reached sunlight again.

I got the speedometer up to 105 kilometers, but the road was only two lanes, full of blind curves and I kept having to use the brake. We passed a concrete retaining wall and you could still read the faded, dripping words out of the past—*Credere, Obbedire, Combattere.* It was the dead voice of Mussolini, except that nothing ever seemed to die in Italy.

We stopped for gas in Piacenza. I couldn't hope to make better time than Major Ricasoli's Alfa Romeo, but by passing up lunch I thought we might have picked up some time on him. While the car was being gassed Pia walked across the street to a grocery store and returned with a half-dozen hard Italian rolls, a thick wedge of Bel Paese cheese and a bottle of Fiuggi still water. She said I'd been driving too fast to drink anything stronger. The Austrian border was still a long way off and I planned to pass up dinner as well.

My only chance was to catch up to Major Ricasoli and head him off. There was only one pass through the Alps to Innsbruck and I thought I stood an even chance of meeting him on the highway. I hadn't yet doped out exactly what I would do when that time came.

Pia was in the back seat when we reached the frontier. She lay asleep wrapped in her fur coat. It was past four in the morning, and it was cold in the car. I had refused to use the car heater; it would have put me to sleep at the wheel. I had been fighting the Italian Alps since Verona, and I hadn't made very good time.

I had the Tokarev automatic at the small of my back, tucked under the belt. Unless they decided to give me a personal shake-down, a thousand-to-one shot, I'd get it across the border with me.

I got Pia's passport out of her bag without waking her and handed it to the passport control officer, together with my own. He stamped them and I carried our luggage into the customs house.

The inspector was in no mood for thoroughness; it was an ungodly hour to be crossing the border. He looked as though he'd been sleeping upright in his chair and wanted to get back to it. He poked through Pia's things and grunted.

"Busy tonight?" I asked.

He shrugged and started in on my bag.

"I'm trying to catch up with a friend of mine," I said. "He's driving an Alfa Romeo. Has he—"

"It just left."

"A few minutes ago?"

"Perhaps fifteen."

My heart vaulted. Major Ricasoli must be only a few miles ahead of me.

My questions must have aroused a hazy brand of suspicion; he decided to give my bag a second going over. I stood there and began to sweat out the seconds I was losing. Finally he finished. I picked up the bags and got them into the luggage compartment. Pia had roused and was sitting up sleepily. She struck a match and lit a cigarette as I got behind the wheel.

"Where are we, Jim?"

"Brénnero."

"I'm freezing to death."

She climbed into the front seat; I started the engine and drove across the border to the Austrian side. A young Tyrolean, surprisingly awake and fresh looking, bent his head to my window and touched his feathered, velour hat.

"*Pässe, bitte.*"

I handed him our passports. The road ahead was empty; it couldn't be far to Innsbruck and I had to catch up to Major Ricasoli before the city could swallow him.

I lost several maddening minutes in red tape with the *carnet,* clearing the car and changing some money into Austrian shillings to pay the entry tax. The inspector showed no interest in my bag since I was travelling on an American *pässe*. But Pia had an Italian passport and he went through her things carefully. He spoke only a few words of English, and I spoke less German. I couldn't make him understand I was in a hell of a hurry.

At least, I thought, Major Ricasoli had lost some time with the Austrians too. We finally got out of there and I saw a marker beside the road. Innsbruck, 38 kms.

Somewhere on the road behind us Max had gotten himself killed chasing after Borsilov. I was going to need more luck than he'd had. I got the Tokarev out of my back and put it in my overcoat pocket.

The slopes of the Brenner Pass rose sharply on either side, with here and there a dark farmhouse on a high, Alpine meadow lit up by the moon. We reached the crest of the pass and began the long descent. It was all vaguely familiar, but it had been too many years since I had been on this road.

"Must you drive so fast, *caro?* It frightens me."

"It frightens me too," I said.

"Look—"

I saw them too. Headlights on the road ahead. But that couldn't be the Alfa Romeo, I thought. I couldn't have gained on it this quickly.

Then I realized that the lights weren't moving. The car was stopped. It was an Alfa Romeo.

I was almost on top of it before I recognized the situation. The car was crowding one side of the highway, and a man I'd never seen before was changing the rear left tire.

Pia's breath caught as the brief flash of our headlights lit up Major Ricasoli waiting at the wheel.

"You were right, Jim!"

"I was due for a change of luck."

I kept going until the next bend in the road cut us from sight. Then I braked fast.

"This is as far as I go," I said. "Take the car to Innsbruck. Do you know any hotels there?"

"The Europa."

"Register there and stay put. I'll meet you later."

"Jim—"

"Don't argue with me. This time I mean it. Now get going."

I shut the door. The darkness was oppressively cold and silent. When Pia had driven off I could hear the chill babble of a stream to the right of the highway. I hurried up the road until I could see headlights behind the bend. Then I cut over the road shoulder and ran along the bank of the stream, out of sight. There was an inch or two of snow under my feet.

I crawled back to the road behind the Alfa Romeo. It was a right-hand drive, and I hoped Major Ricasoli hadn't spotted me against the snow. The engine idled, probably to keep the heater going inside the car, I thought. The rear was jacked up and the guy was tightening the lugs, a flashlight lying near his foot. He was whistling. I recognized the tune.

I took my time now. I gripped my gun by the barrel and moved around behind him. He was at a crouch. I clamped my hand around his mouth and sapped him with the handle of the gun. He stiffened under me and then his breath died in the palm of my hand. I picked up the tune and kept whistling.

He was wearing a beret and a knee-length black leather coat. I threw away my hat and pulled on the beret. I found the last lug and tightened it on the wheel. I put away the flat tire and tools and pulled the guy behind the car. I picked up the flashlight and went through his pockets quickly until I found out his name. It was Ridolfo Alfieri.

I got into his leather coat and threw my own over him and hoped he wouldn't freeze to death before he came around. I took a last look at his face in the flashlight. It was a beefy face, and I wouldn't pass for him except in the dark. Well, it was dark.

I flicked the light absently across the car windows and saw two men in the front seat. I felt a temptation to blast them both. They'd never know what hit them. But Major Ricasoli knew where to find Borsilov; I didn't. It would have been a waste of time to try tailing the Alfa Romeo with my Fiat. The Italian would begin to notice he was being followed and he'd lead me into nowhere but trouble.

I stood in the cold for a moment trying to get up enough nerve to step into the back seat and try to pass myself off as Ridolfo. It was a hell of a gamble, but the stakes were high. If I won, Major Ricasoli would taxi me right to Borsilov's door. If I lost—well, I had a gun. If they came to realize it wasn't Ridolfo in the back seat I'd try to shoot first.

Like Max, I thought suddenly. This is the way it had happened to Max, and now it was happening to me. I kept the whistle on my lips and wished I had his reckless nerve. I opened the car door on the left hand side. I was scared and I admitted it to myself. I got in. I wouldn't talk unless I had to. The heater was going full blast and the interior of the car was hot and stuffy with cigar smoke.

I closed the door after me and sat back. Then my skin jumped. I had brushed someone's leg. I wasn't alone in the back seat, and my heart dropped. It had been a woman's leg, and she shifted. She was trying to sleep.

I began to make out her features. I'd met her before on the ship from Athens, in the customs house and in Major Ricasoli's office. It was Alexandrine Duvivier. I tried to keep whistling.

Chapter Thirteen

The car heater purred. I let the whistle trail off my lips and put my face against the leather upholstery. I would pretend to go to sleep. I grunted as if unable to find a comfortable position.

I had the gun in my hand, out of sight under the flap of the leather coat. When I needed it I would be in a hurry and I didn't want to have to fumble in my pocket.

It must be at least a quarter to five. I thought. I hoped dawn wouldn't come before we reached Innsbruck. When the Duvivier roused there would be trouble. She would recognize me. But I'd work that out when I came to it.

I glanced at Major Ricasoli, rigid shadow in the glow from the dash. He drove like a mechanical man, his neck stiff in the brace. The road had become a long, twisting downward grade, but he used his brakes sparingly. There was no conversation in the front seat. They had been driving too many hours for that. I could make out only a little of the man sitting beside the major. He looked heavy-set. He wore a camel-hair cap pulled tight over his head, as though he expected a wind to come up and blow it away. He was smoking a cigar. Maybe the gunman, I thought.

Major Ricasoli blasted the horn and passed Pia in my rented Fiat. I stopped worrying about her. She'd be all right.

I had been driving for almost eighteen hours straight and my eyelids burned. But it would be deadly to fall asleep, and I struggled to keep my eyes open.

Duvivier shifted beside me. Her face wasn't more than eighteen inches from mine. Her breath touched my free hand. I wondered why he had brought her along. Maybe he had rounded up anyone he could get in a hurry and she had happened to be on the spot. She was still wearing the sealskin coat and hat.

We passed the walls of a bombed-out village and I began to catch snatches of the broad white valley below and the towering peaks beyond. The sky in the east was beginning to gather light. I wished it would stay dark, dark as hell until we reached Borsilov.

Max. His name began to sing through my head. I had picked up where he had left off all right, I thought bitterly. It was as if I had suddenly begun to relive his life, step by step, and I began to feel uneasy. The only part of it that made it worthwhile was falling in love with Pia. I wondered if he'd been in love with her after all. Really in love. There was no longer any doubt in my mind that he had gone over to Sydney Jardine—money he needed for Pia?

I shook the thought. To hell with Max. We rumbled onto a tall, narrow bridge that crossed the valley. Duvivier awoke.

"I can't sleep," she uttered in sudden exasperation. Her Italian had a Gallic accent, even I could tell that. I wondered if she were really French after all. "How much further?"

"But a few miles," Ricasoli said.

I shifted positions to put my back to her. We reached the end of the bridge and sped along solid ground again.

"An hour ago you said it was but a few miles," Duvivier said. "My legs are too long for your back seat. I'm miserable."

"I will rub the pain out of your tired legs, bambina." It was the other guy talking. "I will trade places with Ridolfo if you wish."

"Shut up."

"Only Ridolfo could sleep in the back seat with such a pair of legs. He is a stupid one. He is good only with a gun and for changing tires. Me, I am a Spaniard. We Spaniards have a talent with women, eh?"

"*Tace!*" Ricasoli.

"It passes the time to talk, *padrone*."

"A pity he lived through his civil war when so many brave ones died." Duvivier.

"You think I am not brave, girl?"

"Give me a cigarette, Jorge. I smoked my last one." I could hear the cellophane crackle as she twisted the empty pack.

"For a cigarette, during the war, a woman would trade her virtue, if she had any."

Major Ricasoli spoke irritably. "Give her a cigarette, fool. She is nervous."

"I have only cigars. Let her wake Ridolfo. We're almost there anyway."

My heart began to pound.

Duvivier. "Let him sleep if he can."

"He is an animal. He would sleep on his own wedding night." Jorge turned in the seat. "*Permesso*, I will wake him for you. It will give me pleasure." His hand reached out and caught my knee. "*Gufo*—it's time to get up! *Hi, bástardo! Attenzióne, cretino!*"

I knew I couldn't fake any longer. I shook myself. "*Basta per Dio!*"

Jorge's fingers dug in with pleasure, and he laughed. "Give the lady a cigarette, comrade." I tore away his hand, and he straightened in his seat, quick laughter in his throat. "Perhaps she will give you a kiss for it, Ridolfo. Take her by the earrings, like a bull by the nose, and make her give you a kiss."

I rubbed my face, glancing through my fingers. The others in the car had become well defined shadows. My only chance was to curl up and pretend to go back to sleep. Damn Alexandrine Duvivier and her cigarette. Make it fast, I thought. I found my pack and handed it over, but even as I did I realized my mistake—American cigarettes.

There wasn't a chance in a thousand that Ridolfo had been smoking American cigarettes.

A moment later she returned the pack. It wasn't light enough that she could read the brand. "*Grazie.*"

"*Prego,*" I muttered softly.

I turned away as she struck the match and lit up. I heard her blow out the flame, and shifted around again so I could keep an eye on her. My hand went back to the gun on my lap under the coat. With my free hand I flipped up the collar of the leather coat and raised my shoulder. In case Jorge turned back I didn't think he'd be able to see enough of my face to matter.

I wondered if this was the way it had happened to Max, masquerading in the other car as Kurt Schindler. Maybe he'd been forced to show his gun too soon, and there had been sudden trouble in the car. At this speed on these narrow Alpine roads, a moment's distraction could take the wheel away from Major Ricasoli. My jaws were clamped. It was a long way down.

Duvivier had taken her third or fourth drag on the cigarette when I knew she was trying to make out the details of my face.

"*Non è possible.* Amer—"

That's when I put the gun against her. Her breath caught and she froze. Jorge laughed.

"I hope I don't have to shoot him, *padrone*. A traitor should know what it is to feel a cold knife in his flesh, eh? I would prefer the blade on this Russian pig of a scientist."

"Later I'll decide how to deal with him," Ricasoli said. He seemed lost in his own thoughts and Jorge's animation had obviously gotten on his nerves. But Jorge had to be humored. Jorge was valuable.

"You must admit, *padrone*, I did a good job with the knife on our former comrade. Like a surgeon. Kurt was dead even before he could take a second breath."

"You did well," Major Ricasoli said.

Duvivier was staring at me. The cigarette had burned down in her fingers. She hadn't taken another puff once she realized that something was wrong. I could see her face clearly now, the thin nose, the intense eyes, the shimmering gypsy earrings. She had recognized me moments ago.

"And the knife is silent," Jorge said, like a salesman trying to interest a customer in his product.

"Either way," Major Ricasoli snapped impatiently, "we must make sure he is dead. I will not be given another chance to carry out this assignment."

Jorge chuckled. "I will cut off his ears for good measure. Like a bullfighter. Perhaps I will save ears. *Sì,* when we get back to Genoa I will pick up the ears of the American agent. You would like that, *padrone?*"

"In time we will take care of him."

"*E gia fatto!* But Pia Brindisi, her it will pain me to kill. It is difficult to make a beautiful woman die. Ridolfo would enjoy it—he has no feelings about such things. Me, at least, *padrone,* I have feelings about a beautiful woman, eh?"

Major Ricasoli grunted. He had other things on his mind. The road swept down out of the mountains and I saw a few scattered morning lights in the valley below. Innsbruck rose out of the streaked darkness, pitched rooftops and church towers taking shape in the enveloping dawn. Snow-heavy mountains guarded the valley as if to box in the city.

I warned Duvivier with my eyes.

She killed her cigarette and Jorge turned to speak to her. "Ridolfo is asleep again? He could sleep in a bagnio, that one! *Ecco,* Ridolfo! We are almost in. You want breakfast in bed?"

Duvivier's eyes left me and she faced forward. Maybe she'd been wondering if I really would pull the trigger if she tried to warn them. I would.

Jorge shifted back, laughing easily.

A river cut through the city, dividing it like a wide paper streamer. We reached the floor of the valley and the outskirts of town. There was a scattering of bicycle traffic on the road, men in work clothes heading for the factory chimneys along the railroad tracks.

We turned left through the edge of town, away from the hotel district, and I began to wonder if this ride was going to end at Innsbruck after all. I could read nothing in Duvivier's face; if she was frightened it no longer showed.

We followed streetcar tracks past still-darkened shops and garages, a light pressing here and there through the painted shutters of living quarters above.

We crossed a narrow bridge and almost at once began to climb again. I caught the sign: Igls. The road hairpinned at a steep grade, tall black pines stepping up the mountainside with us.

We must be getting close, I thought. Even Jorge had stopped talking. The road kept twisting and rising and Major Ricasoli blasted his horn around the curves. We passed a volksvagon with skis tied to its roof.

We must have climbed about four miles when we passed a great wooden hotel, boarded up. Except for the hum of the engine there was no sound in the air. It was already quite light. A moment later the tiny village appeared, tilted on a slope: Igls. Borsilov must be in Igls.

Squat, two-story houses with fretted wooden balconies stood back from the road, their roofs packed with snow. The road took a sharp left turn and we found ourselves in the center of the village. A young girl with blonde pigtails was carrying a pail of milk beside the road. Major Ricasoli stopped across from the church and touched the horn.

"*Guten Morgen*," she muttered softly.

Major Ricasoli spoke very slowly in Italian, expecting her to understand. He asked how to find the Hormayr house, Hormayr, *Hormayr*, but she only stared at him.

"*Ich verstehe nicht.*"

Without shifting his head in the brace, Major Ricasoli snapped out to Duvivier, "Do you speak German?"

Jorge broke in before she could answer. "Ridolfo speaks it. He was born near the border."

"Ridolfo, ask her directions," Major Ricasoli barked impatiently.

My temples pounded. Maybe Ridolfo spoke German, but I couldn't.

There was nothing left to do but show my hand. I already knew what I had to know. Borsilov was at the Hormayr house. I began to turn— but Duvivier bent forward and began rattling off German. The little girl's face lit up and she put down her pail and began giving directions with her arms. I settled back and watched Duvivier in astonishment. She had guessed I didn't speak German, and had jumped in to help me avoid the trap. For Christ's sake, why?

She thanked the little girl, who ran off forgetting her pail of milk, and ran back for it. Duvivier gave Major Ricasoli directions to the Hormayr house. He attempted a U-turn in the middle of the street, but it was too narrow. He straightened out, made the turn in front of the brown Sporthotel, and came back. He turned left beyond the church, ground up a steep hill and followed the road past the Iglerhof, an expensive-looking hotel abutting a long, snow-covered meadow. A man and woman were already out on the slope skiing.

We continued along a rutted road for almost a mile. There was only an occasional house spotted among the pines. The morning was turning bright and the snow sparkled in the sun. Major Ricasoli pointed to a house through the trees on a slope to the left of the road. "That must be it."

"That is the one," Duvivier agreed, glancing at me as she said it. Her face seemed a stolid mask, but her eyes were trying to speak to me. They seemed to be saying: don't give yourself away yet. Your time will come.

I decided to wait. Duvivier's unexpected help was a new element to consider, and I didn't understand it. I would have to start shooting when I made the break, and she might get killed. I had taken her for an agent of the Russians, but now I couldn't be sure.

Major Ricasoli drove beyond the house to a bend in the road. He found a place to turn the car around and parked out of sight of the house above.

"*Buonissimo!*" he said smartly. "We have already discussed what to do. The *signorina* goes to the front and knocks while you, Jorge, and Ridolfo cut through the trees to the back. Inside, they will be misdirected to the front, and you burst in."

"*Sì...*"

"It should be very easy. I will wait. When the Russian is dead, I will come in and look at him. This time, I must be sure."

"In five minutes it will be done, *padrone*." Jorge laughed and opened his door.

I stumbled out of the car as though still half asleep. I understood now why Duvivier had wanted me to wait. My odds with Jorge were going to improve in the woods. "Come on," I mumbled impatiently, starting into the pines.

"I'm coming, comrade."

I kept ahead of him, my back to the car, my hand tight around the gun in my pocket. After a moment I caught a glimpse of Duvivier walking down the road. Anticipation sharpened my mind. I had found Borsilov. There was only Jorge to stand in my way, and anyone guarding the Russian in the house. I'd worry about them one at a time.

The hillside was packed with a few inches of snow. My feet seemed to drag, but Jorge began complaining.

"Not so fast, *compagno*. We must give her time to reach the front and draw their attention. I will use the knife on the Russian. Don't shoot too soon, Ridolfo. Save him, if it is possible."

"*Sì*, as you wish." We were already deep in the trees and I let him catch up.

"Did I show you my new knife, Ridolfo. I bought it last week in Milan. A beauty, eh?"

"Let me see."

I had a good grip on the barrel of my gun as I turned. I let him have it almost before our eyes met and he saw I wasn't Ridolfo at all. I cracked the gun butt into his temple. His arms flew out and the knife in his hand gleamed. It fell even before he did. I'd put enough behind the blow to jar his brains, if he had any, and I saw I wouldn't have to hit him again. I looked down at him. He was out cold.

By the time I reached the yard behind the house, my shoes were wet and my feet and hands felt frozen. Espaliered fruit trees clung to the white walls of the house like lacework. A round woodpile stood in a shelter beside the back door, every stick in place as if stacked according to blueprint. I moved quietly to the back door and listened. I had my gun ready, and this time I would shoot at trouble. There were no sounds within. Excitement started up inside me. Borsilov was somewhere behind this door. I tried it slowly and softly. It opened quickly.

"Come in."

Duvivier was standing there. She had a gun in her hand, but it wasn't pointed anywhere. The sealskin cap stood jauntily on her dark hair, and there was a smile on her lips.

"If it had been Jorge, I would have shot him." She spoke English now. "Is he dead?"

"I didn't want to make that much noise." I shut the door and walked through the kitchen. There was an unnatural silence about the house and I sensed that something was wrong. I walked into the living room and saw that the house was empty. There wasn't a stick of furniture in the place. I turned.

"Where is he?"

"Borsilov has never been here."

"*What?*"

"There's no one here but you and me."

I stared at her. "What's the gag?"

"This isn't the Hormayr house."

"I'm stupid this time of the morning."

"It is only an empty house. For rent." She made a gesture with her hand. "See?"

"I see. But I don't understand."

"I would like a cigarette, Mr. Welles—no, you are using the name Cabot. Forgive me, Mr. Cabot, but I am famished for a cigarette."

I dug out my pack and tossed it to her. She lit up and handed it back. She seemed to enjoy my confusion. "It surprises that I helped you, eh?"

"Have fun, baby."

"I have helped you before. I hope you don't mind."

"Keep helping me."

"Do you think I would have gotten on that train to Florence if I wasn't anxious for you to lose me. I wasn't fooled. Did you flatter yourself that I was fooled?"

"All over the place."

"Yes, of course. You are impressed with your own cleverness."

"At the moment I'm not impressed," I said. "Consider me taken down a peg. Now tell me what the hell's going on."

She studied me through a thin cloud of cigarette smoke. "No, you are very clever, I admit it. But I didn't like you to think I was so stupid, Mr. Cabot."

"I apologize. You're way ahead of me."

"Not far. I thought it would be best to settle with Jorge and Major Ricasoli away from the Hormayr house. There may be trouble enough for us there. But I was afraid you would get impatient in the car and ruin our chances."

"I almost did."

"Yes. I not only asked the little girl where the Hormayr house was, but also if she knew of an empty house for rent. We were lucky she did. This house belongs to her uncle in Innsbruck, and she said he would rent it cheaply."

"Where is the Hormayr house?"

"It is a pension, a few blocks up the hill from where we were."

"You're on the ball, Duvivier."

"Perhaps we had better relieve Major Ricasoli of his impatience now."

"What's your interest in Borsilov? You're not with the Russians."

"They pay me, Mr. Cabot. But I am of French Intelligence."

"Double agent."

"We French mean to find Evgeni Borsilov as well as you Americans."

Chapter Fourteen

I aimed for the ceiling and pulled the trigger twice. "Give me a few seconds head start," I said.

Duvivier nodded. We'd worry about which government got to pick Borsilov's brains when we turned him up. Until then we'd work together.

"All right," I said. "Major Ricasoli's heard the shots. Once I leave, go back to the car and tell him he can view the body."

"Yes. It's a good plan, but it might be better simply to kill the Italian."

"I'm not kill-happy yet. Let his Russian masters liquidate him as a bungler."

"You're content merely to out-maneuver him?"

"That's right."

I left by the back door and made a wide circle through the trees. I didn't want to see Jorge again and avoided the spot. I came out of the trees well behind the Alfa Romeo. Duvivier was just coming up to the car, and she nodded as if to tell Major Ricasoli it was all over.

He got out of the car with a springy step, his narrow shoulders stiff. But there must have been a hell of a smile on his face. They talked for a moment, and Duvivier must have been describing the battle that hadn't taken place. She was quite a kid, I decided. She knew the business.

Major Ricasoli finally left her standing and began to lope down the road, looking somehow like a marionette without strings. Maybe he thought Moscow would give him a medal for this.

When he was out of sight around the bend, I moved up to the car.

"Did he leave the keys?"

"Of course. All he could think of was the sight of blood. He is an animal, like the others. A traitor to his own country."

I got in behind the wheel. I gave him about a minute and a half to reach the house and started the car.

"By the time he can walk back to Igls," I said, "we ought to have Borsilov in the back seat."

"There may be trouble at the Hormayr house."

The road straightened out and I saw Major Ricasoli on the porch of the house. He turned at the sound of the car and froze as he watched his Alfa Romeo speed past. But before we had gone out of sight he had drawn his gun. We heard the explosions, but there were too many trees between us.

I glanced at Duvivier. "You'd have been better off if you'd let Major Ricasoli get wise to me in the car. Don't you take me as serious competition? You'd have a clear field on Borsilov if I were out of the way."

"The important thing is to get him to safety—then we can fight over him. Do you speak Russian?"

"No."

"I do."

"I think I catch on." Sure, I thought, she could speak to him in his own language. She could convince him that I was only a hot-shot while I waved my arms trying to make him believe I represented the U.S. Government. She could lead him around by the nose. She'd rather outwit me than kill me.

I'd have to get rid of her, but not yet. She'd known she might need me at the Hormayr house, and I might need her. For the time being we'd have to get along together.

We passed the Iglerhof again and a few minutes later we were in the village, a cluster of nursery-rhyme houses on a narrow cobbled street.

"Turn right at the Sporthotel," Duvivier muttered. "The Hormayr pension is a short way up the hill."

The pension Hormayr stood behind an outcropping of rock above the road on the left side. Smoke trailed from the chimney into the clear, cold sky. I drove onto a muddy driveway and came in along one side of the house. I set the brake and took the ignition key. "Maybe you'd rather wait here," I said.

"I will come."

"There may be trouble."

"I'm used to trouble."

"Suit yourself."

We left the car and walked around to the front of the house. A Teutonic religious mural, the blue paint faded, covered the upper story wall. The morning air was crisp but peaceful, and not far off a falcon soared above the pines.

I knocked. Then I knocked again.

The door finally opened and we faced a shrunken old woman with a shawl across her shoulders. You could smell the schnapps on her breath and see the bitterness and suspicion in her eyes—protruding eyes, like Kurt's. "*Ja?*"

I turned to Duvivier. "Tell her we want to rent a room."

"*Haben Sie Zimmer frei?*"

The old woman shook her head, and Duvivier gave the translation. "She says it's too early in the season. Her house isn't ready yet for guests."

"She's stalling."

"Of course."

The old woman tried to close the door on us, but I put my foot in the way and then pushed my way into the hall. She began to shout at me. I grabbed her shoulders and yelled back at her in Italian. I saw that she understood what I was saying and went on with it.

"Take us to Borsilov—he's here, isn't he?"

Her eyes took on a threatening squint and she tore herself out of my hands. There'd been a lifetime of hard work behind her and her strength surprised me. "If my son—"

"You're Kurt's mother, aren't you?"

"He will kill you if you hurt me!"

"He's dead."

"Impossible!" she shouted flatly.

"He brought the Russian here, didn't he?"

"My son—"

"He's dead."

"No—"

She had been drinking heavily, probably for days, but the idea began to sink in. Her heavy eyes stared up at me. And the fight went out of her. She sat back in a chair, dazed, but unwilling to sob.

I got her back on her feet and then without a word she led us up a winding wooden stairway. We followed her along an unlit hall on the second floor, her heavy shoes thudding in the silent, overheated house. Kurt was dead and she knew it and nothing else mattered. She seemed anxious now to get it over with.

She had a silver chain of keys around her waist and found the one she wanted. We stopped at a door at the end of the hall and she inserted the key and turned it.

"*Ecco!* There is your Russian," she said bitterly. "He waits for you."

I opened the door and my blood went icy. Vaguely, I was conscious of the old woman's heavy steps as she walked back down the hall, leaving us alone to see the secret she'd been living with for days.

The man who must be Borsilov was hanging by a rope, made of a bedspread, from a ceiling beam. The body was hideously bloated by its own gases. He had obviously been hanging there for days.

"Don't look," I said to Duvivier. "For Christ's sake, get out."

But she was looking. She stared, the color washing out of her face.

I crossed the room and threw open a window. I stood for a moment, taking the cold mountain air into my lungs.

Duvivier hung in the doorway, forcing herself to stay. "So it was all for nothing. We were too late. They hounded him until—"

"At least they didn't get him. He chose his own way to die."

I saw her eyes give the bare room a quick, searching glance, but there was nothing of interest. "No one can get to the secrets in his head now."

"We all lost."

"It's inhuman to leave him hanging that way."

I tried not to look at the puffed body dangling from the center of the room. "Go on back with the old lady and pour yourself a good stiff glass of schnapps. I'll cut him down."

She looked as though she'd faint if she stood there another moment. Maybe she'd been afraid I'd ask her to help me. She moved away without another word. Borsilov was dead, and that was that. Her assignment was finished.

Well, so was mine. Borsilov had probably given up hope soon after Kurt brought him here. And when the old woman found him dead, it had probably frightened the wits out of her. She had looked horribly old to me, but I thought she'd probably aged plenty in the last few days. She'd let him hang there, waiting, hoping Kurt would hurry back. He'd no doubt told her the old man would make them rich and she had agreed to keep him under lock and key. Once dead, Borsilov was another matter. She hadn't even turned down the furnace heat in the room and the gases in his body had begun to work.

I held a handkerchief over my nose and mouth and stood on a chair. I got him down. That's when I noticed that the ends of his fingers were ink-stained. My heart gave a leap.

I went over the room fast, not sure that I wasn't only jumping to a wild conclusion. If he'd written anything, the old woman may have gotten it. But I had a feeling she had locked the door fast once she saw him hanging there and had never come back.

I glanced once more at his fingers. They looked as though he'd written his heart out before he took his life. There were more stains than he could have picked up just writing a suicide note.

I hoped I wouldn't have to go through the pockets of his dirty black suit. But there was no choice. I put the handkerchief back over my nose and got on with it. His billfold was gone—I wondered if Kurt had taken it.

I found a paper-covered novel in his coat pocket and a couple of lose cigarettes: Baltos. At least Kurt had been charitable enough to leave him some cigarettes to smoke.

I flipped through the novel. The title was in Russian, and I couldn't read Russian. But my heart jumped when I saw the pages. Borsilov had written between the lines in a small, squarish hand and covered the margins with diagrams. The first forty or fifty pages were marked with data that was obviously scientific.

I slipped the book in my jacket pocket, out of sight, and considered letting myself out the window and leaving Duvivier behind. No, I couldn't do that. Major Ricasoli would eventually find his way to the real Hormayr house, and she deserved a good head start on him. He'd kill her now just on sight. I couldn't abandon her, not here.

I took a last glance around the room. I didn't know what Borsilov had written in his neat Russian hand, but it would certainly tell Washington how far ahead of the Soviets we actually were. Borsilov must have gambled that the old woman would be afraid to touch his dead body and would immediately call the police. He'd wanted the police to find his notes, thinking his information would reach Western hands. Well, she hadn't called the police. And I had his notes.

I left.

I got the Alfa Romeo going down the winding grade to Innsbruck, and Duvivier lit up a pair of cigarettes.

"What are your plans now?" I asked.

"To go home. It's three years since I've been in France. Are you going in that direction?"

"No."

"Then maybe you'll at least take me to the highway. I don't think it would be healthy for either of us to remain in Innsbruck. You should have killed Major Ricasoli while you had the chance."

"You could take a train."

"I would prefer to hikehitch."

"Hitchhike. Harder to trace your movements that way?"

"Of course."

"You know the angles."

"I will feel safer."

"Suit yourself."

We reached the outskirts of the city and I found my way to the highway. I stopped near a bridge and she got out. I felt like a bastard, but she was asking for it. She'd only been able to give Borsilov's hanging body a brief, sickening glance and with his hands turned in she'd never noticed the ink stains on his fingers. For her money, the whole affair was at an end and she seemed relieved. Now she could go home.

"Good luck, Jim."

"Good-by, Duvivier."

"If you're ever in Toulon..."

"I'll look you up."

We shook hands and almost kissed, but didn't. I made a U-turn and I watched her in the rear-view mirror. Before she was out of sight I saw a Buick stop for her, and I felt better. She was well out of it now and she'd be home by tomorrow.

And me, I'd gotten the next best thing to Borsilov alive, and I had to get it safely into U.S. hands. Innsbruck, I knew was in the French zone of Austria, but there was surely some U.S. military around. I touched the book in my pocket. I wanted to get rid of it fast.

Chapter Fifteen

Military cars and French occupation soldiers in floppy military berets were scattered about the Landhaus Platz. I parked on the street, lit a cigarette and looked up at the modernistic lines of the post-war parliament building. I had stopped earlier on the bustling Maria-Theresien-Strasse and gotten what I wanted to know from a cop. There was no American consul in Innsbruck, but there was a U.S. Army liaison officer, and his office was in the Neues Landhaus. I would turn the Borsilov document over to him and tell him to rush it under armed guard to Washington.

I thought of Pia and tried not to worry about her. I couldn't take time now to see her. I hoped she'd made it okay to the Hotel Europa.

I crossed the square, set back from the street, and began to feel tired as hell. My eyes smarted from lack of sleep, and I needed a good meal. I felt edgy and I felt impatient. I'd be glad to get it over with.

A pair of military guards stood behind the glass doors. One of them directed me to a stairway at the far end of the shiny, dimly-lit ground floor. The place smelled of brand-new red tape and there was a hollow clack of typewriters from the offices.

I was checked by another guard on the second floor and nodded on my way. I was carrying a gun, but all they checked for was my name and business in the building.

I followed the hall to my right. It was a long walk. I reached the door and knocked on the glass pane. There was no answer so I walked in.

America in Innsbruck was three small offices strung together. I was in the center one, a bare small room with a littered desk, a couple of wooden chairs and a wash basin near the door. I could hear a woman's voice coming from the office on my right. She was on the telephone and having a hell of a time with a long-distance operator.

I sat and picked up a magazine. I wished she'd get off the phone. She finally reached her party in Munich, spoke German, and I tuned it out. But when she finished and nodded to me, she spoke English with a lovely French accent. "Good morning, sir."

"When will the general be back?"

"Perhaps I can help you." She was dark and rather pretty, but I wasn't in the mood.

"I'm afraid you can't."

"If you are in any trouble—"

"I'm just sightseeing," I said. "I want to see your boss."

"Captain Ryan isn't here." A slight chill.

Why doesn't the brass ever show up on time, I thought angrily. "I'll wait."

"But that's impossible. He has been called to Salzburg for conference." She turned to her desk and began fingering the papers. "I'm in charge. If I can help—"

"When is he due back?"

"He will be gone three days."

"The hell he will."

"Is there anything else, sir?"

"No," I said. "Nothing else."

I was annoyed and began figuring what to do next as I walked back along the hall. Captain Ryan had pulled a hell of a time to go to Salzburg. The paperback novel in my coat pocket felt as explosive as dynamite. I wanted to get rid of it before it blew up on me.

But I wasn't going to hang around three days waiting for Captain Ryan. Switzerland couldn't be very far, and there'd be an American consul in Zürich. Although I didn't want to leave Innsbruck until I saw Major Ricasoli laid out and had a chance to go through his pockets, I had no right to risk the safety of the Borsilov data. I'd better go to Zürich.

I was halfway across the square before I saw the fleshy man hovering around the parked Alfa Romeo. He was wearing my overcoat—and I was wearing his leather jacket. Ridolfo!

The bastard hadn't frozen to death out in the Brenner Pass where I'd left him. He'd picked up a lift, and now he'd come across Major Ricasoli's car.

I turned but I was too late. He recognized his leather coat on me and the beret. I didn't feel like facing any more trouble. I ran.

I heard the thud of Ridolfo's heels on the cobbles behind. A string of half-size trolley cars was rattling along near the sidewalk, but I crossed just ahead of them and Ridolfo was cut off for a few seconds. All I wanted to do was shake the guy. I didn't want to have to slug it out. He'd recognized me as the guy who'd tried to split his skull out on the highway and there was murder in his eyes.

I made the other side of the street. Hell, it was a long way to the corner. I hurried past a few shops and turned into a shoe store. A little bell tinkled over the door as I worked it.

I walked past the salesman as if I knew where I was going. I entered the stock room and then a factory room. A couple of sewing machines were clacking. I saw a back door and started for it. From the front of the shop, I heard the bell tinkle again. Ridolfo was on the ball.

I came out on a courtyard lined with the back doors of shops. I ran across the stones, but the first door I tried was locked. The second led me into a restaurant kitchen. I nodded to the startled cook and kept walking. A couple of steps down led into the dining room. It was a low-ceiling affair crossed with dark beams and a stuffed boar's head over the fireplace. I took my time now. (A few men were sitting around drinking coffee and reading newspapers on wooden sticks from the rack.) Ridolfo must be wondering which door on the courtyard I'd entered, I thought.

I went up a few steps and found myself on the sidewalk again. I fell in with the foot traffic and walked three or four blocks, but Ridolfo had lost the scent.

I got into a taxi. "Hotel Europa."

"*Danke.*"

I pulled off the beret. It was out of place in Austria and had made me immediately conspicuous to Ridolfo. I'd forgotten I was even wearing it. But it was too cold to give up the leather coat, even for Ridolfo.

The hotel stood across a wide street from the depot. I saw my rented Fiat parked in front. Pia had made it.

I paid off the driver and a bellboy opened the hotel doors for me. The lobby was bright and spacious. The bar was off to the right and I spotted Pia at a table by the window. It gave me a lift to see her again. I walked over. She began to smile, as if she'd been sitting there afraid I'd gotten myself killed. My God, she was beautiful, even early in the morning.

"Hello, baby."

"*Caro mio.*"

I lifted her chin and kissed her lips. She was nice to come back to.

"You look like you've had a night's sleep," I said, sitting beside her.

"Don't make me wait again, Jim. I couldn't stand it."

The bartender came out from behind the bar and I told him to bring me nothing but black coffee. I looked at Pia again, and she seemed happy and fresh, even after the lousy night. For the first time in my life, I wondered if I were getting old.

"Is everything all right now, Jim?"

"Lovely," I said bitterly. "Borsilov's dead."

The bartender began to grind my toffee in a small chrome gimmick and across the street there was the clatter of riveting on a new hotel going up.

"Are you sure, Jim?"

"Of course I'm sure. The poor bastard killed himself."

"I'm sorry, Jim. It's a blow for you."

"I'm still ahead of the game."

"What?"

"Never mind what. We've got to do some more driving. Are you really as fresh as you look? You're going to have to spell me at the wheel."

"I'm a good driver."

"We're going to Zürich."

The bartender brought my coffee and we waited until he had gone.

"But I don't understand, Jim."

"You don't have to. Major Ricasoli is around town, so I think I'd better take you with me. Safer that way."

Her eyebrows rose suddenly as if an afterthought had struck her. "But Jim, the car must be fixed before we can go."

"What?"

"There is something wrong inside. Under the bonnet. I almost didn't make it here. There is a loud knocking."

I swore.

I was taking the coffee black, but it stopped doing any good. What the hell—was my luck running out? Captain Ryan was out of town the one day in my life I needed him. Ridolfo had come across the Alfa Romeo and me. And now the Fiat needed fixing.

"I'm sorry, Jim."

"That means we'll have to wait for a train."

I hated the idea of taking a train anywhere. It made too many stops, it lost too much time crossing frontiers and you were never maneuverable enough if you picked up trouble. But I didn't want to hang around waiting to get the Fiat fixed. I glanced at the clock over the bar. It was almost nine-thirty.

I got out of Ridolfo's leather coat and left it on the banquet. He had known me by the coat, not my face, and even if I ran into him again on the street it wouldn't matter.

"I'll be right back," I said. "Have another cup of coffee."

"Must you leave me again, Jim?"

"Sit tight."

I stopped at the reception desk, exchanged more money into schillings and found out the nearest travel agency, Cooks, around the corner on Brixner Strasse. The station was only across the street, but I knew better than to try to buy tickets in a language I couldn't handle.

The crisp Alpine air went through me on the street, but I walked fast. It was a long block and Cooks was almost at the other end. I felt uneasy walking the bay-windowed streets at all; I'd be glad to get out of Innsbruck. Major Ricasoli was sure to be on his way down from Igis, and I didn't like the risk of bumping into him the way I had Ridolfo. But until I got the Borsilov report safely consigned to Washington, I had to keep my nose clean. If there wasn't an early train out, I'd have to put the Fiat in a garage and sweat out the repairs.

I was in luck. There was a train to Zürich at 10:20. I got a compartment. I might be able to grab a little sleep at that.

During the walk back I realized I couldn't carry Borsilov's book in my pocket. I had to conceal the information somehow on the off-chance I ran into more trouble. A Russian book in my pocket might seem suspect even to the frontier inspectors, and one flip through it with all its diagrams in the margins would alert them fast.

I passed a sign over a shop that said *Tabak*, but the jutting window had a little of everything in it. I went in, asked for a couple of packs of American cigarettes and looked over the newspapers. There were none in English. I settled for a local tabloid and pointed to a tube of paste under the counter. I bought that too and left.

I headed for the self-service elevator when I got back to the hotel. I took it up and stalled it between floors. I wanted to make damned sure I was alone. I got down on my knees and went to work. It wouldn't take long.

I ripped out the thirty or forty book pages Borsilov had covered with ink. I opened the newspaper past the middle, laid the stack of torn leafs toward one corner, and began to paste a concealing sheet of newspaper over it. Someone began to buzz for the elevator, but I ignored it. The report held together in a sort of closed pocket of newspaper. The tabloid wouldn't bear much reading or any inspection, but it would look innocent in my pocket.

I folded it up and put it there. I was sorry the newspaper had to be in German; the Paris *Herald-Tribune* would be more in character, but I hadn't wanted to walk through town hunting up a copy.

I raised the elevator to the top floor and got out. There was a sand vase for cigarettes near the doors. I buried what was left of the Russian novel and the tube of paste deep in the sand. Then I took the stairway down to the lobby and rejoined Pia in the bar. It was ten to ten.

The station had obviously been rebuilt after the war. A large sign stretched across the face of it—HAUPTBAHNHOF. There was a café terrace along the wall and it was doing a spotty business in beer and coffee. I scanned the snow-tanned faces, vacationing Austrians mostly in ski clothes and knapsacks, and hoped I wouldn't spot anyone familiar. Once we made the train, I'd stop worrying.

"Not so fast, *caro*. I can't keep up with you."

She was having trouble with her heels on the cobbles, and I made myself slow down. There was no doubt in my mind that Major Ricasoli had made his way to the Hormayr house and found Borsilov. One look at those ink-stained fingers and he'd jump to the same conclusion I had. If he'd gotten any sort of description of me from Kurt's mother, he'd know who to come looking for: Not Ridolfo but Jim Cabot. My broken nose would be enough of a tip-off.

The station entrance was beginning to crowd up with porters pushing carts of luggage and skis and passengers scanning kiosks for last-minute reading matter. But it didn't look to me as though the train was going to be very full. It waited under a shed on Track 4, and we had to go through a tunnel under the tracks to get there. We found our car and got squared away in the compartment. I tipped the conductor and locked the wooden door. I was glad I had paid for a sleeping compartment; it would be a hell of a lot more private.

But the room was icy. I turned the knob for heat. Pia lit cigarettes, handed me one, and we got settled across from each other beside the window.

"Just like home," she smiled.

"If you were brought up in an icebox."

"Do you read German, *caro?*"

"What?"

"Your newspaper. It's a language I refused to learn, even when the Nazis were everywhere in Italy during the war."

"I just bought it to look at the pictures."

There was the distant cry of the train whistle up ahead, and after a few moments the station began to drift by. My muscles relaxed. We were moving and sometime this afternoon we'd be in Zürich and then I could forget I'd ever heard the name Borsilov. Then I could grab some real sleep.

Pia stretched her legs to my seat and crossed her ankles. I knew I'd never be able to go to sleep with those legs before my eyes. The kid was built.

We had crossed the river and were creeping through the outskirts of the city. The mountains seemed to open up ahead of us and I saw we were going to stick with the river valley. I'd wait until the conductor came for our tickets, and then close my eyes a bit.

It was almost half an hour before he knocked at the door. When he finished, I locked the door again, shoved Pia's ankles off my seat and stretched out. The compartment had heated up and I made a pillow of the leather coat. I turned on my side, the side with the newspaper in my pocket. I'd feel better sleeping on the Borsilov report.

We had picked up speed and occasionally the train broke out into a thin, piping whistle through the pass. I fell asleep with the sound in my ears.

I don't know how long I slept. I slept and dozed during the stops and starts. My muscles ached and I couldn't get comfortable. I finally gave it up; threw my feet to the floor and sat up. I couldn't really sleep with the Borsilov material in my pocket. I reached for a cigarette and looked across at Pia.

But it wasn't Pia. She wasn't in the compartment. It was Sydney Jardine.

Chapter Sixteen

The train wheels sang under me.

Jardine sat across from me, his knees apart, a squinting smile on his florid, English face. His curly blond eyebrows lowered with amusement. He'd been combing his beard to pass the time, but now he slipped the comb in the breast pocket of his coat.

"Where's Pia?" I snapped.

"I shouldn't worry about her, Mr. Cabot. She'll be along in a moment."

"If you've done anything to her, I'll kill you!"

"That might prove difficult and it would be wholly unnecessary. I've taken your gun. So relax, sir, and be a good fellow, eh?"

I threw down my unlit cigarette and took a sharp look at him. This was the guy who had corrupted Max, this was the guy who had once saved my life, this was the guy who had picked Borsilov's brains for cash. I touched the newspaper sticking out of my pocket with my elbow. It was still there; I'd been sleeping on it.

"All right, you've taken my gun," I said. "Where do you think that leaves you?"

"Top man, sir. We need to have a chat, you and I. Plenty of time. We won't be rolling into Zürich for almost four more hours. All the time in the world to reach an understanding. Do relax, sir. Violence is quite out of order here, you know. And we're going to be friends, you and I."

"What have you done with Pia?"

"Ah, you're a man in love. I can see it, sir. Delightful. I haven't done a thing with her—I'm not such a scoundrel as you think. I expect she'll be back in a moment. She was nice enough to leave the compartment. Fine girl, sir. Makes a man wish he were twenty years younger."

"How do you happen to be on this train?"

"I usually manage to be in the right places at the right time. It's a gift."

"Sure."

He gave me that pirate's grin of his.

I said, "Why me, Jardine?"

"You're it."

"Spell it out."

He shifted, leaning his bulk closer. "See here—Borsilov's dead, right? You take off for Zürich, a very improbable place. Unless—unless, sir, you picked up something of value. Something big. Something that needs delivering to high American authority. Zürich's the place for that. A pity indeed about the Russian."

"News travels fast."

"We live in an age of communication, sir."

"You could have searched me when I was asleep."

"In a perfunctory fashion, I did. But it's not really important. You'll volunteer your little prize, and you'll join up with us."

"If not?"

"Why, I shall kill you. Come off it, sir. I offer you life and wealth in exchange for your future services. A generous offer it is when the alternative is death, eh?"

"I'll take my chances."

"See here, Max was the best friend you ever had. It pained him to see you risking your neck for a pittance. He wanted to make you rich—rich, sir—I promised him I'd give you the chance. Don't be a stubborn ass."

"I'm just killing time," I said. "Four hours to Zürich."

"The truth is, your talents impress me. You recovered the golden egg Max had pawned for safekeeping, even though you were outwitted at the last moment. I can forgive you that."

I looked across to his raffish eyes under the curly, blond brows. Sydney Jardine was uncanny. He seemed to know everything. I thought quickly of the scene in Pia's apartment. I'd been knocked out while I stood over the recording machine listening to Borsilov's voice. "Are you trying to tell me Ugo is drawing his pay from you?"

He seemed surprised and then briskly amused. "Don't be a fool. The last I saw of Ugo he was sleeping things off rather badly in a closet of Pia's bedroom. We'd hardly have any use for a man of his small abilities. Good lord, sir, don't underestimate us!"

"You're bluffing," I snapped angrily.

"Upon my word I'm not, sir!"

"Pia saw him leave the apartment—"

"Did she?"

I stared at him; his words hit and they jarred. Ugo. I'd believed it was Ugo who knocked me out and took the recording. But Jardine was going out of his way now to open my eyes. Ugo had ended up in the closet. *Pia!* The whole picture began to shift in my mind. He was trying to tell me it was Pia who had come up behind me and knocked my brains loose—and taken the recording.

"You're lying in your teeth!"

He lifted his bushy chin and laughed.

And yet Pia had known I was driving to Innsbruck, and Jardine was in Innsbruck. And Pia had known I was going to Zürich, and Jardine was on the train.

My head was spinning. Jardine rested his shoulders against the seat, his eyes twinkling as he watched me. "What do you say, sir?"

There was a light tap on the door and I turned as it opened. Pia stood in the doorway. She hung there only a moment, her eyes passing to Jardine for some sign. He nodded. She didn't look at me, and it was as if she couldn't. The bottom fell out of my hopes and the truth came crashing into my head. *Pia!*

I'd break her neck. She was a beautiful, titian-haired bitch, and Jardine had been trying to soften me up for the news. It had been Pia who struck me, not Ugo. It was Pia who had the recording, not Major Ricasoli. She had been playing me for a sucker all the way.

She put a cigarette between her lips and closed the door softly. She sat beside Jardine and looked at me for the first time.

"Hello, *caro*."

"Cut it out, baby."

My eyes must have been blazing. For a moment she looked uncertain of herself, but Jardine patted his hand with the gun in his pocket, as if to reassure her that I was under control. Well, I wasn't going to play it that way. I got a fast grip on myself.

"You did fine," I said coldly. "You had me right under your beautiful thumb. You've got talent, kid."

"You're very sweet, Jim."

"You covered all the angles, didn't you? Ugo—all you had to do was drag him into your closet."

"I had to strike him again."

"You're real handy with a Cinzano bottle."

"We wanted the recording, Jim. It's worth money to us. We want you, too. You can take Max's place."

"And the taxi below with your suitcase in it, baby. That was really convincing. You set it up while I was out and I swallowed the whole business. I began to trust you again."

"You're taking it well, Jim."

"Like the seven-year-itch."

"Truly, I'm in love with you. There's no reason why we can't go on being in love, *caro*."

"Sure, baby, sure. You've had the recording all along. In the pension at Monte Carlo when I made love to you. You have it now, but it's only a drop in the bucket, isn't it? What hurts is I didn't catch onto you."

Jardine broke in with his eager-beaver grin. "No use standing on your pride. She's an irresistible creature and a man would be a fool not to know it. The past is past. We're your friends, sir. We've recovered only one of our golden eggs. I daresay you came away from Borsilov with a pot of them."

My eyes swept over the two of them; I felt a certain wild exhilaration in being able to hate them both. I'd let her make a fool of me even as we made love.

"What made you so sure I'd find Borsilov?"

"You were just one of my irons in the Borsilov fire," Jardine said. "But if you did find him—and you did, sir—we'd be ready for you. But there's more to this than Borsilov, don't you see? There's other business to be had. We must expand and good people like you are hard to come by. That's why Max sent for you."

How rotten had Max become? Like a narcotics user, I thought, he'd wanted to drag me into the habit. Money. We'd never particularly liked each other, but we'd respected each other's abilities.

"Well, there you have it, sir. What do you say?"

I ignored him and caught Pia's eye. "You tipped this punk off that I was driving to Austria?"

"When you stopped in Genoa to phone the Italian."

"Because you truly love me."

"Because I would like to be very rich, Jim."

"And when I went out to buy train tickets, you got in touch with him again. He was already in Innsbruck."

"Upstairs in the hotel."

"I seemed to have tipped my hand all the way."

"She's an ambitious girl, sir. And very lovely. You'd be a fool to chuck a future with her."

Alpine peaks moved slowly past the window, the snow glistening under the high sun. "Pia has what it takes."

"Indeed she has. I daresay, one day she'll take over the syndicate. I promise to watch her closely—especially when my back is turned."

He chuckled coarsely, but I realized he was a little afraid of her. Maybe she was too money hungry even for Sydney Jardine.

Pia was watching me, anxious for the matter to be settled. "You have been hurt, and I'm sorry. But am I not desirable, Jim?"

"You're the Venus di Milo," I said, "with the impulses of a chippy."

"Don't think—"

"I'll tell you what I think," I snapped. "You were rolling in bed with Piero and a case of Cinzano because you thought a fortune had slipped through your fingers. You probably hated Max, the way you hate me and even Jardine here. All you want to do is go back to the streets of Florence and show off a million lire to the other girls. What streets did you work, baby? The Lungarno? The Via Roma? I'll bet trade was brisk around the Grand Hotel."

"Shut up!"

"You're a goddamned whore. Your fine family villa in Fiésoli was probably a tenement room around the Piazza Ognissanti."

Quick rage burned in her eyes. "You think it is very funny, eh Jim?" Her voice was full of loathing and contempt. "You think it's funny to be fifteen and so hungry that a bar of chocolate looks like a filet mignon to you?"

"I've heard it before, baby."

"You think it's funny to give yourself to drunk American soldiers who have just won a war? Yes, it's funny. See, even I can laugh at it now. It was such amusement to have these pigs throw up even when they were in bed with you, while your family waited on the street for you to finish in the room."

Jardine turned to her impatiently, as if he'd heard the story before. "Are you finished, my dear?"

"I think we can do without Mr. Cabot."

"If you don't mind, I'll make those decisions." He turned to me, and the grin was back in place. "Look at it this way—opportunity's knocking at your door."

"With brass knuckles."

I turned to Pia. "I'm curious, baby. What did you do with the wire recording? I'm still not entirely convinced you outwitted me."

She smiled with deadly contempt. "It cuts you to be outsmarted by a woman, doesn't it? Yes, I have it."

Jardine pulled the gun out of his pocket: the Tokarev. "And I'll take it, my dear. Good work. Very good indeed." He held the gun on me. "Don't get any ideas, sir. This interesting weapon of yours is loaded."

I nodded. If I got out of this alive, I wanted to make a clean sweep. I had the Borsilov report, but I wanted the recording as well.

Pia gave me a cutting, victorious glance, got the compact out of her bag, lifted the powder screen and there was the wire, coiled like a thin snake. I looked, and it was all I could do to hold myself back, even with the eye of the Tokarev staring at me, black and deadly.

Jardine took the coil, smiled at it and slipped it in his pocket. "Now then," he said, bending slightly toward me. "I'll take what you picked up from the unfortunate Borsilov." He held out his hand. "If you please, sir."

I was being crowded and tried a long shot. There was no doubt in my mind that he'd carry out his threat and kill me if I refused to play ball. He'd get the Borsilov report over my dead body if that's the way I wanted it. "For Christ's sakes," I snapped. "You don't think I was fool enough to carry it with me. I mailed it ahead to Zürich."

"The hell you did!"

"Kill me now and you'll never lay hands on it."

Pia began to laugh, a mean, needling laugh. "You mailed nothing to Zürich. Do you take us for fools?" Her voice became strident with loathing. "We don't need you and we shall kill you—"

"Be quiet, girl!" Jardine growled.

"Shut up, idiot. The compartments in this car are almost all empty except two at the other end. Don't you think I checked? Look at him—see the German newspaper in his pocket? He doesn't read German. Don't be so stupid, Sydney!"

Jardine's eyes lit up. "You may have hit on something, my girl."

"Why don't you get it over with," she muttered.

Jardine got to his feet, the grin gone from his eyes. The stakes were high and he was willing to take the risk of murdering me on the train.

"All right sir. We gave you your opportunity. You're a pig-headed fool."

"You'll have the whole train on your neck if you fire that gun," I said.

"Don't worry about the noise. I'll worry about that."

Pia was on her feet, swaying with the movement of the train, and she had blood in her eyes. "I want to see you die, *caro*. Truly, I will enjoy seeing it."

We entered a tunnel. The windows went black and the compartment lights came on. The noise of the train became a roar and I knew he'd pull the trigger without hesitation now.

I leaped. I heaved myself against him and the gun exploded wild. I lashed out for his gun hand, only to keep it clear, and jammed a hard fist into his bearded jaw. He fell back against the seat. I laid into him, got a better grip on the gun and turned it out of his hand. Jardine had run to fat and it was no match. He spread his arms in a quick gesture of defeat once I got the gun.

"All right, sir. Don't shoot."

I saw then that Pia had taken off a shoe, for lack of anything else to hit me with, and had moved in with her arm raised. But I had the Tokarev now and she stood there looking at it. She'd been yelling for my blood, and maybe she thought the gun would go off in her face.

"Sit down, baby."

She sat down. I held the gun against Jardine's temple, and he knew better than to move. I found his own weapon in a shoulder holster and got the wire recording out of his pocket. We were suddenly out of the tunnel and daylight shot through the windows again.

I backed to the door and fought down the impulse to kill them both. Well, I wasn't built that way and during moments like this I was sorry. It was going to hurt just walking out on them.

"Sit tight," I said, "and you'll both live."

"That's sporting, sir," Jardine said, rubbing his jaw. "We'll sit tight."

All I wanted was to get off the train. The highway wouldn't be far from the tracks. Duvivier was right. Trains were a lousy way to travel. I'd hitchhike the rest of the way to Zürich.

I looked at Pia, but didn't tell her off. She no longer seemed that important. I backed out of the door and closed it. The corridor was deserted. Without a gun, Jardine wouldn't try anything, I thought. He valued his neck too highly. He had other irons in the fire beside Borsilov, and he'd mark it off as a business loss.

I walked toward the vestibule. I'd wait until the train slowed on a curve and jump off. I reached the vestibule. A face appeared through the windows in the pair of doors that divided the two cars.

It was a face with dark, deep-set eyes. It was a face over a neck brace. It was Major Ricasoli.

Chapter Seventeen

He wasn't more than five feet away.

Our eyes met and for a moment neither of us moved. Two doors separated us, we were each standing in a different car, and the wheels clicked away under us. I was armed, but he'd have a gun too and I didn't want to risk shooting it out. If I stopped a slug I'd lose more than some blood. I'd lose a pocketful of secrets.

My impulse was to run. I didn't stop to ask myself how he knew I was on this train; I had to shake him and I had to keep alive. But it would be deadly to attempt a run back along the train corridor. He'd be crazy enough to shoot.

He began opening the first of the heavy doors. I glanced around me quickly. The lavatory. I reached for the door and it opened. I slammed it after me and locked myself in the lavatory. I got hold of my gun, but I wanted to think before I began shooting. In another moment I heard Major Ricasoli's voice through the door.

"Ah, so I found you, *signore*."

"You found me."

"*Sì*, an American is easy to trace. You were noticed by many at the station. I had only to hire a car and catch up with the train."

He must have gotten on at the last stop, I thought, and been checking the compartments for me. "You wasted your time."

"I think not, *signore*. I saw the Russian. I saw the ink stains on his fingers. What did he write? You have taken it—*sì?*"

"Go to hell."

I glanced at myself in the broken mirror. My face was drawn and pale. I looked tired. I was tired.

There was a lavatory window painted white and I lowered it. He'd get tired of talking to himself and catch on that I'd gotten out of the lavatory. Let him catch on. I put my foot on the wash basin and threaded out my head and arms. My eyes caught the flash of gravel and rail racing beneath. The wind smothered my breath. I twisted and got both my feet on top of the window sill. He'd think I'd jumped out into a snow bank.

But that wasn't where I was going. The sky was blue, patched here and there with starched white clouds. I found a grip for my hands and hoisted myself onto the roof of the car. I shimmied along the cold metal, afraid to trust my legs to the swaying car.

He'd get off at the next stop and go back, I thought. He'd believe I'd jumped out. I decided I'd done the best thing to protect the Borsilov report. If I'd tried shooting it out down below, there'd be a mess with conductors running around and the train would be stopped. The important thing was to get to Zürich.

No—I'd steer clear of Zürich. I'd go to Geneva. Sydney Jardine might figure he could make another try for me before I could dispose of the Borsilov report. And Major Ricasoli might have thought to wire ahead and have friends waiting in Zürich. I'd better stay out of the place. I'd ride the roof almost to the border and make my way to Geneva.

I lay there, feeling the cold sun on me. The car rolled gently on its wheels. Beyond the train I saw a cataract tumbling from a shelf of pines. Not far to my left a ravine paralleled the railroad tracks. In the distance I made out the spidery underpinnings of a trestle where we would cross the ravine.

I hoped I'd guessed right. Then I saw I had guessed wrong. The top of Major Ricasoli's head rose over the sloping metal roof. He was coming up. He might have been willing to believe I'd left the train through the window, but he was thorough enough to want to have a look at the roof. Okay, he was nobody's fool, and he was going to get shot.

My jacket flapped in the wind. I got the Tokarev back into my fingers. He pulled himself up quickly, looking like a thin monster, all arms and legs. He was forward of me, almost half a length of the car away. I saw the gleam of the gun in his hand, and he got in the first shot. Wind sucked away the sound.

He's scared, I thought. That was a wasted shot. He didn't wait to aim. I took a bead on him. Didn't he think I'd have a gun? I got his neck brace in my sight and lowered my aim a fraction. Then I pressed the trigger.

The clacking of the wheels took on a hollow sound. We had reached the trestle.

The slug caught him in the chest and he fell back. There was a brief, terrified moment as he tried to grip something to hold with, but there was nothing. He was like a long-legged bug on his back, and he was slipping. I put another slug into him because it felt good to squeeze the trigger again. His legs started over the sloping metal and his arms flew in the air.

I was alone up there. I glanced through the bridge to the ribbon of water below. It was a long way down.

I left the train as it slowed down for Feldkirch. I cleared customs, picked up a short haul to Buchs across the Rhine, and stuck out my thumb again. I reached Geneva a little after ten that night and headed straight for the American Embassy. I handed over the Borsilov material. It was photographed page by page, and by dawn two copies and the original were on their way to Washington by individual couriers—plus the scrap of information on the recording wire.

I checked into a hotel and had breakfast sent up to my room. I ate and smoked a cigarette—and I thought about Pia. I wished I'd been cold-blooded enough to kill her. All the beautiful women in Europe and I'd fallen for a greedy little bitch. Pia and Jardine—hell, they deserved each other. I'd come out on top with the Borsilov secrets, and that's all that really mattered. I was sorry about Duvivier—she'd worked hard and come out on the short end. Well, it was all in the business.

I went to bed and I slept for a week.

THE END

A. S. Fleischman Bibliography (1920-2010)

NOVELS
The Straw Donkey Case (1948)
Murder's No Accident (1949)
Shanghai Flame (1951)
Look Behind You, Lady (1952) [aka Chinese Crimson, UK, 1962]
Danger in Paradise (1953)
Counterspy Express (1954)
Malay Woman (1954) [aka Malay Manhunt, UK, 1966]
Blood Alley (1955)
Yellowleg (1960) [aka The Deadly Companions, 1961]
The Venetian Blonde (1963)
The Sun Worshippers (2012)

SCREENPLAYS
Blood Alley (1955)
Goodbye, My Lady [as Sid Fleischman] (1956)
Lafayette Escadrille (1958)
The Deadly Companions (1961)
Scalawag (1973)
The Whipping Boy [as Max Brindle] (1995)

As Sid Fleischman

Mr. Mysterious & Company (1962)
By the Great Horn Spoon! (1963)
Ghost in the Noonday Sun (1965)
Chancy and the Grand Rascal (1966)
McBroom Tells the Truth (1966)
McBroom and the Big Wind (1967)
McBroom's Zoo (1969)
Longbeard the Wizard (1970)
Jingo Django (1971)
McBroom's Ear (1971)
McBroom's Ghost (1971)
The Wooden Cat Man (1972)
McBroom Tells a Lie (1976)
Kate's Secret Riddle Book (1977)
Me and the Man on the Moon-Eyed Horse (1977)
Humbug Mountain (1978)
Jim Bridger's Alarm Clock and Other Tall Tales (1978)
McBroom and the Beanstalk (1978)
The Hey Hey Man (1979)
McBroom and the Great Race (1980)
The Case of the Cackling Ghost (1981)

McBroom the Rainmaker (1982)
McBroom's Almanac (1984)
Whipping Boy (1986)
The Scarebird (1987)
The Midnight Horse (1990)
Jim Ugly (1992)
McBroom's Wonderful One-Acre Farm (1992)
The 13th Floor: A Ghost Story (1995)
The Abracadabra Kid: A Writer's Life (1996)
Bandit's Moon (1998)
The Ghost on Saturday Night (1999)
Here Comes McBroom!: Three More Tall Tales (1999)
A Carnival of Animals (2000)
Bo & Mzzz Mad (2003)
Disappearing Act (2003)
The Giant Rat of Sumatra: or Pirates Galore (2005)
Escape! The Story of the Great Houdini (2006)
The White Elephant (2006)
The Entertainer and the Dyybuk (2007)
The Trouble Begins at 8: A Life of Mark Twain in the Wild, Wild West (2008)
The Dream Stealer (2009)
Sir Charlie: Chaplin, the Funniest Man in the World (2010).

BOOKS ON MAGIC
Between Cocktails (1939)
Ready, Aim, Magic! (with Bob Gunther, 1942)
Call the Witness (with Bob Gunther, 1943)
The Blue Bug (with Bob Gunther, 1947)
Top Secrets (with Bob Gunther, 1947)
Magic Made Easy (as Carl March, 1953)
Mr. Mysterious's Secrets of Magic (1975)
The Charlatan's Handbook (1993)

From the master of cinematic storytelling....

A. S. Fleischman

978-1-933586-12-0

Look Behind You Lady / The Venetian Blonde

$19.95

"Filled with a colorful cast of characters and wonderful noir dialog." – Michael Cart, *Booklist*

978-1-933568-28-1

Danger in Paradise / Malay Woman

$19.95

"The kind of book that's increasingly difficult to find these days—the pure adventure thriller written for the fun of it." – Steve Lewis, *Mystery*File*

978-1-933586-40-3

The Sun Worshippers / Yellowleg

$19.95

The Sun Worshippers is a Raymond Chandleresque tale set in a West unmoored from history, where anything seems possible."
– Paul Fleischman, from his introduction

"Fleischman writes as if it were on the big screen." – Bruce Grossman, *Bookgasm*

Stark House Press, 1315 H Street, Eureka, CA 95501
griffinskye3@sbcglobal.net / www.StarkHousePress.com
Available from your local bookstore, or order direct or via our website.

www.ingramcontent.com/pod-product-compliance
Lightning Source LLC
Chambersburg PA
CBHW070918190726
48292CB00004B/1022